UNDER ATTACK

The Conquest series

an Indian saga **volume four**

James G. Landis

UNDER ATTACK

VOLUME FOUR OF A SEVEN-PART SERIES

This story tells how unrelenting pressure from settlers, traders, heathen Indians, politicians, and soldiers forced peaceful Christian Indians ever westward from Connecticut and eastern New York across the Alleghenies into the Christian Indian villages of Schoenbrunn and Gnadenhuetten in the Ohioland.

This is a tale of God's grace toward Christian Indians as they suffered captivity, injustice, sickness, and repeated exile from their peaceful villages.

[Jesus] walked with me in peace and uprightness, and turned many from sin. Malachi 2:6

© 2018 by TGS International, a wholly owned subsidiary of Christian Aid Ministries, Berlin, Ohio.

All rights reserved. No part of this book may be used, reproduced, or stored in any retrieval system, in any form or by any means, electronic or mechanical, without written permission from the publisher except for brief quotations embodied in critical articles and reviews.

ISBN: 978-1-947319-63-9 soft cover
      978-1-947319-64-6 hard cover

Illustrations by Igor Kondratyuk

Printed in China

Published by:
TGS International
P.O. Box 355
Berlin, Ohio 44610 USA
Phone: 330.893.4828
Fax: 330.893.2305
www.tgsinternational.com

TGS001690

Dedication

Johannes Papunhank

A hero of faith who:

» renounced his false teaching as an Indian prophet.

» repented of his sins.

» walked in newness of life.

» championed the way of peace.

» suffered much injustice.

» faithfully served the brotherhood.

» died at peace.

—James G. Landis

Overview of The Conquest Series

AMERICAN HISTORY THROUGH INDIAN EYES

-James G. Landis

LENAPE HOMELAND ✦ Volume I
This story tells the early history of the Delaware Indians and the coming of the white man to the Delaware River Valley as witnessed by Lenape heroes.

HOMELAND IN MY HEART ✦ Volume II
Recounts the life story of Lenape sage, Meas, as he staggers through the events that engulf him in his homeland in the Delaware River Valley.

TOMAHAWKS TO PEACE ✦ Volume III
Glikkikan, a renowned Delaware war chief and famous orator, brings to light the hidden causes of what is commonly known as Pontiac's Rebellion.

UNDER ATTACK ✦ Volume IV
Details fierce White attacks against all Indians and the heroic attempts of Christian Indians to remain quiet and peaceable throughout.

WAR CHIEF CONQUERED ✦ Volume V
An Indian saga recounting Isaac Glikkikan's struggle to give up his former life as an influential chief, prophet, and orator and find peace in his heart.

BLACK CLOUDS OVER THE OHIOLAND ✦ Volume VI
A story of duplicity and the betrayal of the Delaware nation and the Moravian missions during the Revolutionary War.

THE FINAL CONQUEST ✦ Volume VII
Isaac Glikkikan remains stedfast in his faith amid conflict, deportation, and starvation, and at last finds a permanent homeland for his people.

Contents

List of Illustrations ix

List of Maps x

Credits xi

Foreword xii

Timeline xviii

» volume four «

Under Attack

Chapters

1. » A New Beginning (1772-1773) 1
2. » Under Attack at Shekomeko (1742-1746) 37
3. » Under Attack in the Forks of the Delaware (1747-1755) 91
4. » Under Attack at Wyoming (1756-1763) 151
5. » Under Attack in Philadelphia (1763-1765) 191
6. » Under Attack at Wyalusing (1765-1772) 275

(Appendix A) Cast of Main Characters. 367
(Appendix B) Place Names 371
(Appendix C) How Much of This Story Is True? 373
(Appendix D) The Life Work of Johannes Papunhank 375
(Appendix E) The 1763 Murders in the Wyoming Valley 377
(Appendix F) Christian Village Statutes and Rules 384

Bibliography 386
About the Author 392

Illustrations

by Igor Kondratyuk

CQ401 - Confident 6
CQ402 - The Skeptic....................................... 28
CQ403 - The First Indian Baptism 61
CQ404 - Government Orders................................. 76
CQ405 - Water Power......................................119
CQ406 - Robbery and Murder 168
CQ407 - Peacekeepers..................................... 175
CQ408 - In Great Danger 209
CQ409 - True Brothers.................................... 212
CQ410 - Wise Counsel 220
CQ411 - Backtracking 290
CQ412 - Farewell...351
CQ413 - Clear Vision 365

Maps

by James G. Landis & Gavin Miles

CQM401 - The Canoe Journey (1773) 2
CQM402 - The Journey to Baptism (1742) 36
CQM403 - Key Points for Peace and Witness in the
        East (1755-1761). 90
CQM404 - The Contested Land of Wyoming (1762) 150
CQM405 - The Treks of the Refugees (1763) 190
CQM406 - The Migration of the Released Captives
        from Philadelphia to Kuskusky (1765-1772) 274

Credits

This story draws heavily from the detailed records of the Moravian missionaries: their maps, letters, statements of accounts, and property deeds, as well as their regular reports to the church headquarters in Philadelphia, Pennsylvania, and Herrnhut, Germany.

Based on these numerous reports, the peerless historian George Henry Loskiel wrote and published *The History of the Mission of the United Brethren Among the Indians in North America*. This earliest published work on the subject was first printed in German in 1788 and then translated to English in 1794. Through the wonders of the Internet, I was privileged to read this 600-page book for the first time in 2016. It has brought exciting stories to me that I had never encountered in fifteen years of research. I have borrowed much from this excellent account with only minor variations from the original translation.

Some of the diarists important to this story were the following: John Heckewelder, Johannes Roth, Johann Jacob Schmidt, David Zeisberger, and Count Zinzendorf.

Because of the diaries, we have an accurate picture of the joys and sorrows that accompanied those Indians who chose to follow the Savior. We can also see selfless missionaries boldly traveling unarmed over difficult terrain, amid terrible weather, and in the face of hostility from both settlers and Indians. Some got sick and died, but others came forward to replace them. These messengers of the Savior carried their pens and notebooks with them and recorded their work in neat German script whenever they could.

The eternal reward of these faithful writers will be found in heaven, but the legacy they left in their writings is recorded on the earth. I give credit to these diligent scribes and to those translators and publishers who have made their work available to me in English.

Foreword

This story is based on the Moravian mission diaries and historical accounts. The people were real characters, the mission villages—Friedenhuetten, Sheshequin, Friedenstadt, Gnadenhuetten, and Schoenbrunn—are real places, and the events described are historically accurate.

The Moravians were Germans. Most of their diaries and letters were originally written in German. And I believe that the Bible they ordinarily used in their missions was a German Bible. This means that most of their preaching and teaching was a free translation of the German Bible into Delaware, Mohican, Shawnee, and English. I have followed suit, and where Scripture is quoted in the story, I have rendered it in my own words rather than quoting any one English version.

I believe this story faithfully portrays the character and attitudes of the Indians. It also provides insights into the surrounding white people, beginning with those who founded the Moravian mission at Bethlehem, Pennsylvania, in 1740 and continuing to those who lived at the Schoenbrunn, Ohio, mission in 1774. The story also recounts some of the characters and events that forced the Christian Indians to leave their villages repeatedly. They would make yet another attempt to live at peace in a hostile world.

One cannot understand *Under Attack* or the rest of the Conquest Series—*War Chief Conquered, Black Clouds Over the Ohioland,* and *The Final Conquest*—without knowing something about the spirit that impelled the Moravians to carry the Gospel to Native Americans. To help the reader grasp the Moravian mindset, I will give several key points I gleaned from an excellent description by Gillian Gollin, based on the writing of John Taylor Hamilton in *A History of the Moravian Church*:

» The Moravians possessed a powerful desire to inform others of eternal salvation.

- » Their religious values dominated the economic, social, and political life of the community.
- » Their religion stressed ethical conduct above correct doctrine.
- » They worshipped the Savior, whose sufferings on the cross had atoned for the sins of mankind.
- » Their belief was a matter of *feeling the divine*, not of understanding it. "Salvation depends less on the truth in ideas than on *the truth in sensation*." —Zinzendorf.
- » The faithful are bound together in a community of love.
- » The people of God are separated from the rest of mankind.

In describing the Moravian mission villages and the life therein, I am trying to portray the beliefs and practices of the Moravians rather than my personal convictions. Much of the Moravian teaching is commendable, and I marvel at the changed lives and powerful witness their villages gave to the world. Moravian emphases included repentance from sin and the Savior's power to forgive and bring peace to troubled hearts. I get excited when I think of the nurture they experienced in close Christian community with meetings twice a day. As I consider how they brought illiterate sinners to faith in Christ, it makes me want to know how they did it. Surely the power came from God, but the Moravians had a part in it all. With proper humility, we can learn much from their experience.

Like moths fluttering out of the darkness to a bright light, the heathen were drawn out of superstition and ignorance to the shining light they saw in the huts of grace and peace. How powerful!

Some areas where I personally disagree with the Moravian theology and practices are these: the tremendous emphasis on the wounds of Christ, the belief in sacramental virtue rather than the emblems serving as symbols of spiritual truths, and infant baptism at times. There was also a strong reliance on feelings, such as the statement that the assembly "felt the breeze from the wound in Christ's side."

These Moravian beliefs undergird many actions and tensions found in *Under Attack*. This story also tells of the horrendous violence, bitterness, and hatred that preceded the Revolutionary War. If you think the Revolutionary War was caused by the injustice of a British government, this story will challenge you to examine the real causes formerly hidden in the smokescreen of "freedom from tyranny."

The main character and the one telling this story is Isaac Glikkikan. Glikkikan had been a powerful Delaware war chief during the French and Indian War and Pontiac's Rebellion. He later served as first councilor to Chief Packanke and as a famous orator to many Indian nations.

At seventy years of age, Glikkikan fully converted to the Moravian understanding of faith on Christmas Eve, 1770, at what is now Moravia, Pennsylvania. After his baptism, having taken the Christian name of Isaac, he laid aside all his princely offices and power, and instead suffered the scorn and mockery of former friends. For the remaining twelve years of his life, he labored faithfully for the Savior among his own people. As an influential helper, he aided David Zeisberger and John Heckewelder in beginning the mission at Schoenbrunn in 1772.

Three years later, at the age of seventy-five, Isaac and his friends were at the core of the highly successful Schoenbrunn mission, demonstrating to the world that Indians could be transformed into peaceful, productive Christians as they lived in the land God had given to His special people. Or so they believed.

But the Whites, including some of the missionaries, had a conflicting view of who should own the Ohioland. And the nefarious Satan inspired evil men to destroy any good the missions had nurtured in the hearts of these Indians. Listen in as John Heckewelder, teacher and scribe, tells of his journey with some two hundred Christian Indians to their new home on the

Muskingum River in the Ohioland. The record of this journey comes from his diary and is factually accurate. It is unlikely that Isaac Glikkikan accompanied the wanderers on this journey, but it is clear, from the things he reveals about himself and the times, that he reveled in truth.

Let yourself go now to join this colorful canoe journey into the Ohioland.

The Conquest series

volume four   **Under Attack**

This story tells how unrelenting pressure from settlers, traders, heathen Indians, politicians, and soldiers forced peaceful Christian Indians ever westward from Connecticut and eastern New York across the Alleghenies into the Christian Indian villages of Schoenbrunn and Gnadenhuetten in the Ohioland.

This is a tale of God's grace toward Christian Indians as they suffered captivity, injustice, sickness, and repeated exile from their peaceful villages.

American history through Indian eyes

Despised

"The rabble of the whole neighborhood was roused against us." —Gabriel

Under Attack Timeline

Historical Notes

Story Timeline

William Penn visits Pennsylvania	1700	1700 Glikkikan's birth
William Penn dies	1718	
The Long Walk	1737	
		1740 Christian Henry arrives in New York City
		1741 Bethlehem, Pennsylvania, founded
Delawares evicted from the Forks	1742	1742 First Shekomeko Indians baptized
King George's War begins	1744	1744 Shekomeko chapel closed
		1746 Huts of Grace, Pennsylvania, founded
King George's War ends	1748	
French and Indian War begins	1754	1754 Heckewelder comes to America
		1755 Huts of Grace destroyed
End of war in West	1758	
		1762 Papunhank baptized
Pontiac's Rebellion	1763	1763 Christian Indians flee to Nazareth
Teedyuscung murdered 19 April	1763	
Connecticut settlement destroyed October	1763	
John Penn becomes governor	1763	1763 Christian Indians deported to Philadelphia
Paxton boys murder Conestogas 27 December	1763	
		1764 Trek to New Jersey
		1764 Papunhank held in Germantown
		1765 Released from barracks
		1765 Huts of Peace at Wyalusing founded
Fort Stanwix Treaty	1768	
British abandon Fort Pitt	1772	1772 Beautiful Spring founded
		1772 Converts leave Wyalusing
		1773 Wyalusing Indians arrive at Beautiful Spring
		1773 Huts of Grace II begun
Virginia takes over Fort Pitt	1774	
Lord Dunmore's War	1774	1774 Heckewelder & Glikkikan rendezvous
First shot of Revolutionary War 19 April	1775	
Declaration of Independence 4 July	1776	

Chapter 1

A New Beginning: 1772–1773

Narrated by John Heckewelder

The Portage

16 April 1773

The hour of decision had come. Should the Indian men attempt to run the rapids or portage the twenty-two large canoes around Beaver Falls? Some of the canoes weighed 250 pounds, and an extra day would be needed to manhandle them a half mile around the falls. But if they decided to risk their lives and dash over the rocky rapids in their bark canoes, each canoe could be lowered approximately ten feet to the landing below—and all this in just a few minutes!

We arrived at the falls three days ago on 13 April. Four brothers from the group went overland with the cattle and horses to Beautiful Spring in the Ohioland. Four other men had come with horses to help us portage our huge store of supplies around Beaver Falls.

However, on the morning of 14 April, heavy rain fell from sodden skies. The brothers who had come to help us decided they might be greatly delayed by rising waters if they stayed, so they departed immediately. Goodbye, horses. Because of the rain, we could do little all day

UNDER ATTACK

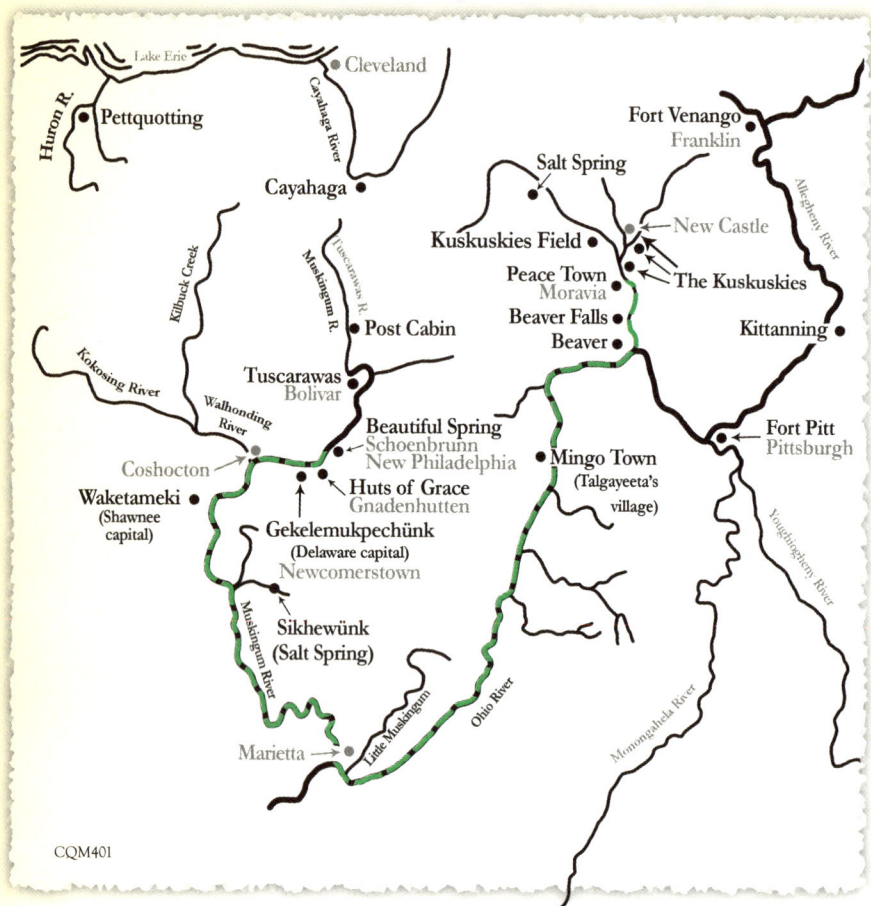

The Canoe Journey (1773)

CQM401 Notes

1. Names in 1773 are in boldfaced type; present-day place names are in gray.
2. In 1773, the Muskingum River extended from its source to its mouth at Marietta, Ohio, and included what is known today as the Tuscarawas River.
3. Today the Tuscarawas River extends from its source to where the Muskingum River begins at Coshocton, Ohio.
4. The colored line traces the route of the canoe journey from Peace Town to Beautiful Spring.
5. Peace Town on Big Beaver to Ohio River: 19 miles
6. Down Ohio river: 144 miles
7. Marietta to Beautiful Spring: 163 miles.
8. Total: 326 miles.

A New Beginning: 1772–1773

other than remain in our shelters.

On Thursday, 15 April, we took three actions:

1. With many of our canoes being overloaded, we decided to build another one. Men began work on that immediately.
2. The women, assisted by some of the men, carried our goods around the rapids.
3. Some of the men went out hunting and returned with five deer.

After our late-morning porridge on this Friday of the week following Easter Sunday, 165 Indians seated themselves on the ground in a semicircle. I used a Watchword taken from Jeremiah 32:41 for the day's devotional. "Yes, I will rejoice over them to do them good, and I will assuredly plant them in this land, with all my heart and with all my soul." I made a few comments on this wonderful promise while Anton translated for me.

After I sat down on a bag of corn, Isaac Glikkikan stepped to the head of the semicircle. It had been eleven years since Big Indian held me captive on the Muskingum River, but he was different now. Instead of a haughty bearing filled with anger as in 1762, his gray head, shining eyes, and giant frame now oozed joy and peace. His resolve, which I knew from those former days, was still there, but it had been saddled by a powerful sense of purpose. The Isaac Glikkikan of today knew he must win his lost people to the Savior and lead them to a homeland where they could dwell in peace and safety.

Brother Isaac flung out his upturned hands as he spoke to the waiting congregation. Everything about him was open and honest, and his hearers hung on to his every word:

> The Savior has been good to each of us in that He brought us from wandering in the desert heat of sin to a life of maize, milk, meat, and water for the soul. Not just in a small measure, but in abundance.

UNDER ATTACK

Now God has brought you out of your wandering where you have been despised and rejected of men—from Shekomeko, the Forks of the Delaware, Wyoming, Philadelphia, Wyalusing, and your short stay at Peace Town.

You have begun your journey to the Ohioland. Watwees,[1] the chief of the Delaware nation, wishes to seat you and your white teachers next to him so that he and his people may hear the good words taught by our teachers. He has declared that no drunkards or any other Indians will molest you as they did at Peace Town.

While you journeyed from your beautiful homes at Wyalusing and Sheshequin last year, ten of your number and Brother Good News journeyed with me over the same path you now travel.[2] We have cleared out the briars and the stumps that would hinder you, and now the way lies open.

We found the Ohioland to be a wonderful land of good earth, flowing waters, and bountiful game where you may build your houses, plant your fields, husband your cattle and horses, tend your poultry, and dwell in peace and safety.

Furthermore, the Wyandots, our cousins, have agreed to give us Delawares this land as our own. This means the Iroquois may not sell it out from under our feet as they have repeatedly done in the past. It means that white settlers may not advance upon you and again drive you from your homes. God has given us this new home in the Ohioland.

I fidgeted on my bag of corn. Why was he telling them all this? Surely he knew they had all heard every one of these words before. It seemed that Glikkikan was just burning daylight. I thought it more

---

[1] *Netawatwees*, his full name, means "wise adviser." In English, he was known as Chief Newcomer.
[2] In this story, we will frequently use "Good News" as the name for the long-term Moravian (German) missionary, David Zeisberger. Only days before this event on 11 April 1773, Brother Zeisberger had turned 52. He was still single and completely dedicated to Indian missions.

A New Beginning: 1772–1773

important to get started carrying those heavy canoes around the falls. By beginning promptly, we might still be ready to go in the morning.

I need not have worried. Isaac Glikkikan knew what he was doing. He was a champion, a chief, a hero of faith, and a trusted leader.

Now his voice picked up in tone and tempo:

> Brethren, sisters, and children, we have begun our journey to the promised Ohioland. The way is open before us, and God has provided powerful rushing waters upon which we may travel. Our canoes are above us, and the way forward is below us. Why should the evil one cause us to cower in fear of the waters? We will climb to our canoes. With God's help, we will ride the waters in triumph!
>
> Jacob Daskund[3] and I will take the first canoe through the waters. I have done this many times before. With the high waters, it will be a frightening ride, but if you follow in our path, all will be well. We will ride the waves to the waters below, and if anyone should suffer shipwreck, we will wait to help them. Forward! To the charge!

The whole company watched as Isaac and Jacob raced off along the river and up to the waiting boats. They thrilled as Isaac and Jacob's racing canoe shot through the foaming sprays and charging currents. Isaac sat alert in the front, guiding the canoe with quick, expert strokes of his paddle. Keen eyes followed the path the canoe took through the dashing waters. The current crashed against a rock, splashing water over the canoe and over Isaac and Jacob. They laughed. Only moments later, the two were in calmer water, Isaac and Jacob holding their paddles aloft triumphantly. The watchers cheered.

Two more men raced along the river toward the waiting boats. Soon

---

[3] Jacob Daskund was a young chief baptized on the same night as Isaac Glikkikan.

UNDER ATTACK

Confident

"*I have shot through the foaming sprays and raging currents many times.*" —Isaac Glikkikan

A New Beginning: 1772–1773

another canoe successfully shot through the rapids to the bystanders below. Many of the bark canoes were half full of water and the paddlers soaked when they arrived on the shore. But in the excitement of the ride, they hardly noticed the ducking they had received. Many hands overturned the heavy boats and emptied the water while the drama continued.

Isaac and Jacob waited in their canoe below the raging waters and watched each boat charge over the falls. It was well they did, for two men were thrown completely out of their canoes and disappeared in the undercurrents. Isaac and Jacob were right there to fish them out before they drowned.

In this manner, all twenty-two boats and their occupants arrived safely below the falls. The rains continued throughout the day.

Riding the Ohio

On Saturday, 17 April 1773, we loaded our goods, including the chapel bell from Huts of Peace, 165 Indians, and 10 dogs, into the 23 canoes (the one we built was now finished). Once again, we set our flotilla on the Big Beaver. After six miles, we arrived on the Ohio and headed west. We camped that evening below an abandoned French fort; we could see the old chimneys standing there like sentinels guarding a forgotten past.

On Sunday, 18 April, we took counsel about how to proceed and decided that since the waters were high, we would keep going till nightfall. From time to time, we passed plantations belonging to Whites on the east bank. They invited us to stop and rest so they could talk with us. We declined their invitation, since we had decided to keep going.

The same thing happened on Monday. We saw more houses and plantations on the east bank and passed up several opportunities to visit

UNDER ATTACK

with friendly people. No sooner had we landed on the west bank and started to set up camp for the night than six Whites appeared across the river and tried to talk with me. The river was so wide that we could not understand each other, so I asked Anton and Boas to take me over to visit with them. Brother Isaac asked to go along as well.

The men plied me with all sorts of questions about our religious beliefs and teachings. My three Indian friends smiled genially at the men, but pretended they did not know any English. In reality, Isaac and Anton understood everything.

Here are some of the questions these men asked, along with my answers:

Whites: "What kind of Indians are these, and where do they come from?"
Answer: "They are a Christian Indian congregation from Beaver Creek."
Whites: "Where are they going?"
Answer: "To the Muskingum River."
Whites: "Are these the Moravian Indians?"
Answer: "Yes."
Whites: "Do they have a minister with them?"
Answer: "Yes, there are two congregations and each has its own teacher."
Whites: "What is the religion of their teachers?"
Answer: "They are Brethren, commonly known as Moravians."
Whites: "Do they receive an annual stipend from the King or some recognized society?"
Answer: "No."
Whites: "Then who supports the teachers?"
Answer: "The believers contribute voluntarily, each giving what he can, and their preachers are supported by these freewill offerings."

A New Beginning: 1772–1773

Whites: "That is praiseworthy," they said to one another. "Can their preachers talk to them in their own language?"

Answer: "Yes."

Whites: "Have any of them really been brought to believe there is a God in heaven?"

Answer: "Yes."

Whites: "Do they accept baptism?"

Answer: "Yes."

Whites: "Have these three been baptized, and what are their names?"

Answer: "They have all three been baptized, and their names are Anton, Boas, and Isaac."

Whites: "Do they remain true to the faith after baptism?"

Answer: "They seldom leave us. Take this man Anton, for example. He has kept the faith for twenty years."

Whites: "You can see by this man's face," they said to one another, "that he is a true Christian." They asked further, "Do they celebrate the Sabbath and keep it holy, refraining from work and even hunting on that day?"

Answer: "They observe the Sabbath the same as other Christian churches do."

Whites: "Which day do you regard as the Sabbath?"

Answer: "The first day of the week."

Whites: "Do they hold services on any day besides the Sabbath?"

Answer: "Yes. They have one and sometimes two services every day."

Whites: "It is clear enough," said they, "that these are true Christians. What do you do if one of your people falls into sin?"

Answer: "We rebuke him, and if that is not enough, he is excluded from the congregation and sometimes sent away."

Whites: "Do you have a school for them?"

Answer: "Yes."

UNDER ATTACK

Whites: "In what language?"

Answer: "In their own."

Whites: "And you do no business with them? Do they give you part of their hunting bag?"

Answer: "We have no business dealings with them, and we get nothing from them. We are content to live very simply, and as long as we see some turn and become believers, we consider ourselves well paid."

Whites: "Surely God is with you and blesses your work. This is just what our minister reported of you. He met and talked with David Good News at Huts of Grace. He knows you are a true Christian community in the Indian country. We wish you success and God's blessing on your work. May your numbers increase."[4]

Anton, Boas, and Isaac said nothing as we paddled back across the river in the darkness. But before we parted, Isaac drew me aside and asked, "Could you ride with me in my canoe tomorrow? I would welcome your company and some time to talk."

"I gladly accept your invitation," I responded.

Before we could break camp the next morning, the same white people we had spoken with earlier crossed the river to have a look at us and our arrangements. They sympathized with the old people, caressed the children, and wished us all a safe journey. They expressed surprise at how quiet our people were. As we departed, our visitors sat on the bank and watched until we passed out of sight.

True to his request, I sat with Isaac in the lead canoe. With the fine, windless weather, the high waters, and the broad river, the canoes could travel close together. One of the men started singing, and many rich voices joined, adding in the various parts. At times, the sopranos

---

[4] Paul A. W. Wallace, *Thirty Thousand Miles with John Heckewelder*, pp. 106–107.

A New Beginning: 1772–1773

took the lead, and at other times the tenor led out. The Indians had sung these same songs many times in the chapels at Shekomeko, Philadelphia, Wyalusing, and Peace Town, and now again in God's chapel on the Ohio River. Sometimes the songs rang across the waters in the Delaware language, sometimes in Mohican, German, or English. Even the music of the German masters Bach and Handel was not neglected. Like an angel choir the travelers sang:

> For unto us a Child is born, unto us a Son is given,
> And the government shall be upon His shoulder;
> And His name shall be called,
> Wonderful, Counsellor, the Mighty God,
> The Everlasting Father, the Prince of Peace . . .
> Come unto Him, all ye that labor,
> Come unto Him, all that are heavy laden,
> And He will give you rest.
> Take His yoke upon you, and learn of Him,
> For He is meek and lowly of heart,
> And ye shall find rest unto your souls.

The Indians sang with feeling that can come only from those who have experienced these things in their hearts. When it was time, Isaac sang a solo, slowly and forlornly in his strong tenor:

> He was despised and rejected of men,
> A man of sorrows and acquainted with grief . . .
> Surely He hath borne our griefs, and carried our sorrows.
> He was wounded for our griefs, and carried our sorrows.
> He was wounded for our transgressions,
> He was bruised for our iniquities;
> The chastisement of our peace was upon Him.

When he finished his solo, I wanted to weep, as did the whole choir.

UNDER ATTACK

A period of silence followed, and then by some imperceptible cue, the whole choir burst into song:

> *Worthy is the Lamb that was slain,*
> *And hath redeemed us to God by His blood,*
> *To receive power, and riches, and wisdom,*
> *And strength, and honor, and glory, and blessing.*
> *Blessing and honor, glory and power,*
> *Be unto Him that sitteth upon the throne,*
> *And unto the Lamb, for ever and ever.*
> *Amen. Amen. Amen. Ah - men.*

I have heard a great deal of Moravian music at Bethlehem and Lititz, accompanied by their spinets, violins, horns, and trumpets, but these Indians singing on the river without accompaniment created the finest music I had ever heard. It continued for two hours while we drifted down the Ohio.

"Where did these people learn to sing like that?" I asked Brother Isaac.

He responded, "Many of these people and their fathers have been singing together like that for twenty years in the chapel at Shekomeko, in the halls of Bethlehem, on the forced march to Jersey, and in the chapel at Huts of Peace on the Susquehanna. These pilgrims and their fathers have been taught to sing by several Germans who were trained in Europe. Those like me, baptized only recently, sing together once or twice every day. And for an Indian, it is not hard to join in and sing the parts and learn the words. The music has a tremendous tug on the strings of the heart."

I thought upon the music for a while, and then Brother Isaac began his questions. Well, maybe they weren't really questions, because the way he put things allowed only one right answer. As we floated along in this idyllic setting, Isaac Glikkikan began his teaching session with

A New Beginning: 1772–1773

me. It reminded me of our interactions ten years earlier, only this time we were free friends.

"Brother John, what did you think of the Whites and all their questions?"

"I thought them friendly and well-meaning folks. They just wanted to know more about the Christian Indians. You heard them bless us and the mission, did you not?"

Isaac kept his eyes on the river as though he pondered my answer. Then he locked those piercing black eyes on mine and asked, "Would you like to ask those people all the same questions they asked you? *Who are you? Where are you from? What are you doing here? Are you true Christians? How do you support your preacher? What do you do with people who fall into sin?*"

I smiled and held up my hand. "Certainly, certainly," I answered rather lightly.

"Then why did you not ask them those questions?"

"I feared they might be offended," I replied.

"John! Didn't they fear offending *us*? Were you not offended?" Glikkikan asked.

"No," I answered. "They were just curious and meant us no harm."

Glikkikan smiled easily and nodded his head up and down and then sideways in an indecisive manner. "Brother John, explain to me why those six men would have been offended if you had asked them the same questions they asked us?"

"I see what you mean. They would probably have considered it rude and none of our business to ask them why they were here and where they had come from. They thought we were passing through *their* country rather than they living in *ours*."

Glikkikan smiled again. "Exactly. But how did the Ohioland come to be *their* country?"

"The Iroquois sold it to them. As I understand it, the treaty at Fort Stanwix gave to the Whites in Pennsylvania, Virginia, and Maryland

UNDER ATTACK

all the land east of the Ohio River. It was the same treaty that sold the land at Wyalusing out from under the feet of these very Indians."

"But Brother John, did the Iroquois really have the right to sell the Ohioland? Didn't it belong to the Delaware, the Shawnee, and the Wyandot?"

Now it was my turn to raise a question. "The Iroquois claim the right to sell all the land by right of conquest. Long ago, they soundly defeated the Susquehannocks and the Delawares and made women out of the Delawares. Is that not true?"

He answered quickly, "I have been trained as an orator, and I know the history of the Delaware and many other nations. The conquest of the Delaware by the Iroquois is a complete myth. In fact, long ago during the Beaver Wars, the Hurons and the Delawares soundly defeated the Iroquois. As for the Delawares being called "women," that simply referred to their role as peacemakers among the nations and their refusal to go to war. In Indian history, this was an honor, not a thing of weakness or ridicule.

"What is true is that Pennsylvania just took the land by force. First the traders came and built forts to protect themselves. Then the settlers came, with or without the approval of the British or Pennsylvania or the Iroquois. When the Indians resisted the taking of the land, the British and the settlers brought in large armies to drive the Indians away or destroy them.

"This is the way it has happened for the Christian Indians at Shekomeko, in the Forks of the Delaware, Wyoming, Philadelphia, Wyalusing, and the Kuskuski River. When we are comfortably settled in Beautiful Spring and Huts of Grace, our two new towns on the Muskingum, I will tell you how and why the Indians were driven away in each of those settlements.

"Even those who live at peace are destroyed by the likes of those six men who talked with us last night. They sound so interested in the Christian religion, but it is a religion that allows them to take the land

A New Beginning: 1772–1773

by gun and knife. And unless God intervenes, they will do the same in the Ohioland."

"That's a promise," I told Brother Isaac. "When we are comfortably settled in Beautiful Spring, I will eagerly wait for you, the master storyteller, to tell how these very Indians were driven to the Ohioland."

In the afternoon, some of the brothers wanted to stop and hunt as we were out of meat. But we wished to take advantage of the beautiful weather, and so we continued on our way.

Later Isaac spied a small island with trees and brush upon it in the river ahead. He felt certain some deer had to be hiding on it. We surrounded the island with our boats, and the men loaded their guns. Then four boys took the dogs and noisily entered the island. Immediately, four deer bounded into the water. The guns cracked, and three of the deer fell victim to our assault. The experts quickly dressed the deer, and within minutes, we were on our way once more.

Early on Wednesday the 21st, we continued our travels. Again, the fine weather through beautiful countryside made our journey a pleasant one. Some of the bottom lands looked like orchards. I did not recognize many trees and plants, and the Indians said, "We are strangers here. The landscape, trees, and plants are all different."

Glikkikan had another story to tell me as we floated blissfully through this lovely country. "Brother John, do not yearn to live here and own this land. If you want to remain in the Ohioland as a teacher, you must be very careful what you say about the land.

"Only last October an English preacher named David McClure came to Newcomerstown and used Joseph Peepi as his interpreter. He preached to the Delaware Indians several times and talked to them very carelessly. These are some of the comments Preacher McClure made:

> You Indians have so much beautiful and good land, but it is lying in waste. You do not use it because you Indians are lazy people and do not want to work; yet you do not

UNDER ATTACK

like it when the Whites use it. In a few years, all the land will be taken from you. The white people will establish cities and towns here and drive the Indians away or even destroy them.

"The Council then called Preacher McClure in and told him, 'We are pleased that you have come to us and preached while you were here. Now there has been enough preaching, and you should stop. It would be best for you to return home.'

"Preacher McClure was very upset about this, and he spit out, 'You will have no more good fortune if you do not accept the Gospel. God will send judgment upon this city and eradicate you from the face of the earth.' No wonder he had to flee for his life."

Very sober now, Glikkikan warned me again, "John, if you want to remain in the Ohioland, you must be very careful what you say about the land. The Indians have been driven out of their homes too many times."

As we floated peacefully down the Ohio, we saw more houses belonging to Whites, some of whom were standing on the bank. They called to us and asked, "Where are you people going?"

"Up the Muskingum to settle," I replied.

One of those standing on the bank answered, "I wish it were ten thousand times farther away."

Another person next to him rebuked the speaker and said, "You are wrong about these people. Don't you see how quiet and well-behaved they are? Not one of them is painted; they are just their natural selves." After that, the group wished us a safe journey.

We shot a bear today, and everyone rejoiced.

On Thursday the 22nd, the ninth day since we left Peace Town, we traveled through the most delightful countryside of the whole trip. Here, the Ohio ran a perfectly straight course through level bottoms on both sides. Most of the leaves were in full foliage with many flowers in blossom. The grass was shoe-high.

A New Beginning: 1772-1773

We were told that on the east side of the river, a short distance inland, there is a settlement of 200-300 families. They do not want to be along the river because they are afraid of the Indians.

Pushing up the Muskingum

At noon we left the Ohio and entered the Muskingum. For a few miles above its mouth, the river is very deep and must be navigated by paddles or oars.

We shot another bear today.

On the 23rd the country became very hilly, and the bottoms were quite swampy; they were almost entirely grown over with beech trees. Several of the brothers did a little hunting and shot another bear.

The push up the Muskingum was very tiring to the men, so at noon on the 25th, we stopped and immediately built a sweat oven. There the men sweated out their fatigue and soothed their tired muscles. I am a firm believer in the sweat oven. Last fall I was suffering so badly from rheumatism that I could not go outside for three weeks. Treatments in the sweat oven completely cured me.

A few went hunting late in the afternoon and saw some buffalo. They shot at them but didn't get any.

That night we got little sleep because of innumerable toads that jumped all over us. Around midnight a violent thunderstorm and heavy rain caused us to seek shelter under a rock. Although some of our grain got wet in the heavy rain, we had good travel conditions on the river and pushed ahead for the next two days. Then on the 28th we found some of our grain beginning to sprout and decided to stop at Sikhewünk to dry our grain.

While most of the men worked at drying the grain, Glikkikan and I and a few other brothers traveled ten miles up a side creek to see the

UNDER ATTACK

famous salt spring. Glikkikan told me that this spring has always been neutral ground where people from any nation may come to make salt at any time without fear of being harmed. The spring had no visible outlet, and it appeared to rise and fall through underground channels. Whenever it is emptied, it quickly fills again.

The next day we headed north from Sikhewünk. From this point on, the countryside changed. Fine bottomland appeared again, and the farther we went, the more attractive it became.

We encountered three bad rapids and had a great deal of trouble drawing our canoes up. At noon that day we came to the Shawnee town of Waketameki. Brother Isaac told me he had visited this town last fall. Several brothers went ashore, but they found only a few people at home. They were kindly received, although most of the inhabitants had moved away. Isaac said he would tell me about the town when we camped for the night.

We encountered some bad stretches in the river where we had to drag the canoes up over the rapids and pull them through shallow places in the river. We made camp early because everyone was feeling weary. This gave Brother Isaac a chance to tell about his visit to this area and why so many had moved away. Most of the congregation, including the women and children, gathered around to hear the story. Listening to storytellers was one of the favorite Indian pastimes, and an opportunity to hear the great Glikkikan was not to be passed up.

> Only one year ago, six families accompanied Good News on the same pilgrimage you are now making. We wanted to be closer to the Delawares so they might hear the good words of the Savior. When we arrived at Beautiful Spring, we built houses and planted gardens to prepare for your coming.
>
> But in the middle of the harvest month, when the women were gathering in the crop from the fields and the

A New Beginning: 1772-1773

men had already gone for the fall hunt, Good News asked Joseph Peepi and me to go with him to the Shawnee towns and see what they knew of the Gospel. We were delighted to do this.

First we went to Newcomerstown to secure permission from Chief Newcomer to go among the Shawnee. The Chief said, "The road to them should be open so that anyone who would like to hear the Gospel is free to come." He gave us two strings of wampum as a gift.

We left Newcomerstown on the morning of 12 October 1772 and passed through two large stretches of flats where there is nothing but grass for miles. We passed through the campsite of Colonel Bouquet's army where, eight years earlier, Packanke, Newcomer, and I had met with him and he had forced us, the Delawares, to release all our White captives. This happened at the same time you languished as captives of the Whites in Philadelphia.

Then Bouquet marched his army on to Waketameki, where he forced the Shawnee to give up their White captives before he took his army back to Fort Pitt in November 1764. The colonel died less than one year later.

Waketameki was the Shawnee town Good News, Joseph Peepi, and I wanted to go to on this journey. The first Shawnee village we came to consisted of only three huts, but the son of Chief Paxinosa lived here. The son recognized us all immediately, welcomed our visit, and was happy to see us. All three of us preached the Savior to him for half the night, and he seemed to receive this well.

He said, "I surely believe your teaching is the right one and that you preach the correct way to salvation. We have tried for a long time to find the way to eternal life. Now

UNDER ATTACK

we see that all our efforts are in vain. We have almost given up because we cannot think of more good things to do. I will go with you in the morning so I can hear more."

We were very glad to take Paxinosa's son with us because he understood the Delaware and Shawnee languages very well. I could understand Shawnee but could not speak it fluently. He also advised us that when we arrived at Waketameki, we should stop at the Indian preacher's house first because, he said, "His word counts the most and governs everything. The Chief only takes care of Chief affairs."

As we traveled to Waketameki, we passed through several small towns of four or five huts. In each town, we told the people who were home that if they would like to listen, they should follow us, as we had precious words to tell them. They did so, and at noon we arrived at Waketameki with a nice crowd.

We stopped first at the preacher's house, and he received us cordially. We told him, "We have come to visit the town, and we have something to tell the people."

The preacher asked, "What kind of things do you have to tell us?"

"The words of eternal life," Paxinosa's son answered.

"We are happy about this and would like to hear it," the preacher answered.

Immediately the people began clearing a house and getting it ready for a meeting. However, because many people, especially the women, were busy in the fields harvesting their corn, it got too late for a public service that day. In the meantime we began preaching to the Indians in the house where we were staying. Our house was always

A New Beginning: 1772–1773

full, and the people listened very attentively until the roosters started crowing. Then we had to lie down and rest a little, but as soon as day broke, we began again.

The next morning we gathered in the house that had been prepared for our meeting. The chief, the captain, and the preacher were present. Up to this time the preacher had listened attentively but wordlessly. Now he began to speak. "I have not been able to sleep all night. I just kept meditating about what I heard. Now I want to share my thoughts with you.

"I believe everything you preached is the truth. For a year it has been clear to me that we are all poor, sinful humans despite all our accomplishments. However, we did not know what else we could do to be saved. I have always consoled my people by telling them that someone would certainly come and tell us the right way to salvation. We knew we were not on the right path. Just the day before you arrived, I told the people they should have a little more patience because someone would surely come soon. Now that you have come, I believe God has sent you to proclaim His Word to us.

"As you know," he continued sadly, "for some years the Shawnee have practiced ritual vomiting. We did this to free ourselves of sin and to cleanse ourselves. We ceased doing this a year ago because we could see that it had not taken away our sin. Then we began, in our own way, to lead a good and pious life. I instructed the people not to dance, fornicate, steal, lie, and get drunk. I told them we would stick to doing this until God proclaimed something better."

I saw many tears in the eyes of the congregation as they listened to Isaac's recounting of the Shawnees' sad plight as they groped for truth.

UNDER ATTACK

Indeed, tears moistened Glikkikan's eyes as he recalled the Shawnee preacher's story. "It still touches my heart when I think about those blind, hungry souls," he said.

Then Brother Isaac told our band of traveling pilgrims how he had given his own testimony to the preacher and the assembled Shawnee.

> "My brothers," I told them, "this day I must tell you how miserable I was while I groped in darkness and sin. When I finally heard the brothers speak for the first time at Lawhannek[5] about Jesus' death and suffering, it tugged at my heart so that I immediately affirmed publicly that it was truth."
>
> After my testimony, Brother Good News began to speak. First he requested that they not ask questions during the sermon as they had done the day before at the house. "After the sermon is over, you may ask all the questions you want to," he said. After that, things proceeded in a quiet and orderly fashion. Brother Good News had his heart open to the Savior, who granted him grace to extol Christ's death and blood as the source of our salvation.
>
> After the sermon, Joseph Peepi and I explained more things to the crowd. They asked various questions, all of which Joseph and I answered to their satisfaction. In the afternoon, they let us know that they wanted to hold a council among themselves, so we left them alone.
>
> In the evening, the Waketameki Council sent for Joseph and me to appear before them. They told us what they had decided among themselves. Their decision gave us great joy and pleasure, and we let them know this. Then they asked us, "What else should we do?" Joseph

---

[5] An abbreviation for "Lawomakhannek." Read the full account of this Moravian mission on the Allegheny River in Volume V of the Conquest Series, *War Chief Conquered*. See also Chapter 6, pp. 338-342 in this volume.

A New Beginning: 1772-1773

and I told them they should ask Good News what steps they should take next.

It was already too late that night to present their case to Good News, so the next morning the Council gathered in our house. The preacher, who was serving as the spokesman, said, "Brother, we are very happy that you have come to visit us and have brought us God's Word. Now we want to let you know what the Council decided unanimously yesterday.

"I said the decision was unanimous. It is true that the women were not present because they are very busy harvesting their fields now. However, they agree with what we men have decided.

"We agreed that from this day on we want to accept God's Word and live according to it. We say this not only with our mouths, but also from our hearts. Our hope and wish is that not only Indian believers, but also white brothers will come to us, live with us, and instruct us how we can be saved.

"We present our request to you. We are poor, bad people, but do not scorn us because we are so bad. Please do not deny our request."

Brother Good News replied, "We brothers are always happy to hear about Indians who desire the Savior and His Word, regardless of which nation they are from. We will be happy to serve you. You shall remain steadfast in what you have set upon, and I will ask the brothers at Bethlehem to send more help. However, I must tell you how things will have to be in your town if we are to live with you. There can be no sign of dances, pipes, drunkenness, gaming, and other commotion as is common in some Indian towns.

UNDER ATTACK

Everything must be quiet and orderly."

"We have already managed this on our own for a long time," answered the preacher. "We will not be bothered by such bad things because we ourselves do not like them. We welcome people who will tell us what we need to do. We truly want to live as believers should."

We discussed how it might work for them to be a Christian Indian village since Waketameki is known among the Indians as Vomit-Town. We concluded that it might be good for them to choose a new site for their village, and they said they would do so when they returned from their fall hunt. After we had agreed on everything, we exhorted the Shawnee not to forget what they had heard. Then we left them around noon.

On our way up the river toward Newcomerstown, we looked at a stretch of beautiful land suitable for a settlement. Brother Good News said, "When our brothers and sisters from Huts of Peace join us on the Muskingum, I think we should build another settlement here. This would do more good for the Savior's work than if they all lived together."

It was getting late. Isaac closed his account of the visit to the Shawnee by telling the assembled travelers, "Tomorrow you will travel past the beautiful site for a village that we saw last fall. As you pass by, remember the hunger of our brothers the Shawnee for the good news we promised them. Now rest in peace."

The next day, as we slogged our way up the river, I pointed out the beautiful stretch of land Good News had selected for a possible settlement close to the Shawnee. It was almost a mistake, as many of the weary travelers wanted to stay right there.

I persuaded them to continue on to towns that were already started

A New Beginning: 1772–1773

and waiting for them to arrive. So for two more days we pushed on, often wading and hauling the canoes up the rapids and over the shallow places. We passed several friendly Indian towns. At a Delaware village, they gave us their best entertainment and saw to it that everyone had plenty to eat.

I asked Glikkikan, "How is it that the Indians in all these towns treat us so kindly, since we are strangers and they are so poor? Some are even from different nations: Mohican, Shawnee, or Delaware. Furthermore, I am a hated White. How can this be?"

Glikkikan smiled. "Brother John, you have heard many evil things about the heathen Indians: drunkenness, carousing, dancing, immorality, laziness, fighting among themselves, and warring. Some of it is true until they come to know the Savior. Now I am going to tell you something good about the Indians—all of them.

"Indians consider themselves to be created by an all-powerful, wise, and benevolent Manito. They look upon all they possess and enjoy as given to them by the Great Spirit who gave them life.

"To illustrate, one young Indian whom I know still follows the custom of his ancestors and occasionally climbs to the pinnacle of a high mountain. There he thanks the Great Spirit for all the benefits bestowed upon him and prays for a continuance of his favor.

"Furthermore, the Indian believes he is highly favored by the Great Spirit who made him, not only in having been created different in shape and in mental and bodily powers from other animals, but in being enabled to control and master them all.

"The Indian also believes that the Great Spirit made the earth and all it contains for the common good of mankind; when he stocked the country, he provided them with plenty of game. It was not for the benefit of a few, but of all."

Then I said to Glikkikan, "You have not answered my question. Why are these people so generous to strangers?"

UNDER ATTACK

He responded, "With the Indians, there is no sense of class such as the English have. No one is higher than anyone else. There are no lords, princes, or kings. Each individual's sense of brotherhood compels him to share his private possessions with anyone who has need of them.

"Indians give and are hospitable to all and will share their last morsel with each other and even with a stranger. They would rather lie down at night with their own stomachs empty than be charged with neglecting their duty by not satisfying the wants of the stranger, the sick, or the needy.

"This generosity of the Indian is rooted in the belief that everything on the earth comes out of a common storehouse. If the meat they have been served comes out of the woods, it belonged to everyone before the hunter took it. If they have corn or vegetables, these grew out of the common soil, not by the power of man but by that of the Great Spirit."

"Such generosity of spirit is seldom found among white Christians," I commented, "for they often become very possessive of material things and refuse to share them with others. It is no wonder that Christian Indians can live so peaceably together when they feel the Savior in their hearts."

Glikkikan answered, "Brother John, you have put it well. The same thought is true of the land. The Whites refuse to share the land, wanting to claim it all. Yet they share the air, the waters, the plants, and the animals, all of which they neither made nor sustain. Oh, that all men might share the goodness of the Savior and the things He has made."

The Delaware Capital

On the third day of May, we passed Newcomerstown, where 103

A New Beginning: 1772–1773

people gave us the customary shout of joy. We camped at the upper end of the town and were barely situated before the friendly residents brought food to satisfy our hunger.

I went with a few brothers to visit Chief Newcomer, the head chief of the Delaware and one of the leaders who had invited the Christians to come to the Muskingum. He and all who were with him showed us great kindness. As we took our leave of him, the thought came to me, *Someday he, too, will belong to the Savior.*

I went next with Glikkikan to visit Killbuck. This son of Chief Newcomer had always been skeptical of inviting white teachers to come live on the Muskingum. During our visit, Killbuck asked Glikkikan, "Does this man really love the Indians?"

"Yes," Glikkikan replied, "not only he, but also all the Brethren who live among us. They do not have to live in this humble way. Many among us have seen how comfortably they could live at Bethlehem, but because they love the Indians and want to acquaint them with the Savior, they are content with a simple life and rejoice when Indians are brought to the Savior. They desire nothing more of us than that."

"Well, well," he replied, "now at last I know."

That seemed to satisfy Killbuck for the time being, but when we left, Glikkikan said, "His mind is still uneasy with having *any* white men among us." Before we left the next morning, many visitors from Newcomerstown came to our camp, and the Brethren got in many a good word for the Savior.

Gnadenhuetten: Huts of Grace II

We finally set out on the morning of 4 May. Everyone was rather worn out after the tiring journey up the Muskingum, so when we met

UNDER ATTACK

The Skeptic

"Does this man really love the Indians?" —Killbuck, Sr.

A New Beginning: 1772-1773

some young brothers from Huts of Grace and Beautiful Spring who had come to assist us, we greeted them with great joy. Many of them were family members who had traveled overland with the cattle and now had come to throw their fresh energy into this final push.

In the afternoon, we arrived at Huts of Grace. Everybody had been looking forward to our arrival and had been busy preparing food to refresh the tired and hungry. Joshua welcomed us to his town, and three Mohican families decided to stay at Huts of Grace and make their homes there in the Mohican village.

The next day as we worked our way upstream on the last twelve miles to Beautiful Spring, I asked Glikkikan, "How did it happen that there is a Mohican town and a Delaware town? I thought all the Christian Indians were one nation. Haven't the Delaware and the Mohican Christians been living together on the Susquehanna for seven years?"

Brother Isaac enlightened me.

> Joshua first came to Beautiful Spring with Brother Good News in April one year ago. But Joshua had occasional disagreements with Brother Good News. He had been baptized in 1742 at Bethlehem when the Moravians first came to Pennsylvania and before Good News had arrived. Before his baptism, Joshua had been a Mohican chief. His role as a guardian of his people meant that he often placed the good of the Mohicans above his deference to the younger Good News.
>
> In the Christian Indian villages on the Delaware and Susquehanna Rivers, the Mohicans and the Delawares with their different languages had not always lived together in harmony. So now, in this new mission village of Beautiful Spring, Joshua decided it would be better to have a separate town for the Mohicans. At first Good News resisted the idea because the missions did not have

UNDER ATTACK

enough teachers for another village, and possibly because he was afraid an offshoot Indian village would not be properly Moravian.

To help Brother Joshua carry this out, I went with him to visit Chief Newcomer in Newcomerstown, and Joshua asked him about starting a separate village. Chief Newcomer listened carefully but gave him no answer.

Joshua then returned to Beautiful Spring and examined a site three miles to the north and found it a favorable place. Less than two weeks after our visit with Chief Newcomer, on 24 September, Joshua took his fellow Mohicans and moved to the new site where they began building a town. This upper town lay close enough to Beautiful Spring that teachers could easily go to them, and they could also attend services at the lower town.

Then Killbuck brought a message from the chiefs at Newcomerstown to the Mohicans: "My grandchildren" (this is what the Delawares call the Mohicans), "thirty-six days ago I learned that you had arrived here. We had designated a site for you at the old town of King Beaver along the Muskingum.

"However, now we see that you wanted to settle and build somewhere else. This is not your rightful place, and you should move away from there. We wish our grandchildren to live closer to us."

Good News returned this message to the chiefs: "The reason the Mohicans settled above us is that they still do not have a teacher with them, and therefore they wanted to live close to us. We will consider your words together and send you an answer as soon as possible."

The Mohicans from the upper town came to Beautiful

A New Beginning: 1772-1773

Spring for the sermon on a Sunday in October of 1772. After the sermon, we held a helpers' conference to consider the message from the chiefs. Good News said, "We must make it clear to the chiefs that we are not two people, but one. They must know that none of us does anything without the prior knowledge of the others.

"Besides, King Beaver Town is too far from us. During winter or spring, the waters often cannot be crossed, and it is possible that no one will be able to reach it for long periods of time." Good News was talking more to Joshua than to the chiefs.

Without asking Good News, Joshua and some others went down to the chiefs' recommended site the next day and looked at it. The place lay on a high bank on the east side of the Muskingum with beautiful fields across the river. The former town was about midway between Beautiful Spring and Newcomerstown.

Joshua and those with him liked the site and decided to move there. On 9 October the Mohicans and those living with them moved to King Beaver Town and erected temporary bark huts until they could build more permanent houses. Since they had no corn to take with them, the Brethren at Beautiful Spring gave them some to help them through the winter.

Brother Good News backtracked. With the approval of the Brethren, he named the mission Gnadenhuetten II (Huts of Grace) in honor of the mission on the Mahoning that had perished in the massacre. He also sent Brother Johann Roth to serve as teacher in the Mohican congregation.

That is the story of how the Mohican town on the Muskingum, Huts of Grace II, was begun.

UNDER ATTACK

Schoenbrunn: Beautiful Spring

On 5 May 1773, we arrived at Beautiful Spring with all our cargo and people intact. Our blessed journey had taken three weeks and a day. Those waiting there received us with all the kindness and hospitality possible.

The residents who had come with Brother Good News a year earlier, and those who had filtered in since, had done a good job preparing for the arrival of the pilgrims who came from Huts of Peace on the Susquehanna.

Palings fenced off the clear outline of a village that kept the cattle and horses outside with clean space on the inside for people. Temporary shelters awaited the travelers, and several necessary houses were already in place. Cleanliness and hygiene were important to their understanding of the Christian life.

With German precision, Brother Good News had laid out the town. He assigned lots for each family to build a house. Near the center, he drew off lots for a chapel and a school.

The added supplies and tools of the newcomers were toted up from the canoes in the river to the new town a quarter mile away. The cattle and the horses had already come overland. Bent on a common purpose, the expanded workforce labored diligently together. The bell, hastily erected on two poles, daily pealed out its welcoming tones in the village. And once or twice a day, the villagers crowded into the meeting hall for worship.

It soon became necessary to do something about the crowded conditions, so the brothers built an addition to the meeting hall. Many willing workers finished the building in only one day.

The first order of business for the entire village was to prepare for spring planting. Just ten days after we arrived, on Saturday, 15 May, the Brethren completed the fencing of more than eighty acres in

A New Beginning: 1772–1773

three different lots. The women will plant all the fenced lots this year, mostly in maize, but also squash, beans, potatoes, pumpkins, cucumbers, melons, and even some cabbages and turnips.

The following Sunday we met in the enlarged meeting hall, and Good News preached how the Savior, who proceeded from the Father and came into the world, accomplished the entire work of our redemption through His sufferings and death.

On Thursday, 20 May, we met early in the morning and read the Bible story (Acts 1:1-14) for Ascension Day. Then we knelt and worshipped Him and prayed for His precious presence and His further walk among us. Many strangers attended the service and heard the sermon that followed.

In the evening service, Brother Good News talked about the Watchword for the day,[6] from Song of Solomon 7:13—"At our gates are pleasant fruits." Then Lazara's husband was baptized into Jesus' death with the name Ezra. This event blessed the brothers and sisters as well as the many strangers who were present.

A week later, the Sunday sermon spoke about those who will be lost because of unbelief. Afterward we held a conference with the helpers. This meeting was special because it brought together the experienced helpers such as Johannes Papunhank from Huts of Peace on the Susquehanna and newer ones such as Isaac Glikkikan. From these helpers we soon heard the Indian perspective on the issues we faced. Today we were particularly concerned about reports that the Shawnees had scalped and killed many Whites far down the Ohio. War with the Virginians seemed inevitable.

Then we heard that two of the Shawnee neighbors, Wawiachtanos and Kickapoo, as well as the Delaware chief in Newcomerstown, had offered to help the Shawnees keep the peace. Furthermore, Chief Newcomer had warned the Shawnee, "If you do not keep the peace,

---

[6] Whenever possible, these same Watchwords were used on the same day in all the Moravian churches around the world.

UNDER ATTACK

you will come to complete ruin because no one will support you."

"Now," Brother David asked, "should we also advise the Shawnee to keep the peace? Peace is important to the mission so we can stay here and teach the Indians about the Savior."

Papunhank spoke first. "Eight years ago," he began, "we were taken from our homes and lands and held in captivity by lying Whites. Only last year we were again forced to leave our homes and lands which had been promised to us by the same Pennsylvania government that then deceitfully sold our settlement. We should have no dealings with the governments of either Pennsylvania or Virginia. They are both as corrupt as the Shawnee. We know only that both Pennsylvania and Virginia wish to steal the Ohioland and drive us away."

Brother Good News answered, "Peace is certainly in the best interest of the mission. We are here with the cooperation and support of Pennsylvania officials. We always speak for peace among all men."

Glikkikan spoke next.

> White men are in the Ohioland only as teachers by the invitation and consent of the Indians. You teachers should remember that. If our teachers want to cater to the officials and settlers of Pennsylvania or Virginia or the British, you should leave the Ohioland at once. These Christian Indians have not forgotten what happened at Shekomeko, the Forks of the Delaware, Wyoming, Philadelphia, and Wyalusing.
>
> You cry, "Peace! Peace!" when you really mean that the Indians do not fight back when the Whites attack them. Who is advancing upon the Indians again? Who is fighting whom for the land? Was it not the French fighting the English? Is it not Pennsylvania now fighting Virginia for the Ohioland? When you stood before their governors and generals and cried, "Peace! Peace!" were you really crying, "Go home"?
>
> Is it not the King's agent, Sir William Johnson, who urges the Indians to fight and destroy each other so the British

A New Beginning: 1772–1773

might take the land? Have you written letters to Sir William and cried "Peace"? Or is it only to the Indians that you say, "Stop fighting and stay home"?

I am for peace of mind and peace of heart, but let it come from the hearts of the Whites as well as from their lips. I long for a safe and secure homeland for the Delaware people, a place of peace.

Many years ago my grandfather, Owechela, urged me to find a gold medallion that held the secret of a safe homeland for the Delaware. Though I have searched long for it, I have not yet found it. Instead, we are always under attack by those who have driven us from our towns and lands. We must find this gold medallion and discover its secret message of peace and safety and a homeland for my people.

I have been entrusted with a copper medallion, but it does not tell how to preserve a homeland for the Lenape. I have been entrusted with a silver medallion, but it does not tell how to keep from being driven toward the setting sun. So after sixty and seven years of searching, it is still the gold medallion that I seek. Will you help me find it?

And then Brother David Good News spoke once more, saying, "I will give in my defense only the words found in Isaiah 52, verse 7: 'How beautiful on the mountains are the feet of those who bring good news, who proclaim peace, who bring good tidings, who proclaim salvation, who say to Zion, "Your God reigns!" ' "

With those ringing words which so clearly stated why we were in the Ohioland, we ended the helpers' conference.

UNDER ATTACK

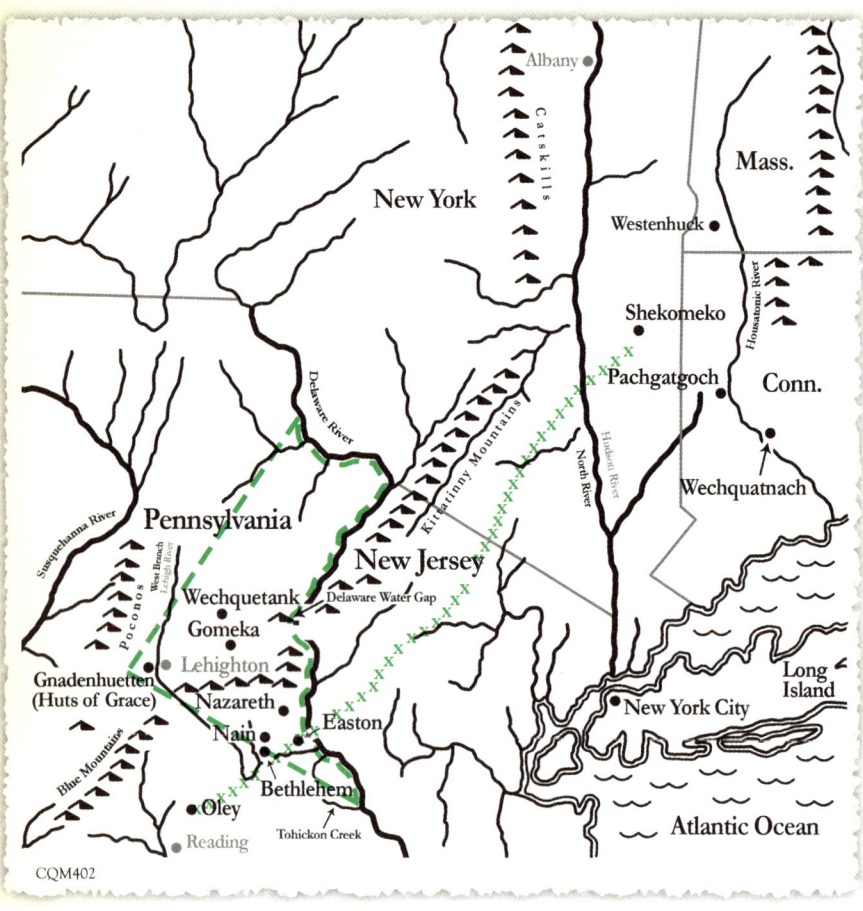

The Journey to Baptism (1742)

CQM402 Notes

1. Green Xs mark the 205-mile, three-week journey to baptism.
2. The broken green line outlines the border of the "Running Steal."
3. Three Moravian Missions: Shekomeko, New York; Pachgatgoch and Wechquatnach, Connecticut.
4. Moravian headquarters in America were in Bethlehem, Pennsylvania.
5. Westenhuck, the Mohican capital, was located in the upper Housatonic Valley, but its exact location is uncertain.
6. In 1740, New York City ranked third in population in American cities with approximately 11,000 people. Boston had 16,000 people and Philadelphia had 13,000.

Chapter 2

Under Attack at Shekomeko: 1742–1746

As recorded by John Heckewelder
At Beautiful Spring, Ohio,
Monday, 2 August 1773

The Machtapassican

After Glikkikan's impassioned plea for peace at the helpers' conference, I could hardly wait to meet with him. My pen was ready to write about some of the attacks he had mentioned at Shekomeko, the Forks of the Delaware, Wyoming, Philadelphia, and Wyalusing.

I also thought that I could possibly enlighten him about the gold medallion. The thing I could not understand was why Glikkikan still did not possess it. More than ten years had passed since Israel Pemberton had commissioned the Philadelphia silversmith to make one, and yet, according to Glikkikan's own testimony, he had not

UNDER ATTACK

received it. I would have to check on its whereabouts.

The famous Glikkikan still commanded such respect for his honesty and speaking ability that he spent much time on external affairs of the mission. Whenever the mission needed to deal with other Indians, Glikkikan went as the mission representative. That's the way it went with the *machtapassican*[7], or "the poison."

Gulpikamen, one of Glikkikan's sons, was a troublemaker from the Delaware capital at Newcomerstown. He had been baptized by the Brethren as Ludwig on 27 April 1749. Gulpikamen had once asked, "Do you know anything about the *machtapassican?*" He had acted very important and had left us a string of wampum which he pretended was coming from the Council at Newcomerstown. The first time he did this, the brothers returned his belt to him, but the second time, he forced it upon us and left. Ludwig had been trying to find the substance known as *machtapassican* for several years, but it seemed to us that his motivation was to gain power among the Indians.

The brothers Johannes, Isaac, Wilhelm, Nathanael, and Joseph were appointed to go and submit a declaration to Chief Watwees at Newcomerstown. Because of Johannes Papunhank's experience with the "poison" charges against him at Huts of Peace on the Susquehanna, we felt it doubly important that he accompany the delegation. The group appointed Isaac, or Glikkikan, to serve as speaker.

On 3 June, the delegation met with Chief Watwees and his Council. In the presence of a great crowd of listeners, Glikkikan delivered the following talk:

> My friends! A year ago we explained to you and your
> Council about our teaching, life, and walk—that we have
> abandoned all heathen ways and all sinful Indian customs

---

[7] This was a secret poison involving sorcery whereby one was supposed to be able to kill one's enemies, including whole towns, if they defied one's wishes.

Under Attack at Shekomeko: 1742–1746

and traditions and do not want to have anything to do with them. We want, instead, to live in the world in a manner pleasing to God. We expected you to give us an answer and tell us whether we could live this way at Beautiful Spring. Instead of giving us an answer, you have caused us trouble with your bad affairs, but we have refused to get mixed up with them. Therefore we think the time has come for you to offer us some explanation.

Glikkikan now presented them a string of wampum before continuing his speech.

> Once again, we are informing you that we have accepted the sweet and saving Word of God, not only with our mouths, but also with our whole hearts. We have brought with us here the Word that God sent to us. We hold firmly to this as to a great treasure and will do so until our end. Anyone among the Indians who would like to hear this and accept it should come to us. We will consider it a pleasure to teach him further.

Glikkikan now presented them a belt of wampum. Then both the first string and the belt were passed around the Council before Glikkikan continued.

> My friends, you have heard enough about what kind of people we are now. One of you forced a string of wampum upon us with angry words and asked us to consider matters which are against our hearts. It is not our business to deliberate about the *machtapassican*. This matter does not belong before us but before you. We have cast all this aside. We do not want to consider this or have anything to do with it.

UNDER ATTACK

At this point, Glikkikan threw the string on the floor in the middle of the Council. There it lay in total disgrace until a woman sweeping the floor took it up and hung it on a peg. The string was still hanging there when the brothers left to return home the next day.

The issue of the *machtapassican* would not go away. We learned from the Chief that the message about the poison had not come directly from him, although we believe it likely that he did have some knowledge of its being sent.

While our delegation was at Newcomerstown, everyone was friendly and polite. But after we left, a large discussion erupted. Some were quite unhappy, feeling that Glikkikan had spoken too directly and sharply in the Council. When he threw the string upon the floor, they interpreted the action as his thrusting evil things, especially the *machtapassican*, upon their heads. Instead, we were trying to help them eradicate it.

But generally, they were surprised that Brother Isaac spoke with such courage and audacity to such a gathering of Indians in the presence of the chiefs. Some said mockingly, "Of course he was so brave and courageous. He was baptized with the brain and heart of a white minister!"

To get the meaning of "being baptized with the brain and heart of a white minister," one must know the Indian legend behind it.

> A certain pious minister lived among the white people. He was a reasonable and wise man. His piety and character were unrivalled. When he died, his followers could not find anyone like him anywhere to minister to them. They took the brain and heart from their departed minister, dried the organs, and pulverized them. They saved this powder to see if it would have a good effect on others.
>
> It happened that someone went mad and was in such a rage that no one could control him. They tried many

Under Attack at Shekomeko: 1742–1746

things without success. At last, the people mixed a little of this powder in a vessel with water and baptized the madman with it. Immediately, he became as reasonable, wise, and pious as their former minister had been.

The heathen Indians say that now we baptize all the Indians who come to us with some of this powder. Nevertheless, the chiefs were still not satisfied about the *machtapassican* and sent a messenger with a string of wampum, inviting our old blind chief, Salomo, to a council. The messenger also said the chiefs wanted to send a twelve-man delegation to the Cherokee to suggest they make peace with the Wawiachtano nation. The Cherokee had just recently destroyed a whole town of these people, killing even the women and children.

We asked Abraham, Samuel, and Jacob Daskund to take Salomo to the Council, and sent with him nearly seventy feet of wampum to assist the peace delegation to the Cherokees.

The chiefs called Salomo to come to them because he is very old, and they wanted to learn what he had heard about the *machtapassican*. He told them all he knew, but emphasized that he had only heard these things without ever seeing them with his own eyes.

Everyone was well satisfied with Salomo's answers, so they gave him a hundred strings of corn as well as other gifts to reward him for his journey. In addition, the Council was very pleased with the gift of wampum from Huts of Grace and Beautiful Spring for the peace delegation to the Cherokee.[8] In short, everyone reacted favorably to Salomo's visit, and for the time being, the matter of *machtapassican* was laid to rest.

---

[8] This giving of wampum to the chiefs was a sort of voluntary tax that gave the chiefs the means to carry out their plans.

UNDER ATTACK

All About the Indians

This spring, a bad cough has wracked the children here and has taken many lives. In Newcomerstown alone, more than fifty children died. Now the sickness has reached into our towns as well. Very few have been spared.

The Savior took young Abigail, the 16-month-old baby daughter of Brother Willhelm and Sister Martha, home to Himself in blessing.

Brother Isaac and Sister Agnes lost their two-and-a-half-year-old baby boy to the ailment. Brother Good News baptized him into Jesus' death with the name Jonathan.

The Savior took Tobias, the little son born to Nicolai and Amalia, home to Himself. He was in his second year.

The following day the same thing happened to Benjamin, a quiet 14-year-old boy who has been sick for a year. His mother brought him to Beautiful Spring at its founding a year and a half ago. After his baptism, he seemed to revive, but nine days later, things suddenly changed, and he went in blessing to the One who purchased him with His blood.

Brother Michael and Sister Charlotte's baby girl, young Sabina, also died. She was one and a half years old.

Then Brother Levi and Sister Salome's baby daughter, Rebecca, who was four months old, died.

All these died in only three weeks' time. We buried them the day after their deaths in the area designated as God's Acre. Conducting a short service at the burial, we comforted the grieving ones as best we could.

Amid all the dying, a baby was born to Brother and Sister Roth at Huts of Grace. The next day Brother David, Brother and Sister

Under Attack at Shekomeko: 1742-1746

Jungman, and some Indian brothers and sisters made the journey so they could attend the baptism of the infant. They named the child Johannes Ludwig Roth.

On another happy note, on 9 July the brothers went fishing and brought home some very large fish four or five feet long. On the 19th of July, they went fishing again and brought home two canoe loads of fish. Some were of the exceptional size of six or seven feet long.[9]

Philippus Jr. from Huts of Grace traveled north on a hunting trip till he reached the lake where the Muskingum begins. Glikkikan told him, "You were only a few miles from where the Cayahaga River begins and only about a day's journey from Lake Erie. I know the area where you were."

On 27 July, Chief Watwees sent for Brother Samuel Moor to come to Newcomerstown and interpret for him. Brother Isaac accompanied him. Three Quakers from Philadelphia had also come for a visit.

First, the Quakers gave a talk in which they reminded the Indians of the longstanding friendship they had maintained since the days they first came into the country.

After this warmup, the chiefs asked the Quakers to send them preachers who could teach them various trades so they might become an orderly people. Furthermore, the chiefs requested that the Quakers would transport some of their people to England to talk with the King.

The Quakers would not agree to these suggestions and made excuses, saying these things were not their concern and it was not fitting for them to do so. Despite much pressure from the Indians, they still refused to promise any money for a journey to talk with the King.

When Brother Isaac returned from his trip to Newcomerstown, I was part of a crowd that gathered around him to hear him tell about it.

---

[9] *Wellenreuther & Wessel*, eds., p. 149. The diary is specific as to the length of the fish caught in this time period.

UNDER ATTACK

I was very well received by Chief Watwees and the Indians. They followed me from one house to another to hear what I had to say. One of them, a headman named Wehund, engaged me in much private discussion.

Wehund told me, "I have already thought about this a lot and considered becoming a believer, but I am afraid of the Indians and especially the chiefs. Then I remembered Isaac, and I thought, *Isaac knows everything about the Indians; nothing is hidden from him. He has been an advisor to the chiefs. He has been a captain, doctor, and preacher. Now he has become a believer. Therefore what the brothers are teaching must really be the truth because he is a reasonable man who can judge whether something is right or not.*"

I answered Wehund, "You have considered correctly. I know everything about Indian affairs because I was among the chiefs everywhere and have gone deeply into every matter. However, I found nothing to satisfy my heart. I can bear witness to you that the brothers' teaching is the truth because I have experienced it in my heart as the truth."

Wehund asked, "What do you think of the suggestions we made to the Quakers for them to send us other teachers?"

I answered him, "The Indians will not complete their projects in many years, and perhaps nothing will come of it in the end. The Gospel will be preached here indeed, and whoever wants to hear it can come and hear it. Why do the Indians want to look further? This is nothing more than obstacles laid in the path so that the Indians cannot hear it."

Wehund agreed with me. "That is what I told the Council as well. What is there to decide? We have the

Under Attack at Shekomeko: 1742-1746

Gospel preached for all those who want to hear it. The brothers teach us how to live and be happy. Why should we go to the King? It would take a long time to carry this matter out, and we could all die before it is done. Then what would we gain? Glikkikan, I would rather come to you now so that I can hear the Gospel before I die."

Then I told Wehund and all those who were there, "Even if you get more preachers and teachers, you will not be any better off. No one will preach God's Word and the way to salvation more clearly than the brothers already have. I, not the brothers, am telling you this. That way, no one can say that the white brothers said this. No, I have said it myself."

"Brother John," Glikkikan said, turning to me, "Wehund will come to us again."

Sure enough, Wehund and several Indians from Newcomerstown came to visit. They attended our Sunday services, and the Indian believers spoke a great deal with them about salvation in Jesus.

The three Quakers and a trader, Honest John Anderson, also a Quaker, stopped by Beautiful Spring on their way back to Pittsburgh. They were very pleased with the reverence and order they saw in our Indian brothers and sisters. I saw Glikkikan corner Trader John Anderson, and the two had a long talk together. Traders often served as walking newspapers, so I strained to hear choice tidbits of news.

As we had agreed on the canoe journey, Brother Isaac met with me on Sunday evening, 1 August, to get some of the past recorded in writing.

We met outside the chapel under the shade of one of the grand locust trees. I sat on a small chair in front of him. As was the Indian custom, he sat cross-legged on the ground in front of me. That gave me a slight advantage in height, which I always enjoyed. When a short man like me

UNDER ATTACK

is dealing with a big, strong captain, a little extra height feels good.

I began our session by asking, "Brother Isaac, did the chiefs really want to have the Quakers begin a mission among them?"

"Brother John," he replied, "the chiefs had little interest in hearing the Gospel or in visiting the King of England. What they really wanted was to pressure the Quakers into giving them gifts in the generous fashion that has been typical of Quakers."

"Did they give you any gifts?" I prodded.

"Like what?" he asked.

"Like the gold medallion you asked us to help you find. I thought maybe the Quakers could be of some help to you in locating it."

"I have heard nothing from them about a gold medallion," Glikkikan replied evenly. Then he stopped and gazed silently off into the distance.

I tried to get things started again, and this time I was more successful. "What did you learn from John Anderson? Maybe he had some information on the gold medallion."

Glikkikan was fully engaged now. "John Anderson is the most honest and trustworthy of any of the traders," he answered. Honest John knows what is going on among the Indians because they trust him."

"Well, what is going on? That's what I want to know."

Brother Isaac grinned. "I guess you know that the King's deputy Indian agent, Alexander McKee, had a mother who was a Shawnee and a father who was a white trader. I don't know how many Shawnee wives he has," Glikkikan answered playfully.

I played along. "Do tell!"

"Yes, and another of your favorite white traders, John Gibson, has a child by a Mingo woman, Koonay. She's Chief Talgayeeta's sister, and she lives over at Yellow Creek on the Ohio. But that's nothing. The King's Indian agent, Many Children Johnson, has a hundred children from Iroquois women."

Under Attack at Shekomeko: 1742-1746

"Is that all the current gossip you know?" I joked. "Let's get serious now."

"Okay. More and more settlers float down the Ohio and settle on Indian lands. British soldiers have evacuated Fort Pitt and promised to destroy it. Instead, John Connolly and local militia took over the Fort for Virginia and its governor, Lord Dunmore. Connolly wants war with the Indians so he can take all their land for Virginia. Deputy McKee wants the Indian land for Pennsylvania. The Shawnee are very unhappy and are prepared to fight. The Delaware and the Cherokee are warning the Shawnee that they will not support them in a war. The Mingos, who own no land and have no right to sell Shawnee territory, have given the Whites some land to compensate them for horses they stole years ago. McKee and Croghan and Gibson are giving a few gifts trying to appease the—"

"Tell me something I don't already know," I interrupted.

He shrugged. "Okay, it's all about land—the Ohioland."

"But that's not why the Moravians are here," I protested. Good News, the Schmicks, the Jungmans, and I—even I—are here to serve the Savior and bring the Good News to the Indian nations. We have no land."

"Brother John, let it be clear. You have done much for the heathen Indians by telling them of the Savior and by teaching them how to live. But maybe you cannot see the truth because your eyes are as blind as old Salomo's. Perhaps if you go back to the beginning when Count Nicolas Zinzendorf first came to America and started Bethlehem, you will find out the Moravians were not as innocent of the land fraud as you want to believe."

"Brother Isaac, what do you know about Count Zinzendorf and the early Moravian missions?" Without giving him time to answer, I forged ahead, confident that I knew what I was talking about.

For a while, Glikkikan gave no hint that he already knew much of what I had to say, but prodded me on with constant eye contact and an occasional *"Kehelle"* of agreement.

UNDER ATTACK

Not Land but Life

As narrated by John Heckewelder

Glikkikan, I know well the story of those first Moravians who came to America. At Bethlehem, Pennsylvania, I thoroughly studied the detailed journals and careful records of those early missionaries of the *Unitas Fratrum*. It has even been my lot to lay eyes on Count Zinzendorf's writings describing his 1742 visit to America.[10]

The story I am going to tell you happened at Shekomeko, New York. Count Zinzendorf himself visited this mission during his travels in Pennsylvania and New York thirty-three years ago. He wrote detailed accounts of the Shekomeko mission.

On 11 March 1754, only twelve years after Count Zinzendorf had been in America, he questioned me, laid his hands on my head, and offered up a prayer. His blessing was my sendoff to America.

The next day, on my eleventh birthday, I boarded the Moravian-owned ship *Irene* under the direction of Captain Garrison. I departed London in the company of men who were to become great leaders of the Moravian Church in America, men like Bishops Ettwein, Spangenberg, and Nitschmann. As we sailed across, we often sang lines like these which I well remember:

> The rugged rocks, the dreary wilderness,
> Mountains and woods are our appointed place;
> Midst storms and waves, on heathen shores unknown,
> We have our temple, and serve God alone.

---

[10] Count Zinzendorf was the founder of the *Unitas Fratrum* (Unity of the Brethren), commonly called the Moravian Church. A German nobleman of rare ability, genius, means, and vision, he inspired and organized a whole cadre of dedicated and zealous worldwide missionaries.

Under Attack at Shekomeko: 1742-1746

Our whole company of twenty-six adults, including my parents and their fourteen children, of whom I was the eldest, called ourselves the Sea Congregation. We arrived in New York without encountering a single heavy gale in a miraculously short voyage of only twenty-one days.

It has been only twenty-one years since I met these early men of faith and vision and was inspired by them. The eyewitness accounts which they have written allow no doubt about the purpose of the first Moravians who came to America. Their record is clear. Unlike most other colonists, the Moravians did not come to America seeking land or wealth. From the very beginning in 1735, when the first Moravians came to Georgia, their express purpose for crossing the waters was to tell the natives of the Savior.

Moravian writings are filled with the purpose of saving souls. Expressions like these permeate the records of the Brethren:

- Send faithful workers for your harvest.
- You, church with little might, make use of your gift for gathering souls.
- The Spirit who created the congregations has certainly invited you to that task. He opens this and that field, even across the ocean in the New World.
- You should get for Him, as a prize, barbarians whom no hunger forces, whom neither push nor thrust disturbs; the word of the cross should gain the victory over them.[11]

Inspired by such fervent beliefs and a commission from a gathered church in far-off Moravia, 22-year-old Christian Henry Rauch boarded a ship and arrived in New York City on 16 July 1740. Except for God, he came alone.

Providentially, he met the Moravian missionary, Frederic Martin, recently returned from St. Thomas, West Indies. Frederic introduced

---

[11] Translated from German <engr.psu.edu/mtah/articles/harvest_home.htm>.

UNDER ATTACK

Christian Henry to several influential people he thought might be helpful to the young man in his undertaking.

But instead of aiding the zealous young man, the contacts all tried to discourage him. "Every attempt to civilize the natives has resulted in failure," they told him. "The Indian savages are illiterate and know nothing of Christian ways. It is impossible to evangelize them," his supposed friends declared.

Christian would not be deterred. "If the heathen cannot read about Christ for themselves, then I must tell them about the Savior and His blood," he insisted.

His friends smiled at the childlike simplicity of the young man and then told him, "Well, since you are so determined to see some savages, there is a delegation of Indians in the city right now, complaining about land matters. Go and have a look at them for yourself. You will find them somewhere near the courthouse."

Christian Henry found the delegation of Mohican[12] and Wappinger Indians. They were in town to complain about the settling of their lands under the Rombout and Philipse Patents.[13] Sure enough, the delegation was a tough-looking lot. Daniel Nimham, with an opossum tattooed on his chest, had just been made chief of the Wappingers. Mohican Chiefs Wamapah and Shabash had multiple tattoos and scars decorating their arms, faces, and chests. Chief Wamapah had another name as well—Hard Warrior. With his constant scowls, fierce countenance, and rough skin clothing, Hard Warrior looked more like an old bear just out of hibernation than a human being.

The New York officials were giving the Indian delegation the runaround by sending them from one person to another. While some of the Indian delegation could speak Dutch, magistrates and clerks

---

[12] *Mohican*, *Mahican*, and *Mohegan* are various spellings for this Lenape grandchild.
[13] These patents for huge tracts of Indian land were given out under former Dutch administrations and were now held or dispersed through these Dutch families.

Under Attack at Shekomeko: 1742–1746

pretended they could not understand their complaints. Instead, generous officials mollified the trio with plenty of rum.

Daniel Nimham was exasperated. Wamapah and Shabash appeared dangerously angry. But young Christian Henry took an interest in their case. He went with them to the officials and was not easily put aside. He made plain his objective to the officials: to evangelize the heathen. These very Indians afforded a good starting place.

The Whites did not like this young foreigner meddling in their business. When he saw Christian Henry would not be easily pushed aside, an official told him plainly, "Young man, you're a fool. It's impossible to civilize these savages. Can't you see that the Mohicans are a confessedly worthless tribe of Indians, naturally fierce, vindictive, and given to excessive drinking?"

Then he continued in a darker vein. "The sorry, worthless, degenerate Mohicans keep grumbling about being defrauded of their land. Just let nature take its course, and the land problem will go away."

But Christian Henry persisted. "Did the settlers pay the Indians a fair price for their land?" he asked.

"What's a fair price?" the official scoffed. "Old one-legged Stuyvesant traded with them for their lands eighty years ago. Why pay for the land over and over? The Mohicans can't do anything about it anyway. The savages know nothing about land titles, and there isn't a magistrate in Poughkeepsie who would rule in their favor. Young man," he concluded ominously, "if you know what's good for you, you'll stay out of this."

Such warnings came from more than just one official. Many Whites (professing Christians) echoed the same sentiment. As one "Christian" expressed it, "The Indians are universally of such a vicious and abandoned character that all efforts for their improvement would be dangerous, as well as utterly in vain."

But Christian Henry knew why he had come to America, and he

UNDER ATTACK

would not be scared off. During one conversation with the Indians when they were sober, Chief Wamapah said, "I frequently wish to know better things than I do, but I do not know where to find them."

Then Chief Shabash proposed, "Would you come to our village and be our teacher?"

This was exactly what Christian Henry wanted, and he readily agreed to the proposition. But the next day, when Wamapah and Shabash were drunk, they cancelled the invitation. When they sobered up, they again invited him to come to their village and be their teacher. The same thing happened several times. When sober, they wanted him to come, but when drunk, they cancelled their invitation. Finally, they slunk off without him.

Christian Henry followed Shabash and Wamapah from farm to farm until he arrived at their home village exactly a month after arriving in New York. Wamapah and Shabash's village lay huddled next to a small stream behind which rose a thickly wooded slope. Nearby, numerous crude shelters housed sixty Mohicans. A large field of herbs, beans, and corn flourished next to the village. The Mohicans called both the nearby creek and their village Shekomeko.[14]

On his arrival, Christian Henry launched right into preaching to the Indians. Favorably prepared for his coming by Wamapah and Shabosh, the village at first heard him gladly, but soon their attitude turned to scorn and derision. Some even threatened his life.

Word of Christian Henry's arrival in Shekomeko came quickly to the home of a nearby farmer named John Rowe. His daughter, Jeanette, had friends in the Indian village and spoke the Mohican tongue with ease. Jeanette told her father of the young German preacher, and John Rowe went at once to find Christian Henry.

The two struck up an immediate friendship, freely conversing in

---

[14] *Shekomeko* has been variously translated as "place of eels" and "little mountain."

Under Attack at Shekomeko: 1742–1746

their native German. They got along so well that John Rowe invited Christian Henry to lodge with him if he would give his children some schooling. Christian Henry gladly accepted on condition that the Rowes would teach him the Mohican language.

Christian found that John Rowe and his family held a different attitude toward Shekomeko than most of the surrounding white settlers. The Whites derisively called the little tract of land inhabited by the Mohicans "The Wigwam." All the surrounding country was already claimed and farmed by Whites who regarded their Indian neighbors with utter disgust. Most of them wanted nothing to do with the village except to profit from them through the sale of alcohol.

In contrast to the prevailing sentiments of the settlers, John Rowe and his family showed concern for the plight of the Indians and made the effort to learn their language. They befriended the Indians and gave them small gifts of clothing, tools, and utensils that the villagers appreciated.

But even then, John Rowe cautioned Christian Henry about the foolhardiness of his avowed goal to save the Mohicans. One day as he traveled with Christian to give medical attention to a sick settler, John broached the delicate subject. "Aren't the Indians like the Canaanites when God told the Israelites to take over the land of Canaan?" he asked. "God forbade the Israelites to mix with the Canaanites lest the Israelites learn their heathen ways. Chief Wamapah worships his grandmother's leather idol. The Mohicans also are wholly given over to their heathen ways. Both Shabash and Wamapah are nothing but worthless drunks. Do you think you can change them?"

John Rowe cautiously eyed his traveling companion and then continued. "Ought not the Mohicans be left alone and nature allowed to take its course? Besides, Shabash and Wamapah's continued land claims only irritate the white settlers."

Christian Henry reined in his horse and surveyed Stissing

UNDER ATTACK

Mountain, mirrored in the glistening waters of Lake Halcyon. Then he responded with fervor of voice and gleaming blue eyes, "The Mohicans are not the Canaanites, and the Whites are not the Israelites. The Whites do not have any God-given right to the land."

"Friend John, you are right," Christian Henry continued, "when you say that I cannot change the Mohicans. But the blood of the Savior can. Do you see the perfect beauty of Lake Halcyon? The same God who made that lake created you and Chief Wamapah. Do you not think the Mohicans have souls that Christ died for? The Bible says that He made all nations of one blood. Yes, God can change the Mohicans if we but teach them the truth about the Savior of all men."

John Rowe studied the attractive and talented young German before him. Christian Henry embodied much of what he admired. "Young man," he said, choosing his words with care, "don't get carried away with your preaching and make a fool of yourself." Then he added rather pointedly, "God forbids the mingling of the races. Christians shall marry only Christians, and not those heathen savages." Then, uncertain that his appeal from the Bible would hold up to Christian Henry's learned mind, John Rowe added, "Besides, there is a great cultural difference between the Whites and the Indians. Any Christian who would marry an Indian is headed for big trouble."

Christian Henry loosened his horse's reins and the two traveled onward with only the clopping of horse hooves to entertain their thoughts.

John Rowe's eighteen-year-old daughter, Jeanette, wasn't sure if the Indians could be saved. She well knew the deplorable conditions the villagers lived in and their despicable treatment by so-called Christians. Furthermore, she admired the noble goals of Christian Henry and had to admit that she did have some special feelings for the earnest missionary. In her mind, one could do worse than marry a Moravian Pietist.

Jeanette set herself to the task of teaching Christian the Mohican

Under Attack at Shekomeko: 1742-1746

tongue. Christian was delighted to have such an apt and likable teacher. He was a ready scholar and fluent in several languages already. But like a horse wearing blinders, he could see only the one motivation of saving the heathen and overlooked Jeanette's interests. Math was math, language was language, and following the Lamb for him meant the saving of souls, Mohican souls.

Not Rum but Blood

Christian Henry learned Mohican quickly while continuing his regular visits to the Mohican village of Shekomeko. He talked much about the blood of the Savior and how it could save the Mohicans from their wretched misery. It didn't make any sense to the Mohicans, and they thought him a fool. He spent his time in Shekomeko in peril of his life, but despite the danger, he persisted in his preaching.

On one occasion, after a long journey back from Bethlehem, Christian Henry arrived at Shekomeko, footsore and weary. He was extremely burdened for Chief Wamapah. Christian had found the Chief in his hut, exceedingly drunk. He sat down beside him and spoke thus to Wamapah: "I come to you in the name of the Lord of heaven and earth. He sends me to let you know that He will make you happy and deliver you from the misery in which you lie at present. To this end He became a man, gave His life a ransom for man, and shed His blood for him. The Creator has died, and the very Son of God, Jesus, has shed His blood so that Mohicans can be saved. Because of the blood, Chief Wamapah can be saved. He must get that blood in his heart. Blood. Blood. Blood."

When Christian Henry finished his discourse, he lay down upon a board and fell into a sound sleep, fatigued by his journey.

UNDER ATTACK

On another day, when Chief Wamapah had sobered up, he called for Christian Henry. "I must tell you something," Chief Wamapah began. "The day you came into my hut and fell asleep in front of me, I thought, *What kind of man is this? There he lies and sleeps. I might kill him and throw him out into the woods, and who would regard it? But this gives him no concern. He must be a good man to trust me so. Maybe I should think about his message.*

"Christian Henry, I have thought much about your words. They are different than the message of another preacher who once came to our village and explained to us that there was a God who made the world and everything in it. We answered him, 'Do you think us so ignorant as not to know that? We know of the Great Spirit. Go back to the place you came from.'

"Another preacher came to our village and began to teach us. He said, 'Man is evil. You must not steal, nor lie, nor get drunk, and so on.'

"We answered him, 'You fool, do you think that we do not know that? Learn first yourself, and then teach your own people to leave off these things. For who steals more, lies more, or is drunken more frequently than your own people?' And we dismissed him.

"Christian Henry, your message is different from anything I have ever heard. What is this blood you speak so much about when you come to our village? Why do you look so pleased when you talk so about blood? Blood. Blood. Blood. When I am awake, I cannot get this blood out of my mind. When I sleep, I dream of that blood which Christ shed for us."

Chief Wamapah leaned his scarred and weather-beaten face closer to Christian Henry and gazed earnestly into his eyes. "Why do you always speak of blood with such emotion and joy of heart?" he asked.

"Ah!" Christian replied, "it is easy to speak of the blood with joy, for I am telling people that the Creator died and shed His blood for the Mohicans and for Chief Wamapah."

Under Attack at Shekomeko: 1742–1746

"Is this true?" Chief Hard Warrior asked. "What must one do to get a share in this blood?"

Christian Henry beamed, and with all the earnestness of his soul he answered, "Nothing but believe, and with one's heart hang upon the Savior, conversing with Him in the mind till one experiences what He did."

"But I am so inclined to drunkenness," Chief Wamapah confessed.

Christian Henry replied, "The reason you have trouble with drunkenness is that you do not yet have that blood in your heart; you must first get that, and then your drunkenness will soon fall away."

From that time on, the heathen Wamapah begged with sighs that God would make this blood real to him as it was to Christian Henry. God gave Wamapah the desire of his heart. The blood of the Savior became real to the heathen Wamapah, and he would not let it go out of his mind. After that, he never had leisure to get drunk any more.

The change in Wamapah was dramatic. He renounced his grandmother's leather idols, abandoned his brutal ways, and to the surprise of all, stopped drinking.

Before Wamapah quit drinking, both his wife and mother had been excessively grieved at his getting drunk so much. Now, however, they were even more displeased that he would have nothing to do with drinking anymore. Instead, he was wholly taken up with things they could not comprehend. They both thought he had gone crazy.

Chief Wamapah's wife and mother were not the only ones who became his enemies after he altered his former course of life. Many Mohicans and Whites were no less angry with him. Wamapah could not understand why this was so, and he asked Christian Henry to explain it to him.

Christian had a ready answer. "All men are corrupt by nature, and it is a very great grace when God takes a person from the bulk of mankind and makes him quite another man," he explained. "Therefore

UNDER ATTACK

people envy someone like that because they are convinced of the matter in their own hearts, and yet, they themselves will not be converted. That is why they hate to see others changed when they themselves continue to live in misery."

Wamapah responded, "Now I know why both the heathen and the so-called Christians persecute you and me, and all my doubts are removed from me."[15]

Wamapah's change in character from an inveterate drunkard and reckless ruffian caused a great sensation in Shekomeko. People saw in him hope of a better life for all Mohicans. Wamapah proved very effective at convincing his own people of the merits of the blood. He said to Christian Henry, "I know how the heathen think. It is not hard to teach them that they need the Savior's blood."

Three other local leaders, Shabash, Seim, and Kiop, soon gave up their fears and followed the teaching of Christian Henry. A great miracle was taking place in Shekomeko as more Mohicans turned to the Savior.

Bishop David Nitschman came from Bethlehem, Pennsylvania, to visit Shekomeko in the fall of 1741. He was delighted with the progress there. When he returned to Bethlehem, he sent another young German to assist Christian Henry.

Gottlob Buettner, only twenty-five years of age, arrived at Shekomeko early in January of 1742. He added fuel to the fire that had begun and preached from Colossians 1:13: "God has delivered us from the power of darkness, and has brought us into the kingdom of His dear Son." After the service, he extended the invitation of Bishop Nitschman and Count Zinzendorf for Christian Henry and those ready for baptism to come to Oley, Pennsylvania, for a church synod.

---

[15] This account is based largely on the diary kept by Count Zinzendorf, the founder of the Moravians, during his visit to America. The account is also corroborated by Wamapah's personal testimony at a later synod (church gathering) in Bethlehem, Pennsylvania.

Under Attack at Shekomeko: 1742–1746

Gottlob, Christian Henry, Shabash, Seim, and Kiop set off on the three-week journey by foot to Bethlehem on 22 January 1742. Chief Wamapah was lame, and much to his disappointment, could not undertake going with them. Instead, he sent a message along with Christian Henry.

Not Idols but Water

As recorded by John Heckewelder

Here Glikkikan's eyes sparkled. His whole body quivered with anticipation. I stopped.

"Brother John," he said, "I would like to give that speech delivering Chief Wamapah's message."

"Please do," I responded. Glikkikan jumped to his feet, and like an orator standing before Packanke's Council, he began.

> I have been a poor, wild heathen, and for forty years I was as ignorant as a dog. I was the greatest drunkard and a willing slave of the devil. As I knew nothing of our Savior, I served vain idols which I now wish to see destroyed with fire. Of this, I have repented with many tears. When I heard that Jesus was also the Savior of the heathen and that I ought to give Him my heart, I felt drawn toward Him.
>
> But my wife and children were my enemies, and my greatest enemy was my wife's mother. She told me that I was worse than a dog if I no more believed in her idol. But my eyes being opened, I understood that what she said was altogether folly, for I knew she had received the idol from her grandmother. It was made of leather and decorated with

UNDER ATTACK

> wampum, and she, being the oldest person in the house, made us worship it. We did this willingly until our teacher came and told us of the Lamb of God, who shed His blood and died for us poor, ignorant people.
>
> Now I feel and believe that our Savior alone can help me by the power of His blood alone. I believe that He is my God and my Savior who died on the cross for me, a sinner. I wish to be baptized and long for it most ardently. I am lame and cannot travel in winter, but in April or May, I will come to you.

When Glikkikan came to the end of the speech, he was so inspired with the story of Chief Wamapah that he could not stop. I knew then that the Chief was one of his heroes. And not only Glikkikan's, but a great treasure in the hearts of all Christian Indians. Yes, Wamapah was a Mohican, but his Christian friends among the Delawares also knew his story well.

So Glikkikan continued:

> The travelers arrived at Oley on the farm of Jan de Turck two days before the synod started. On the morning of 20 February 1742, Bishops Nitschman and Zinzendorf ordained Christian Henry and Gottlob as deacons. On the afternoon of that memorable day, only nineteen months after Christian Henry Rauch arrived in New York City, the three knelt around a large vessel filled with water, and Christian Henry baptized Shabash as Abraham, Siem as Isaac, and Kiop as Jacob.
>
> Abraham, Isaac, and Jacob, along with their leaders, made the long winter trek back to Shekomeko, singing as they went. On 16 April 1742, Christian Henry

Under Attack at Shekomeko: 1742–1746

The First Indian Baptism

"On that memorable day I baptized Shabash, Siem, and Kiop as Abraham, Isaac, and Jacob."
—Christian Henry

UNDER ATTACK

baptized Chief Wamapah at Shekomeko as John, or John Wamapah. Abraham, Isaac, Jacob, and John became model converts and showed that even hopeless drunks and reckless ruffians could become gentle followers of the Savior.

Indians from as far away as thirty miles inland came to Shekomeko to hear the sweet words of life and see for themselves the proof of the incredible stories they had heard. Twenty-seven Indians from Pachgatgoch and four deputies from Potatik, seventy miles away, came to visit and asked for someone to bring them the Gospel.

On one of the missionary journeys to Pachgatgoch, about twenty miles east of Shekomeko, Chief Maweseman asked, "Are you from Shekomeko? Are you indeed Chief Wamapah? We have heard how notoriously wicked you have been, and how the grace bestowed upon you has changed you."

"You are right. I am Chief Wamapah, a great sinner who has been delivered from Satan's power," John confessed. "I am here to tell you that the Lord our Savior desires to grant you the same happiness He has given me. He requires you only to deliver yourself over to Him. Wretched as you are, He will gladly forgive your sins and deliver you from the yoke of Satan."

Chief Maweseman and those with him gladly heard these words of life, staying up till midnight and asking many questions of John and his companions. Before long, six Indians from Pachgatgoch were baptized. Chief Maweseman was now named Gideon. Great grace prevailed among the people, and it was evident that the Holy Ghost was poured out upon them.

John Wamapah had a special gift for making the Gospel

Under Attack at Shekomeko: 1742-1746

clear to the Indian peoples—Mohicans, Wampanoags, and Delawares. He often used a simple object lesson to illustrate his discourse in the Indian manner. Once, at Pachgatgoch, he took a board and drew upon it with charcoal a heart with strings and points proceeding in all directions.

"This is the state of a man's heart while Satan dwells in it," he said. "Every evil thing proceeds from it." John went on to tell them how the blood of Jesus could wash the evil out of their hearts and deliver them from the power of sin.

An Indian woman from Menissing paid John a visit and told him, "As soon as I have a good heart, I will turn to the Lord Jesus."

"Ah," John replied, "that is like saying you want to walk on your head! How can you get a good heart, unless you come first to Jesus?"

Another time, John entered an English town when rumors of war with the French were rampant. The people were all in great dread of the Indians, and they soon surrounded him to inquire what news he brought from the Indian country. He answered, "News of all kinds, but the most interesting news to me is that it is good to believe on the Lord Jesus Christ."

Upon hearing that, the people soon left him so he could quietly go about his business. John was often equally straightforward, in the Indian manner, when dealing with the English. He boldly reproved the Whites for their sinful way of life, and whenever he was interrogated, he spoke the truth without any reserve or caution. For instance, an English clergyman in Westenhuck, the Mohican capital, asked John, "Have you heard the missionary in Shekomeko preach?"

UNDER ATTACK

John answered, "Yes, I have heard the missionary preach quite often."

The English clergyman then asked, "Did you like him?"

John answered, "I would rather hear the missionary's words than attend to you. For when I hear the missionary, his words lay hold of my heart and a voice within me says, *That is truth*. But when I listen to you, you are always playing about the truth and never come to the point. You have no love for the souls of your hearers, and once you baptize them, you let them run wild, never troubling yourself further about them. You act worse than one who plants Indian corn, for at least the planter goes back sometimes to till his corn and see whether it grows or not."

Upon another occasion, a white man asked John, "Are the Brethren papists?"

In return, John asked, "What are papists?"

"Papists worship images and follow the head chief of their church, whom they call the pope," the inquirer explained.

"No, the Brethren must not be papists, for they do not worship images. They worship only the one God in spirit and in truth, and they teach us that Jesus Christ is the head of the church, not some earthly pope. However, I have seen many Whites around us who seem to worship their cows, horses, and plantations. I suppose they are papists," John concluded.

"Then why are the people so enraged at the Brethren?" the White asked.

John answered that question with another question. "Why did the people crucify the Lord Jesus and throw Paul bound into prison?" Not stopping with that, John continued, "And why do you take up guns and bayonets to kill the

Under Attack at Shekomeko: 1742–1746

papists? Does not the Good Book teach us that to fight our enemies with the weapons of this world is sin? We are to be a people of peace, living in love and kindness and forgiving our enemies, not killing them.

Brother Isaac Glikkikan smiled in thoughtful delight as he pondered the boldness of John's answers. I knew they were the same kind of answers he himself would have given.

I, however, threw up my hands. "Brother Isaac, don't you realize that such bold but unseasonable reproofs only increased the enmity of the adversaries? It made it so that those who traveled about in the concerns of the missions suffered much unnecessary oppression and persecution because of similar confrontations. During a war, one must be more diplomatic and considerate so as not to offend his friends."

"But Brother John, should we allow our friends to remain in the sleep of sin and under the power of the devil to avoid persecution? Did our Savior not suffer for us much more than the present light afflictions we now endure for His sake?"

Without waiting for me to answer, Brother Isaac recited the *Lebenslauf*[16] for John Wamapah as recorded in the Moravian journals. John died of the small pox in 1746 and lies buried in God's Acre in Bethlehem, right beside other Whites and Indians who await the coming resurrection of the dead. Taking a deep breath, Isaac continued:

> John was one of the firstfruits, and his life and testimony were a striking proof of his real conversion to the Lord. As a heathen, he distinguished himself by his sinful practices, and as his vices became the more seductive on account of his natural wit and humor, so as a Christian he became a most powerful and persuasive witness of our

---

[16] A recitation of the events of one's life. A type of eulogy.

UNDER ATTACK

Savior among his nation.

His gifts were sanctified by the grace of God and employed in such a manner as to be the means of blessing both to Europeans and Indians. He was without rival when it came to Indian oratory. His discourses were full of animation, and his words penetrated like fire into the hearts of his countrymen.

His soul found a rich pasture in the Gospel, and whether at home or on a journey, he could not refrain from speaking about the salvation purchased for us by the sufferings of Jesus. He never hesitated a moment, whether his hearers were Christians or heathen. In short, he appeared chosen by God to be a witness to his people and was four years active in this service. Nor was he less respected as a chief among the Indians, and no affairs of state were transacted without his advice and consent.

Shortly before his last illness he visited Bishop Spangenberg and told him, "I have something to say to you. I have examined my heart closely, and I know that what I say is true. Seeing so many of our Indians depart this life, I put the question to myself, 'Can I resign my life to the Lord and be assured that He will receive my soul?' The answer was yes, for I am the Lord's and shall go and be with Him forever."

During his illness, the believing Indians often stood weeping around his bed. Even at the end, he proclaimed the Gospel with power and remained faithful until his final breath.

His pains were softened by the consideration of the great sufferings of Jesus Christ, and his departure to Him was gentle, as that of a faithful servant entering the joy of the Lord.

Under Attack at Shekomeko: 1742-1746

The aged Glikkikan added one more line to John's epitaph before he quietly resumed his seat on the grass. "Let me die the death of the righteous," he said softly, "and let my end be like his."

A reverent hush fell upon us there under the giant locust in Beautiful Spring as we remembered the life of John Wamapah. I could not help but ponder the words Brother Isaac had just quoted. Were they prophetic in some way?

The Moravian Heart

After an hour's silence, with the sun nearing the horizon in the northwest, I timidly opened the story once more. I desperately wanted to pursue my defense of the Moravian heart and prove that we had only good motives in our mission efforts. Our only reason for carrying the Gospel to the Ohioland was to save souls. We were not there to acquire land for ourselves.

"Brother Isaac," I asked, "do you think Christian Henry and other young men and women like him risked their lives to get Indian lands for the Moravians? Do you know that the whole town of Bethlehem was organized into selfless choirs[17] so they could support the missionaries they sent out? The work everyone did was for the Lord, not for getting Indian land. In fact, individual Moravians did not even have land of their own; the Unity owned all the land."

Glikkikan mulled over my questions. Then he said, "Yes, I was forty years old when the Moravians first came to the Forks of the Delaware. Although I had already gone further west, we knew of John Wamapah,

---

[17] Each choir represented a different age and sex group—infants, boys, girls, single sisters, single brothers, married brothers, married sisters, widows, and widowers. Married couples had to arrange visiting times in order to see their spouses in private.

UNDER ATTACK

Shabash, Siem, and Kiop. Truly the Moravians did help the Mohicans by teaching them about the Savior.

"Go on with your story," he commanded.

The English Heart

As narrated by John Heckewelder

The problem at Shekomeko was not the German Moravian motives. It was the English settlers and the New York government that drove the Moravians and the Mohicans away.

After the first baptisms in late winter and early spring, the Shekomeko mission continued to prosper. The change in all four Indians was so remarkable that many white settlers, initially out of curiosity, flocked to Shekomeko from miles around. The mission church became a place of worship for Whites and Indians alike.

In the summer of 1742, Count Zinzendorf visited Shekomeko and baptized six more Indians. During the same summer, Johann Martin Mack, a 27-year-old veteran Moravian missionary, came to Shekomeko to assist Christian Henry. Martin Mack wasn't so devoted to his work that he didn't notice Jeanette Rowe's interest and attentions. With her fluency in several Indian languages and many other virtues, Martin decided Jeanette would make a good companion for him. He secured the approval of the church, and on 14 September 1742, he married Jeanette with her father's enthusiastic approval.

By late fall, the Shekomeko mission was firmly established as the first native Christian congregation in America. So many hearts at Shekomeko and Pachgatgoch opened up to the Gospel that the

Under Attack at Shekomeko: 1742-1746

Moravians sent more missionaries. On 1 November 1742, 26-year-old Gottlob Buettner with his new wife, Anna Margaret, rejoined the mission.

Early in 1743, Christian Henry Rauch visited Bethlehem. Church leaders advised Christian Henry that for various reasons, it was not good for a man to be alone at Shekomeko. Under their guidance, he was promptly matched up with a suitable maid, and Christian Henry Rauch returned to Shekomeko married to the former Ann Elizabeth Robins. Two more missionaries with their wives followed soon after.

In 1743, my mentor, Christian Frederick Post, went to the Shekomeko mission at the age of thirty-two and soon showed interest in Rachel, a baptized Indian girl from the Wampanoag nation. The other missionaries questioned the wisdom of a "mixed marriage" and the effect it might have on the surrounding white settlers. Despite the official frowns, Post proceeded happily ahead with his union to Rachel. Their marriage did much to win the approval of the Indians and the disapproval of the Whites.

In July of 1743, the congregation built a small chapel. This little framed sanctuary, covered with bark and nestled amidst the wigwams of Shekomeko, spoke of a new era of life and hope for the Mohicans. By the end of 1743, the Shekomeko congregation numbered over sixty baptized Indians and conducted preaching services at other stations near the Connecticut border.

All these zealous young men and their wives went to Shekomeko to save souls. Land had nothing to do with the missions—that is, land for the Moravian missionaries. Land did have a lot to do with the resentment of other European settlers. In short, the settlers wanted all native lands, and they wanted the Indians gone.

Land may have been the underlying reason for the wicked hatred of the settlers toward the missionaries, but other thorns also needled the resentment. The missionaries gave the natives

UNDER ATTACK

legal advice that kept them from being cheated in their land deals, complained when farmers defrauded them of just wages, exposed traders illegally selling alcohol, and in other ways interfered with "efficient trading." In addition, converted Indians like Abraham, Isaac, Jacob, and John often detected sin in the white settlers and boldly reprimanded the offenders.

Such insults from the "Canaanite Indians" did not sit well with the Whites. They rightly blamed the missionaries for the change in the life and morals of the Indians, and the Whites resorted to any possible strategy to have the missionaries removed. Some went so far as to offer liquor to any Indian who would kill them. So many false rumors—of Indian atrocities, of Moravians being in alliance with the French in Canada, of Moravian priests being secret papists—flew about that the magistrates had to do something to appease the angered and fearful settlers.

Christian Henry Rauch and Christian Frederick Post were recalled to Bethlehem in preparation for being sent to other fields of service. They were replaced by other zealous young Moravian couples.

Early in 1744, Justice Hegeman of Filkentown came to Shekomeko to investigate. Snow covered the ground on this cloudy winter day. With a small fire at his side, Justice Hegeman began his interrogation of Gudlop Buettner, the head of the mission. A crowd soon gathered around to hear the justice and the missionaries.

Justice Hegeman: "How many priests live at Shekomeko?"

Gudlop Buettner: "Please do not refer to us as priests. Priests ask God to forgive the sins of men like they did in the Old Testament. We do not pretend to forgive sins, but preach forgiveness of sin through the blood of Jesus. We are servants of the Gospel of Jesus Christ and are married men. Six of us live together in this one block house of hewn

Under Attack at Shekomeko: 1742–1746

timbers. However, some of us are often gone to preach at other places."

Justice Hegeman: "Do you wear robes and crucifixes when you are preaching?"

Gudlop Buettner: "No, we wear only the same clothing as the common people use. It is the only clothing we have."

Justice Hegeman: "Where do you get your clothing?"

Gudlop Buettner: "Brethren in Bethlehem make clothing for us, the same as they make for all the brothers and sisters in Bethlehem and the other missionaries as well."

Justice Hegeman: "How are you supported?"

Gudlop Buettner: "The Indians allow us to plant a small block of Indian corn from which we harvest much of our food, just like the Mohicans do. What we cannot earn ourselves is supplied by the Brethren in Bethlehem."

Justice Hegeman: "You mean that you do not take any salary and do not demand any tithing from the Indians or the Whites around you?"

Gudlop Buettner: "That is correct. You see, that is another difference between a minister and a priest. A minister serves the people while a priest is served by the people. Look at the miracle God has performed among these Indians. You see they are clothed, quiet, and gentle instead of savage, drunken, and loud as they were before they learned of the blood of Christ."

Justice Hegeman: "Are you not afraid your Indians will unite with the French Indians and attack the English settlements?"

Gudlop Buettner: "We teach the Indians the way of peace and love. Christian Indians do not go to war anymore."

UNDER ATTACK

Justice Hegeman: "I marvel that the most savage of the heathen have been greatly changed. The good conduct of the Indians puts me and many other Christians to shame. Still, many are worried that you are allied with the Jesuit priests and the French Indians. Will you swear allegiance to the English Crown?"

Gudlop Buettner: "I pray constantly for King George, but it is against my conscience to swear; therefore I cannot take the oath of allegiance."

Justice Hegeman: "I am satisfied that the Moravians and the Indians are not a threat to the English Crown or the surrounding settlers. But it will still be necessary for you to come to Filkentown and appear before the magistrates so you can answer their questions."

And so, to Filkentown they went. At the hearing, no reliable testimony appeared against them, but their staunch friend, John Rowe, boldly gave a decisive and noble testimony in their defense. None knew the situation better than he. Therefore the magistrates warned the missionaries not to cause any trouble and then allowed them to return home.

The hearing in Filkentown did not stop the harassment against the missionaries. Repeatedly, the missionaries were hauled before the local magistrates, jailed, interrogated, fined, and released. The harsh, abusive treatment gradually strained the health of even the hardiest German men and women.

The Indians watched all these mean-spirited attacks. One of the officials asked the Indians if they wanted to be present at one of the examinations. John Wamapah replied, "We take neither interest nor pleasure in such malicious proceedings."

Complaints from settlers, who were determined to use every means

Under Attack at Shekomeko: 1742–1746

available to drive the Moravians out, continued to come to the governor's ears. So His Excellency, the Honorable Governor George Clinton, commissioned Colonel Henry Beekman, of the Regiment of Militia for Dutchess County, to investigate what was going on at Shekomeko.

Colonel Beekman, along with a justice of the peace, the sheriff, and eight fully-armed militia members arrived at Shekomeko on 18 July. They found all the Indians and the missionaries at work on their plantations and quite uncertain as to whether they should run and hide or greet their visitors.

The Indians and the missionaries treated the officials with respect and peacefully submitted to a search of all their homes. When the small army could find no weapons other than a few hunting rifles, the justice of the peace roughly demanded that the Moravian priests take the oath of loyalty.

Gudlop Buettner replied, "Our business is only to gain souls among the heathen. We have no other purpose for being here. We take no part in war. Our conscience does not allow us to swear oaths of any kind. Please excuse us."

On hearing this, the justice of the peace sentenced the missionaries to appear before the governor and answer whatever charges should be raised against them.

The missionaries set out at once for New York City, and on 1 August 1744, they appeared before Governor Clinton and the Council. The governor presented himself very rudely and appeared to be a monster of a man, even damning them to their faces. He immediately set forth the charges against them.

"We have heard many complaints against you Moravian priests. You are no more than French Jesuits, papists to be sure. We cannot tolerate any of your collusion with the Indians against the English inhabitants of this country.

UNDER ATTACK

"Reports tell us that you have interfered with English land claims and trading practices, have rejected the preaching of English preachers, and have a stand of a thousand arms ready to give to any Indians who will take up arms for the French. Further, we hear that you pretend to have scruples of conscience against taking the loyalty oath to King George.

"We will now examine you each individually."

The court officer then sequestered two of the missionaries in another room.

Governor Clinton: "Who are you, and why are you here?"

Joseph Shaw: "I am Joseph Shaw and twenty-five years of age. I came over from England two years ago and married a wife in Philadelphia before I came to Shekomeko. I instruct the Indians in the Gospel of Christ and teach school among them. I taught some of the Indians to read English. I understand little of the Indian language, but Indians named John and Isaac interpret for me."

Councilor: "Why do you want to teach the Indians to read English? This works against our best interest."

Joseph Shaw: "We want to help the Indians become civilized so they can adapt to English ways and customs."

Governor Clinton: "Who supports you? Do you get any money from the French?"

Joseph Shaw: "We missionaries work as much as we can, raise corn on a small tract of land, and depend on Bethlehem in Pennsylvania to support us in whatever else we need. We have no contact with the French in Canada and receive nothing from them."

Councilor: "Do you know that you have created such a disturbance at Shekomeko that you may have to be removed from the Indians?"

Under Attack at Shekomeko: 1742–1746

Joseph Shaw: "If we have to move, the Indians will follow us, and the Mohawks might take it ill."[18]

Governor Clinton: "If you are free of the French, as you say, then you must swear the oath of allegiance to King George to prove it."

Joseph Shaw: "I pray constantly for King George, but it is against my conscience to swear, and therefore I cannot take the oath of allegiance."

Governor Clinton then dismissed Joseph Shaw. Next they brought in Hendrick Joachim Senseman, followed by Gudlop Buettner, asking them the same questions and receiving the same truthful answers.

The three missionaries were then brought into the council room together. Governor Clinton again asked them to take the loyalty oath. They politely refused. He sent all three to prison till the charges against them could be examined.

Governor Clinton waited ten days before bringing the three men back into his council chamber. When they stood as criminals before him, in their plain and dirty clothes, he said, "We have not been able to find any evidence to support the charges against you. You shall now return home, live peaceably, cause no further suspicion, and await further orders."

Gudlop Buettner said, "May I ask Your Honor a question?"

"Permission granted," Governor Clinton replied.

"How can we avoid causing any further suspicion when all the charges brought against us so far were false? Will not our enemies bring more false charges against us?"

"You ought to be a lawyer," quipped Governor Clinton, and he dismissed them.

In spite of the governor's clearance, the enemies of the mission did not rest. On 21 September 1744, the Assembly of New York enacted

---

[18] This was a nicely veiled warning that the British Mohawks (Iroquois allies of the British) were already concerned about the conquest of their lands and might vacate to the French.

UNDER ATTACK

Government Orders

"You shall desist from further teaching or preaching and depart this province." —Colonel Beekman

Under Attack at Shekomeko: 1742-1746

two laws that crushed the mission. The first required all suspicious persons to either take the oath of allegiance or emigrate. The second commanded "the several Moravian and vagrant teachers among the Indians to desist from further teaching or preaching, and to depart the province."[19]

The governor's orders went out to the sheriffs and justices of the peace on 27 November 1744. "Give notice to the several Moravian and vagrant teachers among the Indians . . . requiring them forthwith to desist from further teaching or preaching and to depart this province . . . or the acts of the Assembly will be enforced." On 15 December 1744, the sheriff of Dutchess County and three "peace officers" appeared at Shekomeko and closed the chapel doors.

The missionaries stayed as long as they dared. John Rowe, the German settler with a Moravian son-in-law, now stood up for the Moravians against the rabid English settlers, but he was only one man against many. On 23 February 1745, Gottlob Buettner fell asleep in the Lord. Tearful saints buried him at Shekomeko and his epitaph expressed his heart:

> According to the commandment of his crucified God and Savior, he brought the glad tidings to the heathen, that the blood of Jesus had made an atonement for their sins. His last prayer was that

---

[19] *Documentary History of New York*, Vol. III, pp. 1019-1020. The same work contains various other papers, especially "Reasons for Passing the Law Against the Moravians Residing Among the Indians," which show the inveterate prejudice that existed against the Moravian Church.

UNDER ATTACK

they [the converted Indians] might be preserved until the day of our Lord Jesus Christ.

So you see, it was the English and their lust for Indian land that caused the demise of the missions at Shekomeko and two extensions of it on the Connecticut border. I tell you, it was the English, not the Moravians, who wanted the Indian lands!

The Rest of the Shekomeko Story: 1745–1746

As narrated by John Heckewelder

All the non-Indian Moravians were forced to leave Shekomeko. The Whites even posted guards to make sure that no Moravian "priests" visited the Indians or aided them in any way. At times, the Indian assistants traveled to Bethlehem for encouragement, instruction, and direction.

But since they could neither read nor write, they were limited to testimonies of their own experience and remembrance. Here is how one assistant addressed a meeting of the baptized:

> My dear brothers and sisters, I have nothing to say to you but a few words concerning Jesus. Jesus labored hard to gain salvation for us. His pain was so intense that His sweat became great drops of blood falling to the ground.
>
> And now Jesus says to us, "I have redeemed you all; I have given my life and blood for you." Therefore let us give Him our hearts. We may now receive eternal life by virtue of His blood alone.
>
> Whosoever believes in Him shall live eternally, but

Under Attack at Shekomeko: 1742-1746

whosoever does not believe will certainly die in his sins. However, none need die, but all may have eternal life if they come to Jesus, for He will receive him gladly.

The discourses of the Indian assistants blessed the hearers, who knew the speakers were filled with the love of Christ and had experienced the truth of what they taught. They advanced the language of the heart, and consequently, it went to the heart.

These messages could not be called doctrinal. While the missionaries never detained themselves long in discussing doctrinal points, they wished to follow the commandments of our Savior and teach the believers all things as Jesus had commanded His disciples to do. The Indian assistants could not do this because it required Bible knowledge that they had not yet acquired.

It appeared also that the incessant slander from the enemies of the mission had made some impression on the minds of a few of the baptized. The Brethren were so strongly accused of intending to enslave the believers that even one of the assistants began to lose confidence in them. He soon acknowledged his error with many tears, but it proved that these good people were in danger of suffering shipwreck in the faith.

Considering this, the Brethren at Bethlehem wanted to take the Shekomeko believers out of the way of temptation. The leaders thought the Shekomeko Indians should leave the province of New York and settle somewhere in Pennsylvania.

With that in mind, the leaders proposed that the Indians should first come close to Bethlehem and then transfer to Wyoming on the Susquehanna. There they could enjoy perfect liberty of conscience, be less exposed to the seductions of the Whites, and would not be called upon to participate in the war.

In order that no difficulty might be encountered with the

UNDER ATTACK

Iroquois to whom the country belonged, the Brethren sent Bishop Spangenberg, Conrad Weiser, David Zeisberger, and Shebosh to the Great Council at Onondaga. After encountering many hardships along the way, the embassy returned. The Iroquois had given their consent for the congregation of believing Indians to settle at Wyoming.

It now appeared that a good plan for a permanent settlement was in place at Wyoming. However, contrary to all expectations, the Indians in Shekomeko refused to accept it. Abraham, one of the first three baptized at Oley, was particularly zealous in persuading the people not to accept the proposal. He alleged that the governor of New York had commanded them to stay in their own towns. Others feared that if they should emigrate, their unbaptized friends and relations would remain there and resume their sinful courses.

Other reasons or excuses given were that Wyoming lay in the path of Catawba warriors, that it was abounding with savages, and that the women were so wanton they seduced all the men. There seemed to be no shortage of reasons why the believers would not leave Shekomeko. Some of the Brethren suspected that all the reasons given only furnished a smokescreen to hide the real reason the Mohicans would not leave Shekomeko at that time.

However, soon after this, things began to change. The Whites came to a resolution that they would drive the believing Indians from Shekomeko by force. They pretended that the land on which the town was built belonged to other people who would soon come and take possession.

The Indians applied to the New York governor for the protection he had promised them if they would remain at Shekomeko. When the governor did not respond to their petition, they at last felt compelled to emigrate and began to give serious attention to the proposals made by the Brethren. Several of the believers felt they would like to live near Bethlehem, and so toward the close of 1745, they made frequent visits to that place.

Under Attack at Shekomeko: 1742–1746

By now the situation of the congregation that remained at Shekomeko had become very distressing. The Whites seized the land and forcibly prevented all visits from Bethlehem. The war between the English and French caused a general alarm. The Indians were afraid of both the French and the English, but the English mistrusted them because they declined to take sides. The danger was so great that people went armed to church in some places.

The unbelieving Indians in Westenhuck made several attempts to draw the Christian Indians in Shekomeko into their party. With many promises and lots of dancing and drinking, they tried to be as enticing as possible. Those who yielded to temptations soon returned to Shekomeko and admitted that they had led a miserable life while at Westenhuck, having been merry at the expense of an uneasy conscience. All further enticements failed.

Some white Christians in the neighborhood tried persuading the believers to join their congregations by contemptuous insinuations against the Moravians. The believing Indians were poor and were frequently obliged to spend much time working with immoral people for their livelihood. Many of them were deeply in debt, which they had contracted both by their profligate lives before conversion and by exploitation from bad neighbors. These debtors were now subject to much ill treatment and were even threatened with imprisonment.

Not seeing any possibility of paying their creditors or having any other ways to escape, they had no other refuge but to beg the congregation at Bethlehem to assist them. This the Brethren did with willing hearts.

But the greatest grief of all after the removal of the faithful missionaries came from within the congregation. Some believers had fallen back into their old sinful lives. This caused division and slander among them, the result being confusion and misery.

This sad change of affairs caused the most pungent grief to the Indian assistants and the congregation at Shekomeko. The assistants related

UNDER ATTACK

these happenings with great sorrow to the Brethren at Bethlehem, where they united in fervent prayer for this poor, persecuted people.

Even though the Brethren at Bethlehem wanted to help the distressed believers at Shekomeko, they still did not give up the idea of removing the Indians to the free Indian territory of Wyoming. Accordingly, they secured an order from His Excellency George Thomas, the governor of Pennsylvania, that all Christian Indians who took refuge in Pennsylvania should be protected in the quiet practice of their religion. Then they sent missionary Martin Mack[20] to visit Wyoming and assess the situation there. Brother Mack went in the company of two Delaware Indians of great respectability. They carried him on their shoulders across brooks and rivers and showed the most tender concern for his safety along the road.

When Brother Mack returned to Bethlehem, he brought a very favorable report of the land. Everything seemed in place for the Christian Indians to emigrate to Wyoming. But for the second time, the Brethren could not persuade the Shekomeko Indians to move to Wyoming. Therefore they invited them to move to Bethlehem and build and plant near the settlement.

During this period, Christian duties were regularly attended to in Shekomeko. The Indian assistants bore witness to the truth of the Gospel before many travelers who passed through the town. Their discourses were plain but powerful, and they proceeded from their own experience. These left a good impression upon many.

Their manner of singing hymns was particularly edifying. After the discourses, they treated the strangers with fine hospitality. When they had no other place to accommodate them, they spread a table in the chapel, conversing with their guests about the salvation of their souls.

At the same time, the persecution of the Shekomeko Indians

---

[20] Martin Mack and his wife, the former Jeanette Rowe, spent several years in service at Shekomeko and Pachgatgoch. They were both loved and respected by the Indians.

Under Attack at Shekomeko: 1742-1746

intensified. Their enemies reported that a thousand French troops were on the march to the province, with whom the Indians of Shekomeko would join. Then they would ravage the country with fire and sword. The rumor spread such terror that the inhabitants demanded a warrant from the governor of New York to go and kill all the inhabitants of Shekomeko.

Though the warrant was not granted, it was soon known in Shekomeko that it had been demanded. The grievances and oppressions suffered by the Indians rose to such a pitch that, even though their attachment to Shekomeko was very great, some of them at last resolved to accept the invitation of the Brethren at Bethlehem.

Ten families, forty-four persons in all, left Shekomeko with sorrow and tears. They were received in Bethlehem with tenderness and compassion. Several of them immediately built cottages near the settlement. Their morning and evening meetings were regulated, and the service was performed in the Mohican tongue. This helped give comfort for the loss of the regular service at Shekomeko, which was most precious to them.

When the Indians in Shekomeko and Pachgatgoch heard about the Mohican settlements in the Forks of the Delaware, many of them were also induced to join those settlements. Eventually, the number of Christian Indians who arrived exceeded the number of the original inhabitants.

Meanwhile, their enemies who had resolved to expel them from Shekomeko began regretting how many had emigrated to Bethlehem. They resolved to deter the remainder from following by raising a malicious report that the previous party of emigrants had been murdered on their journey.

No one believed these rumors. Several Indian families who were preparing for the journey at that very time set out without fear. One assistant said, "If we must be obliged either to stay here or go to a place other than Bethlehem, you might as well take our lives." One

UNDER ATTACK

family after another departed in such cheerful reliance upon the gracious protection and support of the Lord that all who saw and heard them were edified.

The emigration from Shekomeko and Pachgatgoch to the Forks of the Delaware brought great embarrassment both to the Indians and to the congregation at Bethlehem. Whenever a family intended to emigrate, the neighboring traders brought bills, demanding payment. The Indians, not being able to read or write, were often compelled to submit to unjust charges. The Brethren at Bethlehem, to the utmost of their power, assisted them with aid in these abuses.

Despite the continuing migration to the Forks of the Delaware, quite a few Christian Indians remained at Shekomeko and Pachgatgoch, though life there grew more precarious with each day.

The rumor of war increased. The French Indians made an inroad into the country only a day's journey from Shekomeko. They set fire to the houses and murdered the inhabitants. The English called upon all who could bear arms to rise in their own defense.

The Christian Indians now regretted they had not emigrated earlier, but it was too late. Several joined the army, and the rest lived in continual apprehension and dread. Some men who could not persuade their wives to leave Shekomeko at last left them there. Some women would not be detained by their husbands and went alone to the Forks. Parents left their children, and children deserted their parents. The Brethren spoke strongly against such disorderly conduct, but they were ignored.

The Christian Indians still at Shekomeko grew more miserable each day by the continuation of the war and by frequent messages requiring them to take up arms against the French. This caused great confusion in Shekomeko and Pachgatgoch. The Brethren dared not give any advice because they were already accused of siding with the French. One White publicly asserted that the Brethren were in possession of a stand of arms numbering 3,000 and would give them to any Indians

Under Attack at Shekomeko: 1742-1746

who would join the French and advance into Pennsylvania.

One relative of a believer threatened him with death if he did not disavow all connections with his pastors. The Indian replied, "I know the Brethren are just."

Another believer, threatened with death if he went to the congregation in the Forks, replied, "I will not rest till I am again united to my brothers and sisters in Christ. Though you might kill me, you cannot destroy my soul. It has been redeemed by the blood of Christ and has far greater value than my body."

Such were the attacks that fell upon the Christian Indians of Shekomeko. Their own relatives and friends, whether savages or errant Christians, made life miserable. They were abused by white Christian settlers and clergy. The New York government attacked them through racist legislation. Neighbors and traders stole their lands and their goods.

Eventually, most of the Mohicans, many of the Delawares, and various other nations fled from the banks of the Hudson and the Delaware Rivers to new homes in the Forks of the Delaware. There, they could again be closer to the Brethren who offered them protection from the ravages of the Whites. In that place, hearts of hope could once more envision a land of peace and happiness, until once more . . .

The American Heart

As recorded by John Heckewelder

I thought I had built a rather convincing case for the defense of the Moravian missions and their lack of interest in Indian land. The sun had gone down, and I relaxed in the black darkness that enveloped us.

UNDER ATTACK

Here and there, a light flickered in a cabin window. Heavy clouds blotted out the sky above us. The frogs croaked in the swamp, and swarms of mosquitos buzzed near our faces and hands. Owls hooted.

When Glikkikan spoke, he was highly animated, and I could easily imagine that John Wamapah spoke the same way. "Brother John, I agree that the Moravians did a wonderful thing by bringing the good news of the Savior and His blood to the Mohicans. They preached the same grace I have received. Though I am unworthy of such great grace, I admire John Wamapah. He is my Apollos, and I wish to be like him.

"In your story, you told how Governor Clinton and his Council and the magistrates insisted on the Brethren taking the oath of loyalty to the King. Why was this?"

"Brother Isaac," I replied, "you must know that the English and the French governments were having difficulties over the colonial boundaries. One peculiarity of this case is that the French employed the Jesuits to alienate various Indian tribes from the English colonies. The English wanted to prepare the Indians to fight on their side.

"In this tense time, the Indians were generally looked upon as enemies, and any man who befriended them was regarded as a confidant or spy of the French or of the treacherous and malignant Jesuits. Thus, the governor needed the Moravians to take the oath in order to clear them of any connection with the French or the Jesuits."

"Could it be that some of those same officers who insisted on the Moravians taking an oath of loyalty to the King are now disobeying the King?" Brother Isaac asked.

"Yes," I admitted, "even though this is years later, it could be that some of them are now in rebellion against the King of England." I was unsure what Isaac was leading up to, so I added, "And it could be that some younger officials have recently made an oath to the King."

"Is not every settler who climbs the mountains and settles in the Ohioland disobeying the King's command of 1763 which said, 'No

Under Attack at Shekomeko: 1742-1746

settler shall be allowed to build his cabin west of the Allegheny Mountains'? Didn't the officers of the King promise the Indians the same thing if they would abandon the French at Fort Duquesne? Doesn't that mean that their former oath to the King was worthless?" Brother Isaac probed.

I had to agree with Isaac. "Yes, their oath is not much good. But the oath itself was not really all that important to those who required it of the Moravians. It was just one more law the English government could use to harass the Moravians. They have suffered much because of it, but in Pennsylvania, the loyalty oath has not been required."

"Brother John, should the Indians believe the word of people who have broken their vows of loyalty to the British King?" Brother Isaac persisted. "If generals and government agents come to Fort Pitt and promise not to take any more Indian lands, should the Indians believe them when we know that they break their oaths so lightly?"

"Brother Isaac, the Moravians have suffered much because they would not take the loyalty oath. Other Whites have repeatedly harassed us Moravians because we stood up for the Indians and taught them a better way of life. The whole point of my Shekomeko story is that the Moravians came to America to tell the heathen about the Savior, not to acquire land."

In the darkness, I could almost hear Glikkikan thinking as he mulled over my words. At last he spoke. "Brother John, you raised the question in your story as to whether those who remained at Shekomeko gave the real reason why they would not move to Wyoming. What do you think was the real reason?"

I rolled the question over in my mind, not because I had never thought of it before, but because I wanted to make sure Glikkikan wasn't setting a trap for me. "It seems to me that the Mohicans and the Iroquois were ancient enemies. In this event, the Mohicans did not trust the deceitful, warring Iroquois and did not want to be close to them."

UNDER ATTACK

"At that time (1746), who owned the land of Wyoming?" Glikkikan asked.

I attempted an answer. "Count Zinzendorf came to America in 1742 and was present when Pennsylvania stole the land in the Forks of the Delaware from Nutimus and Teedyuscung. He was in America when Bully Canasetego called the Delawares women and forbade them to sell any land. Furthermore, he ordered the Delawares to go to Wyoming, which was to be their homeland forever. I suppose we could say that after 1742, the land belonged to the Delawares under the dominant Iroquois overlords."

"Did Count Zinzendorf understand that Pennsylvania, through Secretary Richard Peters and Thomas Penn and Conrad Weiser, stole the land in the Forks of the Delaware?" Glikkikan wanted to know.

"I suppose it is possible that Conrad Weiser and the governor's Council hid from the Count the fraud involved in the theft of the Indian lands. But it is impossible that the Count did not know the Indians were dissatisfied after he bought his land from the Penn government. Much to the chagrin of that government, the generous Count paid the Indians again for some of the land he purchased in the Forks of the Delaware."

Glikkikan raised his hand, palm outward. "Correction. The Count paid twice for his land, it is true. But Captain John[21] had never been paid before, so do not accuse Captain John Harris of selling his land twice. Do you think the Mohicans at Shekomeko never heard the story of how the Iroquois, at the bidding and under the pay of Pennsylvania, robbed all Indians of their right to sell their own lands?"

"It is likely that the Mohicans in 1746 knew the whole episode quite well," I admitted.

"Brother John, if you had been a Shekomeko Indian in 1746, would

---

[21] Read the account of the fraudulent Walking Purchase in *Tomahawks to Peace* by James G. Landis. For a reference to Captain Harris, see pages 264-265.

Under Attack at Shekomeko: 1742–1746

you have moved to Wyoming at the bidding of the Brethren?"

"No, I do not think I would have trusted the Iroquois any more than Abraham did."

"So you think the real reason the Shekomeko Mohicans would not move to the Wyoming Valley was that they did not trust the Iroquois?"

"Yes, I would venture that."

Glikkikan sat in a prolonged silence while we listened to the frogs and the owls. At last he rose from the grass and towered over me. "I think you are right. The Mohicans did not trust the Iroquois. But there is also a deeper reason, and if you can unravel that mystery, maybe you can also figure out why the Moravians continued to support the corrupt Penn government. And then you may even be able to decide why the Moravians still support lying and corrupt government officials in Pennsylvania and Virginia. I'll give you a clue—land!"

"Wait a moment!" I protested, but he had already disappeared into the darkness.

UNDER ATTACK

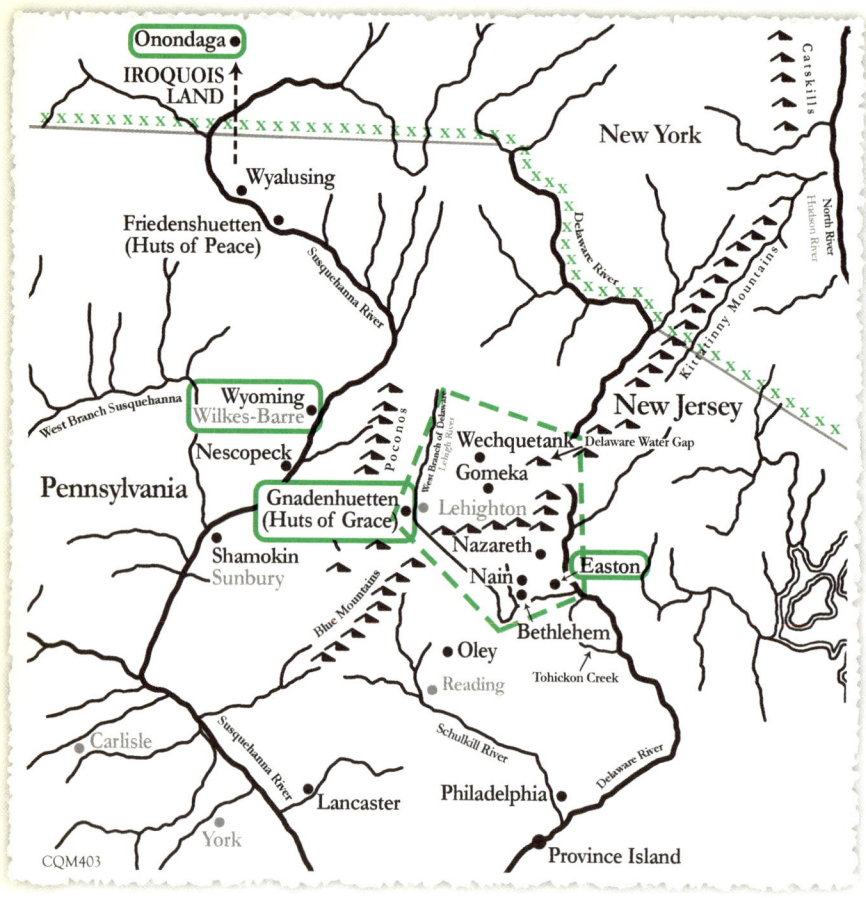

Key Points for Peace and Witness in the East (1755-1761)

CQM403 Notes

1. This map is based on Loskiel's map published in 1794.
2. The two branches of the Delaware River came together at Easton, Pennsylvania.
3. The area enclosed by a broken green line was called the Forks of the Delaware.
4. In later times, the West Branch of the Delaware River was called the Lehigh River.
5. The broken arrow pointing from Wyalusing to Onondaga indicates a greater distance than shown on the map.
6. The green Xs show the present-day New York state line.

Chapter 3

Under Attack in the Forks of the Delaware: 1747–1755

As recorded by John Heckewelder
At Beautiful Spring, Ohio,
Wednesday, 8 September 1773

August was a hard time for Brother Isaac. On the afternoon of the 20th, his aged mother Cornelia went home to Jesus very suddenly. A believer, she had lived with us for four years. She could never thank the Savior enough for what He had done for her, and we all rejoiced over her.

However, last year she became completely childlike. Her mind grew very weak, and she could not remember things or make sense of them. But whenever we spoke with her again about the Savior, she would come back to herself.

Walking was a big undertaking for her, but she attended the services as much as she could. For some days, we had noticed that she was

UNDER ATTACK

not as well. These declines had happened before, but on this day she suddenly lost her speech and gently closed her eyes in death. No one knew her age, but she was well over 100 years old. The next day we laid her earthly dwelling to rest.

I realized that Cornelia would have been at least ten years old when William Penn first came to America. What a different world it must have been! I could not help wondering what memories flooded through 73-year-old Isaac's mind as he helped close the grave. I realized that I still knew very little about this wonderful brother, and I purposed to find out more about him in the days ahead.

Brother Isaac returned from another visit to the Shawnee towns with a stopover in Newcomerstown. There, he was invited to attend a meeting of the Council. Isaac laughed when he told me about it.

"The Delaware Council had sent word to the Shawnees and told them about the three Quakers who visited and admonished them to accept the Word of God. The Delawares said they had promised the Quakers they would accept the Word of God if the Quakers would assist them in sending a delegation to the King of England.

"Brother John, why do you think the Delawares told the Shawnees they wanted to visit the King? The Delawares claimed they were confused; they didn't know which party or religion to join. The French Jesuits claim they have the right teaching. Now there are two towns of Indian believers in their neighborhood who claim they teach the truth. And there are the Quakers and the English Church who also claim to be true."

Here Glikkikan made great big eyes and his voice danced with merriment. "They want the King to instruct them in the matter of which party and religion they should join."

I doubled up with laughter. "They can't be serious."

Glikkikan sobered up suddenly. Without a trace of a smile, he continued, "But they are. The Shawnees agreed to get the Wyandots in on

Under Attack in the Forks of the Delaware: 1747–1755

it so they could help collect hides to pay for the voyage. They should shortly be ready to begin the journey."

Glikkikan eyed me quizzically. My mouth dropped open. "Why, that's preposterous!" I exclaimed.

Glikkikan laughed and laughed till his eyes were wet. "Brother John, the Indians aren't going anywhere. They're just testing each other to see if they're ready to form an alliance. It's the Indian way of speaking."

"Oh," I said sheepishly. I felt humbled and weak. "I sure swallowed the bait on that one," was the best I could manage.

On Saturday, the 4th, we blissfully partook of the body and blood of our Lord in Holy Communion along with fifty-two Indian brothers and sisters. When we wanted to serve Holy Communion to those who were ill, our dear Brother Anton was not strong enough to receive it.

The following morning it pleased our dear Lord to take Brother Anton to be with Him. We held a memorial service for him in the meeting hall where Brother Good News read his *Lebenslauf*.[22]

> Brother Anton was baptized to the Unity in Bethlehem in January 1750, twenty-three years ago. We loved this brother from the very beginning because we quickly realized how attached his heart was to the Savior and to the Unity. This blessed brother served as interpreter among his nation after the Indian congregation had left Huts of Grace and retreated to Bethlehem before establishing another site behind the Blue Mountains in Wechquetank.
>
> The Savior granted Anton special grace and a great gift of expression and wisdom, along with special insight into the Gospel and the Unity. Therefore afflictions did not

---

[22] "Course of Life." A type of eulogy.

UNDER ATTACK

disturb his spiritual life in the least, but brought him ever closer to the Savior and the Unity.

In Huts of Peace, Goschgosching, Lawhannek, and Kaskaskunk, he called many through his preaching of the Gospel. The Indians asked him to repeat in his house what had been taught in the services, and he did this day and night with untiring faithfulness.

The Savior made him worthy to tolerate pain, persecution, and even mortal danger for His name's sake. Brother Anton was not deterred, but left one place to serve his Savior in another. The journey by water to Beautiful Spring was especially difficult for him. When he finally arrived, he expressed his joy and said, "I hope that now I shall be able to rest, because I believe this town shall last at least several years."

He actually recovered quickly from an illness he got on the journey, but soon developed the cold fever which turned into yellow fever. He suffered this ailment for eleven days. Four days before his end, he told a company of brothers who visited him, "I am going to the Savior, and so I ask you not to renounce the faith nor to tear down what the Savior has built among you, but to guard it. Obey your teachers, and do what they tell you. Do not make things difficult for them, and do not let anyone mislead you. Also, do not think that the Savior's work will suffer when I am no longer with you. He will continue His work as He has done until now, and He will also supply the people He needs for this."

During his talk, the hearts of those present became tender, and their eyes overflowed with tears. We did not think his end was so close, and we would have liked to

Under Attack in the Forks of the Delaware: 1747–1755

keep him here longer, but we are happy for his great joy of being at home with his Lord and receiving rest.

A large procession followed the body to the grave, where Brother Isaac added his remarks. "Brother Anton was only a few years older than I, but he served the Savior while I stumbled in darkness in search of truth. I was one of the poor heathen whom Brother Anton preached to about the Savior of men. I was one of the seekers whom Brother Anton stayed up with all night, teaching me the ways of peace. I have been blessed by his faithful life and testimony in the five short years I have known him. He has made me want to know his Savior and his God as he knew Him. May our brother rest in peace."

On Wednesday, we had a helpers' conference where we decided to begin construction on a new meetinghouse. Our plan was to use the present meeting hall as the school for the town, with me as the teacher. The new building was to be forty feet by thirty-six, and we thought it should easily accommodate more than three hundred people.

Brother Isaac also reported to the helpers' conference what he had heard on his recent trip to Newcomerstown.

> Killbuck addressed me and said, "You know your teachers here do not have anything of their own and do not possess any land. Should they continue living here and teaching the Indians like this? That cannot possibly work out. I am going to see Many Children Johnson. When I return, you will see that this will not be allowed, and the white brothers will have to leave."
>
> I answered him like this. "You are right. They have nothing of their own and no land here. They are well aware of this, but they do not desire to own any land. The land is not mine or yours. It belongs to the Wyandots,

UNDER ATTACK

yet we live on it in the same way they also live here. I tell you that as long as there are Indians, the Gospel will be preached unceasingly, for God has decreed it should be preached to all nations. He wishes all humans to be saved, including you. Therefore no one can prevent it or stop it."

Killbuck had no reply to this, but remained silent and left.

After the meeting, I told Brother Isaac, "See, I told you the Moravians don't want any land and never did. Just as you said, the Moravians only want to proclaim the Gospel to the Indians." He looked down at me with a kindly smile but made no reply.

"Look," I told him, "I know you are not convinced that the Moravians were completely innocent of pushing the Indians out of the area they call the Forks of the Delaware. I know a lot about what happened in the land between the Lehigh and the Delaware Rivers.

"I have studied the mission diaries from when the first Shekomeko refugees came to the Forks, and I would like to tell you how the missionaries sacrificed themselves to bless the Indians with the Gospel. I want to tell you what happened to the Mohicans who left Shekomeko and the Connecticut missions of Pachgatgoch and Wachquednach to come to the Forks of the Delaware in Pennsylvania.

"Do you know how the Moravians helped the Mohican believers from Shekomeko establish new homes in the Forks of the Delaware?[23]

"Do you know that eleven Moravian missionaries died in the Forks because they were befriending the Indians? They died, not because they were seeking land for themselves, but because they were helping the Indians find a better life. When can we get together again so I can

---

[23] The Delaware River divided at Easton, PA. The area enclosed by these two branches was known by the Indians as the Forks of the Delaware. Later, the name of the west branch at Easton was called the Lehigh River. With all the various spellings, *Lehigh* meant, "at the Forks."

Under Attack in the Forks of the Delaware: 1747–1755

share this story with you?"

"Brother John, I will be glad to listen to your story. However, Brother Good News, Wilhelm, and I are planning a mission trip to the Shawnee. We hope to leave on the 17th, and we are not sure how long we will be gone. Your story will have to wait for our return."

The three of them returned from their mission trip one week later, much sooner than we expected. Naturally, I was anxious to find out why. I wanted to set up a meeting with Brother Isaac as soon as possible, but he tried to put me off with, "I want to help work on the meetinghouse." He avoided making eye contact with me.

"You can't work on the schoolhouse when it's raining," I countered. "What's wrong?" This was not like Brother Isaac.

"It's no use," he muttered while looking at the ground. "We're both just wasting our time. You will always believe that the Moravians only wanted souls for the Savior and had no interest in land."

"Cheer up!" I told him. "Things can't be that bad. It's a good story that offers us wisdom in the present distress. Sometimes we must look back to see the present and to anticipate the future. The nature of man has not changed over the centuries. We must learn from the acts of the past so that we do not repeat them."

"Nothing," he grunted. "You will learn nothing because your mind is tightly shut. You have set a large stone in front of the door. I see no light in the Forks of the Delaware. The clouds I see carry no water. The trees have borne no berries or cherries, only thorns and thistles."

"Where do you want to meet?" he growled.

"In the schoolhouse, tomorrow morning."

He sulked off, so I took it to mean he would be there. Glikkikan did come the next morning. He sat there in sullen silence looking at the floor. "It's no use," he rasped again. Then he stopped and nodded grudgingly. "Oh, go ahead, Brother John. Tell me whatever you want. I'm still waiting for you to prove to me that the Moravians did not

UNDER ATTACK

want any Delaware land in the Forks."

With Glikkikan still in such a terrible fit of melancholy, I thought it might be good to get his report of the mission trip before going on to the Forks and the land issue. "Tell me about the mission trip to the Shawnees," I requested.

"Every part of it was a disaster," he replied emphatically. "Since you ask, I will tell you how it went.

"We stopped first in Newcomerstown where we had to listen to the criticisms about having white teachers among us. Things there are very disorganized, and there is great confusion among them. They do not know how they should handle the matter, and it is all because they see that Wehund wants to leave them and come to us. They also foresee that if he comes to us, others will follow. They don't care if the people come only to listen, but they should not convert. They are considering ways to control the situation and stop it.

"Although Chief Watwees has so far remained neutral, those who are antagonistic are publicly talking about getting the white brothers and sisters out of the country. They are saying some of our Indians have already been instructed daily in the Word and teaching for more than twenty years. They could certainly instruct others, and then they would not need white teachers anymore.

"Now the Indians cannot live as peacefully as they did before because they hear how various things they do are sinful. Their sacrifices are useless in pleasing God. We left Newcomerstown and went on to stay the night with Captain White Eyes, who used to be my best friend. His brother married my sister, so I know him very well. He is a captain and chief and a reasonable man. If he were ever convinced of the truth, it would be difficult for anyone to change his mind or mislead him. We discussed many things with White Eyes, including the Savior.

"Captain White Eyes advised us not to pay any attention to the

Under Attack in the Forks of the Delaware: 1747-1755

rumors afloat in Newcomerstown unless we heard directly from the Council. Then Brother David ruined it all by telling him how the Six Nations had not put any obstacles in the way of the mission the entire time our Indians lived on the Susquehanna. White Eyes is neither uninformed nor stupid. He knew that was not the truth.

"The next day we traveled on to the town near Woaketammeki that we had visited in the fall and that I visited again in January. If you remember, I told you about that town on our canoe journey here. Everyone had been very anxious to hear the Gospel and to have a teacher come to them. They were prepared to start a new town where they would live as we do. Now the Indian preacher says they spoke too hastily. There is a rift among them. Some of them still want to make sacrifices and dance, and they do not want to abandon the warrior 'poison' they received from God. The preacher said he and some of the people still wanted to become believers and that they could live in a new town with us, but I am afraid it was just idle talk.

"We went on from there to Woaketammeki, the Shawnee capital, and found Chief Natsi (the Whites call him Hard Man because of his hard, anti-White stance) had arrived the day before from a visit to the lower Shawnee towns. He arranged lodging for us and brought Hokolesqua, a Shawnee war chief, and Talgayeeta, a Mingo, along to visit us. All three of them were, like me, very tall men with fine, strong features. Talgayeeta's kindly eyes distinguished him.

"I had known Talgayeeta for a long time. He was the son of Shikellamy, the Cayuga overlord of the Indians placed at Shamokin on the Susquehanna and a close friend of Conrad Weiser. Talgayeeta might be considered the founder of the Mingos, an independent Ohioland offshoot of the Cayugas in New York. In all the wars between the English and the French, Talgayeeta had always sat by his fire and never lifted his tomahawk against a White. I admire him. My wife Agnes was also a Mingo.

UNDER ATTACK

"Since my wife was a Mingo, I speak the language fluently. Furthermore, I understand Shawnee well enough and can speak a little of it. With the aid of Talgayeeta and my grasp of Shawnee, we were able to converse quite freely with the Shawnee chief, Natsi.

"He wanted to know what things were like in Newcomerstown and the affairs of the Wyandot. I gave him all the news I had about these things. Then he launched into a long discourse telling us how things were with the Shawnee."[24]

> There is much drunkenness in the lower Shawnee towns, and it is causing great harm. I urgently warned the young people in my village that it is destroying them, but they no longer want to obey me. I cannot keep them from robbing the traders any more. They are beating each other to death. A great many have died recently, and I do not know what will come of this.
>
> I presume the white man is coming here to tell us good things. You all may go wherever you want. Perhaps you will manage to do more than I have. Perhaps they will listen to you and obey.
>
> The Whites tell us of their enlightened understanding and the wisdom they have from heaven. At the same time, they cheat us to their hearts' content, for we are as fools in their eyes. They say among themselves, "The Indians know nothing! The Indians understand nothing!"
>
> Because they are cunning enough to detect the weak points of our character, they think they can lead us as they will and deceive us as they please, even while they pretend to seek our good.

---

[24] This speech was given to Zeisberger and Glikkikan while on a mission trip to the Shawnees (17 October 1773). —De Schweinitz, *The Life and Times of David Zeisberger*, p. 291.

Under Attack in the Forks of the Delaware: 1747-1755

See them coming into our town with their rum. See them offering it to us with persuasive kindness. Hear them cry, "Drink! Drink!"

And when we have drunk and begun to act like crazed beasts, behold these good Whites, these men of a benevolent race, stand by and point at us with their fingers and laugh among themselves and say, "Oh, what fools! What great fools the Shawnees are!"

But who makes them fools? Who is the cause of their madness? It is men like you who are the cause of our foolishness and madness.

But they always tell us good words. They always "love" us and want to save our souls. "Behold," they say, "thus and so has God taught us. He has given us knowledge. We are wiser than you, so we must instruct you."

Oh, certainly they are wiser than we—wiser in teaching men to get drunk, wiser in swindling men out of their land, and wiser in defrauding them of all they possess!

Whose fault is it that we are in such miserable circumstances? Why do young people no longer want to be obedient to the older ones? Why do they no longer listen to their leaders and chiefs and do nothing but drink, rob, steal, and beat each other to death?

You are the cause of all the unhappiness and harm which has come to the Indians because, I assure you, things were not like this before. Glikkikan, you can go to our towns. I will not forbid it. But if you go, you must expect the Indians to knock out the white man's brains.

"Brother David Good News answered Chief Natsi."

UNDER ATTACK

Brother, I and those like me are not responsible for your miserable circumstances. I told you at the beginning of my visit that there are two kinds of people on the earth, evil and good. Therefore I cannot do anything about it if other Whites cause trouble and unhappiness among the Indians. It is not within my power to keep them away. My concern and intention is to tell the Indians what they should and should not do to be saved.

When someone speaks kindly and brings you something good, you should accept it. If someone brings you something evil, you should not accept it. Therefore when someone brings rum into your town, and so much misfortune occurs, then do as we do in our town: we do not accept them, but send them away with it. Or if they want to stay overnight, we take the rum into our custody until they want to go on. Then we return to them what is theirs and let them go in peace. Why should your chiefs not have as much authority in your towns as we do in ours?

As to the rest of your accusation against me, I will leave it to my brothers to tell you what I teach the Indians and of my walk among them.

"Chief Natsi was silent after that and could not reply. I decided it was time for me to make an answer."

Listen to me once again. You have surely seen and heard that the Indians baptized by the French and English go to war, drink, steal, rob, kill, and continue to live in all kinds of sin. Thus, they have not become any better than they were before. You were also correct that the latter persecuted the Lenape in the last war, killed many of our

Under Attack in the Forks of the Delaware: 1747–1755

people, and burned our cities. It does not follow, however, that we are also like these people.

Those of our people who have become believers no longer do such things. We do not go to war and do not kill people; we do not drink, steal, or lie. We find all such things repulsive, and our teachers instruct us how we can lead a life pleasing to God. We have never seen them do the bad things other white people do. Many of them are no better than the Indians. Therefore you must not think we are like the Indians baptized by other ministers.

Recently, some Indians in Newcomerstown wanted to have other preachers come. I told them that this would not improve them. I know firsthand that the Indians baptized by those besides the Brethren do not lead better lives. Indeed, they become worse than others.

"Natsi had now poured out his heart and emptied himself. It being well past midnight, he pulled himself together, bid each of us a cordial farewell, and then went to his lodging. Chief Hokolesqua and Talgayeeta lingered behind. We wandered outside a short distance from the huts so we could be alone."

" 'Talgayeeta,' I inquired, 'how is your sister Koonay and her little one?'

" 'Ah, Koonay cares well for her beautiful child.'

" 'And Gibson?[25] Does he care for her well?'

" 'He still comes to see them and brings a few gifts, but his attentions are few and far between. You know Gibson is a trader and a fighter. He is not a man of peace, but always attempts to mollify the Indians with gifts and sweet talk so that war is averted. I do not trust

---

[25] See Appendix A and also page 46.

UNDER ATTACK

him, but fear that he will always side with the Whites against the Indians.'

"At this, Chief Hokolesqua spoke, quietly but firmly."

Glikkikan, the Shawnee are headed for war. You have heard the antagonisms of Natsi, and they are not without just cause. Many settlers build cabins and rough forts on our lands right along the Ohio. We have tried many times to plead with the officials to honor their treaties and force the settlers out. They all say they can do nothing about it.

This new Long Knife Connolly at Fort Pitt is worse yet. He openly encourages the people to attack the Indians and get rid of the vermin. Connolly, Gibson, McKee, and Croghan are openly feuding over whether Virginia or Pennsylvania will get the Ohioland after the Indians are gone. The Shawnee have given up on pleading with government officials. We have warned them of reprisals if they do not keep the settlers from crossing the Ohio onto our lands, especially into our hunting grounds in Kentucky.

When Captain Will discovered Daniel Boone and five others hunting in Kentucky, a fight broke out, and one of Boone's men was killed. Boone and the other four were captured and held for a week while Captain Will treated them with courtesy. Then he gave them this speech:

"Now brothers, go home and stay there. Do not come here anymore. This is the Indians' hunting grounds, where we must hunt to provide for our families over the winter. All the animals, skins, and furs were given as a gift by Manito for our support, without which we could not survive. You must go. Consider us to be the stinging bugs

Under Attack in the Forks of the Delaware: 1747–1755

who guard their nests. If you are so foolish as to come here again, you may be sure the wasps and yellowjackets will sting you severely."

With that warning, Captain Will released the trespassers. But the next spring they returned. Surveyors, hunters, and settlers in abundance advanced into the sacred hunting lands of the Shawnee. I tell you, Glikkikan, the anger of the Shawnee is fast raging out of control. The patience of the Shawnee is ended. I believe we can never win a war with the Whites, whose resources appear endless. So should we die as mice and rabbits or as men? I do not want war, but if the Shawnee decide to stand and fight, I will lead them.

"Brother John," Glikkikan continued, "I told the two great chiefs, 'My brothers, my heart bleeds for you. I, too, have yearned for a safe and secure homeland for the Lenape. I have fought for many years to drive the Whites away, and many other great leaders of my people have also strained to capture such a place in their generation.

" 'My grandfather Owechela, a Lenape prophet, told me of a gold medallion that holds the secret of a secure homeland for the Lenape. He charged me to find it. I have searched for it all my life and never found it. Will you help me search for it?'

"I removed the copper and the silver medallions from around my neck. They caught moonbeams on their shiny surfaces and glowed softly in the light. 'Brothers,' I whispered, 'it was revealed to me that the gold medallion is similar in size and shape to these two. The tortoise of the Lenape climbs upon it, and upon his back is laid a cross of gold. Once I was young, but now I am old. The sun is nearing the horizon, and yet there is hope. While I have life and breath, my hand may yet grasp that medallion, my mind yet open its secret.'

UNDER ATTACK

"I continued to hold those medallions out as we three stood there in silence admiring them while each one pondered the lessons of the past and tried to unravel the secrets of the future. In due time, I placed them back under my shirt, and without a word, each one slipped away to his lodging.

"The next morning, our horses were lost, so while we waited for them to be found, we had a chance to visit again with some of the Shawnee we had encountered on our earlier mission trip. They seemed fearful and shy, not so much of us as of the others, and perhaps only of Chief Natsi. They listened very attentively, and when they were leaving, some of them said they were happy they had heard a little bit again. The Shawnee we were with last year have scattered; some have gone to the lower towns, and some have spread out around Woaketameki. As happy as I was to see such a beautiful prospect last year, it now hurts me to see that all has come to nothing and been destroyed by Satan.

"As we mounted our horses to leave, I asked Brother David, 'Are we going south or north?'

" 'North,' he said, and we started the journey home."

Glikkikan sat there in front of me with his eyes on the ground. He waited silently.

I tried to cheer him. "That was an interesting report," I commented. "You never know what good may come from such a journey."

"No," he said sourly. "It's all bad, bad, bad. That is the devil's territory. Even Brother David said so."

"Come on, cheer up," I urged. "You never know what God will do in the hearts of men."

"Yes," he spat out, "Watwees will lead all the Delawares to the Savior. White Eyes and Natsi will join us at Schoenbrunn. Hokolesqua will find the gold medallion, and Talgayeeta will persuade the Mingos to leave off horse stealing and drinking." He grinned a trifle at his own joke.

Under Attack in the Forks of the Delaware: 1747-1755

I took that as a good sign and launched into the story of what happened in the Forks of the Delaware between 1746 and 1755.

In the Forks of the Delaware

A Refugee Camp 1747

"A large burden fell on the white Brethren at Bethlehem when the missionaries were driven out of the Shekomeko mission, and further attacks on the congregation forced the Indians to seek refuge elsewhere. The white Brethren helped the Shekomeko Indians pay off their debts with their neighbors, educated their children, and even bought some additional land for them. Everyone involved bore these expenses cheerfully and without regrets."

Like an interested school boy, Glikkikan raised his hand and peeked out over his arms at me. I nodded.

"Whom did the Brethren buy the land from?" he asked sulkily.

"Why, from the Pennsylvania government, of course," I responded. "It is illegal for anyone in Pennsylvania to buy land from anyone else."

"How did the Pennsylvania government come to own the land in the Forks?" was his next morose question.

"They bought it from William Penn at the Walking Purchase in 1700. And I'm told that Chiefs Lappawinzo, Tishcohan, Manawykyhickon, and Nutimus have all put their marks on the deed the Penns presented to them."

"Really?" he replied. Then he put his head back down and I continued.

The first ten families who emigrated to Bethlehem immediately built huts near the town and began holding

UNDER ATTACK

services in the Mohican tongue. This early settlement adjacent to Bethlehem they named *Friedenshuetten* or "Huts of Peace."

In many ways, the newcomers melded into the congregation of white believers at Bethlehem. Two of the Indian girls were baptized in the Bethlehem chapel. After examining their faith in Jesus Christ, their brotherly love, and their unity of spirit, the Indian believers were permitted to partake of the Holy Communion along with the white believers at Bethlehem.

Being much encouraged by the faith of the believers, the Brethren thought it proper to introduce some good regulations for the conduct of the Christian Indians. In the past, some salutary regulations formed by the men in council had failed, chiefly because of difficulties raised by the women.

Although it was not the usual Indian custom, the baptized mothers and fathers of the families were permitted to come to the council this time. Thus the women heard the reasons for the regulations and were convinced of them. In this way, the regulations met the general satisfaction of everyone.

The Brethren judged that this Indian town, called Huts of Peace, could not be supported so close to Bethlehem. Accordingly, they bought several hundred acres about thirty miles north of Bethlehem and about the same distance south of Wyoming. On this land the Indians could build, plant, and live in their own way. They gave this town the German name of *Gnadenhuetten* meaning "Huts of Grace."

Again, Glikkikan lifted his right hand timidly and supported it with

Under Attack in the Forks of the Delaware: 1747–1755

his left hand at the elbow. I nodded.

"What did the Brethren mean when they said the town could not be supported so close to Bethlehem?"

"I suppose they considered language, the attitude of the neighbors toward all Indians, the amount of land needed for hunting, and some other customs the believers did not know about, both Indian and White."

"Oh," he said, lowering his hand again. I continued my story.

> The situation at the new town pleased the Indian believers, and they cheerfully began clearing the land, building houses, and caring for their crops. They often spoke to each other of the ease with which they could labor since their souls were engaged with the Lord Jesus who labored hard for them. They ascribed the good progress in building this new town and the preservation of their own bodies to the grace and mercy of God rather than to their own efforts and prudence.
>
> The Brethren from Bethlehem joined the Indians in the extensive work of clearing trees and planting and building the town. But since the Indians were unacquainted with husbandry and unable to bear much fatigue, the heaviest work fell upon the white brothers. The Brethren considered this work as an act of service for God, and they spared no exertion in the building of Huts of Grace.
>
> While this work was in progress, the Whites and the Indians shared a common table. Although this was convenient, the practice could not be continued, chiefly because of its appearance to the heathen Indians. The white brothers were in charge of the provisions and found it necessary to be frugal in the distribution of the supplies.

UNDER ATTACK

Thus the Indian believers could not treat their visitors with the usual generosity, and the savages conceived the notion that the Christian Indians suffered want and had become slaves of the Whites. This belief was reinforced when they saw them perform manual labor, for the Indians were not accustomed to such work.

Therefore, as soon as circumstances would permit, each family was put into possession of its own plot of ground and given some instruction on how to cultivate it. At the same time, each Indian family began its own separate housekeeping.

Settling In

In July 1746, the congregation at Huts of Grace received its regulations, the different officers were appointed, the rules of the congregation were made public, and the chapel was consecrated with great solemnity. In the service, Brother Spangenberg prayed, "May the grace and protection of God our Savior rest upon all the present and future inhabitants of this place."

Huts of Grace now became a very pleasant town. The church stood in the valley. On one side, the Indian houses formed a crescent upon a rising ground; on the other side stood the house of the missionary and the burying ground.

The road to Wyoming and other Indian towns went directly through the settlement. The missionaries tilled their own grounds and the Indian families their own

Under Attack in the Forks of the Delaware: 1747–1755

plantations. On 18 August, they had the satisfaction to partake of the firstfruits of the land at a love feast.

Christian Henry Rauch and Martin Mack, both veterans of the Shekomeko mission, were the first missionaries to reside at Huts of Grace. They administered the Word and sacraments to the congregation, and their labor was attended with God's blessing.

The Brethren at Bethlehem believed that frequent changes of ministers might be useful in preventing too strong an attachment to men. They wanted the Indians to fix their hope on God alone.

The Indians who lived around Bethlehem grew in their faith in Jesus as they observed the lives of their European brothers and sisters.

Believers from Shekomeko continued to migrate to Huts of Peace. Jacob was typical of some of the wayward believers who now wanted to come to Huts of Grace and join the congregation there.

He declared, "I am like a child whose father loves him dearly, clothes him well, and gives him all he stands in need of. Afterward, the child becomes refractory, deserts his parents, and despises their counsel. At length, through folly, the child loses all the good things he possessed, his clothes become ragged, and nakedness and want follow.

"Then he remembers how well he fared at home, he repents and weeps day and night, and doubts that he is worthy to return. This is precisely my case. I am totally unworthy."

The Brethren at Huts of Grace and the missionaries heard these Indian believers acknowledge and lament

UNDER ATTACK

> their errors before the public assembly as they begged for the pardon of all present.
>
> The congregation always received the penitents with open arms, and the prodigals were publicly assured of the forgiveness of the congregation. Many tears of love and joy were shed by all present on these moving occasions.
>
> Sometimes the enemies of the missionaries became exceedingly enraged and threatened to kill them.

Up went the schoolboy hand of my audience of one. This time I let Glikkikan hold it there while I finished my thought.

> The missionaries understood that God had greatly blessed their labors among the Indians, and their desire to spread the Gospel among the heathen daily increased. According to Brother Mack's own expression, "The hard fare in a poor Indian cottage afforded us more real pleasure than all the luxuries of the most sumptuous palace ever could."

I nodded at Glikkikan as he looked at me. I thought I saw the trace of a smile while he enjoyed his childish caper. "Why were the Indians angry at the missionaries?" he asked.

"I did not say the Indians were angry at them. I said their *enemies* wanted to kill them. Some Indians did not like that their friends had given up all their Indian customs and ways, but it was the Whites who threw the biggest fits of rage. They did not like Germans, and they did not like Indians."

"Yes," he mused, "it is the way of Satan to hate and kill. Such people do not even need a reason to hate." This time he sat there looking at me until I went on.

> The Indian congregations at Huts of Grace and Huts

Under Attack in the Forks of the Delaware: 1747–1755

of Peace now received their proper regulations, though Huts of Peace near Bethlehem was gradually forsaken. The congregation met twice a day, early in the morning and in the evening after their work, to sing and pray and sometimes to hear a discourse upon the text of Scripture appointed for the day.

By these discourses, the missionaries endeavored to make their people better acquainted with all the saving truths of the Gospel. The missionaries translated portions of Scripture into the Mohican tongue and publicly read and expounded them. As they fellowshipped, they also sang hymns, some of which were in Mohican. This also added to the spirit of the meetings and bestowed a peculiar blessing on all present.

They baptized children of baptized parents soon after birth, but the baptism of adults always took place on Sundays or on festival days. Those preparing for baptism were instructed in the core truths of the Christian faith and then publicly questioned about their views. After they had declared their testimonies, they were absolved by laying on of hands, and then baptized in the name of the Father, the Son, and the Holy Ghost. Solemn prayer and thanksgiving followed, after which the blessing of the Lord was pronounced upon them.

The Holy Communion was administered every month. This great and solemn transaction continued to be attended with the most distinguished blessing, powerfully strengthening their faith and hope. The Indians called the communion day "The Great Day" because it meant so much to them. The missionaries could not find words

UNDER ATTACK

sufficient to extol the power and grace of God revealed on these occasions.

With the cottages completed and all these good regulations firmly established at Huts of Grace, the Brethren wished to send the Indian children in the schools at Bethlehem back to be with their parents. It could generally not be done.

The parents knew that their children would receive a better education in Bethlehem than they would receive at Huts of Grace. One Indian sister even gave her two children to Bishop Spangenberg in order to keep them at Bethlehem. The Indians valued their children greatly, and offering to let them stay at Bethlehem showed the great respect the Indians held for the brothers and sisters.

The children also were extremely unwilling to quit the schools in Bethlehem and entreated the Brethren so earnestly that they at last agreed to keep them. Then some of the children at Huts of Grace begged their parents to let them go to Bethlehem too so they could attend school and be with their friends there. The parents and the children repeated their requests earnestly and frequently, and the Brethren felt cruel to deny them any longer. Therefore the Brethren agreed to place the children in their respective choirs[26] and teach the Indian children alongside the white children of the believers.

Teaching the Indian children in Bethlehem had good effects. The clear proof of God moving in the Indian children's hearts gave great joy to their teachers and

---

[26] This was a system of grouping the children according to age and sex. This grouping applied not only to their time at school, but in all their activities. In the school, they had three groups of each sex with appropriate male and female teachers.

Under Attack in the Forks of the Delaware: 1747-1755

overseers. Care was taken to make sure the children did not lose their native tongue, but in later years, some of these children who had learned the German or English languages became very useful to the missions.

In 1747, supporting the Indian congregation at Huts of Grace became a principal concern of the Brethren. The way the Indians diligently planted the fields allotted to each family proved that a change of heart had indeed taken place. Heathen Indians, especially men, did not usually work in the fields.

However, the fields were not sufficient for the number of Indian believers, so the Brethren bought a neighboring plantation. This gave the Indians great pleasure. One of them said, "It seemed hitherto as if we had lain in a short bed, never able to stretch out at full length, but now we lie in a large one."

The Brethren also erected a sawmill at Huts of Grace. This gave many Indians the means of earning money by cutting timber and floating it down the Lehigh to Bethlehem.

But the chief means of support for the Indian congregation came from hunting. On a good day, as many as fifteen or twenty bears or deer were shot. If provisions became scarce, the people gathered wild honey, chestnuts, and berries from the forests.

Still, the hunting and gathering were not enough to supply what was needed at Huts of Grace. Because of the many visits by companies of Shawnees and Delawares, it had to be supplemented with continual shipments from Bethlehem. The believers received all these visitors with

UNDER ATTACK

kindness, entertained them with meals, and preached the Gospel to them.

The Lord Added to the Church

Nothing made so good an impression upon the savages as to see that peace and harmony prevailed among the believers and that they were content amidst all their troubles. This gave great weight to their testimony of Jesus Christ, for it was evident that nothing but faith in Him could create that display of benevolence and cheerfulness. In contrast, a sullen disposition and a lack of contentment was general among the unconverted.

The missionaries welcomed the savages, hoping that some might be gained for Christ. However, some of the savages proved troublesome because of their wild and disorderly conduct. On one hand, the missionaries had to treat them civilly or they would stop coming. Yet disorder could not be permitted, lest the believing Indians should suffer.

The missionaries and their assistants decided to put certain rules in place. Those who were curious and only came for a day or two, the missionaries welcomed. The Christian walk of the Indians proved edifying to them, and the observance of the rules of the settlement prevented all mischief. But if any expressed an inclination to live at Huts of Grace, the assistants took them aside and told them, "Drunkenness, fighting, games, and the like are not permitted while here." Even with every precaution, these

Under Attack in the Forks of the Delaware: 1747–1755

evils could not be entirely prevented.

With this understanding of the rules, twenty-six Indians came from Pagoch to Huts of Grace and pretended that they wished to live there and hear the Gospel. Since there was no room for them in Huts of Grace, they began to build nearby, but it was soon evident they were not sincere.

These poor people, along with the ones they lured away from the congregation, soon found reason to repent. One, named Gideon, expressed his regret in the following terms: "When I left you, I thought I might still retain life in my heart, but alas, I found it otherwise. My other brethren who have done the same are all spiritually dead and in pursuit of the world. It would have been better for me to have remained with you."

Another dissolute woman came to Huts of Grace and pretended to have the best views, but secretly she wanted to seduce several persons. After they fully exposed her evil intentions, she was called before the assistants and informed that this town was built only for such as were weary of sin and the service of Satan. Then they made sure to tell her that salvation extended even to the greatest harlots, murderers, and thieves if they were truly penitent and desired to be delivered from the power of evil. But Huts of Grace was not a place for those who persisted in sin, and therefore she must now leave the town. However, she would be received into the town with pleasure, should she sincerely change her mind.

As soon as the lady appeared before this venerable company, she was overcome with awe. Her countenance gave evidence of her guilt. She left the house with tears

UNDER ATTACK

and found a home elsewhere. She married a heathen Indian, who was afterward much disfigured in a drunken fight. This misfortune caused the poor man to seriously reflect on his conduct, and his wife reminded him of the Brethren. They both came to Huts of Grace and declared their wish to know by experience the mercy of God who had saved the Indians also. They believed, were afterward baptized, and were named Daniel and Ruth.

I must also tell you of Nicodemus. As a heathen, he was exceeded by none in the practice of evil and was much given to drunkenness. On hearing the word of the cross, he was one of the first who experienced its saving power and was baptized in December 1742.

Formerly of a turbulent spirit, Nicodemus became patient and humble in heart. In his walk and conversation, he was an example to all. Whoever knew him before beheld him now with amazement. By degrees, Nicodemus became much enlightened in the divine truths of the Gospel and was appointed an elder of the congregation at Huts of Grace, in which office he was respected by all.

By contemplating the sufferings and death of Jesus, Nicodemus's walk with his God and Savior was uninterrupted and his faith grew daily. He prayed without ceasing, both for himself and his countrymen, whom he greatly loved. If he perceived any insincerity among them, his concern was evident. His manner of speaking was very figurative, and yet his conversation proved highly instructive and useful to all.

Once, looking at the mill at Huts of Grace, Nicodemus addressed Brother Mack. "Brother," said he, "I discovered something that rejoices my heart. I have seen the great

Under Attack in the Forks of the Delaware: 1747–1755

Water Power

"Surely, all depends upon one wheel!" —Nicodemus

UNDER ATTACK

wheel and many little ones; every wheel was in motion and seemed alive, but suddenly all stopped, and the mill was as dead. I then thought that surely all depends upon one wheel. If the water runs upon that, everything else is alive, but when water ceases to flow, all appears dead. Just so it is with my heart. It is dead as the wheel, but as soon as Jesus' blood flows upon it, it gets life and sets everything in motion. The whole man being governed by the blood, it becomes evident that there is life throughout. But when the heart is removed from the crucified Jesus, it dies gradually, and at length all life ceases."

Upon another occasion Nicodemus said, "I crossed the Lehigh today in a boat, and being driven into the rapid current, I was forced down the stream and nearly upset. I then thought that this is exactly the case of men who know not the Lord Jesus Christ. They are irresistibly hurried away by sin, cannot help themselves, and are in danger of being eternally lost. But as soon as our mighty Savior takes the helm, we receive power to withstand the rapid stream of this world."

When the doctrine of the Holy Ghost became clearer to Nicodemus, he once compared his body to a canoe and his heart to the rudder, adding, "The Holy Ghost is the master sitting at the rudder and directing my vessel."

Glikkikan was following my eyes closely now, but his hand again went up. I paused, and he said, "Those are beautiful figures Nicodemus used. They go straight to the heart of any Indian." Glikkikan lowered his hand and I continued my story.

Nicodemus was very diligent in his attendance on

Under Attack in the Forks of the Delaware: 1747-1755

heathen visitors; his unaffected and solid conversation with them as well as his fervent prayers in their behalf made a lasting impression upon them.

In his last illness, Nicodemus thought much of the resurrection and said, "I am now an old man and shall soon depart to the Lord. My body will be interred in our burying ground, but it will rise most glorious. When our Savior shall call all those who have fallen asleep in Him, they will rise to newness of life and glory."

Nicodemus' countenance appeared at the same time as serene as that of an angel. He repeated his ardent desire to be at home with Jesus and assured his friends that his joy in the Lord had almost overpowered his pain. He added, "I am poor and needy and therefore amazed at the love of my Lord Jesus Christ, who is always with me." Thus he remained cheerful till his happy departure, fully proving the reality of his faith.

Bishop Johannes von Watteville came from Europe to visit the Brethren settlements in North America. In September 1748, he stopped for three days at Huts of Grace, preached the Gospel with fervor, and rejoiced at the grace prevailing there.

Gomeka

In the late 1740s, Gomeka,[27] which meant "a small spot of good land," was a village tucked away in a protected

---

[27] For ease of reading, I have shortened "Meniolagomeka" to "Gomeka."

UNDER ATTACK

valley on the northwestern side of Blue Mountain. Gomeka was the easternmost Delaware settlement in Pennsylvania. It mostly consisted of related groups of Indians who had moved from New Jersey west across the Delaware River. They now sought to remain isolated from Whites and stay on ancestral homelands.

There was a problem, however. Gomeka lay in the Forks of the Delaware, and Pennsylvania claimed it as part of the land taken in the Walking Purchase.

Upon repeated invitations from the chiefs at Gomeka, Bishops Cammerhof and Seidel went there to preach the Gospel. The chief of this place was a young man of rank generally called George Rex. He, along with his wife, was soon after baptized in Bethlehem. Both became useful assistants in the Indian congregation.

Many bitter evils were thwarted in Gomeka because of the firmness and steadiness of Chief George Rex. Renamed Augustus at the time of his baptism, George Rex was a man of sound understanding and strong in faith.

The missionary Grube and his wife went to Gomeka and inhabited a miserable cottage. Among other inconveniences, they suffered their share of a famine that plagued those parts, but were comforted under all outward affliction by perceiving that the Gospel entered with power into the hearts of the heathen.

The missionaries hesitated about baptizing an Indian called Big Jacob who was living in Gomeka. He had been many years an enemy to the Gospel and its ministers, endeavoring with all his might and cunning to retard the progress of the truth. But during a severe illness, the

Under Attack in the Forks of the Delaware: 1747–1755

Spirit of God operated upon his heart. His wretched state was revealed to him, and being in great distress of mind, he asked advice of the Brethren.

Bishop Cammerhof and others visited him diligently, pointed him to Jesus as the Savior of the afflicted, and were convinced that he desired to be converted with all his heart. He owned up to his sinful life. His countenance, formerly savage and fierce, was changed into that of a true penitent, and he constantly repeated his desire for baptism. He said to Brother Cammerhof, "I earnestly desire to be cleansed by the blood of our Savior, and pray Him to have mercy upon me and to enable me to love Him above all things."

Big Jacob was asked whether he believed that none could save him but the true God, who had become a man, died on the cross, and shed His blood as an atonement for sin. He replied, "I believe that nothing can save and cleanse me from sin but the blood of Christ alone. This I chiefly desire to experience."

Brother Cammerhof asked further whether he was willing to devote himself to our Savior, as his entire and eternal property, upon which he answered, "Oh yes, if He receives me, He will also give me strength and grace to live to Him alone that I may no longer serve sin and Satan."

Big Jacob was then baptized and named Paul. God sealed this transaction by a remarkable perception of His divine presence. Paul remained faithful to the end of his life.

The possessor of Gomeka did not proceed so far as to expel the Indian inhabitants, and the cause of the Gospel

UNDER ATTACK

flourished in defiance of all opposition. An Indian assistant came every Sunday to this place to serve as interpreter to Brother Bueninger, who was preacher and schoolmaster.

Brother Bueninger was pleased when a student whom he instructed in writing brought him a prayer written out of the fulness of his heart. It read as follows:

"My dear Savior! My name is Nathaniel. I will open my whole heart to thee, in writing, in thy presence. I am very deficient in everything. I find that I have not yet devoted my whole heart unto thee, and yet thou hast died for me. Jesus Christ! I wish I was so that thou couldst rejoice over me! Dear Savior, I would willingly live so as to please thee."

Wyoming on the Susquehanna

The Brethren had desired earlier to settle the refugee Indians at Wyoming. Thus, Bishop Spangenberg, the director of the Indian Missions in America, and other brothers paid a visit to the Indians in Wyoming.

Upon his return to Bethlehem, the good bishop reported, "The Indians received us as angels sent from God. We preached to them the word of the cross, and they heard our words with uncommon eagerness. We welcomed their interest in the Gospel and their friendliness toward us. On this visit, we established a covenant of friendship between the Wyoming Indians and the Mohican nation to which most of our believing Indians belong."

Under Attack in the Forks of the Delaware: 1747–1755

"As you know, Glikkikan, our Indians refused to go there. It's still somewhat of a mystery why the Mohicans would not move to Wyoming. It's a beautiful place, and it is in Indian country."

Glikkikan said nothing, and it seemed that his dour mood still controlled him, so I continued.

> The bishop, von Watteville, and Cammerhof then proceeded with Martin Mack and David Zeisberger on to Wyoming, Nescopeck, Wabhallobank, and Shamokin. Everywhere they preached the precious Gospel of Jesus Christ.
>
> At Shamokin on the Susquehanna, they renewed the covenant made between the Iroquois chief, Shikkellamy, in the name of the Iroquois and Count Zinzendorf. The visitors delivered him a present and received the following answer: "Tell Johanan (this being the name given to the Count by the Indians) that his brethren, the Six Nations, salute him, for they love him and desire him to salute all his brethren, whom they love likewise."

Glikkikan stiffened. Like a cat getting ready to spring, every part of him tensed. "What did you say he asked?"

"I said that the party went to Shamokin to renew the covenant made between the Count and the Iroquois in 1742."

"What was the covenant made between them?" Glikkikan asked.

"Oh, it was a covenant of peace promising friendship between the Moravians and the Iroquois as long as the sun shines and the rivers run down to the sea. The Count wanted very much to preach the Gospel to the Iroquois."

I saw him relax again. "I just wanted to make sure you knew," he said.

UNDER ATTACK

Penitents Return

The missionaries always assured the penitent that the congregation which they had offended was ready and willing to readmit them to fellowship. This message of consolation had the desired effect. The deluded people confessed their sins with many tears. Nathaniel said, "I know that I belong to my Savior and to His people. My horses often stray far into the woods, but they always return to my hut, and I will likewise return and seek our Savior and the congregation." He added, "If a coal is taken from the fire, it loses its heat and is extinguished. So also my heart has lost its fervor, having strayed from the fellowship of the believers."

Another said, "My heart is in doubt how I should behave in the future. It is unbroken as a stubborn horse. A man may have a very wild horse, but if he can make it eat salt out of his hand on even one occasion, then it will always come to him again. I am not so disposed toward our Savior, who is continually offering me His grace. I have once tasted grace out of His hand, yet my heart still runs away when He holds out His grace unto me. We are so foolish that we lack even the sense of beasts."

All who bemoaned their unfaithfulness received a public assurance of the pardon of the congregation, having previously made known their situation to the missionaries. Soon thereafter, most of them were also readmitted to the Holy Communion, and the Brethren experienced on these occasions something of that joy which is in heaven over repenting sinners.

Under Attack in the Forks of the Delaware: 1747-1755

The missionaries not only welcomed repenting sinners, but often they enjoyed the blessing of baptizing more Indians. On one mission journey in March of 1749 to the old missions in Connecticut, Brother Cammerhof baptized twenty Indians and administered the Sacraments.[28]

Embassy to Philadelphia

In July 1749, deputies from the Six Nations (Iroquois) arrived in Philadelphia to form an alliance with the English government.[29] Brothers Johannes von Watteville, Spangenberg, Cammerhof, Pyrlaeus, and Nathaniel Seidel went along to renew with them the covenant made between the Brethren and the Six Nations. At the request of the Iroquois, the Brethren promised to visit their people.

Glikkikan had been seated on the floor, but now he stood up. His giant frame towered over me. "What did you say?" he asked.

I squirmed in my seat behind the desk. "I said that the bishops went to Philadelphia to renew with the Iroquois the covenant made between the Brethren and the Six Nations."

"And why did you say the Iroquois went to Philadelphia?"

"I said the Iroquois came to Philadelphia to make an alliance with the English government." I did not bend my head back to look up at him, but pretended to be writing furiously.

---

[28] Bishop Cammerhof baptized 89 Indians during his four years in America. The good man was greatly mourned by the Indians when he died in 1751.

[29] This treaty was a part of the Iroquois alliance with the English government whereby they continued to sell Indian lands belonging to all the other Indian nations. Moravian Brethren going to this treaty without Delawares, Mohicans, or Shawnees in attendance was a most uncouth political maneuver. –JGL – Francis Jennings, *The Ambiguous Iroquois Empire*, "Summit and Slope," pp. 347-366.

UNDER ATTACK

"I just wanted to make sure you knew," Glikkikan replied calmly. Then he resumed his seat on the floor and said, "Go on with your story."

So I continued.

Huts of Grace on the Lehigh

The converts from Shekomeko, Pagoch, Westhuck, the Susquehanna, and the Forks of the Delaware continued to wend their way to Huts of Grace, twenty here and twenty there. In May 1749, thirty believing Indians, formerly from Shekomeko, went to live at Huts of Grace.

About this time, the small congregation of Indians settled at Wechquatnach, Connecticut, were driven away by their neighbors. Some retired to Wyoming, but thirty-four of them gave sufficient proof of their sincerity and were allowed to relocate to Huts of Grace.

Visitors swelled the crowd on any special occasion. All held a hope that the Moravians could help them adapt to the new ways being forced upon them and to find a permanent home in Huts of Grace. This town now became an object of admiration to the whole country, and its increasing number of inhabitants gave convincing proof of the Gospel's power to change men's hearts.

The congregation at Huts of Grace kept growing in number as refugees continued flowing in from the churches in Connecticut. Besides those living in the town, dozens of people from Gomeka, baptized and unbaptized, often came there for Sunday and holiday services. Sometimes the missionaries preached to crowds

Under Attack in the Forks of the Delaware: 1747–1755

of five hundred Indians, and the services had to be held outdoors because the chapel built only three years earlier was already too small.

In September 1749, Bishop Johannes von Watteville from Europe came to Huts of Grace and laid the foundation for a new church building. It was to be a large chapel; the resolution was to erect a schoolhouse as well. All the inhabitants took their share in the work with great willingness.

The missionaries were excited and praised God for the grace bestowed on these Indian people, so ready to perform the hardest labor for the cause of the Gospel. When the house was finished and solemnly dedicated to the service of the Lord, the missionaries rendered thanks unto Him that during the whole work, there had not been the least appearance of discord.

The declarations of the Indians proved the effects of the grace of God. Conversing together one day, they were heard to say, "We used formerly to meet for drinking, dancing, fighting, and other reveling, but now we assemble to rejoice that our Savior has delivered us from these things and to thank Him that He has drawn us unto Himself."

When the new school building at Huts of Grace was finished, a school of three classes for boys and three classes for girls was started. Masters taught the boys and mistresses the girls. The Indian youth eagerly applied themselves to learning, and it was a pleasure to their instructors to see their progress.

A regulation was also passed to care for widows and orphans.

UNDER ATTACK

Remove to Wyoming

In March of 1753, an embassy of twenty-two Nanticokes and Shawnees came to Huts of Grace. Many baptized Indians came likewise from Gomeka so they could be present for the transactions of this group. One part of their commission was to thank the Brethren in the name of the Nanticokes and Shawnees for their liberality toward them during the famine the previous autumn. If the Brethren had not sent them timely relief, they would all have perished.

The second point in their commission declared they could not find any place to become better acquainted with the language of the Brethren. It was now the desire of the Iroquois that the Nanticokes would move further inland. However, this did not mean they would no longer be friends of the Brethren or fail to visit them.

Then came the difficulty. In the name of the Iroquois, the speaker made a proposal that the Indians at Huts of Grace should relocate to Wyoming. Yet this was to be a choice for all the people; no one would be forced to move. But it must be understood that if the Indians were later to leave Wyoming, the land must remain in the possession of the Iroquois.

During the last part of the speech, the speaker changed countenance and began to tremble, well aware that this proposal would not be acceptable to the Brethren at Bethlehem nor to the Indians at Huts of Grace. However, both he and the other chiefs were relieved of their fear when they heard the answer of the Brethren "that they

Under Attack in the Forks of the Delaware: 1747–1755

would not determine anything positively against it, but must insist upon this point, that no means of constraint should be used on either side."

Yet some believers doubted their honesty. They wondered why the Iroquois proposed the transplanting of the believing Indians from Huts of Grace without giving any plausible reason. They asked, "Why did the Iroquois not send the message themselves instead of using the Nanticokes and Shawnees to interfere in the business?"

The deputies of the congregation agreed to the proposal, on condition that they should have full liberty to take their teachers with them. They also asked that the land they settled on would be their own as a permanent resting place. The same ceremonies that always accompanied formal treaties were now performed.

The embassy remained at Huts of Grace for one week before returning to Wyoming. During that time, the Brethren held many meetings. All united in prayer that God would cause His Word to bring forth abiding fruit. Some of the visitors did hear and were moved by the blood and the wounds of Jesus and His death on the cross.

Yet, for the inhabitants of Huts of Grace, it appeared that these visits did more harm than good. The people at large became fond of forming alliances with other nations, as did several Indian Brethren who were not yet established and rooted in Jesus Christ. They began to think again of their heathenish customs. Some forsook the congregation and brought themselves into distress of mind and body. Others lost their cheerfulness and serenity, becoming gloomy and shy, and much time elapsed before they were restored.

UNDER ATTACK

Stirring Up Trouble

The course of the Indian congregation had hitherto been, in general, pleasing and unmolested, notwithstanding its various defects. But now troubles began. Many problems originated in the proposal to transplant the congregation from Huts of Grace to Wyoming.

The Brethren in Bethlehem long wished that the believing Indians might withdraw into that country and make a settlement. But now the reason why the savages proposed the removal of the Christian Indians gradually became evident. They planned to commence hostilities against the English and first wished to furnish a safe retreat for their countrymen, the Indians of Huts of Grace. This would make it easier for them to fall upon the Whites in the Forks of the Delaware. When we considered it from this angle, it became apparent that the Iroquois had called the Nanticokes from Wyoming into their neighborhood to make room for the Christian Indians.

The Iroquois had good reason to believe the Brethren at Bethlehem would approve of this step. Nine years earlier, Bishop Spangenberg had made a treaty with them so that the believing Indians from Shekomeko might go to Wyoming. Their plot appeared to be well contrived, and the pressing invitation sent to the believing Indians to go to Wyoming was part of the scheme.

But now things looked quite different to the Brethren at Bethlehem than they had earlier. They no longer wished for the Indians to go to Wyoming, yet they dared

Under Attack in the Forks of the Delaware: 1747–1755

not tell the believers to accept or reject the offer lest they be accused of making slaves of the Indians.

However, the missionaries need not have worried because the Indians were averse to leaving their pleasant settlement, especially after they discovered the true motives of the Iroquois. They saw that if they moved to Wyoming, they would at last be deprived of their teachers and brethren. Several, however, ignored their scruples and resolved to move to Wyoming.

Abraham and Gideon were the most active in promoting this affair. Gideon, formerly called Teedyuscung,[30] had waited long for baptism, and he soon proved that the missionaries' doubts about his character were well founded. He was like a reed, shaken with the wind. Hearing that the heathen Delawares had nominated him as their chief, he began to side with Abraham, who was now a captain of the Mohican nation. Abraham insisted that the converted Indians, having previously accepted the invitation, could not now refuse to go to Wyoming.

These two men sought to form a party, and though they did not meet with much success at first, it caused much contention between husbands and wives as well as parents and their children. They were so convincing that on the 24th of April, sixty-five people moved from Huts of Grace to Wyoming. They went without a missionary and were followed shortly by five more people.

Most of them burst into tears at taking leave and promised they would cleave unto the Lord Jesus and remain faithful. Fifteen more moved to Nescopeck without any

---

[30] For a more complete introduction to Teedyuscung, read *Tomahawks to Peace*, Chapter 9.

UNDER ATTACK

invitation, and all warnings were disregarded.

To see these people leave filled the missionaries with grief. They and the elders of the congregation at Bethlehem could do nothing but wait in silence. They comforted themselves by considering that though the enemy designs mischief, God has all things in His power and can bring good out of evil.

And that is exactly what God did. Huts of Grace had scarcely suffered this great loss of inhabitants before it was partly supplied from another quarter. The new proprietor of Gomeka had ordered the Indians to leave that place.[31] The believing Indians applied immediately to the Brethren, who sent them a cordial invitation by the missionary Martin Mack to move to Huts of Grace.

Their joy was inexpressible. They said, "Let us instantly break up! Our brethren have opened their arms to receive us and have called us to fly to them in our distress." They got ready in great haste, and before the end of April, the whole congregation of forty-nine souls moved to Huts of Grace.

New Huts of Grace

Soon after, it became necessary for Huts of Grace inhabitants to move to the east side of the River Lehigh. The land on the Mahony was too impoverished, rocky, and

---

[31] Fur, *A Nation of Women*, "Meniolagomeka," p. 53. Richard Peters, secretary to the Pennsylvania Assembly, surveyed Gomeka for the proprietors and in 1749 purchased it from the Six Nations. Richard Peters then acquired the property in his own name, and in May of 1754, he forced all the inhabitants of Gomeka to move to Gnadenhuetten.

Under Attack in the Forks of the Delaware: 1747-1755

small for the large number of believers. Therefore it was decided to move the Indian huts and houses across the Lehigh while keeping the mission buildings on the same site.

Jacob, an assistant, expressed himself concerning the future course of the congregation by saying, "When the snakes come forth out of the ground in spring, they have still their old winter coat on, but by creeping through a narrow hole, they rid themselves of the old skin and appear as newborn. Thus I wish that we may leave everything by which we have displeased the Lord in the old place, and bring into the new only what is pleasing to Him."

The congregations at Bethlehem, Nazareth, Christiansbrunn, and Gnadenthal kindly assisted the Indians in moving the buildings. They furnished not only workmen and materials, but also contributions in money. Unanimity and diligence contributed so much toward the progress of this work that the first twenty houses were inhabited by the 4th of June. The foundation stone of the new chapel was laid a week thereafter.

Bishop Spangenberg offered up a most fervent prayer and delivered a powerful discourse on this solemn occasion. The houses were soon after completed and a regulation made in all the families for the children of each gender to be properly taken care of. The dwellings were arranged in such a way that the Mohicans lived on one side of the street and the Delawares on the other.

The Brethren at Bethlehem took the cultivating of the old land on the Mahony upon themselves and made a plantation of it for the use of the Indian congregation.

UNDER ATTACK

They further converted the old chapel into a dwelling both for the use of those who had the care of the plantations and for missionaries passing through on their visits to the unconverted.

Encouraging the Faithful at Wyoming

At the end of June 1754, Brother Mack felt a strong urge to go and visit those who had left Huts of Grace and gone to Wyoming. He encountered many high waters on his journey of thirty miles, but God miraculously brought him through many dangers, and he arrived safely in Wyoming.

He was greatly comforted when he found that the Indian Brethren had not departed from the Lord. Even some who had demonstrated dishonorable conduct at Huts of Grace had now turned to Him with their whole hearts and received pardon and peace.

Those at Wyoming wanted a missionary residing among them. They proposed to send deputies to Onondaga, who in turn should request the Council to grant them land on the Susquehanna as a hereditary property where they might all live together undisturbed as a church of God.[32]

Glikkikan again raised his hand. I stopped and waited. "Brother

---

[32] "The Quakers called attention to the fraudulent Walking Purchase by which the Delawares had been compelled by the Iroquois to surrender possession of their ancestral possessions, and to the purchase of July 1754, by which the Iroquois sold the land of the Delawares and Shawnees from under their feet. The land sales drove the Delawares from one place to another. Wherever they went, the land on which they erected their wigwams was sold by their Iroquois conquerors without their being consulted or having any say whatever in the matter." —C. Hale Sipe, *The Indian Wars of Pennsylvania*, p. 283.

Under Attack in the Forks of the Delaware: 1747–1755

John," he asked, "you say the Brethren went to Philadelphia to renew their covenant with the Iroquois. Do you think they were also there in 1754 when the Iroquois sold the ground out from under our feet? You know that was just a year before the massacre."

"Brother Isaac," I answered, "you look at the wrong thing. The Brethren were neutral in political matters. Look instead at how fervently the missionaries helped the Indians to the Savior and to a better way of life."

Glikkikan lifted his face from his arms and fastened his black eyes on me. I had finally connected.

"Take, for example, the firstfruits of the different nations. Your hero, John Wamapah, was the firstfruits of the Mohican nation. You know what Christian Henry sacrificed to tell him of the blood of Jesus and to bring John out of the misery of sin."

He responded with an affirmative *"Kehelle."*

"We call George Rex 'Augustus,' the Chief from Gomeka, the firstfruits of the Delawares. Like you, Glikkikan, his fame as a warrior of the Delaware nation has traveled far. His gigantic form and terrible exploits as a warrior of the Delaware nation has spread throughout the land. Captain George Rex was also well known as a great drunkard and a monster of iniquity. But true faith in the Lord Jesus changed his conduct.

"George Rex owned with sorrow his former sinful life and found pardon and peace in the redemption of Jesus. After his baptism as Augustus, many visitors came just to see if such a miracle of grace had really happened to him, and to all of them Augustus joyfully declared what the Lord had done for his soul."

Glikkikan spoke another strong *"Kehelle."*

"Anna Caritas was the firstfruits of the Shawnees. Glikkikan, you know how warlike and troublesome this nation has always been. This sensible old woman had long resided among the Whites, but felt an impulse to see the Brethren. Her employers, who greatly esteemed her

UNDER ATTACK

as a good servant and housekeeper, could not persuade her to stay. She went to Bethlehem in the depth of winter, believed in Jesus Christ, and would not depart till her urgent request for baptism was granted."

"That is wonderful!" Glikkikan exclaimed. Then he asked, "Who were the firstfruits of the Iroquois?"

"We're still waiting to baptize the first Iroquois," I answered.

With that, he again laid his head down on his arms, and I carried on.

Brother Mack's visit to Wyoming was an unqualified success. Some believers had borne such vibrant testimonies of Jesus to the neighboring heathen that when Brother Mack arrived, they were prepared to hear him with gladness. One testified, "I am one of those who wish to hear your words, for I believe that I have hitherto been in the wrong and shall miss salvation. I am therefore uneasy and desirous to know the right way."

The missionary found all the people living on the Susquehanna in great fear and dread of both the approaching Catawbas, who were then at war with the Six Nations, and the French who threatened the Indians with fire and sword unless they acted with them against the English. Besides this, the people of New England who laid claim to Wyoming were advancing and intended to seize the land by force.

Soon after Brother Mack's return to Bethlehem, Grube and Gottlieb Rundt set out on a visit to Wyoming and Nescopeck. In both places, their discourses were so well received that the Indians desired the interpreter to repeat them. Though they wished it could be otherwise, the Brethren were obliged to preach to the heathen using an interpreter. They soon began to look for men who might

Under Attack in the Forks of the Delaware: 1747–1755

make it their principal study to learn the language of the heathen to whom they were called. For this purpose, two students, Fabricus and Wedstaedt, arrived that year at Huts of Grace. Fabricus was to learn Delaware and Wedstaedt was to study Shawnee. Brother Schmick had already made such quick progress in the Mohican dialect that he could preach fluently in that tongue.

Growth at New Huts of Grace

In the new Huts of Grace, the missionaries had much reason to rejoice at the growth of their congregation. Bishop Spangenberg, having returned from Europe, took great pains to teach, exhort, and comfort the whole congregation, particularly instructing the parents to educate their children in the fear of the Lord. He even personally attended to the children with the greatest diligence. God abundantly blessed his labors, and the missionaries were much indebted for his advice and assistance in the performance of their respective duties.

Despite the grief and divisions caused by the threat of removal to Wyoming, the Indians now had occasion to rejoice in the many instances of the power of the Gospel on the hearts of the heathen visitors and in the confidence and faith of many Indians who departed this life.

The latter end of a brother called Jeptha, above a hundred years old, was encouraging. He sent for all his children, took an affectionate leave of them, and made them promise that they would faithfully adhere to Christ and

UNDER ATTACK

to His congregation. He urged them to resist the world. After expressing his desire to depart and be with Christ, he soon after fell asleep.

Jeptha had been an Indian of great rank and the lawful possessor of a large tract of land in the district of New York, but he was expelled by the Whites.

A Red-Hot Iron

The external troubles at Huts of Grace continued. The inhabitants were charged with a tax to show their dependence upon the Iroquois. Around this time also a very singular message was brought to them by Gideon Teedyuscung and Paxinosa, the old chief of the Shawnees. It ran as follows: "The great head, that is, the Council of the Iroquois in Onondaga, speaks the truth, and lies not. It rejoices that some of the believing Indians have moved to Wyoming. But now it lifts up the remaining Mohicans and Delawares and sets them also down in Wyoming, for there a fire is kindled for them. There they may plant and think on God. But if they will not hear, the Great Council will come and clean their ears with a red-hot iron. That is, it will burn their houses and send musket balls through their heads."

Paxinosa then turned to the missionaries, earnestly warning them not to hinder the Indians from moving to Wyoming. He said, "The road is free; therefore they may visit their friends, stay with them till they are tired, and then return to their own country if they so desire."

Under Attack in the Forks of the Delaware: 1747–1755

These last words caused much reflection and uneasiness in the minds of the believing Indians, who took them as a sure token that the Iroquois only pretended to favor them while having evil intentions. Therefore the Indians at Huts of Grace gave no answer, but said, "We shall consult our Great Council in Bethlehem concerning this message."

The more the inhabitants of Huts of Grace considered and debated upon the above message sent by the Iroquois, the more their uneasiness and distress increased. Always in their mind lurked the danger of a redhot iron if they disobeyed the orders of the Iroquois.

Meanwhile, the Brethren at Bethlehem had received verification that the idea of moving the Indian congregation to Wyoming had not originated in the Great Council of the Six Nations. Only the Oneida tribe, with the warlike Delawares and Mohicans, had formed this plan. They then falsely ascribed it to the Iroquois in general. It had likewise been discovered that several persons of character in Philadelphia had joined them in endeavoring to move the Christian Indians to Wyoming. These Philadelphia men in high places hoped that if the Christian Indians went to Wyoming, it might prevent the people of New England from taking possession of that place, for these men also laid claim to that place themselves.

The Brethren heard also that the happy course of the baptized Indians at Wyoming had not been of long duration, and that many of these poor people had not only suffered in their own hearts, but had done harm to others.

All this added to the Brethren's concern with regard

UNDER ATTACK

to the removal of the Christian Indians. The Brethren chose not to inform the Christian Indians of the plan devised by the Oneidas, Delawares, and Mohicans, nor of the schemes of the gentlemen of Philadelphia. Yet the Brethren could not refrain from giving a faithful and timely caution.

Brother Isaac did not lift his head from his arms, but raised his hand. "Why did the Brethren not tell the Indians the truth about what they knew?" he asked.

"They needed to remain neutral in the war. If they had told everything, it would have appeared as though they favored the British side against the French and Indians," I answered.[33] Glikkikan made no further comment, so I went on.

As Loving Fathers

The elders at Bethlehem sent a deputation to Huts of Grace in the beginning of February. It consisted of Christian Henry Rauch, Nathanael Seidel, and Christian Seidel. They appointed a meeting of all the baptized to converse with them in a friendly manner, as fathers speak with their children. First, they reminded the Christian Indians of the rich grace they had received from God our Savior. Then they discussed the deep grief the Brethren felt for everyone who had relapsed into heathenism. They

---

[33] In trying to imagine why the delegation did not reveal to the assistants all the information they possessed, my opinion is this: the Brethren claimed to be neutral in the war in that they did not actually fight. Yet their sources probably came from the Pennsylvania/Iroquois alliance. To have revealed the information and the source to the assistants would have totally discredited the information in the eyes of the assistants and probably brought them to an undesired conclusion. –JGL

Under Attack in the Forks of the Delaware: 1747–1755

shared recent examples of the misery experienced by those who spurned the grace of God. They pointed out the true signs of an hour of temptation and told of the imminent danger of giving ear to seducers. They further observed that the Brethren did not prohibit anyone from leaving Huts of Grace, but would only seek to guard them against all hurt to their souls. Thus, on some future day, the Brethren would be able to prove that they had carried out their duty and warned them.

Kneeling down with the whole congregation, they recommended this beloved people to the grace, mercy, and protection of God with many tears.

This declaration produced the desired effect in most of the Indians. Several who had both deviated themselves and endeavored to draw others aside, publicly and of their own accord owned their transgressions. They begged forgiveness of the rest, which the congregation granted with joy.

The missionaries observed in their account that the powerful grace of God was never more evident than when an Indian, naturally obstinate and inflexible to the last degree, appeared before a whole body of people as a humbled sinner, confessed his faults, and asked pardon of God and of those whom he had offended.[34]

Some, however, still supposed that the above-mentioned message was really sent by the chiefs of the Iroquois. Feeling that they must follow the chiefs' dictates as obedient children, they would not yield to conviction.

---

[34] Loskiel, *The History of the Mission of the United Brethren Among the Indians in North America*, p. 340. It appears that the delegation was treating these former chiefs and men of renown as little children by withholding privileged information from them. In this way, they expected adult men to come to the desired conclusion of penitence and agreement in action.

UNDER ATTACK

Murder Without Reason

Many of the white neighbors of the Brethren in Bethlehem feared a sudden invasion from the French Indians and forsook their dwellings. Other Whites raged against the Moravian town of Bethlehem because it sided with the Indians. The whole town ought to be destroyed, they swore.

Instead of fleeing, the Brethren made a covenant to remain undaunted in the place allotted to them by Providence. The peace of God comforted them in a special manner and preserved their hearts from fear and despair.

However, no caution was omitted. Because the Whites considered every Indian an enemy, the Indian Brethren in Huts of Grace were advised to keep out of their way as much as possible. They were to buy no powder or shot, but were told to sustain themselves without hunting, which they willingly did.

Glikkikan bade me stop. "Brother John, who were the French Indians?" he asked.

"I would say they were any Indians who chose to side with the French in their evil war against the British. They could have been Iroquois, Mohicans, Shawnees, or Delawares."

Glikkikan followed up with another question. "And why did the French care about the land in the Forks of the Delaware?"

"They didn't. I must tell you, the war between the French and the English was not about land. It was about religion and trade and power."

He tried once more. "Brother John, would you say that the Moravian dealings with Pennsylvania and the Iroquois had nothing to

Under Attack in the Forks of the Delaware: 1747–1755

do with the land deals in the Forks of the Delaware?"

Glikkikan's voice began to falter toward the end of his last question. So I answered him in the gentlest manner possible. "You have heard how the meanest savages received the grace of God. The Unity gave everything to reach every nation of Indians with the Gospel, even including the Iroquois. Several times the Brethren bought land in the Forks for the use of the believing Indians. So, no, the Brethren did not come to America—"

Glikkikan's giant frame shook with sobs. With his head in his hands, the tears flowed out in torrents. Was this the penitence of the proud Indians the Unity had witnessed twenty years ago?

I touched him lightly on the shoulder. "Brother Isaac," I said softly, "I would like to tell you the terrible price the Brethren paid for befriending the Indians in the Forks. Then maybe you will understand."

He quieted down but did not look up. I took that as a sign for me to proceed with my story.

> At this time, all was peace in Huts of Grace. Suddenly, however, the scene changed. Fear, horror, and inexpressible distress filled the whole country. A cruel Indian war, caused by the contest between the English and the French, burst at once into flames. It spread terror and confusion, especially throughout Pennsylvania.
>
> The first outrage was committed about five miles from Shamokin where the French Indians fell upon six English plantations. They plundered and set fire to the dwellings and murdered fourteen Whites. Two sons of Paxinosa rescued three Brethren at Shamokin and delivered them safely to Huts of Grace.
>
> Every day disclosed new scenes of barbarity committed by the Indians. The whole country was in an uproar, and people did not know what course to take. Some fled

UNDER ATTACK

to the east. Some fled to the west. Some sought safety in places that had been abandoned by others earlier.

On 18 November 1755, some messengers from the Indians at Wyoming arrived in Huts of Grace. With many complaints of threatening and abuse, they delivered the following message: "We, being friends of the English government, are in great fear and do not know what to do. We are in danger of being attacked on all sides by enemies who are much enraged. We are no less afraid of the white people who suspect us of having been accessary to the murders committed in various places. We are in danger of being murdered by the white people. Tell us therefore what to do."

The Brethren in Bethlehem could give no answer to this message because they were in nearly the same predicament as these Indians. They knew the rage of the enemy was directed against them for supporting the Indians.

From this incident, and other accounts received at the same time, it was evident that the Christian Indians at Huts of Grace were considered friends of the British government and were in imminent danger of being destroyed by the French Indians. Dreadful reports multiplied rapidly from all quarters, causing some to be so intimidated that they fled into the woods.

However, the greater number of believers stayed in their towns. They resigned themselves to the will of the Lord and gave the most encouraging assurances to one another. They promised not to forsake each other, but to remain united in life and death.

But God had ordained otherwise. Late in the evening of 24 November, French Indians attacked and burned the mission house at Huts of Grace. They murdered eleven

Under Attack in the Forks of the Delaware: 1747–1755

of the inhabitants: Gottlieb Anders, his wife and fifteen-month-old daughter; Martin Nitschman and his wife Susanna; the married sister, Anna Catharine Senseman; Leonhard Gattermeyer, a widower; and the single brothers Christian Fabricus, George Schweigert, Martin Presser, and John Frederic Lesly.

The missionaries, while eating supper, heard an uncommon barking of dogs. Brother Senseman went out the back door to see what was wrong. On hearing the report of a gun, several others ran together to open the front door.

There the Indians stood with their rifles pointed toward the door. They fired immediately and killed Martin Nitschman instantly. His wife and some others were wounded, but they fled with the rest upstairs into the garret where they barricaded the door with bedsteads. Brother Partsch escaped by jumping out a back window. As he jumped, he cried aloud, "God, save my wife!"

Brother Worbas, who was ill in bed in an adjoining house, escaped by jumping out a back window, and thus he evaded the enemy guard at his front door.

Meanwhile, the savages pursued those who had taken refuge in the garret and strove hard to burst the door open. Finding it too well secured, they set fire to the house, which was soon in flames. A boy named Sturgeous stood upon the flaming roof and ventured to leap off. He escaped even though one side of his head was much burned.

Sister Partsch, who witnessed this, also took courage and leaped from the burning roof. She came down unhurt and unobserved by the enemies. In this way, God answered the fervent prayer of her husband.

Brother Fabricus then leaped off the roof, but before

UNDER ATTACK

he could escape, the Indians instantly wounded him with two shots. He was the only one whom they seized alive. Killing him with their hatchets, they took his scalp and left him dead on the ground.

The rest were all burned alive, and Brother Senseman, who first went out at the back door, had the inexpressible grief to see his wife consumed by the flames. Overcome with fear, Sister Partsch could not run far. She hid herself behind a tree on a hill near the house. From there, she saw Sister Senseman. Already surrounded by the flames, she was standing with folded hands and calling out, "Tis all well, dear Savior. I expected nothing else!" The house being consumed, the murderers set fire to the barns and stables. All the corn, hay, and cattle were destroyed. They divided the spoil, eating a hearty meal of bread soaked in milk, and then departed. All the while Sister Partsch was looking on unperceived.

It was not discovered until later that Captain Jachebus carried Susanna Nitschman away as his captive. Because of cold and cruel treatment, she died several weeks later at Tioga. These all died in faith and received their eternal reward.

Not one Indian died in the attack. Of the hundreds of Christian Indians living on the other side of the river, not one died! Glikkikan, what I have never been able to understand is this: *Why did the Delawares attack and destroy their friends?* Teedyuscung, Abraham,[35] and many others knew how hard the Brethren worked to help them find

---

[35] Teedyuscung (Gideon) and Abraham were renegade believers who drew off seventy believers from Huts of Grace to Wyoming. Captain Jachebus, a Delaware Indian, led the expedition in this attack. On the way to the first Easton treaty, Teedyuscung and Jachebus got into a violent argument of some kind, and Teedyuscung killed Jachebus. It seems very possible that the argument was over this attack on the peaceful Moravians. –JGL

Under Attack in the Forks of the Delaware: 1747–1755

the Savior and improve their way of life. Why did the Delawares kill and destroy the very people who wanted to help them?"[36]

Glikkikan lifted his tear-stained face and looked at me. I looked into his reddened eyes and swollen face. "Brother John," his voice quavered, "do you know that two of the Delawares who joined in the attack on the missionaries recently visited Beautiful Spring? You should ask them that question."

Then he added, while fresh tears streamed down his face, "Brother John, first cast the log out of your own eye, and then you will be able to see clearly the speck that is in your brother's eye."

And then, ever so gently, he whispered, "You can go now."

So I left him there in a forlorn heap, weeping for I knew not what.

[36] "Canasetego stood at the door and waited while the rest of the Delawares in the room filed past, heads down, but with hatred and passion burning forever in their hearts. For Indians from one generation to another will never forget the injury done them, or fail to revenge the wrongs they have received. Never again will the Delawares trust either the Pennsylvanians or the Iroquois. The Delawares returned to the villages of their homeland, gathered their belongings, burned their houses, and made the journey to Wyoming." —Landis, *Tomahawks to Peace*, p. 249.

UNDER ATTACK

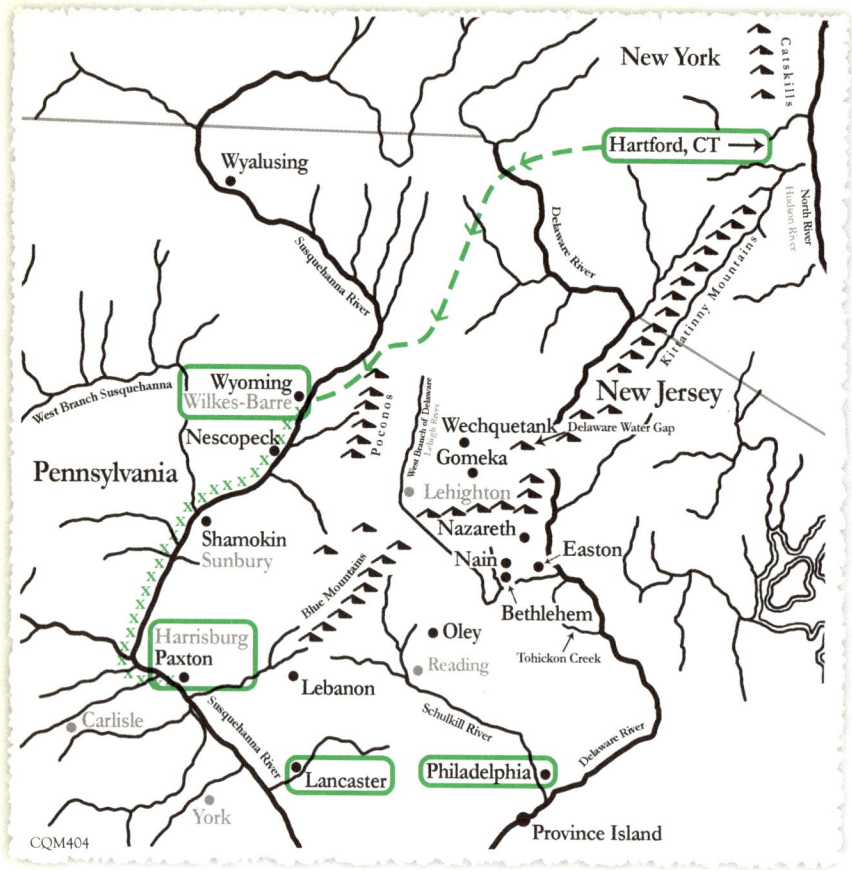

The Contested Land of Wyoming (1762)

CQM404 Notes

1. The North (East) Branch of the Susquehanna River begins north of the present Pennsylvania border and joins the West Branch at Shamokin, or present-day Sunbury, Pennsylvania.
2. The Indian town of Wyoming lay 60 miles from Bethlehem. Wyoming was located at present-day Wilkes-Barre, Pennsylvania.
3. Wyalusing lay 50 miles north of Wyoming along the Susquehanna.
4. The green Xs indicate the possible route of the Paxton Boys to Wyoming, a distance of 120 miles.
5. The green broken line indicates the route of the Connecticut people to Wyoming, a distance of 210 miles.
6. The distance from Philadelphia to Wyoming was 130 miles.

Chapter 4

Under Attack at Wyoming: 1756–1763

As recorded by John Heckewelder
At Beautiful Spring, Ohio,
Monday, 3 January 1774

I didn't quite know how to approach Brother Isaac after our disappointing ending on 8 September 1773. Something wasn't right. We steered around each other for several days at the daily services with little more than perfunctory greetings.

This wasn't the way I wanted things between us, so I stopped him after the evening meeting on Wednesday. "Brother Isaac," I said, "I want to be your brother. Tell me how I have offended you so we can continue the recording of your story."

"Oh, Brother John, we can be good friends and brothers in the Lord, but let us forget about writing this story on paper. It's no use. You are going to believe whatever you want to anyway. You see everything from the superior European point of view. In your mind,

UNDER ATTACK

the Indians have nothing of value. Proud, haughty Indians can only submit to having their lands taken away and being driven from their homes. The Moravians support the governments and the Iroquois who do these things. It is no use to take your pen and dig into festering sores."

"Brother Isaac, forgive me. I do not want to share a proud heart with unbelieving Whites. Believe me, that is why I am here in the Ohioland. I really do want to understand how the Indians look at things. Will you please tell me about the events that transpired at Wyoming after the massacre? I would like to write them down."

"I'll think about it," was all he said.

Welooch, the Delaware chief of Shenenge, had visited us several times. On his first visit, Brother Isaac had stayed up all night with him and answered his many questions. Brother Isaac revealed to us that Welooch was very rich and that his wealth might be a hindrance to his coming to the Savior.

But when he came to Beautiful Spring on the 20th of September, the Chief told Glikkikan, "I have not come to just visit as previously. My intention now is to become a believer in the Savior. I have considered everything adequately and am completely ready. Therefore I hurried to this place to tell you my heart and mind. I wanted to stay with you for a short time until my wife has finished harvesting her fields. Then I will fetch her and my whole family. It seemed too long to me to wait for her, so I came on ahead."

We met with Welooch at a helpers' conference on the 29th of September and considered his request to move here with his family. He expressed himself very well and told us about all his circumstances. We also told him our thoughts. After we had read him our town statutes and explained them, we granted him permission to move here with his family. He expressed his joy over this.

On 26 October, Welooch arrived with his family to stay. Everyone

Under Attack at Wyoming: 1756-1763

welcomed them, and we rejoiced together. He immediately began building a cabin, after which he went back to Shenenge for his belongings and food for the winter, returning to his family on 13 November. This was one Indian family who did not come to us poor and needy as was so often the case with other Indians.

On Sunday, 24 October, we dedicated our new meetinghouse with a sincere prayer. We commended this site to the Savior's grace so that many more Indians might be brought to Him yet through the word of redemption. Then Brother David preached a sermon, and in the afternoon we held a love feast.

A sad and painful event took place in the first part of October. We had to tell Abigail, Peter's wife and our Abraham's daughter, that she could no longer stay because of her bad behavior. We told her she had to leave that very day, which she did. We hope this serves her best interests and brings about her salvation.

Indian Agent McKee came through Beautiful Spring and advised us that Hokolesqua, the Shawnee chief, had sent word to all the traders in the Lower Towns telling them they should return to the white settlements. The Shawnee needed to go out hunting, and they could no longer guarantee the safety of the traders. If the Mingos should kill a trader, the Shawnee would be blamed for it.

The report came to Beautiful Spring that four Shawnee were killed while trying to steal horses. We have no way of knowing if this is a true report or not. So many false reports are coming out of the fort these days that we can hardly believe anything. Agent McKee claims that Dr. Connolly wants to incite the white settlers to attack all the Indians.

Glikkikan brought this word from Chief Watwees in Newcomerstown: "Things look very serious for the Shawnee and the Mingo. I do not know where to turn for help except to the King across the great water. I still hope that through the King we can become a calm and peaceful people.

UNDER ATTACK

"For this reason, I ask both your towns to collect hides to cover the expenses of those who go on this expedition. The Shawnee and the Wyandot have already been asked to do the same."

I sighed. I would have to ask Glikkikan to tell me the meaning of all this. Did the Chief really believe that if he stood before the King of England in person, the Indians would get a guarantee for their lands? His idea of the King of England certainly was different from my own. However, I didn't think the time was ripe for me to speak to Glikkikan about this yet. Thus far, we seemed unable to get close to each other.

Then on 21 December, the "speakings" with the brothers and sisters began. In these very personal examinations, Brother Isaac confessed wrong feelings toward me, and I did the same to him. We resolved our differences, and things were once again as they should be between brothers. After that, I knew the way was open for us to continue with the stories.

The Christmas celebrations blessed us all. They began with a love feast on Christmas Eve in which we reflected on the little baby in the stall and celebrated Him in song and worshipped Him on our knees. The children carried their candles, sang the *Gratias* to baby Jesus, and rejoiced over Him in the manger. Many older people were moved to tears.

On Christmas Day, we enjoyed several sermons and witnessed the baptism of old Sarah the Nantikok, now Rebecca. Afterward, fifty-four brothers and sisters experienced the most blessed enjoyment of His body and blood in the Holy Sacrament. We concluded this blessed holiday with the benediction, after which we also shared the kiss of peace.

On the 29th, Queelpacheno, formerly a great doctor among the Indians, came to us and complained about his miserable condition. He has been living with us for two years and has heard much about

Under Attack at Wyoming: 1756-1763

the Savior, but has remained dead in his heart.

He told us, "Ever since I have been living with you, a little man has been with me constantly. He accompanied me into the services and was always either behind me or beside me, preventing me from thinking about change. When I sometimes wanted to listen reverently to what was said in the services, that little man kicked me in the head so that I almost fell off the bench.

"However, when I came here last spring, the little man left me, and I have not seen him for some time. Now I hope to be cleansed from my sins with the Savior's blood."

We helped Queelpacheno find forgiveness for his sins and the peace he so desired. He was not alone. By the end of 1773, nearly two hundred people lived at Beautiful Spring. In addition to the eighty-one baptized adults, there were unbaptized residents consisting of fifteen adults, four older boys, three older girls, twenty-three younger boys, and thirty-three younger girls.

Since we had confessed our faults to one another, the way now seemed clear to me to spend a day with Brother Isaac. It was still eleven days till I would start school for the children. The harvest was in and the fall hunt concluded. So after the New Year's Day service, I approached Brother Isaac and asked, "What did you decide about continuing the story?"

He smiled. "I suppose I would be willing to tell you Johannes Papunhank's story if you promise to write it down exactly as I tell it."

"I don't think writing the truth will be a problem," I half-promised. "Would you be able to tell me Johannes's story on Monday morning?"

He agreed to meet at the school on 3 January 1774. There I soared with the eagles for several hours as I listened to things no white man had ever heard before.

UNDER ATTACK

Johannes Papunhank

"Brother John," Isaac began in a kindly tone, "since Brother Johannes arrived here last spring from Huts of Peace on the Susquehanna, I have spent a good deal of time with him. During that period, I asked him many specific questions about the events of his life.

"Brother Johannes lived on the Susquehanna at Wyalusing in the Wyoming Valley at the exact time the war was raging there. The memories of what happened to the Christian Indians were still clear in his mind."

Brother Isaac waited while a nearby hen cackled and a horse neighed. Then he continued with a question, "Brother John, do you believe that Brother Johannes tells the truth and that he is a reliable witness?"

"I have known Brother Johannes for several years," I answered. "I traveled with him when the Christian Indians made the journey from Peace Town on the Big Beaver to Beautiful Spring. I believe Brother Johannes is a fine brother. I can accept his witness. But what makes you think that Brother Johannes told you things he did not tell me?"

Brother Isaac studied me for a while before replying. Then he shook his gray head and shrugged. "Brother John, I think that Brother Johannes Papunhank feared that if he told you all, you would not believe him. You would think he exaggerated or lied. Besides, some past injustices and grievances are best forgiven and forgotten. Does not the Savior tell us that if we forgive those who sin against us, He also will forgive our sins against Him?"

Under Attack at Wyoming: 1756-1763

Forced Out (1705-1755)

As told by Isaac Glikkikan on 3 January 1774

A Delaware Indian of the Munsee clan gave birth to a son in 1705. Because she and her mother were Munsees (the Wolf clan), her son also was of the Wolf clan. It didn't matter if the father was from the Turtle or the Turkey clan; the child always became a member of the mother's clan.

Thus Papunhank was born a Munsee, or Wolf. Now the Wolves were the fiercest of the three Delaware clans and most prone to warfare with their ancient enemies, the Mengwe (Iroquois). In light of the Munsee reputation for war, it was surprising how Papunhank, even before he was a Christian, committed his life to the way of peace.

Despite their fierce reputation, the Wolves generally lived in peace on the upper regions of the Delaware River on into New Jersey, Pennsylvania, and New York. But when baby Papunhank was born, the great European invasion of Indian lands had already begun. The French, the Dutch, the Swedes, and the English vied with one another for the trade and the lands of Papunhank's birthplace. Some settlers used guns, others gifts, and still others guile to overpower the natives and force them from their settlements.

As far back as Papunhank could remember, an evil spirit seemed to possess the Whites around him. They seemingly could not exist peacefully with the Indians.

Before Papunhank was ten years old, in 1715, his parents had already migrated from lands in eastern New York westward to lands in the Forks of the Delaware to an Indian village called Wechquetank.

By the time Papunhank was thirty-two years old in 1737, he was

UNDER ATTACK

distressed by the events surrounding the fraudulent walk.[37] After the walk and the resulting false government claims to the land in the Forks of the Delaware, settlers continued to pour into the lands surrounding the Indians. Much talk of violence and revenge stirred among the already displaced Indians living in the Forks. Chief Nutimus tried for a peaceable solution and yet threatened removal of the settlers if justice was not done.

By now, Papunhank had become an influential prophet among the Delawares. He saw the folly of war and preached the way of peace to the insecure Indians.

In 1740, a strange sect of German-speaking people bought lands where Monocasy Creek emptied into the west branch of the Delaware River (Lehigh River). When Nutimus scolded them, the Moravian leader paid some of the Indians for the lands they had already purchased from the Penn family. These Germans were also men of peace.

Papunhank heard of the endeavors of the newcomers who built stone buildings three and four stories high as part of a new town they called Bethlehem. Shiploads of settlers from Europe brought more and more workers and worshipers into the towns these settlers built. The towns thrived. They sent young men out into the Indian villages to learn the languages and thus prepare them to carry the Gospel to the natives.

In 1742, Thomas Penn, the governor of Pennsylvania, took action. The threats of the Indians to attack the settlers endangered his land sales. He hired the Iroquois, those ancient enemies of the Delawares, to drag Chief Nutimus by the hair and throw him out of the Forks of the Delaware. The Iroquois spokesman, Canasatego, not only ordered the Indians to leave their homes in the Forks, but also ordered them to settle in the Wyoming Valley along the East Branch of the Susquehanna River. Some Delawares, greatly humiliated and

---

[37] James G. Landis, *Tomahawks to Peace*, "The Tomahawk of Fraud," and "The Tomahawk of Slavery."

Under Attack at Wyoming: 1756–1763

embittered, burned their homes in the Forks and settled across the mountains at Wyoming with Chief Nutimus and Teedyuscung.

At about the same time that New York and Connecticut forced the closing of the Shekomeko mission, Papunhank took a band of his followers to a stretch of fertile lowland some distance to the north of Wyoming. In this secluded vale called Wyalusing,[38] they constructed a village of twenty well-built Indian houses. There they lived undisturbed while Papunhank preached peace to his followers.

In 1754, Bethlehem sent Christian Frederick Post—the Shekomeko missionary who married the Wampanoag Rachel[39]—to Wyoming to preach the Gospel to Teedyuscung and his followers. Papunhank heard some of Post's message, and he said, "I wish that my people and I might be further instructed by the Moravians in the purpose of God respecting man's release from the bondage of sin, and his happiness in the world to come." Papunhank would have to wait eight more years before his wish was granted.

Post's preaching at Wyoming was cut short in November of 1755 when he was called back by a tragedy at Bethlehem. In this year, the French were giving the Delawares a chance for revenge against the English for having forced them out of their homes in the Forks of the Delaware. Murders and burnings raged throughout the western settlements and threatened to engulf the Forks of the Delaware as well.

In Bethlehem, things were particularly tense. The Moravians attracted many displaced Indians to their village at Huts of Grace north of Bethlehem; sometimes six hundred Indians lived close to the village. As a result, the heathen Indians became angry that so many Indians were adopting the white man's ways and accepting the theft of Indian lands.

---

[38] Papunhank may have migrated directly from his Jersey home to Wyalusing in 1746. Some evidence points to 1746 as the beginning of Wyalusing on the Upper Susquehanna.

[39] Post married Rachel in 1743, and she died about 1745. In 1747, he married Agnes, a Delaware, and she died in 1751. He had four children with his native wives; all died in infancy.

UNDER ATTACK

To complicate matters, many Whites were also incensed by the Moravians (Germans) because they were so obvious in their sympathy for the Indians. Some of the Whites (English) threatened to destroy Bethlehem and all its occupants.

In this hostile war environment, where both Indians and English wished to destroy the Moravians, a band of Delawares swept down upon the unsuspecting mission at Huts of Grace on the Mahoning. They killed eleven white Moravian missionaries and burned all the mission buildings. Only a few of the resident missionaries escaped to tell the tale.

The Prophet in the Valley

In the spring of 1762,[40] our brother Johannes lived in the Wyoming Valley at an Indian village called Wyalusing. Brother Johannes, then known as Prophet Papunhank or simply The Prophet, had been forced out of his homeland by relentless pressure from the Whites who used the traitorous Mohawks, one of the Iroquois nations, as their "arm of flesh" against the Munsees.

Because a beloved parent had fallen victim to the passion for strong drink, Prophet Papunhank often reflected on the evils and punishment of sin. As a result, his people held him in high repute as a teacher of morality. His many gifts made Prophet Papunhank a dominant force at Wyalusing.

---

[40] There is some confusion on the dates of events in the Wyoming Valley. De Schweinitz was unclear whether the events in this chapter occurred in 1762 or 1763. Olmstead apparently used DeSchweinitz's dating and portrayed the events accordingly. I have based the events in this chapter on two fixed dates: Johannes' baptism (26 June 1762) as listed in the *Lebenslauf* and the Moravian diaries, and the death of Teedyuscung (19 April 1763). Teedyuscung participated in recorded treaty negotiations during 1762, so the 1763 date must be correct for his death. (Anthony F. C. Wallace, *Teedyuscung*).

Under Attack at Wyoming: 1756-1763

The Prophet loved the beautiful Wyoming Valley. Its seas of waving grass and fertile fields opened their wombs to the planting of Indian corn, squash, and beans. Besides the fields, the two forks of the Susquehanna River converging at Shamokin enclosed an outstanding hunting area where Prophet Papunhank could freely roam for sustenance and enjoyment. Hunting was his way of life. He loved the valley and made it his home, intending to stay there the rest of his days.

Meanwhile, Prophet Papunhank continued to preach and practice a message of peace that he believed came directly from the Great Spirit. At times, The Prophet was translated to heaven where he could see the Great Spirit face to face. These trips to the other world required great effort and often dangerous purging of the body to try to eliminate sin from the soul. While The Prophet taught that the resulting life must be free from the lusts of the flesh—drinking, murder, and theft—he was not completely satisfied with his own teaching.

Prophet Papunhank visited some of his relatives at Nain, just two miles north of Bethlehem, and there heard some preaching about the Savior. When he returned home, he acquainted his people with this teaching, and they wanted to hear more. He sent a message to Bethlehem, asking for a teacher to come to Wyalusing.

Thus, in the middle of May in 1762, Brother David Zeisberger and Anthony, an Indian believer, set out on foot for Wyalusing to answer Prophet Papunhank's call. With only the dancing needle of a pocket compass to guide them, the two men endured seven days of fearful hardships. They crawled for miles beneath and between the tangled mazes of laurel bushes that made walking impossible, slogged forward through drenching rains, and pushed onward through trackless forests and swamps. Finally, the two arrived at Wyalusing.

The Indians flocked together from every part of the village to hear the Gospel for three days of solid preaching. Tears rolled down the

UNDER ATTACK

cheeks of the villagers, and The Prophet seemed the most moved of all. Once, Brother Zeisberger asked him during a sermon, "Brother, what have you to say to this people?" Papunhank replied, "Nothing, except that they should listen to their new teachers."

The whole town liked what they heard and wanted to hear more about the Savior. The Council asked that a resident missionary might come and establish a mission. The two returned at once to Bethlehem. By the middle of June—about one month after Brother Zeisberger and Brother Anthony had set out on their first trip—Brother Zeisberger was again back at Wyalusing, accompanied by Nathaniel.

The singing of hymns in Delaware, the calls to repentance, and the teaching of free grace in Christ astonished The Prophet. It was all so different from the painful conditions for salvation that he had taught. Prophet Papunhank wanted this Gospel and asked for baptism.

Only two weeks after Brother Zeisberger's return to Wyalusing, he taught about baptism and then examined Prophet Papunhank concerning his faith. After the questioning, Papunhank stated, "The Savior has made me feel my misery and utterly depraved state. I used to preach to you. I imagined myself a good man, not knowing that I was the greatest sinner of all. Brothers, forgive and forget everything I have said and done."

Then Prophet Papunhank fell on his knees and Brother Zeisberger baptized him as Johannes.[41] He arose a new man and joyfully exclaimed, "Now my heart is light. Before, it was heavy, so heavy I could scarcely endure it."

Brother Johannes Papunhank's changed outlook on the world at the end of June 1762 did not change what was going on around him. The

---

[41] David Zeisberger was 41 years of age at this baptism. His readiness to baptize Papunhank so quickly was amazing in light of his hesitancy to baptize natives only six years later.

Under Attack at Wyoming: 1756-1763

western Indians had revolted against the English, and many of the western forts had fallen. The soldiers garrisoned there were massacred. The tragic news traveled east, and the threat of savages striking farther east terrified the Whites across Pennsylvania. Only four days after Papunhank's baptism, the mission board recalled Brother David to Bethlehem because of fear for his safety.

Prophet Johannes was now left to lead the people of Wyalusing on a peaceful path in a time of war. He was determined that his people should "war no more."

The Contested Valley

The Prophet did not live in the valley by himself, but shared it with a loose collection of other Indian exiles: Shawnees, Mohicans, Nanticokes, and the most numerous, Delawares. All of them shared Chief Teedyuscung's vision that the Wyoming Valley was to be their new permanent homeland.

The Indians living in the Wyoming Valley in the spring of 1763 were not alone in their desire to possess it. The Delaware champion, King Teedyuscung, who had himself been forced from his home in the Jerseys and later in the Forks of the Delaware, wanted the lands in the Forks of the Susquehanna to be an exclusive Indian reserve.[42]

The Iroquois wanted the same lands as a buffer to keep white men from encroaching on their New York homelands.

White men from Connecticut claimed the valley under a patent

---

[42] Teedyuscung proposed a two-million-acre reservation that included all the Wyoming Valley on the east branch of the Susquehanna River.

UNDER ATTACK

from one of the English kings, and their representative, Lydius, secretly bought the Wyoming Valley from the Iroquois.[43] From the very beginning, Pennsylvania had no intention of surrendering the Wyoming Valley to anyone else.

Like David standing in front of Goliath, Chief Teedyuscung, or Honest John as many knew him, stood as the champion of ten Indian nations. With his reckless courage, Honest John had resisted the deceit and wiles of the Pennsylvania government at the four Easton treaties that helped end the Seven Years' War between the English and the French. In the treaty negotiations, Honest John could not be bought off or deterred from his determined quest for a new Delaware homeland.

Honest John made public what everyone involved knew was fraud—the theft of Indian lands in the Forks of the Delaware. And then to make matters worse, Honest John had appealed to the English king to judge the land issue. To complicate the issue further, the Iroquois, through Bully Canasatego, had earlier ordered the Delawares in the Forks of the Delaware to relocate to the Wyoming Valley.[44]

Quaker craftsmen, seeking a peaceful and equitable solution to end the war, had built Honest John eleven block houses right in the Wyoming Valley. In the spring of 1763, there sat Honest John and his village guarding the valley under the protectorate of the Iroquois nations. Everything about triumphant Honest John and the Quakers who assisted him irked the cheaters and liars in the Penn government.

The Prophet, like Honest John, wanted to keep the whole Wyoming Valley as a homeland for the Indians, a place where they would be safe from further encroachments by the Whites, and where they could

---

[43] This secret transaction in land matters broke all Indian traditions and protocol. Such matters were to be public and open before all, but this deal was not out of keeping with similar purchases from the Iroquois brokered by Conrad Weiser for the State of Pennsylvania.
[44] James G. Landis, *Tomahawks to Peace*, pp. 245-267.

Under Attack at Wyoming: 1756-1763

continue living the Indian way. The Prophet trusted in the treaties Honest John had crafted with the Whites and made sure that the Indians at Wyalusing did everything they could to keep the peace. He was determined that his people would war no more.

In fact, the governor of Pennsylvania had barely lifted his hand from taking hold of Honest John's peace belt before the Whites killed a Delaware Indian a little above Hays. This news angered the relatives of the murdered Delaware. Four of them immediately set off with intentions to kill some of the white folks. On their way, they called at Wyalusing. When the relatives of the murdered Delaware informed The Prophet of their design, he got all the Indians of Wyalusing—men, women, and children—to join in a collection of wampum. When it was delivered to the aggrieved relatives, this gift pacified them, and they returned home without doing any harm.

In addition, The Prophet knew that some of the people at Wyalusing had purchased goods, horses, and prisoners taken by hostile Indians during the late war. At the close of the war, he saw to it that all of these purchased goods, horses, and prisoners were returned to Pennsylvania. He then sent a message to the governor to make sure he knew what the Wyalusing Indians had done.

But Prophet Papunhank was still uneasy. News had reached him that Many Children Johnson, the King's Indian agent, had sent 400 English pounds to Honest John in order to quiet him down. Another rumor the birds carried to The Prophet was that the Connecticut settlers had also offered Honest John a large sum of money if he would allow them to settle quietly around him.

Prophet Papunhank wondered what all this money meant. Could it be that Honest John had at last yielded to bribery, or had Pennsylvania and the Iroquois really given him some assurance of a new homeland for the Delawares in addition to the money?

Papunhank wanted answers to these questions, so he set out at

UNDER ATTACK

once to talk with Honest John. But being a wise and prudent Indian prophet in dangerous times, Papunhank did not set his canoe on the Susquehanna and float down to Honest John's village at Wyoming. Instead, he set out on foot with Job Chilloway, a Delaware from Wyalusing who spoke good English. The Prophet called him Easy Tongue.

The two men knew well the whole area they traveled. They skirted the main paths to Wyoming from the north and from the east. They kept a discreet silence as though on a hunt, and they heard every spring bird that sang and surprised many deer bedded down in the underbrush. As for humans, they saw only two Iroquois rum traders traveling north.

Traveling on the east side of the Susquehanna, the two camped atop the same great hill where White Eyes and I camped many years ago with Iron Man, Jubilant, and Free Son.[45] Atop that hill, the two could look west across the river upon the twenty dwellings that comprised Honest John's Wyoming. From their perch on the bluff, they could also see the mighty, muddy Susquehanna a great way down in the valley. Swelled by spring rains, it made its second bend below the village.

Toward dusk on that April evening, The Prophet spied ten to twelve canoes coming up the river. The Prophet and Easy Tongue could not see the voyagers in detail; at first, the distance was too great, and then darkness settled upon the land. They knew only that they came from the south. The noise of the broad river coursing below them covered all the sounds that might have reached them as the canoes made their way northward.

The Prophet and Easy Tongue began their descent to the river at once. They rushed along the Susquehanna, whistling until they caught the attention of Honest John's son, Captain Bull. Captain Bull and

---

[45] James G. Landis, *Tomahawks to Peace*, pp. 218-220.

Under Attack at Wyoming: 1756–1763

several others immediately jumped in canoes and crossed the broad river to pick them up. The Prophet spoke just a few words to Captain Bull before the canoes raced back across the river.

Hurriedly, the men ran through the village telling everyone to gather by the canoes at the river. Within minutes, twenty huts and the Quaker-built block houses were emptied of their inhabitants who were now running for their lives. Captain Bull and The Prophet ran to the largest block house. They entered the Quaker-built cabin with the wooden floor. There lay Honest John in a disgraceful, drunken heap on the floor. Captain Bull leaned over his father and shook him. "Father, an enemy is coming. Where is the gold?"

King Teedy roused himself in anger. "Wouldn't you like to know?" he roared. "I'm not that easily taken in by your tricks." The King fumbled around for his knife.

At that moment, bloodcurdling war whoops came from the side of the village bordered by the river. The Prophet and Captain Bull exited in the murky dusk and vanished into the surrounding fields and woods. There they listened and waited and watched. Shadowy forms moved about the village. Only a few shots were fired, but here and there, men gathered up everything of value and carried their loot to the river. Then all twenty dwellings burst into flame at once.

Now the attackers were plainly visible to Captain Bull and The Prophet. The men appeared to be dressed as Indians on the warpath, but to the two experts watching from the darkness, they were an obvious imitation. They were not Shawnees or Delawares from the west. They were not Iroquois from the north. They were not Cherokees or Catawbas from the south.

Captain Bull raised his gun and drew a bead on a figure outlined by the fire of his father's house. The Prophet reached over and pressed Captain Bull's gun down. "Now is not the time to be caught up in the war," he said firmly. "If you kill one, hundreds will return and kill all

UNDER ATTACK

Robbery and Murder

"Dad, where is the gold?" —Captain Bull

Under Attack at Wyoming: 1756-1763

our women and children."

As the invaders moved quickly toward the river, an exultant cry rose from the throats of the destroyers of Honest John and his village. In frontier English, they shouted, "We got the gold!"

The next day The Prophet and Easy Tongue quietly made their way back to Wyalusing. The Wyoming people scattered to different places for refuge. Captain Bull and many of his people went to Great Island farther north on the Susquehanna. A few stayed at Wyalusing. Some moved to Shamokin, and some trekked still farther west to join the Shawnees and the Delawares in the Ohioland.

The Prophet and his people wanted peace, not war, and they wanted to remain at Wyalusing. Shortly after Honest John's death and Wyoming's reduction to ashes, settlers from Connecticut returned to the valley. They planted several hundred acres of corn in the open fields and built themselves houses and barns. Before the summer ended, 119 Connecticut settlers had made their home in the Wyoming Valley. Some of them settled very close to the place where Honest John's village had been. They planted their corn in the Indian fields.

In July, the growing corn raced toward a promising harvest. Two military officers from Lancaster County, Thomas McKee and James Burd, appeared at Wyalusing. The two men plied Papunhank and Easy Tongue with all sorts of questions about the settlers from Connecticut. How many were there? What were the names of the leaders? Would the Delawares attack the settlers now that Teedyuscung was gone?

Officers Burd and McKee let it be known that Governor Hamilton had commissioned them to warn the Connecticut settlers that they must leave the Wyoming Valley and allow their habitations to be burned. In language as plain as the summer sun, the officers said, "The Pennsylvania government will never tolerate settlers from Connecticut in the Wyoming Valley." Furthermore, the two officers were authorized to capture three of the leaders, by cunning or force,

UNDER ATTACK

and carry them to the Lancaster jail.[46]

Brother Johannes Papunhank listened politely to the officers but refused to answer any of their questions. He told the two men, "At Wyoming, we desire to live in peace with all men and concern ourselves with nothing but the worship of God." The officers left, disgruntled by the lack of cooperation from the Wyalusing Indians.

That month, five friendly Indians from Great Island on the Susquehanna passed through Wyalusing. The whole village listened to their woeful tale.

> We journeyed to Bethlehem to exchange our furs for valuable manufactured goods such as cloth and cooking kettles and tools such as hoes and axes. Well satisfied with our trade, we began the journey home. Eight miles from Bethlehem, we stopped for the night at a public tavern owned by John Stenton. He is of the Scotch-Irish people who stole the land from Sassoonan twenty years before the Long Walk took place. We paid for our lodging and spent the night in the ample quarters of the large house with a cellar underneath.
>
> We could well understand English, and during the night, we could hear many of the threats shouted against us. John Stenton was gone, but his wife offered to "give a gallon of rum to any guest who would kill one of those black devils."
>
> With so much commotion around us, we spent a restless night, but the next morning we arose unharmed in body to continue our journey. Alas, we discovered that we had been robbed of some of our most valuable

---

[46] *Minutes of the Provincial Council of Pennsylvania*, Vol. 9, p. 29.

Under Attack at Wyoming: 1756–1763

possessions. We complained to the barkeeper, who with threats and curses ordered us to leave the inn at once.

Unwilling to lose so much property, we retired some distance into the woods and appointed two of our number to watch over our remaining goods. The rest of us returned to Bethlehem and registered a complaint with a Moravian justice of the peace named Timothy Horsefield.

After listening carefully to our account and asking more detailed questions, Justice Horsefield promptly issued a letter to Mr. Stenton, pressing him without delay to restore our goods. We then returned to the inn with the letter and handed it to Mr. Stenton.

Mr. Stenton read the letter and then said, "If you set any value on your lives, you must leave this place immediately."

Realizing that we had no other alternative, we departed without receiving back any of our goods. However, on the way here we chanced upon Teedyuscung's son, Captain Bull. After we told him our story, he assured us that other Delawares had been similarly treated, and one of them even had his rifle stolen. Captain Bull advised us to sit still until the Delawares declared war on Pennsylvania. Then he would help us recover our losses. And he added, "Perhaps you will also help me avenge the robbery and death of my father."

Brother Johannes listened to the sorrowful tale. He urged them to make their plea to the governor instead of retaliating with violence. He preached to them the way of the Savior and the peace he now knew in his heart. But the Indians scorned him.

"We have listened to the white man's religion long enough," they

UNDER ATTACK

said. "The Whites cry about peace and treaties, but then they build forts from which soldiers shoot and kill and rob the Indians. We have indeed lost more Indians since the war ended three years ago than we did during the entire course of the last war.

"In the end, the Whites always take our land and drive us away. How long do you think the Whites will allow you to stay in the valley? Look what they did to Teedyuscung. Look at the Connecticut settlers swarming in front of your lodge. See how the Iroquois sell your land and call you women. The Whites will never allow you to stay here in your fur-lined nest.

"We no longer believe the Whites want peace. Even now, the Indians are having great success in the West. Many English forts have been destroyed, and we will soon take more. Perhaps if we strike Brother Onas hard, and he still wants peace, we can then believe him."

There was nothing more Brother Johannes could say. He knew it was all true. Still more disturbing news came to Wyalusing in August.

On 3 August, four young men left Wyalusing to go to the Moravian mission at Bethlehem. They never returned home.

Also in early August, Zachary and his wife and papoose came through Wyalusing on the way from Shamokin to Bethlehem. Zachary proudly led his horse, carrying valuable skins and furs. His wife, with her papoose strapped to her back, trudged on behind. Two years earlier, Zachary and his new wife had left the Moravian Indian mission at Wechquetank, north of Bethlehem, and had moved farther west to Shamokin. Now Zachary and his wife were returning to show their new papoose to the four uncles and the grandparents who still resided at Wechquetank.

Brother Johannes welcomed Zachary and his family to Wyalusing and then sent greetings on to Brother Zeisberger. Zachary had more than trade goods on his mind. He feared for the safety of his four brothers and their families at Wechquetank, and he intended to urge

Under Attack at Wyoming: 1756–1763

them to move farther west where he believed they would be better protected from hostile Whites.

Brother Johannes agreed that great danger from the Whites already existed for the peaceable Indians who had no part in the wars or the raids. Johannes told Zachary of the marks of identification and rules of conduct the governor and the local justices, in conjunction with the Brethren, had already set up. These would help the Whites identify the Christian Indians so they would not harass them or shoot them.

- They are always clothed.
- They are never painted.
- They wear hats or caps instead of feathers.
- They let their hair grow naturally; they do not shave their heads or wear scalp locks.
- They carry their guns on their shoulders with the shaft upward.
- When they meet a white man in the woods, they will call to him and salute him.
- Coming near to a white man, they will carry their guns either reversed or on the shoulder.
- Lastly, when they go out hunting, they must get a pass from Justice Timothy Horsefield or Mr. Bernard Adam Grube, the missionary in charge at Wechquetank.

Zachary was doubtful. "It seems to me that saluting a white man with your gun reversed only invites him to kill you," he said. "And there are plenty of Whites willing to shoot an Indian whether he has a pass in his pocket or not."

"Yes, the danger is real," Brother Johannes agreed, "but the way of the Savior is the way of peace. We do have intelligence that Captain Bull and other wronged Indians will soon seek revenge for the robbery and murder of Teedyuscung, and some of it will come in the Forks of the Delaware

UNDER ATTACK

not far from Wechquetank. There will be bloodshed. Warn your brothers. But we, the Indians at Wyalusing, will have nothing to do with violence and war. We concern ourselves only with the worship of God."

Zachary and his family traveled on to Bethlehem, exchanged their skins for a valuable pack load of trade goods, and went north to Wechquetank for the family visit. Zachary's four brothers recognized the danger of remaining at Wechquetank, but none of them wished to leave their comfortable dwellings or the abundant food and the daily teachings of the missionaries for a more rugged life farther west. Only one relative, Zipora, decided to accompany them.

Having accomplished his mission, Zachary set off to the west, followed by his packhorse, his wife with the papoose on her back, and Zipora. I imagine they looked much like Mary and Joseph and the Christ child on their flight to Egypt. Fourteen miles later, the weary travelers arrived at the Buchabuchka[47] Inn, a short distance north of Fort Allen on the Lehigh River.

It so happened that a company of Pennsylvania soldiers under the command of Captain Jacob Wetterholt also occupied the Buchabuchka Inn for the night. The soldiers could easily see that Zachary and his family and Zipora were friendly Indians who posed no danger to the public peace. There

---

[47] *Buchabuchka* in the Monsee tongue means "where the mountains butt against each other." Today the place is called The Lehigh Water Gap.

Under Attack at Wyoming: 1756–1763

Peacekeepers

"The soldiers wanted my horse and valuable trade goods." —Zachary

UNDER ATTACK

was one problem, however. The soldiers wanted Zachary's horse and his valuable trade goods. During the night, Captain Jacob Wetterholt and his company fell upon the band sleeping under their supposed protection and killed them.

Zachary tried to run away, but the soldiers pursued him and cut him down. Zachary's wife got on her knees and begged for the life of her babe. It was in vain. They slew them both. Zipora, sensing the calamity come upon them, fled to the barn and tried to hide in the grain loft. The soldiers discovered her hiding place and threw her down headfirst upon the threshing floor with such force that her brains splattered out.

Now the murderers reasoned that some of Zachary's four brothers at Wechquetank might seek revenge for the murders. Accordingly, the soldiers showed up at Wechquetank in three parties led by both Captain Jacob Wetterholt and his brother Captain Nickolas Wetterholt. The soldiers fully intended to destroy the whole village. The invaders hesitated only because of the missionary Grube's earnest protests and his appeal to the government's promise to protect the Christian Indians. As a last resort, Brother Grube threatened to report the Wetterholt captains to the governor, their commander-in-chief. Only then did the militia give up on the assault.

Glikkikan stopped and let out a long sigh. Then he wiped tears from his eyes before going on.

"Brother John, one can only wonder; if the government had promised protection to the Christian Indians, why were not these heinous murders reported to the governor and the murderers punished?"

Not waiting for me to answer, he continued his narrative.

Under Attack at Wyoming: 1756-1763

The news of these murders spread like a wildfire among the Delawares, the Nanticokes, and the Shawnees living in scattered villages along the Susquehanna River, as well as to their supposed overlords, the Iroquois. But from the Pennsylvania government came only silence. The governor sent no wampum belts to the mourning relatives. He never wiped the tears from their eyes, and he never attempted to punish the murderers.

Instead, 110 Paxton Rangers, or Brave Boys, as they were called, set out to destroy the Indian town at Great Island on the Susquehanna. The Great Island Indians, including Chief Nutimus and Captain Bull, learned in advance of the coming expedition to destroy their village. The Great Island Indians, with some help from others, caught the militia force by surprise at Muncy Creek Hill and killed or wounded a number of invaders before retiring.

The confused and defeated Paxton Rangers tried to regroup and start for home. In this angry, wandering, and hungry state, they came upon a band of six Indians returning to Great Island from a trade mission to Bethlehem. The Whites forced the Indians to leave the meal they were preparing, confiscated their trade goods, took them prisoners, and marched them along in front of the militia. After some time, six Whites fired on the six Indians from behind and three fell. One of them, named George Allen, fell with his wounded arm atop his blood-covered body.

These "Brave Boys" then scalped the three fallen Indians and made off with their trophies. After they were gone, George Allen jumped up and made his escape. While running down the hill, he fainted, then got up and tried to run again, but the loose skin on his forehead hung down over his eyes so he could not see. George took off his leggings and bound up his scalped head. When he came to a spring, he took

UNDER ATTACK

cold moss, laid it on the top of his head to protect the wound, and then went to Great Island where he recovered.[48]

Now Brother Johannes was fully alarmed. What would happen to him and his people at Wyalusing? He could not tell. The danger of a massacre by soldiers, settlers, or other hateful Whites could no longer be ignored. In the middle of September, Brother Johannes decided to send a message to the governor. Papunhank reminded the governor how the Wyalusing Indians had kept the peace agreement made with Teedyuscung three years earlier, and how they had returned all the prisoners and horses and goods that some of their people had purchased from others in the late war. Brother Johannes also wanted the governor to remember how the Wyalusing Indians had bought off Indians bent on avenging murders against their relatives. In the message, Papunhank carefully pointed out to Governor Hamilton how the Wyalusing Indians depended on the governor to advise them of any danger to them in the future. He closed his message with a firm statement that the Wyalusing Indians concerned themselves with nothing but the worship of God. Then Brother Johannes Papunhank waited anxiously for Governor Hamilton's reply.

While Johannes waited, major events transpired in the Wyoming Valley. Indian brothers from Bethlehem came to Wyalusing to wipe the tears from their eyes and to console them over the loss of the four young men from Wyalusing. The four had been robbed of their rifles and thirty-one pounds of deerskins at Fort Allen by troops under the command of Captain Jacob Wetterholt. As soon as the four had left the fort, twenty soldiers pursued them into the woods, murdered them, and scalped them. "It is said," the messengers added, "that in Philadelphia, one can get money for Indian scalps."

The messengers also detailed what they had witnessed in the woods

---

[48] C. Hale Sipe, *The Indian Wars of Pennsylvania*, p. 452.

Under Attack at Wyoming: 1756–1763

as they traveled up along the Susquehanna from Nescopeck: more than a hundred men dressed in breechclouts, leggings, moccasins, and green shrouds with red handkerchiefs tied around their heads and their faces painted red and black. They appeared as Indian warriors on the warpath.[49] But they were not Indians. Indian warriors would have come from the west or the north if they were moving either toward Wyoming or Wyalusing, the messengers reasoned. And Indians would not have traveled in such a large body. The messengers were sure the army moving northward toward Wyoming and Wyalusing was the Paxton Rangers.

Brother Johannes immediately prepared Wyalusing for instant flight to the north. Then he sent the messengers south once again to spy on the advancing army.

Three days later, the spies returned and reported that the Paxton Boys had tortured, murdered, and buried many of the Connecticut settlers at Wyoming, burned all their habitations, and destroyed all their stores of corn. The spies followed the departing army southward for some distance to make sure the Pennsylvania army would not swing back on Wyalusing.

Brother Johannes pondered the situation. Certainly the governor knew of the army's advance. Why had he not been informed of the imminent danger? Brother Johannes concluded that the governor must have sent the expedition only to remove the Connecticut settlers from the Wyoming Valley. As Officers McKee and Burd had so emphatically told him, "The Pennsylvania government will never tolerate settlers from Connecticut in the Wyoming Valley."[50]

The Pennsylvania army had barely left the Wyoming Valley when the Indians who had been robbed at Stenton's Inn in June visited Wyalusing once again. They bragged, "Captain Bull led twenty of us

---

[49] John Bradford, SCOOUWA: *James Smith's Indian Captivity Narrative*, p. 121.
[50] C. Hale Sipe, *Indian Wars of Pennsylvania*, pp. 460–462.

UNDER ATTACK

directly to Stenton's, and we successfully surprised them early one morning. By the appointment of the Great Spirit, we killed Captain Wetterholt and some of his troops as well as John Stenton. Then we quickly moved on to other farmsteads where Indians had been insulted, wronged, and robbed."

Triumphant, they boasted of having killed twenty Whites while they themselves lost only one warrior. Besides killing these twenty, the war party also destroyed the Whites' habitations and crops with fire and took prisoners and plunder. The warriors freely offered to share their booty with the Wyalusing people.

Brother Johannes strictly forbade anyone to take of the proffered gifts and urged the victorious warriors to move on as quickly as possible. He well understood what the Whites would do next, and he found out he was right when John Curtis brought him the long-awaited answer from Governor Hamilton.

Here is what John Curtis reported to the whole village of Wyalusing.

"After Captain Bull's raid, the White reaction was immediate. Great fear of more raids to come caused many settlers to flock to Bethlehem for protection from the savages. John Stenton's widow—the same woman who had offered a gallon of rum to anyone who would kill an Indian—swore that Renatus of the Christian Indians had been among the raiding party that killed her husband. A few days later, a body of militia accompanied by a mob from the two Irish communities arrived at Wechquetank and threatened to massacre the whole congregation if they did not soon depart.

"The militia and the mob were so hostile that Missionary Grube and Zachary's four brothers, along with all the other Wechquetank Indians, fled to Nazareth.[51] The Indians left their prosperous village and their stores of corn to the mercy of their enemies, who destroyed both."

---

[51] A Moravian town ten miles north of Bethlehem.

Under Attack at Wyoming: 1756-1763

Every eye and ear fixed on John Curtis as he described the plight of their brothers at Nazareth.

"The refugees crammed into the crowded town. Everyone suffered much from the cold and the lack of other necessities. Every day they expected an assault. Suspicion and distrust filled the minds of the settlers, and the militia could hardly be restrained from acts of violence.

"Brother David Zeisberger, so recently recalled from Wyalusing due to urgent warnings by the governor, now lent his assistance to the Indians confined at Nazareth. Under Brother Zeisberger's direction, the Indians built a stockade around Nazareth and kept a constant watch. They set guards at the chapel doors lest they be surprised and murdered while assembled for divine worship.

"At Nazareth, an Indian never left town except in the company of a white man. Even then, when he returned, they greeted each other as though the one who returned had narrowly escaped death. Such is the condition of the Wechquetank Indians huddled at Nazareth."

But John Curtis was not finished yet. The Council at Wyalusing was assembled with attendees from all the scattered Nanticokes, Mohicans, Munsees, and Delawares. The elders were seated in the front of the semicircle with the younger men standing behind them. John Curtis laid out the wampum belts in front of him, and string by string, delivered Governor Hamilton's answer to Papunhank's earlier message:

> *Brother:*
> We do not look on you and your Indians as our enemies, but rather as our friends. We can sincerely say that you form a true judgment on this behavior of the Indians, for we assure you we have not given the least cause of offense since we concluded a peace with the Indians. Since this renewal of hostilities is without the least provocation on our side, and has been carried on in so cruel a

UNDER ATTACK

manner, you cannot but think that it must raise great resentment in the minds of the inhabitants against those who have committed them.

As to you who have had no part in these disturbances, but have given yourselves up to the religious worship of God, we shall still be your friends. We shall endeavor to preserve you in that safety which your conduct deserves, and pray God to bless your religious designs.

You remind us of the services you did for us in the affair of the prisoners and of the horses which were stolen from our inhabitants. We remember it well, and as we did then thank you for it, so we do now again thank you for it.

You likewise remind us of the great service you did in preventing the relatives of an Indian killed soon after the last treaty at Easton from coming down to take revenge on our inhabitants. This we also remember well, and now repeat our thanks for your kindness therein. Such acts of friendship may always be expected from men who act with sincerity on religious principles. And as we hope we are under the influence of the same good principles toward God and man, we shall always behave toward you in the same just and kind manner.

You further tell us that the favor we did you by warning you of any mischief designed against you had made you perfectly at ease and satisfied and that you do entirely depend upon us. Agreeable therefore to our engagements, we now inform you of what lies very heavy on our minds, our apprehensions of your danger.

Brother:

It is true that we concluded firmly and made a peace with the Indians. But now our innocent inhabitants, who think there is no danger and are depending on your good faith

Under Attack at Wyoming: 1756-1763

so solemnly pledged to us, have been seized in their houses. They were barbarously murdered, their innocent little children's brains dashed out before them. This has been perpetrated frequently, and our brother, John Curtis, can tell you that within these ten days, some of these barbarous Indians have been down and killed upward of twenty of our people near Bethlehem. These actions have enraged and provoked my people greatly, and some of them have gone into the Indian country to take revenge. As I do not know where they are gone, I cannot but be under apprehensions, lest, in their great anger, they will not be able to distinguish between those who are our friends and those who are our enemies. And if any such thing should happen, you must blame those Indians who have so unjustly struck us. People who have been so badly mistreated cannot be restrained from taking revenge.

We cannot predict the actions of those enraged people with their desire to avenge the blood of their kindred. Therefore we are not without apprehensions of your being in danger, though we will do all in our power to prevent it. We would, therefore, be glad now to hear from you how you think that can be best done. For that purpose, we now send a white man, James Irvine, along with our brother, John Curtis, as far as Fort Allen. He shall remain there fifteen days in expectation of receiving your answer to that point and also receive any other message you may have for us.[52]

After John Curtis had laid the last string of wampum down, the Council reflected on the governor's speech and how to answer him.

---

[52] According to Indian custom, at the end of each section of this address, John Curtis presented a string of wampum to seal his message. John Curtis' speech was based on Governor Hamilton's recorded speech as found in *Minutes of the Provincial Council of Pennsylvania*, Vol. 9, pp. 67-68.

UNDER ATTACK

Each speaker spoke without interruption till he was finished. Several Munsees[53] spoke first.

"The governor speaks with a great forked tongue," they cried. "His soldiers kill us. His subjects rob us." Carefully, each speaker detailed the outrages committed against peaceable Indians after the treaties had been made. "And yet the governor says we attack without the least provocation. He lies. What shall we do? Shall we again give up our homes and lands and flee? Where shall we go? We are men and not women! We shall fight to defend our homes and our wives and children."

"The governor says the savages have committed barbarous acts against the 'innocent' Whites," another angry Munsee declared. "He says we should not blame the settlers who take revenge against any Indian they can find." A chorus of *"Kehelles"* burst from the attentive listeners. The speaker paused while his eyes studied each of the faces in the semicircle before him.

Then he continued, "Are the governor's eyes closed? Is not shooting peaceable Indians in the back a barbarous act? Are not killing Zachary's family and papoose, as well as dashing Zipora's brains out, barbarous acts? Why does the governor cover the blood shed by his inhabitants and say that they have a right for revenge, while he denies, by his closed mouth, the Indians their right for revenge?"

Another Munsee added, "When the militia drives peaceable Indians from Wechquetank to Nazareth and destroys their homes—aren't those barbarous acts? Does the governor mean that his own soldiers are ungovernable and that he pays his own soldiers to take revenge without his permission? And from whence do the soldiers and settlers get their scalp bounties? I smell the reek of the governor's hands whenever Philadelphia money is paid for an Indian scalp—scalps of men, women, and even children."

---

[53] The Munsees were the Wolf clan of the Delaware Indians.

Under Attack at Wyoming: 1756-1763

Easy Tongue, the Nanticoke, spoke next. "We must remember that the Nanticokes and the Delawares live in the Wyoming Valley by appointment of the Iroquois. Their great chiefs want us to live here, and they claim they have never sold the land to Pennsylvania. The Iroquois will protect us from Pennsylvania. We should live here in peace so that Pennsylvania will have no cause to strike us. The French are now gone, and if we cannot trade with Pennsylvania, our guns will be silent. Our women and children will become but skin and bones."

Then the Nanticoke chief, Newoleka, spoke. "Easy Tongue speaks well," he began. "The English Quakers have used us well. They have been honest in their trades and kind in their speech. They give us no cause to attack them or molest them. Where will we go for powder and ball if the English will not trade with us?"

Another warring Munsee spoke next. "Yes, where shall we go? The Delawares have all been driven from their homelands along the Delaware River. Teedyuscung negotiated with the English for the Wyoming Valley as a homeland for the Delawares. Yet you yourselves know what Pennsylvania did to Teedyuscung. You know that Pennsylvania settlers build their nests among the valleys of the Susquehanna and the Juniata Rivers. Yet the Iroquois, who boast that they have conquered us and claim to own all our lands, only squawk like frightened hens driven from their nests. The Mengwe will do nothing to save our lands for us. We must eat the English eggs before they hatch, and we must destroy their nests with fire. We must stop them now, or they will drive us away.

"You yourselves know that the Iroquois sold the Wyoming Valley to settlers from Connecticut. And you know how barbarously Pennsylvania removed them from the land. Do you think those Pennsylvania soldiers destroyed the Connecticut settlers, their habitations, and their corn in order to save this land for the Indians? I will answer the question for you. No! No! Those barbarous, fake Indians

UNDER ATTACK

want the land for themselves. And they will have this land if we do not drive them into the sea."

The Munsee's words had come fast and strong. Now he stopped. He glared at his listeners. When he spoke next, his words came slowly. "The blood of our four brothers slain at Fort Allen cries to us from the ground. I will go and avenge the death of the four Delawares whose blood was spilt by soldiers at Fort Allen. Nothing will turn me back."

Again the warrior's voice picked up speed and rhythm. "And to those who seek to turn me back, I say, 'I will lay your heads upon the logs and cut them off with the hatchet. I will bind your hands and feet and refuse to give you food and water. I will take your young men away and tie them up until they learn that innocent blood unavenged only makes one's enemies bolder. I will teach the English governor that if he is unable to punish the barbarous murderers of innocent Indians, I will.' "

Brother Johannes spoke last to the Council in this manner:

> My brothers, I do not deny that the clouds hang close to the ground and the thunder rumbles continuously. Strong, evil winds blow from every direction. Yet we must keep searching the sky for the sun and the moon and the stars.
>
> We should not be overcome by the darkness of the present or yearn for the days when our ancestors dwelled in friendship with the Great Miquon. We must look much further back than that. We should look back to the beginning when God Almighty made us and placed a good spirit in our hearts. Then we must endeavor to remove the evil spirit that stands between us and the English. Otherwise, we poor and weak Indians will lead a very miserable existence.
>
> Governor Hamilton has sent James Irvine to Fort Allen to wait fifteen days for an answer to his message. But we

Under Attack at Wyoming: 1756–1763

cannot send our message through a white man, and it is not safe for an Indian to go to Fort Allen. Therefore Easy Tongue and I will go to Philadelphia and meet with Governor Hamilton. I will ask him to work on his side to remove the evil spirit between us.

And we will work on our side to remove the evil spirit among us. That means that those Indians who clamor for vengeance and killing must wait for my return. Perhaps if we can bury the hatchet deep underground and overlook, for a time, the injustices poured upon us, peace may again be restored. We may yet see Teedyuscung's vision of a homeland in the Wyoming Valley.

But to those who seek revenge and justice and a homeland through tomahawk and knife and fire, be aware that the English dogs have teeth and hearts filled with hate. There is no place to hide from them when they run in packs, and they will hunt us and kill men, women, and children. The scalp of a peace-loving Indian brings just as much as the scalp of one who hates and kills. And the English dogs do not take prisoners.

Wait, I say, until I return, but be vigilant. The English dogs may come upon you at any time. Do not let them surprise you while eating or sleeping.

And if, after I have talked with the governor and he is still unable to remove the evil spirit from among his people, I am not sure where to go or what to do. But I am thinking that I will make a straight path to Many Children Johnson and see if he will not take us into his house and protect us from the mad dogs that would destroy us.

Now I have said all I have to say.

UNDER ATTACK

Who Killed Honest John?

Glikkikan stopped and just sat before me shaking his head. I waited. The cold penetrated the schoolhouse. I went for some more sticks to throw on the fire while he sorted out in his mind the things he had heard.

When I sat down again, he asked cautiously, "Brother John, who killed Teedyuscung?"

I stalled for time. "Would you repeat the question?"

This time he added another question. "Who killed Teedyuscung, and why did they murder him?"

I looked at Glikkikan sitting before me with uncharacteristic dejection and sadness on his face.

"All the evidence is inconclusive," I answered.[54] "It could have been the Six Nations. They hated how King Teedy challenged their right to sell Delaware land, and by extension, also challenged their authority over all the Indian nations. King Teedy's conduct at the Easton treaties was a brazen affront to the Six Nations. They did not take lightly to his braggadocio and could have murdered him.

"Or it could easily have been the settlers from Connecticut. They plainly warned Honest John and the Six Nations that they would settle the Wyoming Valley and defend their habitations by force if necessary. It is evident that Connecticut settlers moved in unmolested after Honest John was gone. For myself, I favor the conclusion that it was the Connecticut settlers who murdered Honest John and burned the village."

Glikkikan rose to leave. "Brother John," he said sadly, "you still believe that Brother Johannes was a liar. Just remember your vow to write

---

[54] See Appendix E for the evidence I have gathered to answer this question. –JGL

Under Attack at Wyoming: 1756–1763

everything exactly as I told it to you."

"Wait! Wait!" I cried. "I will write the story down exactly as you have told it to me. What I believe has nothing to do with what I write down as your scribe. Please remember that you have not yet told me anything about the Philadelphia captivity or the gold medallion. To be fair, you must also tell me about all the good people who have tried to help the Indians—the Moravians, the Quakers, the Mennonites, and even Governor Hamilton."

"You are not yet ready to receive the truth," Brother Isaac said in cold judgment. "Perhaps another day you will be ready." With that, the mighty Glikkikan stepped out into the falling snow and quietly vanished.

UNDER ATTACK

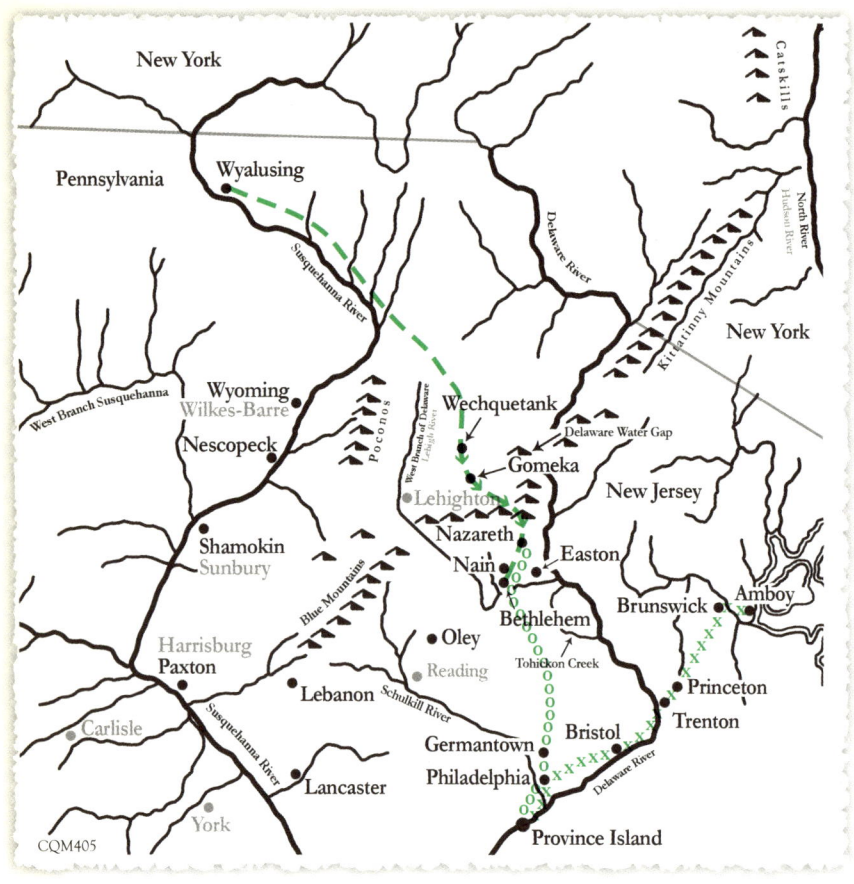

The Treks of the Refugees (1763)

CQM405 Notes

1. Nain was an Indian village two miles north of Bethlehem. It was built after the massacre at Huts of Grace forced the Christian Indians to flee that settlement.
2. ➔ ➔ ➔ = the flight of Wechquetank Indians to Nazareth.
3. o o o = the forced march from Nazareth and Nain to Philadelphia and Province Island (80 miles).
4. — — — = the flight of Papunhank's band to Bethlehem from Wyalusing (130 miles).
5. x x x = the forced march from Province Island to Amboy, New Jersey, and back to barracks in Philadelphia, Pennsylvania (95 miles each way).
6. The quarantine house lay on Province Island in the Delaware River five miles south of Philadelphia.

Chapter 5

Under Attack in Philadelphia: 1763–1765

As recorded by John Heckewelder
At Beautiful Spring, Ohio,
Monday, 23 May 1774

E arly in the morning, a Shawnee delegation of eight led by Hokolesqua, head chief of the Shawnee, and Pucksinwah, Shawnee war chief, rode into Beautiful Spring for a short stay. Someone from their party had two knife wounds, and Glikkikan doctored them while other brothers refreshed the travelers with victuals.

The travelers paid no respects to Brother Good News or me, as was customary. As soon as they had eaten their porridge, they rode solemnly away. Each one looked straight ahead with a determined face set in stone.

I forced myself to wait till they were out of sight before setting out to

UNDER ATTACK

find Isaac. He was nowhere to be found. Jacob Daskund assured me, "He has gone off with the delegation to find Chief White Eyes."

"That was a delegation?" I asked.

"Of the highest Shawnee level," Jacob answered. "You know Pucksinwah and Hokolesqua. The wounded one was Silver Heels, a brother of Hokolesqua and of the six-foot woman, Nonhelema. She often accompanies war parties, and she can fight so well the Whites call her the grenadier squaw. Both Pucksinwah and Silver Heels speak fluent English.

Yellow Hawk is chief of the village of Chalahgawtha, located near the spot where Paint Creek empties into the Scioto River. The sturdy woman who rode beside him was his wife, Duck Eggs.

The two young men bringing up the rear were Elinipsico, son of Hokolesqua, and Blue Jacket, the adopted son of Pucksinwah.

"That does sound like an impressive array of Shawnees," I commented. "What happened while they were here?"

"When Glikkikan returns, he will be able to answer all your questions," Jacob responded. He would say nothing more. Neither would anyone else tell me anything other than the same words Jacob had given me, "When Glikkikan returns . . ."

Starting a War

Since there was nothing more I could learn until Glikkikan returned, I fretted away in my cabin and started writing what I did know about the worrisome situation we were in.

Since the first of the year, we have had many opportunities for preaching, baptisms, communions, and burials. In between all this, we always had to contend with fear of Indian uprisings, rough traders,

Under Attack in Philadelphia: 1763-1765

and aggressive Whites invading Indian lands.

Major Connolly was a commandant at Fort Pitt and served under the Virginia governor, Lord Dunmore. He had incited the settlers to attack and destroy the Indians. To do this, he sent out circular letters similar to this one:

> A party of land claimers had been making improvements near the mouth of the Kanawha. They met another party of Whites, who told them they had fallen in with a party of Shawnees who had been hunting on the southwest side of the Ohio River. The two groups argued until a fight broke out. The Whites then killed all the Shawnees and took all the Indian horses and goods. Knowing an Indian war would be the result, the land-claimers, with the exception of a few who went upriver by boat, fled overland eastward.

Agent McKee claims that in the letters from Connolly, no dates were given nor names mentioned, so it was always impossible to verify the incidents had actually taken place. Whites accepted each story without question, and in each retelling, the stories became more frightening, the peril waiting down the Ohio more deadly.

This spring, the huge number of boats and crafts of all kinds going down the Ohio exceeded anything previously seen. The Indians were watching. Whites sometimes shot the Indians without cause, and sometimes the Indians retaliated. The Shawnee and the Mingo suffered the most, and everyone in the Ohioland feared an all-out Indian war.

Some Indians from Mochwesüng on the Walhonding came here for a visit. They told us a Shawnee chief apparently was killed by Whites on the Ohio. We also hear that the Virginians on the Ohio are threatening to attack the Shawnee in their settlements and destroy their towns. This rumor proved correct. Both the governor of Virginia and

UNDER ATTACK

Dr. John Connolly issued proclamations of war against the Indians.

On Saturday, 7 May, we heard much about war from strangers who were visiting here. One of them asked our Indians, "What would you do if your teachers could no longer be here with you?"

"Then we would go with them wherever they go," Papunhank answered.

The questioner then asked, "Are your teachers your gods then?"

"No," Papunhank returned, "but they have acquainted us with the one true God and His Word. If they had not done this, we would still be as blind as all the Indians who know nothing about God. We love them and will not leave them."

Shortly thereafter, the worst news possible came to us. On Sunday evening, an express messenger from Newcomerstown arrived sounding a horrible cry that the Indians use only in times of greatest danger. In quick succession and in a high-pitched voice he shouted, "Aw, oh! Aw, oh! Aw, oh!" People came running from all over the town and quickly gathered around him. "Eleven out of twenty Mingos were murdered by a gang of thirty white men at Yellow Creek! This happened at the village of Talgayeeta (John Logan), a respected and peaceful Mingo leader!" Everyone gasped.

The messenger continued, "Jacob Greathouse, by cunning and intrigue, invited the men to a shooting match. After all the guns of the Indians were discharged, men jumped up out of hiding and shot the Mingos and butchered the women. Talgayeeta was not there at the time, but when he arrived, he found his brother Taylaynee, his son Molnah, his sister Koonay, his wife Mellana, and seven of their friends all dead. In addition, his sister's belly had been cut open and her unborn son torn from her and scalped. The baby girl she carried in her backpack was gone. Koonay was John Gibson's wife, and he was the father of the children!

"When Talgayeeta arrived on the dismal scene, the eerie death cry

Under Attack in Philadelphia: 1763-1765

tore from his throat. When the death cries had died away, Talgayeeta raised his tomahawk and vowed, 'I, Talgayeeta, give my vow. For every life taken here, ten of the Shemanese will die under my hand. I, Talgayeeta, vow it. By my hand alone, twenty lives for my unborn nephew!' "

The same messenger also brought us a hopeful message from the Shawnee chief, Hokolesqua, which the Delaware Chief Watwees asked him to deliver to us.

> Our grandfather, the Delaware nation, should not be worried. They should remain completely quiet and calm. They should also allow the traders to trade among them and not put any obstacles in their way or in that of other white people who are there. The women should start planting already. They don't have to wait until they see what is going to happen.

The message made it sound as though the Shawnee had resolved not to hurt the Pennsylvanians or the Delawares and were concerned only with the Virginians. We doubted the Shawnee would keep their resolution. We decided to meet with the brothers of the conference to discuss what could be done to protect the Whites at Beautiful Spring and Huts of Grace.

We also decided to ask some Indian brothers to take a message to Chief Watwees in Newcomerstown. Of course, we know the chiefs cannot protect us. They don't even have power over their own people. Yet we know they will not abandon us but assist us with good counsel.

Even in this dangerous time, we know that our help and protection must come from the Lord alone.

The next evening another white trader, Mr. Anderson, and Chief White Eyes arrived from Pittsburgh. They had almost fallen

UNDER ATTACK

into the hands of the Mingo who were camping on the road to Newcomerstown. Fortunately, they had been warned and arrived here safely after detouring around them. These two men had been sent to the Shawnee in another attempt to bring them to peace.

We now hear there is a gang of Whites on the Ohio who not only committed the murders of Indians but would also kill White traders because they furnish goods to the Indians. A number of traders still reside among the Shawnee. Should there be a war, they would all be killed.

Straining to Avoid a War

On the evening of the 13th, we got the unpleasant news that the Shawnee had not received Captain White Eyes and his peace message, but had shot at him and Mr. Anderson when they were returning to Newcomerstown. Now Chief Watwees wants to take a large party with him and go to the Shawnee to see if he can get them to listen.

Early on the morning of the 15th, a messenger came and called Brothers Johannes Papunhank, Isaac Glikkikan, Jacob Daskund, Augustinius Leekey, Wilhelm Chelloway, and Joseph Peepi (all former chiefs) to come to Newcomerstown. When they returned late in the evening, they told us that things looked very grim. Instead of agreeing to make peace, the Mingo and Shawnee had stormed out of the Council, threatening to kill all the White people they met. The Delaware are warning the Shawnee and the Mingo that if they make war on the Whites, none of the other nations will support them. They will have to fight by themselves. May the Savior overrule and guide in all of this and destroy all their evil attacks. May He stop Satan's plan to destroy our work among the Indians.

Under Attack in Philadelphia: 1763-1765

We uttered countless sighs to the Savior's heart for ourselves and for all of His work here. We prayed that the Savior would rule over the hearts of the chiefs and leaders and guide them to do what is best.

Brother Isaac slipped into my cabin late that night and told me, "I had a private talk with Hokolesqua today. Would you like to hear about it?"

I laid my pen aside and turned to face him in the close quarters. He seated himself on a footstool and looked directly at me.

> Brother John, I thought you would want to know about the meeting the Shawnee and the Mingo held a few days ago. You will be glad to hear that the Shawnee are still trying to make peace.
>
> Only a day or two ago, nearly thirty chiefs and their assistants gathered in the council house at Wapatomica. Representatives were there from the Delawares, Shawnees, Wyandots, and Mingos, including Hokolesqua, Pucksinwah, and the enormously influential Talgayeeta.
>
> For several hours, each one told his story of the unprovoked attacks they had experienced from the Shemanese. Then Pucksinwah told the Council of the messages they had received from their friends Croghan, McKee, Elliott, Gibson, and others.
>
> The messages begged them not to make war on the Whites and assured the Council that the recent acts of violence had been undertaken by irresponsible individuals, not the government, and those individuals would be punished.
>
> Would they please send a delegation to Fort Pitt under the mantle of peace and try to reach an accommodation,

UNDER ATTACK

rather than dash their nations into war with a very deadly foe? The messages all assure the delegation safety.

Pucksinwah said, "We have all been provoked beyond what any of us should bear. We Shawnees have lost good people, as have the Wyandots and Lenni Lenape and certainly the followers of Talgayeeta. Yet we are asked to come to Fort Pitt and see if we can repair the damage done by both sides. We Shawnees are on our way there now.

"Talgayeeta, some time ago we asked you to help us make war on the Shemanese so we might drive them back from our lands. You declined to help us. Now we have turned around and wish to try for the peace that is offered. We ask you to lay aside the harm that has been done you and join us. Tell us what is in your heart."

When Talgayeeta rose to speak for the first time in the Council, a deep hush fell over the assembly. His face was etched in deep grief, and he stood silently for a time before speaking. "My heart grieves for the losses that have been inflicted upon you here," he said at last. "I would not lead you into a war that would do you even greater harm, but the losses and injury done to us are beyond accommodation. I have vowed vengeance, and I will carry it out. My hatchet shall not be grounded until I have fulfilled my vow."

Brother John, Pucksinwah's reply gives us hope that a war in the Ohioland may yet be averted. He said, "We here respect what Talgayeeta has said, and considering the injury done to him, we cannot find fault in his vow. But we have given our promise to talk with Salamander

Under Attack in Philadelphia: 1763-1765

George Croghan[55] at Fort Pitt. If accommodation can be reached, we will lend ourselves to it, but not to the detriment of our Mingo friends. And if accommodation cannot be reached, then we, too, will raise our hatchets in war."[56]

After that speech, Chief Watwees, who must be around ninety years old, advised the Shawnees and Mingos in a fatherly manner. "You should consider the blessings of peace and the folly of war. I appeal to your powers of reason to consider what misery you may bring upon yourselves and others by your madness. But if you insist upon such a course, you must know you cannot expect any help or assistance from the Delawares. But you should let the road to Philadelphia be clear and free."

Chief Hokolesqua answered Chief Watwees thus: "We believe your words to be good, and we will take notice of them. Please advise our wives that they should plant corn for us rather than move away in fear."

It was getting very late when Brother Isaac finished his report, but I couldn't resist the temptation to ask him a question. "What do you think? Will peace be restored?"

"Brother John, understand one thing." He spoke very slowly and emphatically. "The Indians do not want war. They are being pushed into it by White atrocities. It is not the Indians but the Whites who will determine whether we have peace or not. Do you believe this?"

"Glikkikan," I protested, "it is not the Whites who will kill us white teachers, but the Indians. If the Savior does not protect us

---

[55] Col. George Croghan, a well-known Indian trader and the King's deputy Indian agent under Sir William Johnson. In this story Croghan was known to the Indians as Salamander George. His reputation as a heavy drinker, land speculator, and unprincipled opportunist traveled with him.
[56] Allen W. Eckert, *That Dark and Bloody River*, pp. 70-71.

UNDER ATTACK

from the Shawnee and the Mingos, we are lost."

"I would say just the opposite," he retorted. "If the Indians do not protect us from the Whites, we Christian Indians will be destroyed."

The next day a messenger arrived from Salamander Croghan at Pittsburgh. His message to the Delaware, Mingo, and Shawnee stated, "Everyone should remain calm and not have thoughts of war. You should go about your lives and not offend the traders. In Pittsburgh, they are trying to find and capture all the white people who have committed the murders, and they have caught one already. Everything in Pittsburgh is calm, and the Indians come and go undisturbed."

Have You Spoken for Peace?

All of us at the mission are greatly relieved to hear that there is no more danger from the white settlers. The way things stand now, we hope that there will not be an open war. In the meantime, however, the Shawnee and Mingo could still take revenge on the Whites, and many innocent people would suffer from this. May the Savior soon grant us peace and calm and spread His wings over us so that the evil enemy does not carry out his tricks on us or trouble us in body or in spirit. Herewith we commend ourselves and the entire Indian congregation to the remembrance of all the congregations before the Savior.

Glikkikan confronted me again. "Heckewelder, Salamander George is lying again. He says all is quiet in Pittsburgh, that the Whites have stopped killing Indians and have already arrested one white man. In reality, an Indian messenger approached Pittsburgh one morning, carrying wampum in one hand with the other

Under Attack in Philadelphia: 1763–1765

upraised in the sign of peace. Before a watching crowd, Sam Meason shot the Indian dead. At Salamander Croghan's insistence, Dr. Connolly had Meason arrested, put in irons, and locked in the guardhouse. The crowd, outraged that a white man had actually been jailed for killing an Indian, broke into the guardhouse and set Meason free.

"But that's not all. Down on the South Branch Potomac near Moorefield, two white men coldly gunned down four friendly Indians who were known and respected in that area. No action was taken."

Glikkikan was not happy, and I braced for what was coming next. "With your approval, I went and spoke very sharply to the Munsees at Mochwessüng, imploring them not to go to war. Some of us told the Delaware and the Shawnee the same thing. The way of peace is best.

"Now," Glikkikan continued, "are you going to go to Fort Pitt and tell Dr. Connolly the Virginians should not go to war against the Indians? Is there nothing you can do to make the Whites stop their rampages or keep them from raising an army?"

I didn't know what to tell him, so I remained silent. How could we teachers go to the military officers upon whom our safety depended and tell them what not to do? The thought was preposterous.

I shook my head and mumbled, "No, we can't do that. Why, the settlers and the soldiers would kill us."

Glikkikan turned his head and slowly walked away.

Sometimes Glikkikan baffled me, so I had to let it go at that and turn my attention to other things. Glikkikan's close friend, Captain White Eyes, discovered the butchered remains of a white trader near his town and buried them. The Mingos dug them up and warned White Eyes they would do the same to all white traders they could find. Furthermore, they promised to treat him the same way if he interfered further.

UNDER ATTACK

White Eyes then sent word to Wapatomika and warned the trader William Butler and his friends of their danger. The traders there detoured and came to White Eyes' town, where he informed them of the tense situation. White Eyes told the traders he would hide them for several days until he could find a safe way to get them to Fort Pitt. Furthermore, his friend Glikkikan was hiding several traders at Beautiful Spring.

It was at this same time that the Shawnee peace delegation came through on the way to Fort Pitt. Chief Hokolesqua agreed to safely escort the white traders whom both White Eyes and Glikkikan were hiding.

At the time, I knew nothing about the sheltered traders or the peace delegation. But when the Shawnee delegation returned by way of Beautiful Spring with the wounded Silver Heels, my suspicions were fully aroused. What was going on? And then Glikkikan disappeared with them.

When Glikkikan returned to Beautiful Spring, I tried to find out what had happened. He would tell me nothing. "Heckewelder, he said, "you know nothing about war and peace. If you better understood the past, you could possibly understand the present. This time we are living in is just like the time when our dear brethren here were under attack in Philadelphia. I thought you wanted to hear that story."

I was eager for all the details of the recent events, but I had long wanted to hear this story that Papunhank had told to Glikkikan. "Okay," I agreed. "I'm all ears. The details of your journey can wait."

Under Attack in Philadelphia: 1763–1765

The Philadelphia Captivity: 1763–1765

As told by the Prophet Papunhank to Isaac Glikkikan
Transcribed by John Heckewelder

Fleeing Wyalusing

By mid-November of 1763, so many threats and warnings from friend and foe alike had come to Wyalusing that I no longer considered it safe to remain there any longer. Twenty others left Wyalusing with Easy Tongue and me. We followed a northern route and used every stratagem we knew to avoid detection. We hoped to arrive safely at Bethlehem and find Brother Zeisberger there. He had baptized me, and I held great confidence in him.

The twenty-two of us arrived at the three-story stone building on the hill above Monocacy Creek that served as the Moravian headquarters. It was the last part of November, and the chilled, bedraggled group waited a little distance behind while Easy Tongue, speaking in good English, informed Bishop Peter Boehler of the purpose of the group's dangerous journey from Wyalusing. "Brother Johannes Papunhank and I wish to confer with Brother Zeisberger, my trusted teacher, before giving an answer to Governor Hamilton."

The good bishop quickly arranged for the travel-worn party to be brought indoors and fed. Even in such dangerous times, the Moravians were not afraid to shelter me and my band. He brought us into the community house, the large stone building. According to the command of Christ, he took us strangers in and gave us Indian food and drink and a chance to rest. The bishop and his wife served the food themselves.

Then Bishop Boehler took me and Easy Tongue aside into a sparsely furnished room where two young men, Gabriel and Michael, were

UNDER ATTACK

also present. "Was the food and drink to your liking?" Bishop Boehler asked.

"Ah," Easy Tongue answered, "it was served by angels and tasted as though our own women had made it."

The bishop smiled easily. "And so they have," he replied. "We have six single Indian sisters who have lived here in their choir for years, and they like to prepare Indian food for our Indian guests.

"Now," Brother Boehler continued, "there are some things that I must tell you. Brother Zeisberger is not here. He is very, very busy caring for the Christian Indians from Nain and Wechquetank who now live under the protection of the Penn government on Province Island. This island abuts the Delaware River five miles south of Philadelphia.

"These Indians were, by order of the government, taken from their homes, disarmed, and moved to the island. I am going to let Michael and Gabriel give you a firsthand account of the journey from Bethlehem to Province Island. These young men drove two of the wagons that moved the Christian Indians to Philadelphia.

"Meanwhile, I shall busy myself making some arrangements for you." With that, the good bishop excused himself, and the two young wagon drivers told their story to Easy Tongue and me.

Arrested, Despised, Rejected

Gabriel was the talkative one, while Michael listened closely and nodded his head approvingly. "After Captain Bull's party raided John Stenton's Inn, Mrs. Stenton swore out a warrant accusing Renatus of being one of the Indians in the raiding party. Probably Renatus was the only Christian Indian she knew by name or else someone

Under Attack in Philadelphia: 1763–1765

maliciously supplied his name for her. It was impossible that Renatus[57] was at the raid on that early morning, for at that tense time, the missionaries at Nain and Wechquetank kept track of every Indian's whereabouts every hour of every day. And on the morning of 8 October 1763, Renatus, his wife, and his venerable father, Jacob,[58] were all in Renatus's house at Wechquetank.

"Never mind the facts. A judge in Philadelphia, not a local judge, issued a warrant for Renatus's arrest, and near the end of October, John Jennings, the sheriff of Northampton County, seized Renatus and sent him off to the stone prison in Philadelphia.

"According to Renatus, just as he, his lawyer, and the deputy sheriff approached Philadelphia, a severe earthquake and a loud roaring noise scared the inhabitants quite badly. Renatus thanked God for the sign of His overpowering presence. The next day he learned that the earthquake occurred just as the new governor, John Penn,[59] was stepping off the ship from England onto the wharf.

"The new governor, backed by the Assembly, lost no time in dealing with the Christian Indians. One week after his arrival, Governor Penn sent an express to the mission board at Bethlehem ordering all the baptized Indians to come to Philadelphia for their 'protection.'

"When informed of the orders, the Indian congregations at Nain and Nazareth could not refrain from weeping. The Indians feared they

---

[57] The massive form and gigantic strength of this celebrated Lenape warrior had made him a terror to his foes. But his dissipated life at home and bloodthirsty fierceness in many a drunken brawl had gained him a disgraceful notoriety even more widespread than his warlike fame.
  In 1748 he came with tears of penitence to the missionary at Gnadenhuetten on the Mahoning and begged to be baptized. It seemed the Brethren almost doubted that such a great change of heart was possible and thus delayed his baptism a long time, but at length they yielded to his earnest pleading and baptized him as Christian Renatus.
  His subsequent life proved his sincerity, though it never ceased to be a wonder to all who had known him. Both white men and former companions among the Indians came from afar purposely to convince themselves of this miracle of grace. His conversion made a deep impression for good on his tribe.
  – Donald R. Repsher, *Meniolagomeka - Annals of a Moravian Indian Village*.

[58] Jacob was the last remaining convert of the first three Mohicans that Christian Henry Rauch baptized (Abraham, Isaac, and Jacob) from the Shekomeko Indian mission.

[59] John Penn was a son of Richard Penn and a grandson of William Penn, the founder of Pennsylvania. At the age of 33, he became governor of Pennsylvania.

UNDER ATTACK

should be separated from their teachers and their dearest friends at Bethlehem. When assured that their teachers would accompany them, they rested more easily.

"But orders were orders. On 8 November, Sheriff John Jennings of Northampton County, the same man who had seized Renatus, arrived to take charge of the new prisoners and conduct them safely to Philadelphia. The first order of the sheriff's business was to collect all of their arms—guns, knives, and tomahawks."

Gabriel frowned thoughtfully before going on with his story. "I could not believe how readily the Indians gave up their rifles. Their rifles were the very means of their livelihood, and they greatly prized them."

"True words, indeed!" I told him. "I am only newly baptized, as of last June, and I have done everything I can to keep the peace with Pennsylvania. But to give up my rifle and trust the governor to feed and protect me? I cannot do it."

Gabriel continued, "Well, the Christians calmly surrendered their rifles to Sheriff Jennings. The only thing I can say is that those Indian men loved the Savior more than liberty or life, and in this act of complete surrender, they cast themselves upon the mercies of God and the uncertain promises of the government.

"The Indians then gathered in the church at Bethlehem. Bishop Boehler preached a farewell sermon, 'Make Thy Way Straight Before My Face,' based on Psalm 5:8. The congregation listened intently and again renewed their commitment to follow God's way, come what may. Sheriff Jennings witnessed the whole spectacle.

"After the service ended, the Delaware and Mohican believers gathered on the south bank of the Lehigh River. The people from Bethlehem came to see their departure and brought them much needed gifts of blankets and clothing. It was November, and a heavy coat felt good to me. The refugees now numbered 125 and were

Under Attack in Philadelphia: 1763-1765

comprised of women, children, the elderly, and the sick. Eight of us white drivers guided our open wagons overloaded with goods and refugees. The Indian men and the brothers Grube, Zeisberger, and several others walked. Our pathetic procession, headed by Sheriff Jennings on his horse, got under way about the middle of the afternoon. As the procession plodded along, the missionaries passed from rank to rank with words of encouragement and peace.

"The hatred intensified toward all Indians and any Whites who aided them. The same night we left Bethlehem, the oil mill burned to the ground, and the expensive waterworks[60] would have suffered the same fate had not vigilant residents put the fire out. Nothing was ever done to punish the evildoers.

"We spent the first night at a farm, and the next morning we pursued our way amid a pelting rain. The rutted road became greasy, and the mud splattered over everything, but the oxen plodded forward. We hired an additional wagon, but even with the added space in the uncovered wagons, it was impossible to remain dry or warm or comfortable. Thus our bedraggled, miserable procession pushed laboriously and quietly onward toward Philadelphia.

"We spent the second night at two adjacent taverns and then continued our journey the next morning. The dreary weather continued, with cold rains falling on everyone. To add to our misery, in every hamlet we passed through, people shouted curses at the Indians, declaring that hanging and burning ought to be their doom. Nearly every traveler we met treated us to insults and made threatening signs with their hands that clearly showed their intense hatred of the entire company. Sheriff Jennings looked straight ahead and paid no attention to

---

[60] A creative Moravian engineer designed and built this first municipal waterworks in America. It used water power from an undershot water wheel to lift water more than 100 feet to the top of the highest building. This updated system had only been completed in 1762, the year before this night when the oil mill was fired. This house and the pumps have been recreated and can be toured in Bethlehem, Pennsylvania, today (2016).

UNDER ATTACK

the reviling bystanders. The Indians and the missionaries suffered the reproaches silently.

"By the time we reached Germantown, the rabble of that whole neighborhood was roused, and angry threats were made to kill us all. This time, Sheriff Jennings could no longer ignore the threats and the curses. He dropped back and rode between the angry crowd and his charges. In the name of the King, he ordered the crowd to drop back, but the mob only pressed in closer and the shouts became louder. It seemed to us that the mob, emboldened by their numbers and the commotion, would break in among us at any moment with sticks and stones and knives and axes. But at the very moment when it seemed Sheriff Jennings could no longer restrain the mob, God sent a heavy rain that sent many seeking cover until we had safely passed through the town. Thus we arrived safely, but much wearied and distressed, at the edge of Philadelphia.

"Governor Penn had appointed that the prisoners should be housed in the British barracks which encompassed a hollow square with two-story brick buildings surrounding three sides. A three-story brick building housed the officers on the fourth side. Early on the morning of the eleventh, Governor Penn's four authorized representatives—Marshall, Schmick, George Neisser, and Commissary Fox—went on ahead to prepare the way for the refugees.

"Michael and I drove two of the first three wagons loaded with women and children. They rolled through the gates into the barracks at 9:30 that morning. Suddenly, the British Highlander soldiers grabbed their muskets and rushed upon our three

Under Attack in Philadelphia: 1763–1765

In Great Danger

"The rabble of the whole neighborhood was roused against us." —Gabriel

UNDER ATTACK

wagons with a great tumult. The soldiers stopped the rest of the wagons outside the gate. Then they threatened to shoot the cowering women and children in the yard if we did not leave at once.

"It was strange that the governor's officers had gone ahead to the barracks to prepare the way for the prisoners, and yet no officers were present giving orders during the tumult. But the soldiers insisted that the wagons must leave. So our three wagons joined the other six wagons and the rest of the company waiting on Second Street. Commissary Fox rushed off to report to Governor Penn."

I stopped Gabriel in his tale and asked, "Are you saying that the soldiers were acting under prearranged orders? Do you think the whole uprising was planned?"

Gabriel answered me, "Papunhank, it's quite possible."

Then I asked Gabriel, "Do you think the soldiers really would have killed women and children?"

"Papunhank, I believe they would have shot them if we had not taken our loads outside." Michael nodded his head in agreement.

I told Gabriel and Michael, "That proves that the officers gave the orders. Otherwise, the soldiers would have been afraid of punishment."

Gabriel continued, "Meanwhile, a large crowd had assembled, which soon swelled into an excited mob. Shouts and yells as fierce as the war whoops of any savage Indians terrified the defenseless band. Bloodthirsty threats passed from mouth to mouth. 'Shoot them! Hang them! Burn them! Scalp the accursed redskins!'

"The presence of the missionaries, Zeisberger, Schmick, and Grube, and of clergymen from other churches was no restraint upon the rabble, but inflamed them still more. From ten o'clock until three in the afternoon, the converts and their teachers endured every abuse which wild frenzy or ribald vulgarity could clothe in words.

"However, in these hours of trial, many Quakers with their plain

Under Attack in Philadelphia: 1763-1765

clothes and honest faces braved the scorn of the rabble, took the Indians by the hand, and called them friends.

"The Indians made no response to the threats and abuses of the crowd. Instead they talked together of Him whose name they bore. 'Jesus was despised and rejected of men,' they said. 'What else can we expect? Jesus was buffeted and spit upon, yet He opened not His mouth. Why should we not patiently bear these indignities?'[61]

"At last Commissary Fox returned with some members of the governor's Council and directed that we should proceed down Second Street. We prodded our oxen forward, only wishing we could get out of there faster. The women and children drew their blankets more tightly around them on that chilly November day. The men paced dutifully behind the wagons carrying their loved ones. Thus our forlorn company, surrounded by a howling mob, moved forward to the outskirts of the city. There the mob finally dispersed while the refugees and their meager belongings were loaded on flatboats. We bid them all Godspeed and began our long journey back to Bethlehem."

The quiet Michael added, "I cannot get the picture of them, floating away in the dusk, out of my mind. Sheep among howling wolves—despised, forsaken, lonely—yet they opened not their mouths. God bless them . . . and protect them."

When Bishop Boehler returned, he told Easy Tongue and me of the current state of affairs and of the arrangements he had made. "We will care for the rest of your band here in Bethlehem until you return from your meeting with the governor. I have issued passes to the two of you, and Gabriel and Michael will escort you to Philadelphia.

"I also want to inform you that Governor Hamilton is no longer governor of Pennsylvania. John Penn, a grandson of the great Miquon, is now the governor. He is still quite young, but we are hopeful of more

---

[61] DeSchweinitz, *The Life and Times of David Zeisberger*, pp. 288-289.

UNDER ATTACK

True Brothers

"Many Quakers took us by the hand and called us friends." —Gabriel

Under Attack in Philadelphia: 1763-1765

honest help from him than we received from Governor Hamilton.

"I have also written letters to Israel Pemberton, Jr., that true and kind Quaker friend of the Indians, asking him to arrange lodging for you while you are in Philadelphia. Friend Israel has a brother James who is chief of the Pennsylvania Assembly, and between the two of them, they know what is happening in Pennsylvania.

"It is hoped that Friend Israel will also be able to arrange a meeting with Brother Zeisberger before you give your answer to the new governor. I bid you Godspeed, and may the Savior guide you as you decide where to go for refuge in these perilous times."

Where Should I Go?

I would describe Israel Pemberton, Jr., the King of the Quakers, as decisive, modest, wealthy, wise, diplomatic, and honest, honest, honest. I instinctively knew Friend Israel was to be trusted, and to him I opened my heart. Easy Tongue translated for me.

"We thank you for your kindness to the Indians and the efforts of your society to help restore peace during the late war. At Wyalusing, we commend you, and we ourselves have done everything possible to keep the peace you helped fashion with Chief Teedyuscung. But the clouds of war have again come close to the ground. The lightning strikes all around us, and the thunder becomes louder and louder.

"I come to you for counsel. The hatchet has again been raised against us. What shall the Indians of Wyalusing do? Where shall we flee? Shall we follow the setting sun and hide among the warring Indians in the West? Shall we clothe ourselves in heavier furs and go to Many Children Johnson? Perhaps he will take us in and shelter us among the Mengwe. Shall we give up our rifles and our homes and

UNDER ATTACK

come in to our brothers on Province Island? Will the governor care for us in the bear's own den? Will he protect us and bring us food and raiment? Or should we simply trust God to protect us and remain in our houses at Wyalusing?

"I have sent a message to Governor Hamilton reminding him of our deeds done to maintain peace with the English, even when his people murdered and robbed our people. Still, Governor Hamilton claimed that the Indians have so cruelly struck his inhabitants without any cause that now his soldiers and his people cannot be blamed if they go into Indian country and satisfy their desire for revenge. The governor says that these angered white savages are not to blame for not being able to distinguish between good Indians and bad Indians. If we want to blame someone for our danger, we must count it against the savages.

"So Governor Hamilton has warned us that we at Wyalusing, the peaceable Indians, are in great danger of an attack by his soldiers who operate beyond his control. We think that Governor Hamilton is lying. He says the Indians struck his people first. He denies that the Indians suffered cruelties at the hands of his people. He denies that the British built forts in Indian territory and that British soldiers killed more Indians in peacetime than they killed even during the last war. Now the governor says that he cannot control his own soldiers! We almost believe him because of what happened at the barracks.

"How should I answer the governor? Where shall the Wyalusing Indians go? Or is it safe to stay at Wyalusing?"

Friend Israel was not one to speak quickly before he had the facts. The King of the Quakers considered my questions while Easy Tongue and I sipped a cup of tea with him. "This tea is special," Friend Israel began. "I just received a fresh shipment on one of my ships directly from the Orient. The British want to regulate and tax the tea trade. The English King's navy makes it difficult to import fresh tea without coming through Great Britain. But thankfully, there have been ways

Under Attack in Philadelphia: 1763-1765

around the British controls so far.

"It is the same with the Indian trade," the King continued. "The British want to control the Indian trade so that only approved traders can deal with the Indians. The war has made it very difficult for us to supply the Indians with anything. Some of our goods have even been waylaid and destroyed by Paxton Rangers at Sideling Hill. When the British commander at Fort Loudon, Captain Grant, attempted to punish the robbers, three hundred riflemen from the settlements came to Fort Loudon and actually took Captain Grant prisoner. I tell you this to show you that there is some truth in the governor's claim that many settlers are beyond his control.

"Now let us consider your last question first. Should the peaceable Wyalusing Indians remain in the Wyoming Valley? Let me tell you a few facts that I believe will answer the question for you. At the very time the Pennsylvania militia was launching the raid on the Great Island Indians, Governor Hamilton made a request to the Assembly for additional funds to pay the soldiers. Please wait a moment and let me see if I can find a copy of that bulletin."

Friend Israel swung around on his chair where he could reach the drawers of his massive oak desk and went straight to the proper file. He was that kind of ordered man. "Yes, this is the bulletin I wanted," he said. "I shall read it to you." The King placed two lenses connected by a wire on his nose. He looked at his guests and smiled as he explained, "Tis a wonderful contraption Dr. Franklin has invented that helps me to read. For a 48-year-old man who reads a lot, my arms just aren't long enough anymore. Friends, hear then Governor Hamilton's message to the Assembly on 15 October:

> I do, therefore, gentlemen, in the most earnest manner, recommend to your immediate consideration the distressed state of our unfortunate inhabitants on the

UNDER ATTACK

> frontiers, who are continually exposed to the savage cruelty of a merciless enemy; and request that you will in your present session, grant such a supply as, with God's assistance, may enable us, not only to protect our people, but to take a severe revenge on our perfidious foes, by pursuing them into their own countries, for which purpose there prevails at present a noble ardor among our frontier people, which in my opinion, ought by all means to be cherished and improved.[62]

The Quaker King laid his lenses on the desk, bowed his head, and placed his hand upon his brow in sober contemplation. Easy Tongue Chilloway and I waited. At length, the King spoke quietly as if to himself, "Severe revenge . . . noble ardor . . . cherished and improved." Friend Israel looked up at Easy Tongue and me. "I await the leading of the Inner Light," he said. His thoughtful mood continued as he spoke.

"Let's think about this. Governor Hamilton made this speech on a day when he knew that the Paxton Rangers were on the way to the Wyoming Valley. And the governor had straightly warned the commanders that the Wyalusing Indians were under the protection of the government. But our guess is that had the Rangers not come across the horrible massacre of the Connecticut settlers by Captain Bull's savages, the Rangers would have gone on to destroy Wyalusing regardless of the governor's orders. And yet, in this speech the governor is saying that these brave soldiers ought to be rewarded and encouraged. Something does not add up."

I held up my hand, palm outward. "Permit me to speak, my brother." Friend Israel nodded, and I began. "The King is right. His thoughts sound true, but some information is false. The Wyoming

---

[62] *Minutes of the Provincial Council of Pennsylvania*, Vol. 9, p. 59.

Under Attack in Philadelphia: 1763–1765

Valley is not such a large place that the birds cannot carry their songs from one end to the other. One hundred thirty-five soldiers cannot come upon us suddenly without the crows cawing, even if Whites are painted black and wear the garb of Indian warriors.

"The governor's soldiers came to the Wyoming Valley to destroy the Connecticut settlers, their habitations, and their corn, and they very cruelly did so. If there had been 135 Indian warriors in the Wyoming Valley, we would certainly have known about the presence of such a large force, and we would have tried to turn them back as we have at other times. But there were no Indian warriors in the valley at the time of the massacre.

"Captain Bull and his raiding party of only twenty warriors had nothing to do with the destruction of the Connecticut settlers. Captain Bull had avenged the death of his father and the plundering of his village. They carried their goods and captives far to the north and west of Wyoming.

"As surely as a trail of blood leads to the wounded deer, the trail of blood follows the Pennsylvania soldiers to the governor. In June, the governor's messengers came to us and told us they bore a clear warning to the Connecticut settlers. They said to us, 'The Pennsylvania government will never tolerate the Connecticut settlement in this valley.'

"It is as clear as spring water. Pennsylvania destroyed the Connecticut settlers and blamed it on the cruelties of the Indians. There is yet more evidence. As soon as these brave soldiers finished their murderous work in the Wyoming Valley, they returned home.

"One thing that I, Prophet Papunhank, do not understand is this: why does Pennsylvania murder settlers in the Wyoming Valley on land which Pennsylvania has never purchased from the Indians? Why does Brother Onas not also remove all settlers west of the Susquehanna on the Juniata? This also is land that has never been purchased from the Indians."

It did not take long for the King to begin his answer. "Prophet

UNDER ATTACK

Papunhank, your question is a good one, and I shall try to explain. The King of England granted the land north to 42° latitude to the Penn family. This is a line north of the Wyoming Valley. Never mind that an earlier English king had also given the same land to the people of Connecticut."

Again I held up my hand. The King stopped and nodded at me. "But how does the King of England have the right to grant Indian land to anyone?" I asked.

The King of the Quakers hung his head in sober contemplation. At last he spoke quietly and with carefully measured words. "Friend Papunhank, you and I are people of peace. We do not war. But the truth is that the English King claims all your land by right of conquest. He may dress all his words in the finest French silk and say that God gave him the land, but in the end, he took the land from the Dutch and the French and the Spanish by force. Indeed, the English are no different than the Six Nations who claim all Delaware lands by right of conquest."

The King of the Quakers paused, and I spoke again. "Friend Israel, I see that you speak the truth. It is as you say. But if we look down the gun barrel, might we not also see that the English will also take the land of the Six Nations by right of conquest?"

"Friend Papunhank, I see that you are indeed a prophet. If I were to prophesy, I would prophesy exactly the same thing. At some time in the future, the English will take over the lands of the Six Nations. Many Children Johnson is only using the Six Nations to divide and conquer the Indian nations. It is an old English tactic.

"Returning to your original question, you asked why Pennsylvania would drive Connecticut settlers from the Wyoming Valley. Why do Whites kill their own people in the Wyoming Valley, but allow other Whites to settle on other Indian lands? It's all about land. The Penn family claims the land in the Wyoming Valley, and they want to sell it to their friends so they can resell it to settlers. They cannot sell it to

Under Attack in Philadelphia: 1763-1765

Pennsylvania settlers if people from Connecticut settle it.

"Prophet Papunhank, there is another thing you must consider. The King of England has just issued a royal proclamation forbidding the settling of all lands west of the Alleghenies . . . for a time." Again, Friend Israel swiveled his chair to his desk and drew a paper from his file. "Prophet Papunhank," the King continued, "you will also want to know that this same Royal Proclamation authorizes Governor Penn to grant land to his soldiers. Listen to this:

> We are desirous to testify of the conduct and bravery of the officers and soldiers of our armies, and to reward the same, and to grant, without fee or reward the following quantities of land: field officers—5,000 acres; captains—3,000 acres; staff officers—2,000 acres; non-commissioned officers—200 acres; each private man—50 acres.[63]

"Johannes Papunhank, do not forget that those murderous Paxton Rangers want land, and they will get it. Not from lands Pennsylvania has already bought and paid for, though. It will be granted to them from unsettled Indian lands.

"So it is clear that you and your people must leave Wyalusing. Regardless of your help in turning back warriors, regardless of the governor's promises, and regardless of your good intentions to only worship God, you are not safe in the Wyoming Valley.

"Where you should go, Friend Johannes, is a harder question. But why don't you come to Philadelphia? I will take it upon myself to speak for the Society of Friends. We will shelter you and care for you until the war is over.

"Or, with the governor's permission, you could go to the Moravian

---

[63] Authorized by the Royal Proclamation of 1763 and published by Governor Penn, 8 December 1763. *Minutes of the Provincial Council of Pennsylvania*, pp. 81-85.

UNDER ATTACK

Wise Counsel
"*Where shall we go?*" —Johannes Papunhank

Under Attack in Philadelphia: 1763-1765

Indians on Province Island under the protection of the government. I have been in close contact with Brother Zeisberger, and he is having great difficulty securing ample supplies for the 120 Indians already under his care. How many Indians do you think would be willing to leave Wyalusing with you?"

"Friend Israel, there remain at Bethlehem twenty Delawares from Wyalusing who would leave with me. The Mohicans from the valley may be able to join their friends in Jersey under that governor's protection.

"What do you think of going north and strengthening the chain of friendship with Many Children Johnson? Would he not see to it that the King's armies would protect us from raging Pennsylvania settlers?

"What do you think? Should we cross the Alleghenies and dwell amongst the Western Indians? We do not fear they will attack us without cause. We know Captain Glikkikan, the hero of Fort Pitt and the Battle at Bushy Run. Captain Glikkikan is an orator, and he concerns himself with finding a homeland for the Delawares. Perhaps he and Chief Packanke will grant us a refuge among the Delawares and a place where we can concern ourselves only with the worship of God."

Again the Quaker King bowed his head in silent thought. When he spoke, it was with calmness and certainty. "Friend Johannes, all the King's horses and all the King's men cannot bring peace to the heart or kindle the Inner Light. Might does not make right or bring light to the soul. Do not go to Sir William Johnson. Many Children Johnson works for himself and the Crown. Remember that his job is to appease the Indians, including the Six Nations, until the English are strong enough to conquer them.

"I have heard of Captain Glikkikan and of his desire to find a homeland for his people. It would be well for you not to mention his name to the governor. The governor and the Council, and indeed many in the Assembly, already believe that the Christian Indians are in league

UNDER ATTACK

with the savages. If you so much as mention Glikkikan's name to the governor, he will believe the rumors. We must be very careful. But if you choose to go west to the captain, I hope to have a present ready to send to him. Be sure to tell me before you go west."

Glikkikan stopped the telling of his story in Papunhank's words for a moment, and then he asked, "Brother John, do you see how the road Papunhank's band traveled ten years ago lies right alongside the one we travel today? They wanted to live in peace, but they were attacked from all sides. It was not safe for them to live in their own land. The Whites committed horrible murders against the Indians. The murderers were never punished. The Whites declared war and sent soldiers and armies to destroy the Indians."

I waved my hand, urging him to stop. "No armies have come to the Ohioland yet," I countered.

"They will come from Virginia soon enough," Glikkikan prophesied. "Mark my word. And you will do nothing to stop them. Or will you have the courage of Friend Dreamer and stand before the rabble to declare the way of peace?"

"I cannot stop the armies if they come. Only God can do that," I declared. "There is nothing more I can do about the evil around us than to pray for peace."

"Then why do you send us to the Indian councils to urge them not to go to war, but you will not speak out against the evils of war to the white people?" he asked.

We left the question hanging unanswered, and he continued with his story of ten years earlier.

Under Attack in Philadelphia: 1763-1765

Life on Province Island

I drew Brother Zeisberger to myself in a long embrace. "I have longed to see your face and to hear your voice once again," I cried. "There is so much that you must yet teach me about the Savior. And we at Wyalusing do not know which way to turn, for the darkness is thick about us. Ah, Brother, can you but light a candle for us and brighten the path for us to walk?" I let the tears roll freely down my cheeks.

After a long period of giving silent comfort to me, his distressed brother, Zeisberger spoke freely in the Delaware tongue. "Brother Johannes, Friend Pemberton has arranged this meeting while I am in Philadelphia trying to secure supplies for the Christian Indians on Province Island. I cannot spend too much time with you, or I will not be able to return to the island before dark.

"Friend Israel has told me that you must take an answer to the governor. If Governor Penn will allow you and your people to join the Christian Indians on Province Island, we will then have much time to teach you more about the Savior. On the island with us, you would be under the protection of the Penn government."

"But, Brother David," I asked, "what is life like on Province Island? I have talked with Gabriel and Michael, and they told me how the soldiers in the barracks refused entrance to your Indians and even threatened to shoot women and children. They told me how the mob cursed you, your fellow missionaries, and the Indians. How can Governor Penn even protect you if the soldiers will not obey his orders?"

"It is true that life on Province Island has not been easy," answered Brother Zeisberger. "As you know, the governor had planned to send us to the English barracks. No preparations had been made to receive us on the island. By the time the last of our company floated down the Delaware

UNDER ATTACK

and arrived at the island, the weak winter sun was nearing the horizon.

"The two large hospital buildings designated to us had been used in the summertime as a place for quarantining immigrants coming into Pennsylvania. Both buildings now stood vacant, appearing as specters in the winter dusk. Though everything looked bleak, we paused and thanked the Savior that He had delivered us out of the mouths of howling wolves and that, once again, we could enjoy quiet and peace.

"The first day, all we had to eat was the small mess of fish we caught in the Delaware. For four days, we had only rotten stumps to burn that gave off more smoke than heat. Brother Grube fell sick, and I had to serve as minister, purveyor, and superintendent for 130 people. I thanked God that, like the Apostle Paul, I am not a married man. The care of all these people weighed heavily on me.

"I reestablished all the regular worship services held at the mission: the daily Watchword morning meeting, the prayer bands,[64] the evening service, the Sunday worship services, and the special event celebrations such as communion.

"Taking two young men with me to help row the boat, I made the five-mile trip up the Delaware River to Philadelphia several times to plead with the officials for needed supplies, especially firewood. Several other times, the Brethren made exploratory trips up and down the river to see if we could find a place to cut firewood. But no one would allow it. Each morning, some of our sisters went along with the boat when it crossed the Schuylkill River to the farm of Jacob Weiss. They milked his cows and returned with some milk to share among our many mouths. But it seems the supplies for so many soon run out, and again I must beg for more.

"So Brother Johannes, if the governor does grant that you can come

---

[64] *Bands* were small groups of believers meeting to share and pray. Men always met only with men, and women only with women. From the diaries, I would understand that this could mean only two men talking and praying together in a time of very close fellowship. —JGL

Under Attack in Philadelphia: 1763–1765

to the island to stay with us, we will share with you what we have, but it is always in short supply. Perhaps you and your family will be better off to stay in Philadelphia and let Friend Israel look out for your needs.

"On the other hand, if you come to us, we will have much time to share with you more about the Savior. You can also enjoy the riches of fellowship with other Delawares and Mohicans who have given up their homes for the Savior's sake. When Brother Grube and his wife held blessed prayer bands in preparation for communion, the brothers and sisters emptied their hearts about how it was to leave Nain and Nazareth. A few said it was very hard for them in the beginning to leave their nice homes, but now they are totally free, and they are happy that they can sleep peacefully again and eat their bread without fear. And they are happy that the Savior has sustained them peacefully and blessedly up to now.

"Brother Johannes, I do not know how you are going to answer the governor, nor can I tell you what is best to do. I can only say that if you are able to come and be with the other captives on Province Island, we can bear the Lamb's reproach together as the Savior also suffered for us.

"But, Brother Johannes, remember there is much evil in the world. We do not struggle against the governor or the Paxton Boys or the Scotch-Irish. We wrestle against Satan and all his evil spirits. Whatever you decide, remember when you talk to the governor that the Lamb is the Prince of Peace. And it is only through the Prince of Peace that we will overcome all evil."

A Statement to the Governor

I remembered Brother David's advice when Easy Tongue and I met with the governor and his Council in the State House on 1 December

UNDER ATTACK

1763. This is part of what I, the recently baptized Indian preacher, told the recently appointed Governor Penn:

Brothers:

We desire to use our mutual endeavors to live in friendship together. We can see very well, brothers, that the evil spirit stands between you and us, and as a result, we cannot see each other. Therefore we urge you to join us in our endeavors, that we may remove this evil spirit on one side. If you cannot remove him out of the way, we shall live but a miserable life.

You know and can see that we Indians are poor, weak, miserable people of ourselves, but if you join your endeavors to ours, we can remove the evil spirit out of the way.

You told us to remember how our forefathers and grandfathers did and the method they used to make friendship. You look but a little way, but I look further. I look as far back as the creation, when God Almighty first made us and placed a good spirit in our hearts.

Brothers:

I desire to see that you are endeavoring to live in friendship. We will do the same and use our endeavors to maintain peace. On the Susquehanna, four of my people lie dead, killed by your people. But I will overlook this fact and shall still use my endeavors to preserve our friendship.

I am very glad that I have heard from you. I am glad to find you have taken pity on me and spoken to me so kindly. I am now going to give an answer to your message you sent me by John Curtis.

I am glad to hear your speeches. I am here at present, but I myself can scarcely determine which way to turn or

Under Attack in Philadelphia: 1763-1765

how to lead my family, but I will let you know which way I think to remove. I shall go away to Sir William Johnson, among his Indians, where they hold treaties of friendship. I, therefore, deliver you this belt, as other Indians used to do, to let you know my mind.[65]

We have now said all we have to say.

Quakers or Moravians?

After the visit with Governor Penn and his Council on 1 December 1763, Easy Tongue and I returned to Bethlehem to await the governor's answer. At Bethlehem, we found that the sheltering of our Indian wives and children made life very difficult for the Brethren. Many from the surrounding community publicly threatened to destroy the entire town if they did not rid themselves of the Wyalusing Indians. So my band and I left Bethlehem and journeyed to Philadelphia. There, we again trusted ourselves into the care of the Quakers under the guiding hand of the King of the Quakers.

Easy Tongue visited some of his Delaware friends on Province Island. When he returned to Philadelphia, he reported to me that one day the refugees had received thirteen cords of firewood, and it took nearly a whole day for the Indians to carry all of it from the wharf to the house. Everyone was very thankful.

The joy over the wood supply was dampened the next day by a surprise disappointment. After the morning service, the sisters had gone with the boat, as they had done every morning in the past, to Jacob Weiss's farm to milk their cows. When they arrived that morning,

---

[65] Job Chilloway then presented Governor Penn a belt of seven rows.

UNDER ATTACK

however, the cows had all been herded to Philadelphia to be sold. No one knew why they were sold.

Easy Tongue also reported that Brother David had told the refugees that, for the time being, they must suspend their trips to the city to go shopping. The people are angry again.

The bright spot in Easy Tongue's report was the worship services. In the evening, the captives had a most blessed service from the Daily Text,[66] "For our conversation is in heaven." At midday, Brother Grube preached, "I have a desire to leave and be with Christ, which is far better."

The teaching of Brother Zeisberger tugged at my heart. I longed to be near him once again where I could learn the way of the Savior more perfectly. Then I thought of my wife, Rhodendrun, and our two daughters, Lirio and Nandina, hidden among the Quakers in Philadelphia. What would be best for them? They were not yet committed to the Savior. How would they fare on a long journey through the cold to Many Children Johnson and life among the traitorous Mohawks?

Who would Lirio and Nandina marry? Would they marry Mohawks or Munsees or Mohicans? Would they marry warriors? I shuddered. That settled it. I made up my mind. If possible, I would send my wife and daughters to join the Christian prisoners on Province Island.

While I waited in Philadelphia for the governor's answer, I visited Brother Renatus in the stone prison. Renatus' father, the patriarch Jacob, also visited him the same day. Both of them assured me that Renatus had been at the mission when Captain Bull's raiding party attacked Stenton's Inn. Brother Renatus showed Brother Johannes the children's books that he spent much of his time poring over.

Then poor Renatus—huge, scarred, and tough warrior that he had once been—broke down and wept. "Why cannot I be with my wife and the others on Province Island?" he sobbed. "Why must I be locked in

---

[66] The Moravians used the same Daily Text in all their worldwide missions.

Under Attack in Philadelphia: 1763-1765

with these mean people? Where is the Savior? Can He not deliver me from this prison as He delivered Peter?"

I tried to console poor Renatus. "I am going to see Governor Penn in the next day or two, and I will put in a plea for you," I promised.

The Governor Speaks

On 10 December, three Indians from Wyalusing, the Nanticoke John Curtis, the Delaware Job Chilloway, and I as Munsee representative, met with John Penn and his Council. Governor Penn addressed us thus:

> Brethren, you have behaved like persons who are sensible of the engagements they are under, to perform faithfully all that they have promised in their public treaties of peace and friendship.
>
> Were we to enumerate the particular cruelties and barbarous murders committed against our inhabitants, it would astonish you. But since you have told us you are determined to forget everything of this nature, and we see by your good speeches you have pleasant dispositions, we shall not, on our part, mention any of these disagreeable matters again. By this string we bury them and cover them out of sight.
>
> I now address myself to Papunhank. Brother Papunhank, you and our other brethren at Wyalusing should consider and advise what method would be best for protecting you and all other Indians who are against the war and desirous that there should be mutual good

UNDER ATTACK

> understanding between us and everything else that characterizes good friends.
>
> I, therefore, now request you to let me know what you think should be done in this matter which will not admit of longer delay. Likewise, tell me, if you can, who these enemy Indians are who are committing the present ravages and murders upon the frontiers; and as I look upon you to be my friend, I desire you will open your heart very freely to me, and tell me what are their reasons for so doing.

My counselors and I then retired for half an hour to consider what answer I should give to the governor's questions. When we returned, I spoke as follows:

> Brother, I can scarcely find what to say in answer to you. As to my own part, I cannot answer for the behavior of any of the Indians who live to the westward at and about Allegheny, and in the Seneca country. What I know is chiefly respecting some of the Delawares and Munsees. As for us and the few Indians in my neighborhood who speak a common language, the Delawares and Munsees, I know their minds.
>
> Since the last war, when we entered into our treaties of friendship, we, the Indians on this side Allegheny, thoroughly purged ourselves and buried all the blood that had been spilled.
>
> After the English built the forts and garrisoned them, the Indians became uneasy, and they and the English began to kill each other. We intended to live in friendship, agreeable to our treaties. Yet whenever our people went hunting, they were killed by the soldiers.

Under Attack in Philadelphia: 1763–1765

After the friendly and good speeches were delivered at the treaties, we on the Susquehanna were inclined to live at peace with the English on the strength of those friendly speeches. We went trading and hunting toward the Allegheny, and the soldiers there, not knowing our good intentions, killed our people. Later, some of the Indians at Allegheny came and fell on the people on the frontiers. This provoked your soldiers at Fort Augusta and Fort Allen to kill some of our Indians, who are your friends.

It gives me pleasure to tell my mind to my brother, the governor, as he has spoken so favorably and kindly to me. Brother, I will now acquaint you with what I have heard with my own ears, and not from hearsay. The Indians say that even though the English have entered into a treaty of peace, their people still continue to kill our people. They do not understand this conduct, and are therefore determined to strike the English themselves. If after they have struck them, the English declare themselves willing to live in friendship, we shall then believe them.

Now I will tell you what a company of the Munsee warriors who are now striking you said to me on my coming away. "Now brothers, you are going down among our brethren, the English. All the warriors should be very glad to know whether the English treat you kindly or not, and how you are used."

And now, Brother, I am exceedingly obliged to you that you have received me so kindly and spoken so favorably to me. I should be glad if you will let me return to the Indian country that I may let the Indians there know how kindly I have been received and that I may make them acquainted with what you have said on those two things.

UNDER ATTACK

In order to do this, I desire you will convey me safely through the inhabitants.

You desire to know in what manner we and those friendly Indians we have left behind proposed to live in security. We now tell you that we have not any better method to take for the security of all such Indians as are kindly disposed to you, than to invite them in as you have done to us. The message you sent us on this account by John Curtis was not delivered to us in the manner you mentioned. If it had been delivered in the proper manner so that we could have considered this matter in our Council, we should have done it, but it was not.

Brother, you desired me to inform you what steps can be taken to secure our friendly Indians from being hurt by your warriors. For my part, I cannot think of any, and I desire your advice and assistance; particularly, that you will not suffer any of your young men or soldiers to hurt the Nanticoke, Newoleka, or any of his people. He is your hearty friend and was one of the first Indians to take hold of the belt of friendship after the last war.

Because of your kind treatment toward me, I have laid open my heart to you and informed you of all that I have heard. Now, Brother, I desire you will take pity on me, and not confine me in your jail on account of false reports or stories that you may hear, as you have done to one of our brethren, Renatus, who is even now confined here. I am very glad to find the governor takes pleasure in hearing me, and thank him for it. I have now finished what I had to say.[67]

---

[67] *Minutes of the Provincial Council of Pennsylvania*, Vol. 9, p. 86.

Under Attack in Philadelphia: 1763-1765

But I was not yet finished. After delivering my answer to Governor Penn's message, I made no move to leave the chamber. After an awkward silence, Governor Penn asked me if I had more to say or whether I was ready to leave. I then, in a dignified way, replied that I would like to whisper in the governor's ear. After some hesitation, my request was granted, and the governor, Easy Tongue, a guard, and I all retired to another room.

"Let us speak plainly and not with a forked tongue," I told the governor. "You asked that I tell you the names of those who commit ravages and murders upon the frontiers. Since you are young and new as governor, you may not know what has happened. I will tell you who some of these savages are. It is the Paxton Black Boys and your own Paxton Rangers who commit these demonic ravages. They pretend to be savages by disguising themselves as Indians, and savages they truly are.

"After Pennsylvania and Sir William Johnson made clear peace treaties with Teedyuscung, they robbed and murdered him and burned the entire village. It was these same white savages who murdered and destroyed the Connecticut settlers in Wyoming. This same people committed numerous robberies and murders against the Indians, and yet your people never punished any of them.

"You asked me to give you the names of those who attack you. I will give you a name. It was Lieutenant Jonathan Dodge at Fort Allen who robbed and killed my four Indians from Wyalusing.[68] If you really desire peace, you must treat those accused of killing innocent Indians the same as you treat Indians accused of killing a white man.

"Release Renatus, or imprison Lieutenant Dodge. Then you will prove that your heart and your mouth dwell in the same house. I promise you that the warring Indians who await my return will open their ears and gladly lay down their hatchets if you prove that the

---

[68] C. Hale Sipe, *Indian Wars of Pennsylvania*, p. 456.

UNDER ATTACK

Pennsylvania government will protect them. But if your people continue to kill and murder innocent Indians, even the Iroquois will rise against you."

Governor Penn listened carefully to me. I studied his clean-shaven face, his bobbed hair, his mild blue eyes, his dominant Penn nose, his tightly wound white neck scarf, and the gold embroidered on his scarlet coat. Was the governor honest and sincere, or naive and foolish? What would he say?

His mild and pleasant manner masked his intentions when he responded. "Thank you for the information. I will take all of it into consideration. As I said, you and your people may join the Indians on Province Island. There you will be under my government's protection. But if you choose to remain at Wyalusing or go west or north, you will be seen as joining the enemy.

"I cannot release Renatus. See that you tell no man that you have made the accusations you shared with me today, or you may be accused of treason and imprisoned with Renatus."

Thus ended my whisper in the governor's ear.

"Do you see, Brother John?" asked Glikkikan, pausing in his retelling of Papunhank's own words. "Governor Penn would not punish those Whites who murdered and stole. He had no interest in seeing justice done. Renatus was held in prison while known white killers continued at liberty. His grandfather, the great Miquon, would have done differently.

"It is the same today. Dr. Connolly punishes none of the killers of Indians. Rather, he encourages those who kill Indians, he beats the drum, and he does the war dance."

Under Attack in Philadelphia: 1763–1765

"You forget about our friends," I objected. "Gibson, Anderson, Elliott, Croghan, and Mckee are trying to make peace and prevent war."

Glikkikan snorted. "So they are. Our friends," he continued sourly, "do not want the Virginians to have the Indian lands. They want them for themselves and for Pennsylvania. And when the armies march in to destroy the Indians, our 'friends' will unite with the worst white killers in both armies to destroy the Indians. Is it not true?

"Brother Isaac, I must tell you again, not all Whites are evil. God controls the armies, and in evil times we must look to Him for deliverance. He is our rock and a very present help in time of trouble. Did He not deliver Papunhank from the Paxton Rangers? Now let us hear how God worked to preserve the Brethren while they were in Philadelphia."

Life on the Island

In the words of Johannes Papunhank

Two days later I met briefly with Brother Zeisberger and Brother Grube in Philadelphia. Supplies on Province Island were again running dangerously low, and they had come to the city to beg Mr. Fox[69] for more provisions. After the two had made their visit, I, my wife Rhodendrun, our children Lirio and Nandina, and two old men went along to the island when Brother Grube returned. The six of us had to share a single room, since it was the only space left for us newcomers.

The next day Brother Zeisberger arrived with a boat from the city. On board were three cords of wood, ten barrels of salt meat,

---

[69] Joseph Fox was appointed by the Pennsylvania Assembly to look after the needs of the Indians under the protection of the government.

UNDER ATTACK

five barrels of cod fish, 2,200 pounds of flour, and two kegs of rice. Almost everyone rejoiced, but a few grumbled over the distribution of the provisions. It didn't seem fair to them that the newcomers should get a portion equal to those of people who had been on the island the past month.

After the morning service the next day, Brother Zeisberger and Brother Schmick gathered all the adults together and gave them an earnest reminder that they must be grateful for what God has provided and must share with everyone.

The night of 14 December was unusually cold and stormy. After Brother David held the morning service, both he and Brother Schmick went to Philadelphia, hoping to secure more provisions and wood. That same day seven more Nanticokes came from the city to stay with us.

The Nanticokes brought frightful news. The day before at daybreak, amid sleet and snow, the Paxton Boys raided Conestoga Manor and murdered all six of the Indians present and burned their cabins. The other fourteen Conestogas were placed in the Lancaster jail "for their protection."

I sadly shook my head. "Except for the grace of God, it could easily have been us," I told the others. "The Paxton Boys have no scruples over murder of any kind for any purpose. If I have discerned the governor's heart rightly, the murderers will not be punished for this devilish killing. Oh, he will make some fair speeches and wipe away a few tears from Iroquois eyes so as not to excite them, but the murderers will not be punished. And I predict that the fourteen Conestogas in the Lancaster jail had better prepare to die. The Paxton Boys will return."

I found life on Province Island to be quite different. Now I could drink in the spiritual teaching of my beloved Brothers Zeisberger, Schmick, and Grube. And I could observe how they dealt with so many people living so closely together. Rhodendrun, Lirio, and

Under Attack in Philadelphia: 1763-1765

Nandina all loved the companionship of Sister Schmick and Sister Grube, who shared the prisoners' hardships.

With my band of Delawares from Wyalusing and the Nanticokes who had also come from the Susquehanna, the number of Indians on Province Island under the protection of the government now numbered more than 140. The supply situation became even more critical, so on 19 December, Brother Zeisberger again went to Philadelphia to beg for more wood and provisions. The next day our dear Brother David returned with thirty pairs of shoes.

A couple of disobedient young men went over the borders to the neighbors on the rest of Province Island to drink alcohol. Brother Grube then went to the entire neighborhood and asked the people not to admit any Indians or to give them any strong drink. All of the neighbors agreed to this.

On 21 December, Brother David and I held a heartfelt band.[70] Brother David then left Province Island and carried the sincere greetings of everyone to the church at Bethlehem.

After the evening service, the room overseers came together to speak earnestly with the disobedient young men about their souls. Abraham repented immediately and begged for forgiveness, but Phillipus did not ask for forgiveness until the next day. The sick Sister Verona said today, "Ah, if only the Savior would soon take me to Him. I am so tired of living here."

On 22 December, Brother Schmick took four Indian brothers to Philadelphia to buy a few necessary things. Everyone was uneasy about their safety in the city, but the next day they all returned without harm.

On Christmas Eve, Brother Schmick held a love feast with the children in which he told with feeling the story of the Savior's birth.

---

[70] *Bands* as used here refers to an intense period of sharing and prayer among very close friends.

UNDER ATTACK

The children then sang several pretty verses to the little Jesus child, while young Joshua played the spinet and Elias played the citter.[71] I observed that our older daughter, Lirio, seemed quite taken in by the music. Or was it the talented young spinet player, Joshua, who held her black eyes? I liked the thought of Lirio marrying a Christian from among the Mohicans.

Afterward, the adults had their love feast with wafers and tea. Brother Grube spoke from the Daily Text. Finally, we all kneeled before our most dear Jesus, thanked Him from our hearts for His painful birth and incarnation, and then Brother Grube recommended us all to His faithful heart.

On Christmas Day, Brother Schmick held the holiday service over the message of the angels. In the afternoon, there was a children's hour, and in the evening, Brother Grube held the service about the Daily Text, "Blessed are the poor."

The short supplies continually pressed down upon the captives. Mr. Fox, the government supply agent, sent twenty-five pairs of shoes to us as a present. We were very happy about this, as some of us were going barefoot. Brother Grube and I traveled four miles downstream to Galloway Island to see if there was any firewood to be had there. We returned empty-handed.

The Paxton Boys Strike

Then the real storm broke. My prophecy was right. We captives received word that the Paxton Boys rode into Lancaster, broke into the jail, and murdered, dismembered, and scalped the remaining fourteen

---

[71] A spinet resembles a piano but plucks the string instead of hitting it with a hammer. A citter was likely a cithara, an ancient precursor of the zither that resembled a lyre.

Under Attack in Philadelphia: 1763–1765

Conestoga Indians, three couples and their eight children. Worse yet, the brazen murderers vowed to come to Province Island and kill all the Indians there.

Our hearts failed us from fear, and we spent a restless night. But the next morning Brother Grube spoke from the Daily Text: "And the peace of God, which passes all understanding will guard your hearts and your minds in Christ Jesus."[72] We were somewhat comforted.

All Philadelphia was in an uproar over the murders. Several Nanticoke Indians came from Philadelphia seeking refuge, but because they brought no official letters, Brother Schmick and Brother Grube sent them back to the city.

At midnight, two boats came to the island from Philadelphia with a letter from Mr. Fox indicating that everyone should be brought away quickly by water. The Irish Rebels had come down from Lancaster County in order to kill all the Indians. The leaders woke everyone and told them they should make ready to leave the island at once. Everyone got ready the best they could at such an hour, but all were quite dismayed. Brother Schmick and Brother Grube sought to console the refugees with today's Daily Text: "For you alone, O Lord, make me dwell in safety." After a few hours, a messenger on horseback arrived from Philadelphia with letters from Mr. Fox concerning the flight.

As soon as the morning service was over the following day, everyone was busy with packing, and each hour they expected orders to go on board. The people who had come to assist them with the boat kept watch. At midday, Brother Marshall, the Moravian mission board representative to the Penn government, came from Bethlehem and brought pleasing letters, along with the new Daily Texts for next year. Several influential men from the city and even a colonel and two captains visited during the day.

[72] Philippians 4:7

UNDER ATTACK

Friend Israel, the King of the Quakers, also came. He assured me, "Friend Johannes, the government will do everything that can be done to help secure the safety of the captives."

Despite such assurances, all were uneasy, and the men kept diligent watch throughout the night. Soon after Brother Grube held the morning service, an express came from Mr. Fox with the news that the rebels were only twelve miles from Province Island in great numbers. He ordered that the refugees should retreat immediately on the three boats that had been sent for that purpose.

We managed to get everyone on board in a quarter of an hour, but we had to leave most of our belongings behind. We took flight to Leek Island, three miles from Province Island, where we laid anchor and waited for further orders. The wintry air chilled everyone to the bone while we huddled there without fire or hot drinks to warm us.

In a few hours, some gentlemen came and brought a letter from the governor to Brothers Schmick and Grube:

> His Honor, the governor, has ordered me to report to you that the alarm that we heard this morning—the rebels were said to be on their way to Province Island—has been found to be false. Therefore the governor's desire is that you will go back to the house on Province Island immediately. As soon as possible, a certain protection will be sent there to protect you against all attacks.
> - Joseph Shippen

As soon as Brother Schmick and Grube read the letter to us, we gladly hoisted the anchors and began the journey back to Province Island. We arrived home at 3:00 that afternoon and were soon enjoying fires, warm food and drinks, and another chance to rest in peace.

Brother Schmick held the evening service at the close of this

Under Attack in Philadelphia: 1763-1765

remarkable year. His Daily Text was, "The Lord is my strength and shield; my heart trusted in Him." In the service, everyone kneeled and thanked Jesus, tearfully begging Him for forgiveness for everything. The communion that had been planned for that day could not happen because of the commotion of flight.

I thus closed the year in a refugee camp. In only one year, I, Papunhank, had moved from being a Delaware preacher and chief trying to live at peace with the English, to become a baptized member of a Moravian sect. I had left my earthly home and fled to this strange place, completely alien to the life I had lived at Wyalusing. Even so, I found a sense of great calmness in my soul to be under the guidance of teachers who gave themselves so readily to helping their converts, and because I was able to be with others of my people who had also found the Savior precious. All the refugees seemed to hold a complete confidence that the Savior would make everything in the coming year bearable to them with His nearness.

It was good we did not know how much grace we would need in 1764. On the very first day of the new year, Mr. Fox and two other gentlemen from the city visited us and assured everyone that there was no more danger. The three large boats we had used yesterday were to remain at our disposal, and Governor Penn promised that if he should hear something, he would let us know immediately so that we could instantly board the boats and flee.

Israel Pemberton, Jr., the valiant Friend, also sent a message to us through Easy Tongue, saying, "The Indians can all be dispersed among the Quakers in the city. The Quakers will shelter them."

Easy Tongue returned to the city with the following answer to the message. "We wish to remain together under the protection of the Penn government; if it cannot protect us, we prefer to suffer together."

The second day of the new year was also difficult. Brother Zeisberger arrived with a message from Brother Marshall of the mission board.

UNDER ATTACK

The Quakers, through Friend Valiant, made a proposal to transport all the refugees to Nantucket Island where only Quakers live. Since there is no wood on the island, the Quakers support themselves by fishing.

I shook my head. "No trees, no hunting! Will not the dear Father show us some other way that we can be together and still dwell in security?" We declined the kind offer right away.

In the evening, Brother Schmick held a blessed service over the Daily Text, "Majesty and power are due you, magnificence, victory, and thanks be unto our God. For everything in heaven and earth is yours. You are the ruler of all things."[73]

On the third day of January, the blessed Savior allowed the communicants to go ahead with the *Abendmahl*—the love feast of the communicants, the public confession and absolution of sin, and then the blessed taste of the body and blood of the Lord.[74] The participants thanked the Lord with tears for the great blessing, as they had despaired of ever enjoying the "Great Thing." Only the Lord knows if they will ever have such a blessed day again.

I, as well as many other refugees not yet considered communicants, watched quietly during all the services of the day. The guards were amazed at the devotion of the teachers who held so many services and took such special care of all the Indians.

Once again, many birds sang evil rumors, and I pointed out, "The governor is not doing a very good job of putting down evil on his side. He has offered a scalp bounty if someone brings in the leaders of the murderers of the Conestoga Indians. Not likely," I remarked. "Where are the soldiers and the sheriffs who imprisoned Renatus? They could go get the murderers and bring them in if they wanted to."

---

[73] Although not an exact translation of the German text, I believe the text was based on 1 Chronicles 29:10-13.
[74] The German word *Abendmahl* included all three aspects detailed in the sentence (Love Feast, Absolution, and Communion).

Under Attack in Philadelphia: 1763-1765

Deported

Everyone was very uneasy throughout the day. Toward evening, Brother David Zeisberger returned with the disturbing news that the captives were no longer safe on Province Island and that we must go away yet that night to Philadelphia. From thence, Governor Penn planned to send us to Many Children Johnson, the Indian agent in New York.[75]

We all packed our things together, taking only what we needed for an emergency, and we set out at midnight. Brother and Sister Schmick and their child remained on Province Island and planned to join us in the morning with the rest of the luggage. We crossed the river in the three boats to a farmer's land. There, Brothers Ludwig and Jacob Weiss were waiting to assist us onward on our journey. They loaded a cart and wagon with the blind, the sick, the children, Sister Grube, and some luggage. The rest of us tramped though the frigid air for five miles until we arrived in Philadelphia.

Our procession moved so quietly through the city that the guards scarcely noticed us. Thus, with little undue attention, we arrived at the Brethren's meetinghouse at 7:00 in the morning. The Philadelphia Brethren provided us with a love feast, and Commissioner Fox, when he saw our condition, immediately provided thirty more blankets. We rested about an hour at the meetinghouse before beginning the journey to New York.

We had to leave Renatus's wife, Geschee, in Philadelphia, as she was very heavy with child and birthed a son shortly after we left. Her mother, Jamitz, stayed with her. The patriarch Jacob, Renatus's father,

---

[75] Sir William Johnson was the Royal Northern Indian Agent. He is said to have fathered over a hundred children, most of them from Indian women, and amassed a very large fortune in land. He favored the Iroquois to give them supremacy over other Indian nations.

UNDER ATTACK

also took his leave from the group with many tears. He did not want to leave his son alone in prison, and he also realized the journey would be too much for him. The rest of us loaded the sick, the old, and the children, along with the necessary baggage, onto four wagons.

By this time, however, a crowd of people had assembled so that the refugees could barely force their way through. The crowd cursed and reviled us in a dreadful manner, but we were able to get through without receiving any personal injury.

The terrible harassment continued until Captain Robinson with seventy Highlanders arrived to accompany our caravan. The crowd then dispersed, but a new problem developed. The soldiers cut quite a shine, dressed in their pleated kilts, red and white socks, polished shoes, red coats, dark blue sashes, and white packs. They carried their long guns as though they were on parade, acted quite wild, and harassed the young women.

My two young daughters, Lirio and Nandina, drew special attention from the marching young soldiers. Easy Tongue and I stepped up our pace till we marched alongside Captain Robinson. "We are very grateful for your protection on this journey," I told him. "The mob nearly tore us apart before we got out of Philadelphia."

"Aye," the captain responded, "it is a pleasant task to be of some service. This soldiering is often a grimy business when one must leave his manners and morals in England. Take these Highlander boys. They're far from their beloved Scotland, lonely, and without much purpose in life. They endure long periods of rough camping in these God-forsaken woods and hellish forts. I ask myself why they endure it. Is it for the hope of a good fight with the skulking savages that may pounce upon them at any moment and then slip stealthily away? But why should I be telling you how or why the godless savages fight? I am told that from birth onward they are taught to love war, murder, and

Under Attack in Philadelphia: 1763–1765

torture. Bravery in war is the way the men prove their manhood and attract the women. Is it not so?"

Captain Robinson eyed his marching companions thoughtfully, called a halt, and then glanced backward over his whistling and catcalling troops. "They're some of the King's bravest and best soldiers," he said proudly. Things quieted down somewhat, and after a brief rest, he signaled for the company to move forward once again. Captain Robinson encouraged his thoughtful, attentive listeners to stay with him on the march and then continued his soliloquy.

"Or do these young men fight for the sake of a few crowns that may wind up in the hands of some English lord or the Penn family? Or could it be that they are enduring all this in the hopes of getting fifty acres of unclaimed land? As a captain, I can get three thousand acres of this wilderness. But do I want it?" Captain Robinson drew his lips together and shook his head contemptuously.

"Captain Robinson, has your regiment been fighting in the West?" I asked. Easy Tongue translated for me.

"Aye, the Highlanders lost a number of good men at Bushy Run, but that crafty little Swisser, Colonel Bouquet, outdid the savages and beat them at their own game. Then our regiment came east and was stationed at Lancaster for the winter until the governor asked General Gage for British troops to help him in Philadelphia. After the affair on Sideling Hill and the Conestoga murders, he didn't trust his crude Royal Americans and Paxton Rangers to obey his government any more.

"So now the governor has the best of the best British troops, the Scottish Highlanders, marching along to protect you and yours," Captain Robinson added proudly. Then he switched to his thoughtful mood again.

"The Conestoga murders in the Lancaster jail should never have happened. There were plenty of rumors that the Paxton Boys were

UNDER ATTACK

coming to murder the fourteen prisoners. My Highlanders and I were stationed in Lancaster, and I offered to guard the jail, but Edward Shippen, the chief magistrate, forbade me to do so.[76] Oh, how my Highlanders would have loved a good fight with those Paxton cowards! Breaking into the jail and scalping babies, children, and defenseless adults! How low can they get? I say they're cowards of the lowest class. If we had been there, we wouldn't need to be escorting you to New York today."

I thanked Captain Robinson for the protection of his special soldiers on the march and then dropped back into place to march alongside my family. The soldiers gradually tired of their harassment of the maidens, and by dusk, the tired refugees arrived at Bristol. Since leaving Province Island at midnight, we had traveled twenty-five miles.

The soldiers immediately went to inns, but we could not go there. Half of the party found some places in the Quaker meetinghouse, while others had to crawl up in a hayloft. The sick and blind lodged in a cooper's shop where they were provided with some bread and cheese that the captives had brought along.

Truth Censored

Mr. Fox and Mr. Logan, two of the governor's counselors, met the captives at Bristol and delivered the governor's surprising orders: "Papunhank and his family must return to Philadelphia."[77]

---

[76] Kevin Kenny, *Peaceable Kingdom Lost*, p. 141.

[77] The diaries place the delivery of the governor's surprise recall to Brother Johannes at Bristol. The Moravian diary certainly sounds as though Johannes Papunhank and his family returned at once to Philadelphia by unknown means from Bristol. This is more than a whole day before Mr. Logan and Mr. Fox delivered the message from the governor to the refugees at Trenton and then returned to Philadelphia. Thus, Brother Johannes' forced return to Philadelphia makes it quite certain that Governor Penn did not want Papunhank present when his speech was read to the other exiles nor when the captives delivered his message to Sir William Johnson.

Under Attack in Philadelphia: 1763–1765

The governor sent me and my family to the German enclave of Frankfurt.[78] Our conditions there did not outwardly appear bad. Our brusque hosts provided us with ample German food and enough wood to stay warm. However, they spoke no Delaware, and we spoke no German and little English. Without Easy Tongue present to translate for us, our family was shut off from the outside world.

The terms of our orders were to remain within the house and not appear in public. I did not really want to be seen outside, as I remembered quite well Gabriel's story of the murderous hostility toward the captives as they passed through Germantown. Nor had we forgotten the threats and curses heaped upon us by the mob on our march through the streets of Philadelphia. If the soldiers had not come, who knows what might have happened? To lie low in Frankfurt was better than to helplessly suffer the Conestogas' fate.

Truth Out of Lies

During the long, housebound days, I wondered repeatedly why the governor had recalled us, but I never found a certain answer. After three tedious, anxious weeks in confinement without any contact with our friends, a government official brought strange news to us. "The governor of New York has forbidden the captives to set one foot in New York. Therefore the refugees have returned to Philadelphia and are housed in the English barracks with the soldiers instead of on Province Island. Would you and your family like to rejoin them there?"

I did not hesitate for one minute. "Yes, we want to rejoin the captives

---

[78] The location of Frankfurt was on the northeast corner of Philadelphia, some six miles from City Center. William Penn sold the land for the town to a German company, The Frankfurt Company, on his founding visit to his colony. Today, this suburb of Philadelphia is called Frankford.

UNDER ATTACK

in the barracks as soon as possible," I told the official. On 29 January 1764, Brother Schmick came to Frankfurt and brought me, Papunhank, along with Rhodendrun, Lirio, and Nandina back to Philadelphia where we could again be with our friends. We could barely contain our joy at again being with our own troubled people. Many hugs and kisses passed between us, and the deep feelings stirred by hearing our own Delaware tongue freely spoken brought forth many tears.

I could not wait to talk with Easy Tongue. A lot of questions and thoughts went through my head during three weeks of isolation. I still wanted to know why Governor Penn had recalled me and my family and held us in Frankfurt. Perhaps Easy Tongue had some answers.

Easy Tongue was glad to tell me what happened during our forced stay in Germantown. "When Mr. Fox and Mr. Logan brought you the governor's orders to return to Philadelphia, they also carried another message from the governor for the captives to deliver to Many Children Johnson. But they did not deliver the message the next sunrise.

"Instead, the soldiers rousted us out early and marched us from Bristol, Pennsylvania, to Trenton, New Jersey, in the cold.[79] Each of us received only three ship's biscuits to live on for the whole day. Mr. Fox was supposed to be the one who supplied our needs, and although he was nearby, he failed to help us.

"We arrived at the Delaware River in the afternoon, but it was so full of ice that it took the soldiers two hours to get across while we stood around in the cold and awaited our turn. We stayed that night in the same barracks as the soldiers, but we had to wait a long time before we could have some firewood to warm ourselves with. The soldiers got all their needs supplied first.

"The next sunrise, while we stood outside in the frigid air, Mr.

---

[79] A distance of twelve to fifteen miles depending on the route.

Under Attack in Philadelphia: 1763-1765

Logan read the governor's long message, complete with kerchiefs, match coats, and wampum belts. Brother David Zeisberger translated the message for the Delawares, and Joshua Sr. translated it for the Mohicans.

"Here is what the governor's message said:

> Brethren, I should have been pleased to have had the opportunity of speaking to you before you went out of town, but the great hurry you were obliged to move in, to accompany Captain Robinson, prevented me. I therefore desired Mr. Logan to go with you part of the way and take the first opportunity of delivering you my message. I request you to attend to that message closely and deliver it to the Indians who live near General Johnson as well as those in the Six Nations country.

"Mr. Logan then presented a string of wampum before giving us the message the governor wanted us to deliver.

> You well know that there has always been a fixed agreement between us, that whenever any accident or evil befell either of us, we should take the first opportunity to inform each other of it. I now take this opportunity to send you a message by some of our brethren who are coming to you at their own request. It is with great sorrow I inform you that some of your people have, in the most cruel manner, murdered a great number of my people. These people have now returned to their settlements, and I am sure that you wanted to know about it.
>
> This unexpected, unexplained barbarity has so embittered the minds of their relations and friends who live on our frontiers that they formed themselves into a small body.

UNDER ATTACK

> They came down without my knowledge and have killed those Indians who lived at Connoytown near Conestoga, being twenty in all—men, women, and children.
>
> Their manner in coming down to that town was so sudden and private, that neither I, nor any of my Council knew of it till it was all over. Otherwise, I should have endeavored to prevent it.
>
> I am now taking all the measures in my power to expose the people who have committed the murders. I have issued my proclamation and offered a reward of 200 pounds for apprehending each man, that they may be put to death according to our laws. I desire you will find out and inform the relations of those Indians of what has happened to their friends, and the steps I am taking to bring the offenders to justice. I now send them twenty-one black strand matchcoats to cover their graves and twenty-one handkerchiefs to wipe the tears from their eyes.

"The matchcoats and the handkerchiefs were delivered. Then Logan resumed the governor's message to the Iroquois.

> Brethren, I allow that when anything of this sort happens on either side, it is very sorrowful and aggravating, but you must own that your unruly young men have been the first cause of all the troubles and murders which have happened since we made peace with each other.
>
> It is now about nine months since they first struck us near Pittsburgh without any cause given by my people, and many have since that time been cruelly killed. I therefore desire you will take the hatchet out of your young people's hands, and tell them that by their unwillingness to heed the

Under Attack in Philadelphia: 1763-1765

advice of their elders, they have brought all these troubles on themselves and us. Let what has passed be forgotten on both sides, and let the hatchet be buried so deep in the ground as to be out of the reach of your young men.

If you do this, we shall then live in peace and plenty as our forefathers used to do. To prove that I desire to live in peace with you, I send you this belt of wampum of seven rows.

Our brethren, the Indians who lived at Bethlehem, hearing of the death of their brethren at Conestoga, were very uneasy lest some mischief should also befall them. I have therefore, at their request, sent them under a guard of soldiers to New York, to go from there to General Johnson to live near him. All these Indians can inform you how kindly they have been treated here by me and my people, and our good dispositions toward them, and that the mischief which has lately happened must not be imputed to me nor any of my sober people, but to the angry young men on the frontiers whose relations have been killed by your Indians.

Our Brother Papunhank and the Indians who lived at Wyalusing, who had lately come down to live near me, are now gone to live with their friends in Jersey below Burlington. I have no doubt they will live there very happy, as the governor of the Jerseys has promised them his protection. I desire that you will, as soon as possible, inform the Nanticoke and Newoleka, who lives near Wyalusing, of this. Otherwise he might think some accident has befallen Papunhank. To assure you that what I have said is true, I give you this belt of six rows.[80]

[80] <http://bdhp.moravian.edu/personal...papers/letters/indians/1764governor.html>

UNDER ATTACK

I listened carefully to the governor's message. Then I told Easy Tongue, "I understand now why the governor sent me back to Frankfurt. His message had all these lies: that the Indians started the war without provocation, that the murder of the Conestoga Indians could not be helped, that he was doing all in his power to apprehend the murderers, that the captives were going to New York at their own request, that Papunhank and the other Mohicans were safely among their friends in New Jersey. And I am sure the governor did not want me along when his message was read to Many Children Johnson. He knew I would tell Many Children the truth.

"Now the captives have returned with the wampum belts, the matchcoats, and the kerchiefs, and the governor's message has never been read to Many Children Johnson. I am troubled. Neither has the governor ever given a reply to those warring Delawares who awaited a message from him. The Iroquois and the western Indians have heard nothing of what became of their brethren, the peaceable Indians.

"Easy Tongue, it is possible that hostile Indians will attack the settlements again in retaliation for the murder of the Conestogas and the disappearance of the peaceable Indians. Easy Tongue, will you go with me and carry a message to the western Indians? Perhaps further war may still be averted."

Glikkikan paused in his retelling of Papunhank's story and started pressing me again. "Brother John, why did Governor Penn knowingly tell lies? Why did he remove Papunhank from the captives before his officials read the message to them? Did his officials not know they were reading lies?"

"Sometimes government officials must tell lies to protect the people.

Under Attack in Philadelphia: 1763-1765

They have no choice," I replied.

"Then you would likewise excuse other people who tell lies for a good reason. Is that right?"

"No!" I answered. I am excusing no one who lies. I am just saying that government positions force people to lie. That is the very reason Christians do not hold positions in the government. That is not the Savior's work."

Life in the Barracks

In the words of Johannes Papunhank

Meanwhile, the uneasy life in the barracks went on. After Brother Schmick held the evening service, the officers posted a double watch for the night because they suspected trouble was lurking nearby.

On 30 January, Brother Grube preached a memorable sermon from the Daily Text: "And I will provide a place for my people Israel and will plant them so that they can have a home of their own and no longer be disturbed." There in the austere barracks kitchen, the sighs and the tears and the *"Kehelles"* gave vent to the deep yearnings of all hearts. How we longed to soon find a place of rest where we could again live in peace.

The Paxton Boys and their fellow rebels were getting ever bolder. The ones with a reward on their heads appeared regularly in public, but nothing was ever done to capture them. I did not believe the governor wanted to punish the Conestoga murderers. I said, "If Governor Penn really did want to capture the known leaders, he would send Captain Robinson and his Highlanders after the ones who have a

UNDER ATTACK

reward on their heads and bring them in."

To support my contention that Governor Penn was only brushing aside the Conestoga murders, I pointed out that the captives never had delivered the wampum belts and the silk cloths the honorable governor had commissioned them to take to the Six Nations. As a result, Brother Grube returned the belts and silk cloths to Mr. Logan, the governor's counselor who had given them to the refugees. In this manner, the governor was reminded that his message had never been delivered.

With all the hue and cry, I thought it urgent that the government should send a message to the hostile Indians lest they come to believe that all the captive Indians had been killed. I feared that if the message was not sent soon, warriors might attack the settlements again. In light of my concern, Brother Schmick and Ludwig Weiss drafted a letter for me to the honorable governor urging him to get a message to Indian land as soon as possible.

The confining, troublesome life in the barracks continued. Brother Grube held a short service for the fourteen widows in the group. Afterward, the widows held a love feast where they discussed the recent pilgrimage to Amboy. The old, blind Thamar and Hanna said, "We well remember the time when no houses stood at Amboy or Brunswick, and many hundreds of Indians lived there. Now there are hundreds of houses and no Indians."

After Brother Schmick held the morning service, each of the rooms received a fourth of a cord of wood. All were very grateful, as many rooms did not have even one stick of wood left.

By mingling with the soldiers and officers in the barracks, I learned that many of the soldiers stationed there had earlier been scattered among the western forts taken from the French. In the present war, the Indians have taken most of the forts, and the officers and soldiers alike told me that where they had been, there were so many Indians it would be impossible to wipe them out or bring them under the yoke.

Under Attack in Philadelphia: 1763-1765

On the afternoon of 4 February, fearful reports of a great mob marching toward Philadelphia from Lancaster reached the refugees. The rebels hoped to be joined by thousands in Philadelphia, who would then descend upon the barracks and kill all the Indians there.

The soldiers now mounted eight cannons and threw up breastworks in the middle of the square. Late that day, Captain Schlosser told the Indians that they should move to the second story with the soldiers because there were no locks on the doors if the barracks should be broken into. Great confusion resulted as the soldiers chased the Indians from one upstairs room to another until the refugees and the soldiers all had rooms.

Then a couple shots were fired in the dark outside the barracks, and everyone was alarmed while the soldiers made ready to fight. The captives had a hard time quieting their minds and getting to their rooms. They constantly reminded themselves of the Daily Text they had heard that day: "You shall not shout, or make your voice heard; neither shall any word go out of your mouth, until the day I tell you to shout. Then you shall shout.[81] The Lord will guide us, prepare the path, and with His eyes point to many things, if it be time to fight or if it be a day of rest."[82] We were openly saddened by the circumstances, but we turned to the dear Lord Himself for comfort.

We slept very little during that troubled night. The honorable governor himself visited us in our rooms at midnight and paid particular attention to the children. Two hundred citizens were also there for defense during the night, and they were replaced by others in the morning. Due to the unrest, we could not meet in our regular place for worship, but Brothers Grube and Schmick held services in the rooms.

The soldiers fired the eighteen-pound cannons, and the explosions

---

[81] Joshua 6:10
[82] 1764 Daily Text book hymn citation: 1208.

UNDER ATTACK

shattered some of the windows. The tremendous noise so close to the houses frightened us terribly, as most of us had never heard anything like it. With all the other uproar around us, we did not go outside our rooms that day.

At midnight, a great alarm was sounded. The bells of the city rang, and the citizenry awoke and went to the city hall, where it was announced that the rebels would be there at daybreak. Everyone took up arms and got ready to repel them. Two citizen companies, including many Quakers carrying arms, arrived at the barracks. Word came that a party of the rebels had arrived in Germantown, only six miles away. A peaceable and good man there, David Rittenhouse, sent an express to us describing the rebels:

> About fifty of the scoundrels marched past my workshop. I have seen hundreds of Indians traveling the country and can with truth affirm that the behavior of these fellows was ten times more savage and brutal than theirs. The Paxton Boys paraded through the streets and frightened the women by running the muzzles of their guns through windows, swearing and hallooing. They attacked men without provocation, dragged them by their hair, and pretended to scalp them. They also shot numerous dogs and fowls.

The express also carried a description of the rebel forces by an anonymous writer who claimed to be a Quaker. He estimated the rebels to be about three hundred in number rather than the fifteen hundred rumored to be advancing on Philadelphia.

> This "formidable body of forces" consists principally of a set of fellows, dressed in blanket coats and moccasins, like our Indian traders or back-country wagoners. They are armed with rifles and tomahawks, and some of them

Under Attack in Philadelphia: 1763-1765

have a brace of pistols besides.

Amid all the hubbub, Brother Grube and Brother Schmick comforted us with the Daily Text: "Nothing can hinder the Lord from saving, whether by many or by few."[83]

The next day, 7 February, the brothers again held services in the rooms and spoke about the beautiful text for the day: "Hitherto hath the Lord helped us."[84] Then Brother Schmick prayed, "Oh, now let Him continue to do so."

Now we again heard rumors that the rebels were advancing. The city bells called the citizens together, and the soldiers mounted four more cannons in front of the house and loaded them with grapeshot.

When the rebels understood the punishments promised them if they advanced further, they halted and met with a government delegation headed by Ben Franklin. The rioters insisted that the government was sheltering in the barracks Indians who had been seen at Fort Pitt and other places. Because of this and other accusations, the rebels wanted all Indians turned over to them.

To prove this claim false, Franklin's delegation agreed that a Paxton man in the company of Commissioner Huse would visit the barracks and see if he could find any Indians against whom he could lay specific charges. The hostile ruffian came into the barracks with Mr. Huse and inspected everyone closely, but he could find no one he recognized. Then the rebels made the charge that the Quakers were sheltering six guilty Indians in the city. Even the officers of the soldiers asked me if this accusation was true. I said, "It certainly is not." Brother Grube and Brother Schmick, with the aid of the records, then proved this charge to also be false.

While the rebels negotiated with Mr. Franklin, they raided the place

---

[83] 1 Samuel 14:6
[84] 1 Samuel 7:12

UNDER ATTACK

in Frankfurt where my family and I had been staying when the rest of the Indians had traveled to Amboy and back. Thankfully, I was not there. Because the Paxton Boys made threats against Mr. Fox and Friend Pemberton, the two men left the city for the Jerseys.

Finally, the rebels disbanded and went back home. The tension eased, and everyone was pleased that the matter had been concluded without bloodshed. But even after the rebels disbanded, we still had many problems.

While Renatus languished in prison awaiting his trial, his aged father, Jacob, the only remaining patriarch from Shekomeko, died of the smallpox and was laid to rest. Then Renatus's wife, Geschee, went blessedly to the Savior from the pox. Renatus wept much. Then his baby son, little Jacob, was kissed home by the Lamb. Poor Renatus. When he heard the news in prison of his son's passing, he wept bitterly and said, "It is very hard for me that I have lost my father, wife, and child. Ah, if only I also would be released."

We suffered much from the cold as there was little firewood to be had. A dear man from Skippack brought a sack full of axes and gave them to us.

We became a gazing stock for the city of Philadelphia. So many people came to see us and to hear our singing that on certain days we had to bar the doors so we could have some rest. On one day, I thought there might have been a thousand visitors.

The Secret Peace Mission

My anxiety over sending a message to the western Indians finally got through to the governor. In the middle of February, Colonel Clöthen

Under Attack in Philadelphia: 1763-1765

and Colonel VVorck,[85] accompanied by Easy Tongue as their interpreter, came to see me in the barracks. They questioned me closely about how I would make contact with the western Indians and how I would arrive safely at my destination. I assured the officers that if they would get me safely to Fort Allen on the Lehigh just north of Bethlehem, there would be no need of any further escort. I insisted that the danger to me and my mission was from white settlers and soldiers, not from enemy Indians.

Colonel Clöthen pressed me about how I knew the hostile Indians so well that I could carry a peace message to them without fear. Then he asked, "Will you bring back names and information about the condition and numbers of the western Indians that might help the army bring the war to an end?"

I told the colonels, "I can enter Indian territory without fear because of the Indian respect and honor for any messenger. Unlike the Whites, the Indians will never hold or murder a messenger."

I stuck to my proposal: "My mission is only to assure the Indians in the West that the Christian Indians in captivity have not all been murdered as the Conestogas were. Beyond that, I know nothing."

I held to my statement when Brothers Grube and Schmick visited me and Rhodendrun the next day. "We know your desire to return to Indian country is strong," the brothers said. "But there is also great danger to you in this mission. Do you not know that you could easily be taken for a spy and held or murdered by the savages? We want you to know that a wrong move on your part could jeopardize the safety of all the Indians held here under the government's protection. As a Christian, you must not take up arms in self-defense, but rather, trust

---

[85] Military rank in the British army from lowest to highest was as follows: privates, sergeants, lieutenants, captains, colonels, and generals. The importance of Papunhank's proposed mission to the Indians was shown by the high rank of these two officers. Only General Gage, the British commander of all soldiers in the colonies, would have been of higher rank.

UNDER ATTACK

entirely on the Savior to care for you. We fear that you might decide to stay in Indian country and leave your wife and daughters here."

"What you say is all true," I replied. "Do you want me to give up my mission into Indian country and let the savages sweep down upon the settlements to avenge the Conestoga murders and the supposed murders of all the Indians in captivity? You know that the hostile Indians will never believe the lies the government agents tell them. Or do you not want the savages to know the truth that the government protected captive Indians from being murdered by wicked rioters?"

"Brother Johannes, we cannot prevent you from going if you choose to do so," the two brothers concluded. "But do remember whom you belong to and that the Savior has suffered much for you."

With that admonition and a parting prayer, the two brothers prepared to leave. I stopped them. "Friend Pemberton wanted to send something with me if I went west to meet Captain Glikkikan. Would you let Friend Israel know that I am planning to go west?"

Brothers Grube and Schmick both frowned. "Do you not know that the governor and all the frontier settlers blame the Quakers for meddling in Indian affairs? For you to deliver anything to an enemy Indian in the West would be considered treason. We cannot help you in this."

"But the Indian custom has always been to give presents to each other at treaty conferences," I objected. "As a peace envoy, will I carry no wampum belts to prove that the governor has sent me?"

The brothers offered no further direction or blessing to me as I prepared to begin my journey westward. Four days after the colonels first visited me, Colonel Clöthen, Easy Tongue, and another Philadelphia gentleman appeared at the barracks. The third gentleman was the governor, without any marks of office to give him away. The governor laid out my orders in the following plain language:

> First, I want to make clear that this entire mission was

Under Attack in Philadelphia: 1763-1765

Papunhank's idea. I have only consented to the peace mission. There will be no wampum belts for you to carry. If anything goes wrong, I know nothing about it.

Brother Papunhank, only Easy Tongue will go with you and serve as your translator from the Delaware to the Mohican tongue. Colonel Clöthen will escort you as far as Fort Allen on the Lehigh, and from there, you will be on your own.

You must make it clear that the western Indians started the war without any provocation on our part. The cruel and unjust attacks on the settlements by the savages so excited the frontiersmen that I was unable to restrain them from taking their just revenge into Indian country.

Brother Papunhank, you must wipe the tears from the eyes of the savages and tell them that I am sorry about the murder of their brothers, the Conestogas. But I knew nothing about it, or I would have taken steps to prevent it. Be sure to also tell the savages what courageous steps I have taken to prevent the Christian Indians from being murdered in like fashion.

In the interests of peace with the Delawares, you may also mention that the British King has made a proclamation. For a time, there shall be no English settlements west of the Allegheny Mountains. All settlers beyond the Alleghenies must return east.

The savages must also understand that British troops under Colonel Bouquet will mercilessly carry the war into Indian country until the savages agree to return all the white captives taken in this war and the last.

Brother Papunhank, you must be made aware that your mission is of a very delicate nature and requires the utmost

UNDER ATTACK

secrecy. You are not allowed to discuss your mission with any Quakers or allow any reports to appear in the papers. Do you give me your pledge to remain silent?

Colonel Clöthen remained with me while the governor and Easy Tongue visited a number of the other Indians in the barracks. When they returned, I had some questions and some answers ready for the governor.

Honorable Governor, I call you to remember that I asked you and your Council to help take away the evil spirit that separates us so that we cannot hear each other. Now you ask that as a messenger of peace without wampum belts, I become the mouth of a lying evil spirit. This I have never done and cannot do now. The tongue of Johannes Papunhank will only speak the truth.

Again, I ask you to work to remove the evil spirit in your people, a spirit that causes them to steal and war and murder Indians so unjustly. And I, likewise, will work among the western Indians to remove the evil spirit that causes them by cruel and violent acts to seek revenge and justice and a place to live unmolested.

Honorable Governor, if by my mission to the Indians in the West, I am successful in stopping the attacks on the settlements east of the Alleghenies, can you pledge that all the Christian Indians in captivity will be released and allowed to return to the Wyoming Valley? Will you pledge that your government and British soldiers will protect them from the Paxton rebels?

In the end, neither I nor the honorable governor made any pledges to each other. But on 21 February 1764, I bid a tearful farewell to my

Under Attack in Philadelphia: 1763-1765

wife and daughters and to all the Brethren in captivity in the barracks in Philadelphia. Colonel Clöthen rode with us through the settlements till we reached Fort Allen north of Bethlehem on the Lehigh. There, the colonel remained behind to keep any soldiers from following us into Indian country and murdering us.

We left our government-provided steeds at Fort Allen, as there would have been no way to feed them on the barren winter journey. Also, the clop of horse hooves would have given news of our presence to any listening ears for miles around.

Chilloway and I passed silently across the familiar trails to Wyoming on the Susquehanna and beyond. With our guns, knives, and flints, we easily provided for ourselves. This was the life we had always known, and we exulted in the sighing of the wind in the trees, the silence and solitude of the woods after a new snow, or the howling of the wolves and the scream of the mountain lion. Rousing the bear out of his winter den, stalking the deer, snaring the rabbits, and beholding the otter and beaver all blessed our hearts with peace. Many times we knelt and thanked the Creator for giving us the wonder of it all.

Slowly we made our way west to Shamokin near the confluence of the two branches of the Susquehanna River. There, we met with Boss Man, the Iroquois overlord.[86] In the name of the governor, we wiped the tears from his eyes for the murder of the Conestoga Indians, a people who spoke Iroquois. We informed Boss Man that the Christian Indians were still safe in the barracks in Philadelphia.

Then, by mutual consent, we swung to the northeast instead of continuing west. We decided that winter was not a good time to cross the Alleghenies. And why should we bother? We bore no official words to

---

[86] Pennsylvania's Indian policy upheld a forced dominance by the Iroquois over all the other Indian tribes. In keeping with that policy, the Iroquois placed a ruler at the forks of the Susquehanna. But as the tensions with the Whites increased, the Delawares and even some of the Iroquois, especially the Senecas, disregarded the Iroquois overlord.

UNDER ATTACK

the Indians in the West. Besides, hunting and fishing was a lot more interesting than telling lies to our own countrymen.

We moved freely through the area Honest John had requested as a permanent homeland for the Delawares. We met with small pockets of Delawares who lived in miserable huts after being driven from their village at Great Island by the Paxton Boys. Everywhere, we found hunger and misery. Last October, the marauding Paxton Rangers had done a thorough job of destroying all the corn in the region. Because of the war and a hatred of all Indians, the Indians in this region could not obtain gunpowder for hunting. Without corn and powder, great hunger prevailed in Indian country.

We also found that great uneasiness existed everywhere over the possibility of another murderous attack by hostile Whites. In their weak and poor condition, the Indians knew they would be as helpless as a cottontail with a broken leg. Among the few Indians left at Wyalusing, I found my own daughter suffering from want and in poor condition. I decided to take her along back to my wife and daughters in Philadelphia.

We lingered at Wyalusing beyond the expected time of our return. We shared our remaining powder with the few able men remaining, and then left the Susquehanna and followed the trail across the mountains to Fort Allen on the Lehigh River. By prior arrangement, we found Major Clayton and Captain Ervins waiting to escort us to Philadelphia.

Even with the military escort, in every hamlet our small party suffered the taunts and threats of an angered citizenry. Bitterness and boldness were everywhere evident, and we could not hesitate in our ride or an irate mob would quickly gather. To the relief of all the Brethren, my daughter and I arrived safely at the English barracks on Sunday, 25 March 1764. For several days, all the captives had feared that evil had befallen us on our journey.

Brother David Zeisberger had returned to aid in the care of the

Under Attack in Philadelphia: 1763–1765

captives and to accompany us to the land of the Iroquois in the event the government granted us permission to leave Philadelphia. Brother David spoke Iroquois quite well. He told me, "We are very worried about our poor Indians because it seems that no one wants to take care of them anymore. Almost daily, more writings are published that tell of many accusations and great enmity against our Indians. Through such writings, the people are enticed to be more and more against us, and if our dear Lord does not specifically protect us, then we must still become victims."

I entered once more into the life of the barracks. I watched closely as the faithful and proven believers once again prepared their hearts and minds for the *Abendmahl* and bared their souls to one another. A few said, "We do not fear dying any more. Now we belong to the Savior and will go to Him when we die." Others said, "During the recent commotion, we were seized by fear, but we lay by the bed and prayed to the Savior, and He comforted us in our hearts so that all fear and anxiety disappeared." Of course, we all long for a place where we can live with a measure of safety again.

This time there were thirty-seven communicants. They all participated in the love feast, were absolved, and then received "the blessed taste of the body and blood of our Lord."

I listened to the testimonies and drank in the blessings of the *Abendmahl*. I was moved to tears as Brother Schmick read the story of the suffering of the Lord. It was the first time I had ever heard it.

I was not the only one who liked to hear the preaching and the singing of the captives. That talented young man Joshua, the one Lirio had her eyes on,[87] played the spinet for many. Even the governor once requested that Joshua play for him. So many people kept coming to

---

[87] Brother Grube married Joshua, Jr. and Lirio, Papunhank's daughter, on 26 June 1764. The wedding took place in the barracks. Lirio was not baptized until 11 June 1765, so it is not clear when she began using her Christian name of Sophia.

UNDER ATTACK

see the captive Indians that Brother Schmick asked the soldiers to put a stop to their coming for a while.

I also knew when Captain McIntosh went through the barracks and cleaned out all the dissolute women keeping company with the soldiers. There were so many of them that the soldiers were almost worthless.

I joined the other men in making spoons while the women spent their time making baskets so they would be able to earn some money to buy bread for their children. Many boys from the city brought hickory wood to the Indian boys, who made them into bows and arrows. In this way, the boys earned a few pennies to buy bread.

Friend Israel came again to the barracks. He bought many spoons and conferred with me. "How was your trip west to Indian country?" he asked. "Did you get to see Captain Glikkikan? As I told you, I have a very special present I wish to send him."

Friend Israel Pemberton listened carefully while I recounted the events of my recent trip to Indian country. "I tried to contact you before we left on our journey, but it was not possible," I explained. "And since we carried no wampum belts from the governor, we did not try to cross the Alleghenies in the winter. Winter time is not the season when war parties from the Ohioland travel east, so we did not see Captain Glikkikan.

"Easy Tongue and I went no farther west than Shamokin, but spent all our time hunting in the Wyoming Valley. There is great distress in the valley because of the powder shortage and the destruction of all the corn. The Indians still living in the valley greatly fear that the Paxton Boys will return in the spring and stake out land claims.[88] Do

---

[88] Later events confirmed that the Paxton Boys certainly intended to have free land in the Wyoming Valley. The Pennamite Wars proved this fact. A curious incident two years after this story clearly shows their bully-and-bullet morality. In 1766, a gang of about fifty of the Paxton Boys turned up at Conestoga Manor (personal untaxed Penn property) and ran off a Mennonite farmer whom the Penns had engaged to look after the land. The Paxton Boys claimed that because they had killed the Conestogas, the manor now belonged to them "by right of conquest." —Kenny, *Peaceable Kingdom Lost*, p. 209.

Under Attack in Philadelphia: 1763-1765

you think this is possible?"

"Yes, it is possible that the Paxton Boys will continue to terrorize not only the Indians in the Wyoming Valley but also all of Pennsylvania," Friend Israel answered in his direct way. "My brother James tells me that the Assembly has repeatedly warned the governor that to stop the present murders, lawlessness, and war, the known leader in the murder of the Conestoga Indians, Lazarus Stewart, must be brought to justice. But the governor refuses to bring him in. Why? I believe it is because the governor is in league with the bandits.

"The lawlessness and disdain for the Penn government increases. The Paxton Boys become bolder every day. They publicly say that a white man should not be punished for killing an Indian . . . any Indian. In the words of their known leaders, they have done Pennsylvania a service by ridding her of vermin in her midst. The Paxton Boys spit in the governor's face by saying they should be rewarded for killing the Conestoga Indians, not punished.

"Ben Franklin is now advocating making Pennsylvania a royal colony like Virginia. He thinks this would overthrow the alliance between the Scotch-Irish Presbyterians (the Paxton Boys) and the Penn government. Franklin believes this would allow the Assembly to restore order and respect for law and justice in Pennsylvania.

"But I don't know. Franklin is a very clever fellow; he will ride whichever horse carries him best, and it may not always be for peace and righteousness and truth. I stick with George Fox and the Scripture, 'Follow the Inner Light. Always do good to all men, as you would have them do good to you.'

"Friend Johannes, I cannot tell you how it will all end, but I will do all I can to help you return to Wyalusing. Beyond that, it is up to God, who can overrule even the most evil of men."

Friend Israel's insights gave scant comfort or hope to me. Like

UNDER ATTACK

many others among the refugees, I became sick. The highly seasoned victuals, the salted meat, and the fish did not agree with my stomach. I could get no exercise. I was completely deprived of hunting.

I said to the other refugees, "Having so many people confined in a small space only spreads ill will, not to mention the pox and fevers. When we are very sick, the white man wants to bleed us. The problem is not in the blood. It is in the stomach, and we know how to treat stomach ailments if we are free.

"Such close confinement cannot last. The supplies are always short. This is no better than being in prison. The Moravian teachers only support the lies and pretended kindness of the government. We should be set at liberty and simply go back to Indian country. Our lot there can be no worse."

I spoke for many, especially for the young men. Indeed, the discontent among all the Indians was so strong that Brother Schmick and Brother Zeisberger went to the honorable governor and conveyed the concerns of the Indians to him. In response, the governor sent Secretary Shippen and Councilor Logan to the barracks to hear how I thought the Indians could get through to Sir William Johnson and live among the Iroquois.

I assured the governor's councilors, "If the government will simply convey us safely to the frontier, we can go farther on our own."

On 12 April 1764, the Honorable Governor Penn sent this message back to me by the mouth of Mr. Fox:

> The honorable governor with his Council has considered your circumstances. We cannot give you permission to go to New York and settle there. In the current situation, you cannot be sent to Indian country because you would lack for food and could quite easily come into danger of being attacked by enemy Indians. Also, you

Under Attack in Philadelphia: 1763-1765

could easily be blamed if a murder should be committed on the border.

The governor and his Council have concluded that the best thing to do is to allow you to return to Province Island, and a watch of soldiers would be provided there. However, at this season of the year Province Island could be treacherous.

The soldiers will soon leave the barracks in Philadelphia, and then there will be more room for you right where you are.

I mulled over the governor's words and looked for some sunshine beyond the torrents. I could find none.

The governor said the captives could not return to their homes at Wyalusing, Nain, and Wechquetank, as he could not keep the settlers from murdering them.

The governor would not allow us to go to the western Indians in the Ohioland, as they were at war with Pennsylvania, and he was afraid our young people might join them.

He said we could not go to live with the Iroquois, as we might be murdered by other Indians, and the Christian Indians might be blamed if a settler was killed. And we might run out of food, he said, even though our food (and clothing, firewood, and other necessities) in the barracks were always in short supply.

The governor said we could not return to Province Island because it would be unhealthy. Yet we were dying in the confinement of the barracks.[89]

Our dear teachers told us the Savior had a good plan in mind for

---

[89] Out of approximately 140 captive Indians, 56 (21 children and 35 adults) died during 1764. Most of the deaths were attributed to smallpox and fevers.

UNDER ATTACK

us somewhere, and yet they did not have any idea what it was.[90] They told us to "just be patient." I feared that my beloved teachers only sang the governor's song and whistled his tune while the governor busily destroyed our nest. I wondered why our teachers and friends did not tell the people the truth, choosing instead to remain silent while their enemies spread so many lies about us.

I suffered the anguish of watching the children and friends needlessly die while our dear teachers sought to comfort us with pious phrases.

Our teachers closed one month "with thanks and joyful tears for the blessed visits of our dear Lord who took twenty souls out of our midst into His arms."

Sister Johanna Schmick was "kissed home by the Lamb."

Dear old, blind Sister Thamar, who fourteen years ago had been carried by her sons forty miles from the Susquehanna to the Lehigh that she might hear the Word, became sick with dysentery, which "served to be her blessed release."

Easy Tongue's eight-year-old daughter died from the pox, and thus she "went over into the Savior's arms."

Dear old Brother Joel went blessedly and gladly "over into the healthy realm."

I concluded that the only hope in this place was in dying. Thus, I left the captives, my Moravian teachers, my wife, and my daughters and went hunting on the Susquehanna."[91]

---

[90] The entry in the Moravian Diary for 20 October 1764 reads: "Joshua, Johannes Papunhank, and Sem Evans, an unbaptized person, went to Mr. Allen, the Chief Justice, to speak with him regarding their departure. Almost all our poor people have the intention of leaving, and therefore they work very hard to bring it about yet this fall. We ask them often to have patience and leave it to the direction of the Savior, but it has little effect."

[91] The entry in the Moravian Diary for 13 November 1764 reads: "The old Joshua, Johannes Papunhank, Bartholomeaus, and Joshua junior also went to the Susquehanna. They have acquired a pass from the honorable governor without our knowledge [but there was nothing we could do about it] and claim to look for a place for future settlement on the Susquehanna. Their main goal, however, is the hunt. The other young people were very disappointed not to be allowed to go with them."

Under Attack in Philadelphia: 1763-1765

Captivity or Exile?

Recorded by John Heckewelder

Glikkikan stopped and waited. "Is that all for today?" I asked.

"Did you learn anything from Papunhank's story?" he countered.

"I learned that Whites unjustly forced the Christian Indians from their homes in Wechquetank and Nain. They grossly reviled and threatened them in Germantown, Philadelphia, and on the march to Bristol. Governor Penn and his officials publicly lied, secretly sponsored the Paxton Boys, refused to punish the evildoers, held Papunhank's family in detention, and only partially provided for the physical needs of their charges. The Moravian missionaries selflessly ministered to the spiritual needs of the captives, but they also colluded with the Penn government to hold the believers in confinement. Quakers at all times stood with the captives and were not afraid to be identified with them."

"Is that all?" Glikkikan probed.

"I learned that you believe the story foretold what is taking place today in the Ohioland. Land speculators, soldiers, and traders stake out claims on Indian lands. They sell them to settlers who swarm in like locusts. Whites defend their claims and attack Indians—any Indians—and rival governments fight each other over who can sell the Indian lands. When the armies come, evil men on all sides unite to destroy the Indians, Christian and heathen alike."

"Brother John, both your ears and your heart have been open to truth. If you doubt any of what I have told you, you may ask Brother Johannes Papunhank, his wife and daughters, and Brother Good News. They are all with us to this day."

UNDER ATTACK

"Oh, I forgot that you also forecast war in the Ohioland," I added. "I thought Hokolesqua and Pucksinwah led a Shawnee peace delegation to Fort Pitt. What happened?"

"Brother John, whether you know it or not, White Eyes and I secretly harbored white traders for several weeks to shield them from the wrath of the Mingos, who were terribly upset by the massacre at Talgayeeta's village. They sought to kill all white men they could catch outside the villages.

"When Hokolesqua and his band came up the Muskingum on the way to make peace, he agreed to conduct all ten of the white traders to Pittsburgh. All went well until the group approached Pittsburgh. Then the protected traders became the protectors of the Shawnee. Five traders marched ahead of the eight Shawnee leaders, decked out in their finest attire with their heads held high and riding their beautiful horses, while five white traders marched behind them.

"However, as soon as the Shawnee reached Pittsburgh, the traders disappeared while a nasty mob congregated around the Shawnee. Threats and insults forced them to dismount, and a melee occurred. In the noise and confusion, Salamander Croghan, white with anger, rushed up with a pistol in each hand. He fired into the air and shouted, 'Get away from these people. I will shoot any man who makes a move to harm them.'

"The crowd backed away, but Silver Heels lay on the ground gasping frothy red bubbles. Blood flowed profusely from two knife wounds, one in his right shoulder and one in his chest.

"A squad of militia ran up and dispersed the crowd. Croghan ordered Silver Heels to be taken to the post surgeon for treatment and apologized profusely to Hokolesqua. Agent McKee offered to take the delegation to the quarters that had been prepared for them.

"But it was too late. Hokolesqua refused. With his face set in grim lines, he said, 'We will not stay. Now there can be no further talk of peace.'

Under Attack in Philadelphia: 1763-1765

"Heckewelder, that is why I can prophesy that there will be war in the Ohioland. What will you do to prevent it? Will you send messages to Dr. Connolly begging him to call off the Virginians and make peace with the Shawnee and the Mingos? Will you go to the fort in person and condemn the bloodshed as evil? We have done this with the Indians. Will you and Good News do this with the Whites? What will you do?"

"We will pray," I responded.

With that, the orator for the Lenni Lenape turned to go.

"Wait one moment," I cried, "I have another question. Did Brother Johannes have any idea what the gift was that Friend Israel wanted to send to Captain Glikkikan?"

Brother Isaac replied that Brother Johannes had given no indication he knew what the gift might have been.

I promised myself, *Someday, I'll let him know it was the gold medallion Friend Israel wanted to send to him. But not tonight.*

UNDER ATTACK

The Migration of the Released Captives from Philadelphia to Kuskusky (1765-1772)

CQM406 Notes

1. ➔ ➔ ➔ = the journey of released captives from Philadelphia to Wyalusing (1765).
2. ─ ─ ─ = the journeys to the Iroquois seeking permission to settle at Wyalusing (1766).
3. X X X = the route of the group leaving Wyalusing by water (1772).
4. ● ● ● = the route of the group leaving Wyalusing by land with cattle and horses (1772).
5. ═══ = the trans-Alleghenies route both groups took from Muncy to Kuskusky (1772).
6. From Wyalusing to the prospective mission at Goshchuenk involved crossing the Allegheny Mountains as far north as the source of the Ohio River and then floating down the Ohio (now named the Allegheny) to Goshchuenk (1767).

Chapter 6

Under Attack at Wyalusing: 1765–1772

As recorded by John Heckewelder
At Beautiful Spring, Ohio,
Monday, 18 July 1774

On July 1, a party of Indians came to Beautiful Spring from near the fort. They told us, "The Virginians are there in great numbers, and more are arriving every day. It is unsafe for Indians to come anywhere near the fort because the Whites are stirred up against them."

We do not know what it is like among the Whites in Pittsburgh, but we have not heard any news favorable to us. We worry that gangs of white people might possibly be formed to go out against the Indians. This would be the most dangerous thing for us because people like this are not under anyone's command. There is a party of Virginians like this on Beaver Creek. They rob and plunder in the fields where people have fled, and they make the road here unsafe.

UNDER ATTACK

Under such circumstances, we commend ourselves and our entire people to the Savior for grace, and we pour out our worry and concern to His faithful heart, according to our Watchword for today, "Redeem Israel, O God, out of all his troubles and protect us from all sin and all earthly turmoil" (Psalm 25:22).

The Indians who came here yesterday told us they had tracked a party of Virginians who are patrolling as far as halfway here. We concluded they were becoming familiar with the roads near us and were planning something against our towns. Therefore we sent four brothers a day's journey to the northeast to watch the bush and the roads until we receive more certain information from Pittsburgh.

On 2 July, more bad news arrived. Some of our people told us the Virginians will attack Huts of Grace tonight. We paid little attention to this warning because most of these lies are meant to frighten us. Also, we heard that the Delawares in Newcomerstown are wavering and want to join the Shawnee.

Because we heard so much bad news, we sent Glikkikan to Chief Watwees in Newcomerstown to find out what is going on and how things look to him. When Glikkikan returned, we held a helpers' conference, and he reported to us what he had found out. One by one, he disbursed the many rumors and lies that made us fearful, but he also calmly faced the very real possibility of attacks on our towns. He stood before us as a tower of strength when all around us the earth trembled and men's hearts failed them.

"When Joshua and I arrived in Newcomerstown," Glikkikan began, "the people immediately crowded around us in the Chief's house. They had already exhausted the Chief with so many rumors of impending disaster from the Whites and the Shawnees and the Mingos that he had told them to prepare to flee to Walhonding. We told them it was a good idea to keep a watch, but most of the rumors were enlarged, and likely nothing would come of them.

Under Attack at Wyalusing: 1765–1772

"One of the main reasons the people in Newcomerstown were so upset was because Captain White Eyes and most of the head people had gone to the fort. They had already been gone too long, and the people were afraid they had either been taken prisoner or killed. We considered this to be extremely unlikely and urged the Delawares to wait a little longer for their return before fleeing or joining the Shawnees.

"The Shawnee are running from one town to another carrying countless lies with them and horrifying the Indians with their terrible tales of mayhem and murder. We told the Delawares that the Shawnees are doing everything they can to find allies in their war against the Whites. They claim the Wyandots, Twichtwees, and Cherokees have already joined their alliance, and the Six Nations will soon join their western children, the Mingos, in the war of retribution. The Shawnees have even sent to the French on the Illinois and asked them to help in the war. The French replied, 'You must first bring us many skins. Then we will help you.'

"We know the Shawnees have few allies. Only the Munsees, the Mingos, and the Shawnees have agreed to war together as revenge for the Yellow Creek murders and to stop the Whites from encroaching on their lands.

"However, the young people in Newcomerstown are very agitated because they believe if they were to join the Shawnees, the Indians would get the upper hand against the Whites. But if they do *not* join, both the Shawnees and the Whites will be against the Delawares. Therefore they are blaming us Christians for making the Delawares retreat because we do not want war.

"I assured the would-be warriors, 'I have seen the blood, I have heard the screams, I have felt the pain. In war, the little man within throws his evil tomahawk about, weighing our hearts down with guilt. But in peace, the little man within us sits still. I know. Only in the

UNDER ATTACK

blood of the Savior does one find forgiveness and peace.'

"My speech seemed to have a calming effect on their ardor, but that evening we heard several shots at a great distance. Everyone raced about saying, 'The Whites are coming!' I said, 'If the Whites were coming, they would certainly not fire warning shots to announce their arrival. The shots must have been fired by hunters taking their game.'

"Another message that supposedly came to the Delawares from the Shawnee said, 'Bring all your women and children to our lower Shawnee towns where they will be safe. All the men should guard their fields well so they will have something to eat when they return from the war.'

"I told them, 'I doubt that such a message came from the Shawnee since most of the Delaware living close to the Shawnee have already moved to Newcomerstown. No one feels safe in the Shawnee towns. My guess is that the message came from the Munsees living at Mochwesüng on the Walhanding.'"

That ended Brother Isaac's report to the conference. Brother David then said, "On occasions such as this, you can feel the power of Satan and the darkness that rules the Indians.

"Despite the evil, the Savior does not fail to reveal Himself and to profit from this. Our beloved Simon's brother (Netawastond) used to be an enemy of the Gospel and did not want to hear anything about God's Word. He came to Beautiful Spring eight days ago, heard the Gospel for the first time, and was powerfully convicted and touched. Upon his request, we granted him permission to move here with his family. Then he expressed his heart as solidly as any brother who has already lived with us for years.

"Brother Isaac has confirmed that the Delawares are wavering between war and peace. But a bigger danger to us are those among us who are unsettled by the lies and rumors. We already noticed that the strangers who have been filling our towns have been frightening

Under Attack at Wyalusing: 1765-1772

our people and trying to get them to move away from here. Although we knew they were trying to misguide their friends by telling them we would be the first to be attacked by the Whites, there was nothing we could do to get rid of them.

"Now, the old blind chief, Salomo, wants to leave here with his family and live among the Shawnee. It hurts us to watch them intentionally throw themselves into physical misery and spiritual ruin. At the same time, this will free us from much trouble and distress because of their bad friends. It would not be good for us to try to persuade people like this to stay here because we could turn the Indians into enemies by keeping their friends.

"Trying to hold Indians in our towns could make it twice as dangerous for us white brothers and sisters because then we would have both the Delaware and the Shawnee at our throats. The danger to us white teachers is real, so we have decided to send Brother Roth, his wife, and their young daughter back to Bethlehem."

Brother David then closed the helpers' conference with this plea: "Let us call to the Lord and remember that this day's Watchword tells us, 'Arise, O Lord, let not man prevail. Help us, Lord God, in this distress, so that those who do not consider, who despise your Word and teach others to do so, might also convert.'"

In the Sunday evening service on 10 July, there was talk about the text for today, "For ye are bought with a price: therefore glorify God in your body, and in your spirit, which are God's." Netawastond, who moved here for good, was buried into Jesus' death through holy baptism and received the name Seth.

Three Shawnee and two Mingo passed through here on their way to the Six Nations to ask them for help in their war against the Virginians. They told us the Iroquois are planning a huge Council in Onondaga with Many Children Johnson. To our dismay, these warriors carried three white scalps on a stick. Several brothers escorted

UNDER ATTACK

them through our town and beyond our borders.

On the 17th, Captain White Eyes and the Indians who had gone with him to Fort Pitt returned and brought us the happy news that there is nothing to fear from the white people. They promised the Delawares that no Whites shall come across the Ohio onto their land. However, the Whites did not promise the Shawnee this because the Shawnee have not yet decided if they want to make war or peace. We are so thankful the Delaware are thus encouraged to stand firm for peace, for if the Delaware do not remain steadfast, the missions will not survive.

After the announcement, I saw Glikkikan and White Eyes engaged in what appeared to be an intense conversation, maybe even a heated argument. A knot of Indians surrounded the two, and I could see neither one. The whole group sheltered in the shade of a giant locust tree. I decided to climb up a few branches into the tree where I had a good look at their faces and could easily hear the conversation.

> Glikkikan: "When you said *they*, who did you mean? Who said, 'We have nothing to fear from the Whites'? I know Colonel Connolly would never make such a promise."
>
> White Eyes: "It was the King's agent, McKee. He also promised that the Whites would not cross the Ohio except to get the Shawnee if they want war."
>
> Glikkikan: "Do you believe such tales? McKee already claims tens of thousands of acres west of the Alleghenies. He cannot guarantee the safety of anyone from the Virginians. They want the same land McKee and his companions claim."
>
> White Eyes: "McKee and Croghan are trying to restrain the settlers and the Virginians from fighting the Indians. They are the only ones at Fort Pitt who might help the Indians preserve peace in the Ohioland. McKee told me the Shawnee were informed there could be no more thoughts of peace unless the

Under Attack at Wyalusing: 1765-1772

guilty on both sides were delivered and punished."

Glikkikan: "I do not doubt that Colonel Connolly said Talgayeeta and his raiders must be delivered up for punishment. But if you believe the colonel will even think of turning the Greathouse gang over to the Mingos, you will also believe McKee can fly across the Allegheny Mountains or swim across the Great Salt Sea. That will never happen. The only reason Agent McKee and Salamander Croghan are taking up for the Indians is to keep the Virginians from getting the land they steal from the Indians. Do not trust the word of Virginians or Pennsylvanians or the King's agents, McKee, Croghan, or Many Children Johnson. Peace is in the hands of God."

White Eyes: "I am not completely blind to the deceitfulness and lies of the Whites. I told Colonel Connolly, 'The Delaware want peace. Newcomerstown, Huts of Peace, and Beautiful Spring want peace.' I warned him, 'If you are planning something against the Shawnee, do not come into our area. That would be a breach of peace.' Glikkikan, you are right. Peace is in the hands of God. We are all in the hands of God, even Many Children Johnson. He died in his chair at the great Iroquois Council where over three thousand Indians had gathered. Now it is clear the Iroquois will not fight with the Shawnee against the Whites. They also are for peace."

Glikkikan: "I am glad you are for peace. It will be very dangerous for the white brothers and sisters here if the Delaware should go to war. Tell the brothers here what I heard you tell the Delawares in the Great Council."

White Eyes: "We are friends of the white brothers and the Indian believers. We should act peacefully and cordially toward them and not speak badly of them because we are their friends. The

UNDER ATTACK

Delaware nation is already known for having accepted God's Word, and even though it is not yet true of everyone, there is already a large group of Indian believers. It will be better if we do not speak badly of our own nation because someday you may want to call upon God's name, especially when you get into trouble or distress. Or if you see you are going to die, it may occur to you that there is a God in heaven who created all things, and you may want to turn to Him then. Therefore you should not be hostile toward the believers, but should love them, so that when you need help and comfort, you will know where to turn. You also could surely believe that if you hurt them, you will be doing the same thing to God."

I climbed down from the boughs of the giant locust and joined the Indians gathered beneath it. What a powerful thought! If you hurt someone else, you are doing the same thing to God. Surely the Savior had raised up this man for such a time as this. He can speak so confidently to the people for us. If the Indians were against us in the present circumstances as they had been earlier, what would our chances be now?

Only last month, in the Delaware Council, evil plans were discussed to chase us white brothers and sisters away. The Delawares are unhappy that they cannot do whatever they want with our Indians, and they have concluded it is because we are here. They think if they can get rid of the teachers, the Indians will then be in their grasp.

However, Captain White Eyes ruined their plan to attack us. He told the Council he would not support them at all if they were not acting reasonable. He said, "If you hear anything bad about these people, you believe it right away and make no effort to find out if it is true. But if you hear something good about them, you make no effort to even consider it." The Council was unwilling to discuss the matter further.

Under Attack at Wyalusing: 1765–1772

As recorded by John Heckewelder
At Beautiful Spring, Ohio,
Monday, 26 September 1774

On 24 August, Brother Zeisberger went with the brothers Cornelius, Isaac, Jacob, and Augustinus to Huts of Grace for a conference with the brothers there about Chief affairs. We have been overwhelmed with these since spring. It seems the Indians and chiefs in Newcomerstown no longer want to undertake anything without our Indian brothers. They claim they are too weak, there are too few of them, and they do not have enough wise men. We realize we are in Indian country now, and we have a lot to learn, but we must be sure we do not become so involved with the chiefs that they gain power over us and can then order us to do things opposed to our congregational rules.

On the 26th, Indians came here with a message from Governor Penn in Philadelphia. "Admonish the Delaware Indians to do their best to talk the Shawnee into peace. We understand the Virginians in the fort have stopped all trade with the Indians. Therefore Pennsylvania will open a new trading center north of Fort Pitt at Attike."

On the 28th, Brothers Isaac (Glikkikan), Augustinus (Leekey), and Jacob (Daskund) were called to the Council at Newcomerstown. Brothers Jacob and Augustinus returned on the 30th, while Brother Isaac remained at Newcomerstown.

On the 31st, Jacob and Augustinus left again to attend the Council in Newcomerstown. After it is finished, they will go on to the lower Shawnee towns to hold a council with them and see if they will not incline their ears to peace.

In the early service on 5 September, we talked about how it is not

UNDER ATTACK

sufficient to be baptized and cleansed of your sins; it is also necessary to become obedient to God's Word, to learn all that goes with this, and to live according to His teaching. The Savior said, "Baptize them and teach them to observe all things whatever I have commanded you."

Our Indian brothers, Jacob and Augustinus, returned from the Council with the Delaware and the Lower Shawnee. They brought us the happy news that the Shawnee want to keep the peace. They have heard the whole story now, and the Shawnee blame the whole trouble on the Mingo or Six Nations who talked them into the war. The two brothers would say nothing about Brother Isaac except that he was often seen keeping company with Captain White Eyes and Chief Hokolesqua.

On 13 September, a messenger from Kaskaskunk passed through here on his way to Newcomerstown. He bore the disagreeable news that notorious villains had stationed themselves near the roadside and had slain two friendly Delawares in cold blood.[92]

On 20 September, another messenger on the way to Newcomerstown informed us that the governor of Virginia had arrived at Fort Pitt with 1,200 soldiers. Besides that, another 900-man army was camped at the mouth of the Great Kanahwa River awaiting orders to meet with Lord Dunmore's army and punish the Shawnee.

The next day Johannes Papunhank and two other believing Indians accompanied me to Bethlehem by way of Great Island on the Susquehanna. Brother Johannes was homesick, so we wanted to pass, if possible, through Wyalusing after visiting Great Island.

Before we left, the brothers prayed with us and commended us to the Savior's protection and to His dear angels. We decided to take the overland route from Beautiful Spring to Kaskaskunk. This was the same route the cattle drivers had followed in the spring a year ago when the rest of us had taken the canoes and the cargo by way of water.

---

[92] Wellenreuther & Wessel, eds., p. 228, note 508.

Under Attack at Wyalusing: 1765–1772

This route had the advantage of staying well to the north of Fort Pitt and the 1,200 soldiers of Lord Dunmore. We knew the route well, for we had traveled it numerous times. Our four-man party expected no trouble from Indians or Whites, so when we arrived at our usual camping spot, we built a small fire, turned our horses loose, and collected a few fresh boughs for the night. A crescent moon furnished a pale light, and crisp fall air settled upon us.

While silently relaxing by the fire, Papunhank motioned us not to move while he placed his ear to the ground. "Indians," he whispered and held up three fingers. All three of my Indian companions slid noiselessly off into the dark. I held my breath and waited to see what would happen next. Suddenly a tall Indian sat down beside me. I started. "Glikkikan!" I gasped.

"You had better be more careful when traveling in wartime," he chided me. "You post many signs of your whereabouts; horses, smoke, and crackling boughs. Why are you going to Philadelphia?"

I jumped again. "How did you know where I was headed?" I asked in amazement.

"Oh, the signs are written all along the trail," he replied mysteriously.

"Okay, I'll play the game with you," I told him. "Where are Hokolesqua and White Eyes? Bring them in. I'd like to know what Lord Dunmore told you."

"Our secret meeting with Lord Dunmore is not for the birds to carry to other ears. The agreements we reached will unfold soon enough if the governor can be trusted."

"And if his word is no good? Then what?" I asked.

"Then Captain White Eyes and Chief Hokolesqua will put tomahawks in the hands of all the nations. His armies are a long way from home, and the united Indians will destroy them.

"That is not what Hokolesqua or White Eyes want. They want

UNDER ATTACK

peace, and they are prepared to meet some unreasonable demands if that will allow for peace. Now we will see if the governor can safely disperse his armies before they try to wipe out the Shawnees. His armies are made up of determined men who do not know the Savior, but are filled with hate and greed. The general has a very difficult task, but his life is in the hands of God.

"Now I see you have a long journey ahead of you with Brother Johannes. I am sure he can tell you the story of Huts of Peace at Wyalusing better than any other. Listen well. God be with you!" And Glikkikan vanished as suddenly as he had come.

A Memoir of Huts of Peace at Wyalusing, 1765–1772

As told by Johannes Papunhank to John Heckewelder

Banished!

The captives were free at last! At least, those who had not been released by death while in captivity were now freed.

Poor Renatus! Brave Quakers and Moravian brothers had stood with him against a rowdy mob at his trial. He had rightly been declared innocent and set free, but he remained in prison for a night while the crowd who wanted to murder him dispersed. The next day friends whisked him away to rejoin the captives at the barracks. His aged father Jacob, his wife Geesche, and his infant son all lay in unmarked pauper graves in Philadelphia.

But Renatus was not the only one who lost loved ones. Out of 125 captives from Nain who had been taken to Philadelphia and the 21 souls

Under Attack at Wyalusing: 1765–1772

from Wyalusing who had gone there voluntarily, 56 had died in captivity.

Because of the losses the captives had endured in the earlier French and Pontiac wars, and in consideration of their loyalty, the government agreed to furnish them flour until after the corn harvest. The Quakers carried out the government's promise.

The captives pled in vain to return to their former peaceful settlements at Nain and Wechquetank. But the Penn government decreed, "All Indians must immediately remove beyond the bounds of all lands held by the Whites by right of purchase."

I was adamant. "There were no purchased Indian lands other than those rightfully purchased by William Penn," I said. "The former homes at Nain and Wechquetank have been stolen." Nevertheless, everyone knew that to return to these old towns would probably mean death.

So where could they go? I invited the released captives to come to my home on the Susquehanna at Wyalusing. I told them, "The land here belongs to the Delawares. We have lived here for many years, and no one has troubled us. It is ours."

The mission board agreed that the fertile flats surrounded by the hills at Wyalusing could be their new home. Brother David Zeisberger, to the delight of everyone, was assigned as the resident missionary, and Johann Schmick agreed to accompany the group on the journey to their new home.

But Brother Zeisberger had questions. "What will the Iroquois say about having the converts seated in their territory?"

I answered him, "It is not their territory." So Brother David let it rest for the moment.

Thus it came about that about eighty hopeful pilgrims with ninety happy children[93] left the barren barracks in wagons supplied by the

---

[93] The exact number of pilgrims is uncertain. It is likely that other Christian Indians from the area joined the migration after the captives were set free. Otherwise, there would have been only about 100 left from the original captives. A fixed number for the mission found in Zeisberger's diary entry for 31 December 1765 lists a total of 148 souls.

UNDER ATTACK

Quakers and traveled to their old homes at Nain. They arrived there on 22 March 1765 amid a blustery snowstorm that laid two feet of snow on the ground. Their forlorn cabins greeted them without warmth or welcome. The group rested in their old homes for eleven days before leaving Nain to continue their journey to the promised land of Wyalusing.

Armed government officials escorted the despised Indians through the white settlements to the foot of the Blue Mountains where the roads ended. Then the escort left the pilgrims to make their own way on foot unmolested.

The Indians built a hamlet of bark huts amid the cheerless ruins of their former town of Wechquetank. They camped there by Pohopoco Creek for a week while they held Passion Week services.

On 11 April 1765, the pilgrims resumed their journey northwest. They crossed steep ridges, climbed Broad Mountain, and came to the Great Pine Swamp. They estimated it to be fourteen miles across the swamp.[94]

Several old men agreed to serve as guides, and the Indians began cutting a path through the swamp. They hacked their way through dense thickets and tangled underwood, bridged creeks, and laid tree trunks over deep sloughs. At times, they suffered drenching rains. The pilgrims could advance only about two miles a day because they then had to return to carry their goods forward with them.

Frequently they suffered painful hunger. Much time was lost because of hunting. Still, their want of food was so great and the cry of famished women and children so heart-rending that something had to be done.

---

[94] It is uncertain why the pilgrims followed this route and why it was so strange to most of them. It certainly was not the route they were used to in former times. Also, I am not sure that Johannes was with the migrants at this time. With his wife and daughters along, it is highly possible that he had returned to Philadelphia or Bethlehem to accompany them. But if he was along, why would he not have known a better route?

Under Attack at Wyalusing: 1765-1772

At dusk one evening, all the expert hunters went out to shoot game. Brothers David and Johann stayed in the camp and prayed. God heard their prayers, and the hunters returned with six deer.

The hardships of the journey were so severe that aged Magdalene and the boy Anthony died.

After two weeks of strenuous labor, the old men led the weary Indians to the edge of Pine Swamp. But much to their distress, on the other side of a large creek, a very steep mountain rose before them. There was no way they could cross the creek and climb the mountain, neither up or down the creek.

All gathered to decide what to do. It appeared that they would have to retrace their steps to the beginning of the journey and go southwest till they came to the Susquehanna River. Then they could go up the Susquehanna to their destination. They knew this route would be one hundred miles.

In the midst of their difficulty, Brother Zeisberger remembered that there was a young man along who knew the area. The young man, David, had been with them for the whole journey.

He called the young man to him and asked, "David, are you familiar with this area? Do you know a better and shorter road to the Susquehanna?"

"Yes," David replied, "I am perfectly acquainted with this place. Six miles back lies a road where we can easily pass through the mountain. It is much shorter than the proposed road. I am sure of it."

"What?" Brother Zeisberger asked. "Do you mean that we have all been going wrong while you are with us? Why did you not tell us about the road before we toiled over these futile miles?"

"I did not say anything because the guides are older than I am," David answered. "They took the lead and never asked me whether I had any knowledge of the country. If they had inquired, I would have told them."

UNDER ATTACK

Backtracking

"Why then, did you not tell us we were on the wrong road?" —David Zeisberger

Under Attack at Wyalusing: 1765-1772

"Will you tell them now?" Brother Zeisberger asked.

"No indeed," David replied. "Unless they ask me, I will not. It does not become an Indian to instruct his elders."

Brother Zeisberger then held a small conversation with the old men who had been leading the party. They promptly asked David to take the lead, and he readily agreed.

First, David had them retrace their path for six miles. Then he directed the pilgrims to follow a path northeast instead of northwest. This path brought them to a gap in the mountain where the whole party could pass through with ease.

By agreement, David then led them the rest of the way to Wyoming on the Susquehanna River. There they borrowed canoes and braved the swollen rushing waters of the Susquehanna for fifty miles. But this frightened them not at all. Here in this place they knew what to do, and they did it. I welcomed them to their new home on 9 May 1765.[95]

Starting Over

We were together again, my wife and daughters! Yes, all of us brothers and sisters were reunited, and with teachers to guide us in truth. We were free to work and worship. Free to live.

Cheerfully we went to work clearing and fencing in ground to plant. Quaker friends helped us obtain seed corn, and thus we were able to plant our new fields on 26 May, only seventeen days after the pilgrims arrived.

Hunters took to the woods for meat. The women and children dug

---

[95] The Indian's name was David, and the route he followed through the difficult part of the journey is called David's Path to this day. —Rachel Wheeler, *An Eighteenth-Century Trail of Tears: A Translation of the Travel Diary of Johann Jacob Schmick of the Moravian Indian Congregation's Journey to the Susquehanna, 1765.*

UNDER ATTACK

wild roots and plants to serve as substitutes for bread and sauce. The Society of Friends bought flour from farmers in the Craig settlement. The Indians transported it by pack horse to the mouth of the Lackawanna and then loaded it on canoes and paddled it upstream to Wyalusing.

Only three weeks after the pilgrims arrived at Wyalusing, a party of brothers from Bethlehem arrived with more needed supplies. In addition, they drove four cows ahead of them. You were with them, John.

We had only been at Wyalusing long enough to choose a location for our new town, name it Huts of Peace, and hold a few worship services under the open skies when Brother Zeisberger insisted that we send a message to Togahaju and ask his permission to seat ourselves on his land.

"But why do we need his consent to live here?" I asked him. "This is my home. The Wyoming Valley is where the Iroquois Bully Canasetego ordered us to live. This is where Brother Onas wants us to live. Why should we beg Togahaju to let us live here?"

But Brother Zeisberger would not yield. "Togahaju is the Cayuga overlord of this area and represents the will of the Five Nations. We want to dwell here in safety and peace, and we must secure his approval," he insisted.

"Those are your words, not ours," I declared.

Zeisberger sent the message anyway. Within a month, a messenger arrived bearing a string of wampum. He summoned Anton, Joshua, and me north to Cayuga Lake to meet with Togahaju.

"Now what shall we tell him?" I asked of Brother Zeisberger. "Suppose that Togahaju tells us we cannot stay here? Then what will we say?"

"Let us hope for the best," Brother Zeisberger urged. "Here is what you must tell Togahaju: 'The Mohican and Delaware here are not as other Indians. They do not fight or drink, and they want to live at

Under Attack at Wyalusing: 1765–1772

peace.' You must also tell them you desire to have your white teacher, Ganousseracheri,[96] reside with you."

"They are your words, not mine," I answered. "I will tell him your words."

I left with two others to answer Togahaju's summons the middle of June. Two weeks later, we were back at Wyalusing. I reported to Zeisberger.

"Togahaju told us, 'I am pleased to have the praying Indians in my territory, but they should come closer to me and live at the headwaters of Cayuga Lake. The Wyoming Valley is stained with blood,[97] and it is not a good place for you to live. More bloodshed in the valley is sure to follow.'

"I answered him, 'Chief Togahaju, I have no objection to living closer to you. However, I am familiar with the area you describe, and there is no game around Cayuga Lake. Our people are hunters, and we need meat to sustain us. Nevertheless, we will lay your suggestion before our people, and we will respond when the corn is ripe.' "

Brother Zeisberger agreed that I had given Chief Togahaju a good answer. Then he said, "We will continue to build our town here. Perhaps the Chief can be persuaded to change his mind."

Despite Togahaju's warning, the settlement moved ahead with building their town. During the month of June, the busy Indians constructed thirty bark-covered huts and four log cabins. At the end of June, they began using one of the cabins for the daily worship services instead of meeting out in the open.

The daily services and the busy scramble for provisions continued

---

[96] Years earlier, Zeisberger had been adopted into the Onondaga clan of the Six Nations as *Ganousseracheri*, meaning "on the pumpkin." The use of his Iroquoian name was an attempt to quiet Togahaju's fears of having a white man living in Indian country.

[97] Some sources say this refers to a long-ago time when the Iroquois conquered the Susquehannocks; others think it was the war trail taken when fighting the Cherokee. I side with those who think Togahaju referred to the recent bloodshed when the Connecticut settlers and Teedyuscung's village were destroyed.

UNDER ATTACK

on through July. The stock of bread bought from their neighbors was soon consumed, so a party of forty men set out for Fort Allen on the Lehigh to fetch part of the corn given them by the government of Pennsylvania.

When the men had gone halfway, they decided to return to Wyalusing. They heard that the Whites in the Irish settlement, the Paxton Boys, were again exasperated against them. Two Whites had been murdered in their settlement, and they blamed the deed on the Christian Indians, even though it was impossible that they had the least share in it.

Upon their return to Huts of Peace without the corn, the community used herbs and roots to take the place of bread. Then word came that Sir William Johnson, the King's Indian agent, had established peace with all the Indian nations in the name of the King of England. So once more, nearly all the men in the village set out for Fort Allen and soon returned with enough corn to last them until their own crop was ripe. The believers prayed for blessings on the English government because of its liberality toward them.

I was not deceived. I prayed blessings on the heads of the Quakers in the government. I knew who supplied the bread. It did not come from the governor's men. Nevertheless, I prayed a blessing on the head of my enemies as well.

A Shining Light

Brotherly love and concord prevailed among the believers. As in a swarm of busy bees, each one knew his proper task and performed it readily. Some were employed in building houses and others in clearing the land. Some went hunting and fishing to provide for those at work,

Under Attack at Wyalusing: 1765-1772

while others did the housekeeping chores. The missionaries were not idle either, and among other things, they made their own gardens and plantations.

Twice daily the brothers and sisters assembled for worship and exhortation. The Lord's presence and peace surrounded us as we sang and praised God for His mercies.

My large circle of acquaintances and the fame of Huts of Peace drew a great number of visitors from all parts. This gave the missionaries the opportunity to extol the grace of Jesus before large numbers of heathen. Many believed the glad tidings, turned to the Lord, and received joy and peace in the Holy Ghost.

Every day it became more evident that God Himself had truly converted me. Since I had been the first one to be baptized at Wyalusing, I was now the first one to be made a partaker of the Lord's Supper in this place.

Also, at the end of July, less than a month after I returned from my visit to Togahaju, one of his councilors came to Wyalusing. This Cayuga chief, Tajannoga, was a good friend of Zeisberger's from years past when he lived with the Iroquois. The two friends talked about moving the settlement to Cayuga Lake. Tajannoga agreed with my observation that Cayuga Lake would not be a suitable location due to the scarcity of game.

Life at the mission grew busier as the time neared when the government flour shipments would be discontinued. After the summer hunt ended in the first part of September, the Indians built a larger meetinghouse and a substantial manse of round logs, complete with cellar and attic, for Brother Zeisberger to dwell in. They dedicated the new chapel on 15 September.

The harvest ended and the flour shipments ceased, but still no one sent the promised word to Togahaju.

On 20 October 1765, the sacrament of baptism was administered

UNDER ATTACK

for the first time to the wife of an Indian named Sakima. After her baptism, she said, "I feel very happy, but have not yet enough. I long now more than ever for our Savior."

Her husband was present during her baptism, but could scarcely bear to stay because of his emotions. He immediately went into the woods to give vent to his tears. Upon his return, he saluted his wife, and bursting into tears, said, "Oh, how I do rejoice that you are cleansed in the blood of Christ! Ah, when shall I have that favor?" Sakima had this grace imparted to him on Christmas Day when he was baptized.

Such a general emotion occurred during his baptism that the whole company wept together. Thus without words, the whole congregation expressed their joy and gratitude for how graciously Jesus received sinners. Many unbaptized were powerfully awakened and now desired the same favor. One of them observed, "If I should see the water for baptism brought into the chapel and hear the missionary say, 'Whoever wishes to be baptized, come hither,' I should not hesitate a moment to accept so great an offer."

By the end of December, the seated village now consisted of 54 baptized adults, 37 adults not baptized, and 57 youth and children, 148 souls in all.

But still no one sent a message to Togahaju. I did not want to recognize the Six Nations ownership of our land, and Zeisberger was also reluctant.

In January, chilling snow-laden winds blew down from Browntown Mountain upon Wyalusing. Deep drifts of snow made all traveling difficult. The Susquehanna froze solid. A wolf was killed in the town. Hunters brought in ten deer, and the young men went on a bear hunt and returned with seven bears. The meat was all apportioned among the heads of families.

Among the visitors who came were those belonging to the Cayuga

Under Attack at Wyalusing: 1765–1772

nation, a member of the Iroquois. The Cayugas seemed better prepared to receive the kingdom of God because they were less entangled with political affairs than the other Iroquois. Once during Zeisberger's absence, Brother Schmick asked some of the visiting Cayugas if they knew Zeisberger. As soon as they heard his name, they expressed much joy, and placing two fingers together, said, "We are one. Are you also one with him?"

Brother Schmick replied, "We are brethren."

The Cayugas then went to the chapel, saw and heard what they never before had been witness to, and were powerfully struck with the Gospel of Jesus Christ our Savior. They said, "You must come to us and build your house in our town."

Getting Seated

Still, Huts of Peace sent no message to Togahaju. This time he sent us a strong message. "Cousins! What kind of corn have you at Wyalusing? You promised you would give an answer to my proposition when your corn is ripe. The corn has been ripe a long time already. It is nearly consumed. I think of soon planting again. Why do you not fulfill your promise?"

Zeisberger now sprang into action. He sent Brothers Anton and me to seek the aid of two Delaware chiefs, Newallike and Echgohund, in dealing with the Cayuga chief.[98]

When we two returned, I reported to Zeisberger with an evasive, "They declined to advise us. Those two chiefs do not want to recognize Iroquois ownership of our land any more than we do."

---

[98] Both of these chiefs later joined the Ohioland missions for a time.

UNDER ATTACK

In the first part of April 1766, Zeisberger traveled to Bethlehem to consult with the mission board. Two weeks later when he returned to Wyalusing, his mind was made up. He gathered up Anton, Abraham, Jacob, and me and set off with us to Cayuga to settle the matter.

After two days of travel, the group arrived at Togahaju's village on Cayuga Lake. He welcomed us and promised to call his Council to a meeting the next day.

The Council began with all the Indian ceremonies and customs normally observed in a formal council. Tagahaju figuratively cleaned our eyes and wiped the dust off our feet. I presented five strings and two belts of wampum at the beginning of my speech. Then I assured the Council, "The path to Wyalusing has been cleared. The road is now open."

Anton presented a large wampum belt of ten rows, after which he declared, "We are different from other men. We do not engage in drinking, revelry, and fighting. We are only concerned with the worship of our God. We have much trouble when the wild Indians come to our village."

Then I spoke again. "Uncle, you made known to us last year that you wanted to remove us from Wyalusing and place us at the upper end of the lake. However, we desire that you would permit us to remain at Wyalusing. We have already built houses, and the place which you cleansed for us a year ago is agreeable. We would like to live there quietly and undisturbed."

Togahaju responded, "Up to this time you have had no abiding place, but now I will take you and seat you permanently. You can therefore remain there, and the land shall be yours. As your number is many and may increase, so I have further thought of you. We will therefore give you all the land from Wyalusing to beyond Tioga, which is by land a good two days' journey."

Three days after the Cayuga Council, my embassy and I arrived back

Under Attack at Wyalusing: 1765-1772

at Wyalusing. The good news of a permanent seat in the valley sparked joyous singing of Delaware hymns. It also brought on a discussion of moving the town to a more suitable location where the inhabitants would be closer to wood, water, and their plantations.

After choosing a site close to a good spring and planning the layout of the town, the move began on 26 June. The old town and the new site were not far apart, so we moved thirty-five huts and cabins to the new site. Having finished transporting the dwellings, we set the meetinghouse near the center of the town next to the spring. Beside it, we constructed a strong dwelling of logs for our teachers. The builders attached a wing and covered the whole with a roof of split plank. All was in readiness for the teachers to move in by the end of August.

On 23 June, Zeisberger had announced that Johann and Johanna Schmick were coming to replace him as head missionary at Huts of Peace. All who had been in captivity in Philadelphia knew the Schmicks well and knew they would love them. The Schmicks arrived at Huts of Peace in July of 1766 and began keeping the mission diary a month later.

Late in July, a Six Nations Indian who carried no wampum brought disturbing news to Wyalusing. He told me, "The Six Nations Council scolded Togahaju for permitting you to settle at Wyalusing."

I laid the news aside as only a rumor. However, when Zeisberger returned to Bethlehem, he obtained the blessing of the mission board to go to Onondaga and investigate. He took 21-year-old Gottlob Senseman on a difficult ten-day journey from Bethlehem to Huts of Peace. Normally, the trip would have taken only four days, but because of swollen rivers and streams, they encountered numerous detours and difficulties.

When they finally arrived at Huts of Peace, I tried to discourage Brother David from continuing his journey to Onondaga, the capital

UNDER ATTACK

of the Six Nations. I chided him, "You ought not to interfere in the Six Nations/Pennsylvania/Delaware politics that involve the land issue. We should mind only the things of God and be at peace with all men. All is quiet now, and it is not good to take a dog by the ears."

But Brother Zeisberger stubbornly refused to give up his mission to the Six Nations. He remained at Huts of Peace five days before continuing his journey north to Zeninge.[99]

At Zeninge, he attempted to speak to the inhabitants about our Lord and Savior Jesus Christ, but he found there were no ears to hear. The Chief observed, "Though we have heard no sermons and know not God, yet we are the best of Indians." Ironically, that very day, the whole village was drunk to such a degree that they committed the most shameful excesses.

Zeisberger and Senseman pushed on to Onondaga where the Great Council of the Iroquois met.[100] After meeting with both the Council and Togahaju, Zeisberger received the confirmation of the land grant and permission to preach the Gospel on the Susquehanna. But he also received a hint that the Brethren should not attempt to carry the Gospel too far into the country of the Iroquois. The speaker said, "As soon as we choose to have the Gospel preached among us, we will let you know. But for now, you may return to your own house."

A triumphant Zeisberger and his companion Senseman returned to Huts of Peace on 7 November 1766. "It was all a mistake," he told me. "The message was not sent properly. Togahaju told us, 'I have given you the land, but not for the purpose of allowing Whites to build storehouses on it. Do not give the traders place among you, and do not permit them to build houses.' "

---

[99] An Iroquois town on the Chenango River, close to where it emptied into the Susquehanna. Zeninge was about thirty miles north of Huts of Peace.

[100] Onondaga was the Iroquois capital where Zeisberger had lived eleven years earlier. The house where he had lived was still standing, and the Chief allowed the Brethren to stay in it during their visit.

Under Attack at Wyalusing: 1765–1772

The Great Council of the Six Nations at Onondaga confirmed the land grant Togahaju made to us. This is what the Council of the Iroquois told us:

> We let you know herewith that the matter which Chief Togahaju in Cayuga treated and concluded with you meets with our consent, and we all know what he has done. We are not only satisfied therewith, but it pleases us very much that the believing Indians live in Huts of Peace and that they shall have a council fire there, which is no small matter.
>
> The Great Council has heard your mind in regard to living among the Indians. We very much approve of the white teachers dwelling among the Indians on the Susquehanna. You do well that you instruct them in good things. They need it, for the Delaware, our cousins, are very much inclined toward the bad. This could be plainly seen in the late war.

And I, The Prophet, said, "All their words and wampum belts are as hot air. You have prostrated yourself at their feet, and they will again sell the land out from under our feet."

Doing Good

By John Heckewelder en route to Bethlehem

The trip over the mountains on the path that Papunhank and the refugees from Huts of Peace had traveled in the spring of 1772 had

UNDER ATTACK

gone well. The yellow poplars, red oaks, and scarlet maples shone in their fall glory. The weather held. Once across the Alleghenies, Papunhank was again at home. It seemed he knew almost every path, spring, and hideout in the whole area.

Each evening as we stopped to rest after a hard day's ride, he would tell me more of his story. The previous evening, he had thrown out a hard question to me. Now as we skirted Bald Eagle Mountain and clopped along toward Great Island, I had time to ponder his question.

"Brother John," he had said, "the Moravians have been good to the Indians. They told the Indians of the Savior and what the Lord required of them. The Moravians not only cared for the Indians' souls, but they also met their physical needs. I remember how you even drove four cows to Huts of Peace in our hour of need. Many men and women, like Buettner, Post, Rauch, and Zeisberger endured much hardship against the body to live with the Indians and teach them. Some died, while others were murdered at Huts of Grace."

He went on, "The Moravians truly did much good for the Indians, but did they have a part in driving the Indians out of their homeland? What do you think, Brother John?"

I answered cautiously, "The heathen Indians who continued in their idolatry, revelry, and warring and did not adopt the civilized ways the Moravians taught them could not coexist with Whites. They did have to leave their homelands."

But Papunhank did not let the question rest with my evasive answer. "Brother John, I am talking about the praying Indians. Did the Moravian support for the Pennsylvania government's policy of making the Iroquois lords over the other Indian nations have anything to do with forcing the Delawares out of their homelands? To be specific, why did Brother Zeisberger insist on going to the Iroquois and getting their consent for us to live on our own lands when all the Delawares, Mohicans, and Shawnees opposed his going?"

Under Attack at Wyalusing: 1765-1772

Then Prophet Papunhank added one more unanswerable question. "If Brother Zeisberger was so intent on dealing with the Six Nations, why did he not open a mission at Cayuga or Onondaga?"[101]

I answered truthfully, "I don't know the answers to your questions. Perhaps we should ask Brother Zeisberger."

With these questions hanging in the air, we rode into Great Island and greeted all of Papunhank's friends there.

A Memoir of Huts of Peace at Wyalusing 1765-1772
(continued)

As told by Johannes Papunhank to John Heckewelder

The About-Face

Huts of Peace prospered. The inward and outward state of the settlement was truly blessed, and an extraordinary number of Indian visitors came from all parts to see it. They were struck with the outward appearance of Huts of Peace, with its orderly huts, clean streets, miles of fences, gardens, boats, cattle, horses, swine, and poultry. They declared it to be the most beautiful Indian town they had ever seen.

The visitors also paid great attention to the Gospel. Its power in their hearts was often remarkably evident. Frequently, the whole assembly was so moved, the weeping of the congregation so widespread and loud, that the missionaries were obliged to stop and

---

[101] Earl Olmstead has this to say on page 145 of his book, *David Zeisberger, A Life Among the Indians:* "To this day, it is a mystery why the Moravian Church authorities gave up their effort to found missions among the Six Nations, especially the Onondaga. I have questioned numerous church officials, and all are at a loss to provide an answer. Edmund De Schweinitz, a long-standing and respected bishop of the church who wrote the only definitive biography of Zeisberger (published in 1870) noted: "None of the authorities we have examined explain this change in the policy of the Church."

UNDER ATTACK

give vent to their own tears.

Some who heard the Gospel for the first time seemed suddenly roused from the sleep of sin, and having mourned over their transgressions, found pardon and peace with Jesus. By faith, they began to taste in Him the sweetness of the Gospel.

This awakening was generally followed by a desire to dwell with the believers. For instance, Menatschis and Mamtscha spent Passion Week and Easter at Huts of Peace. When it was over, Mamtscha said to her husband, "I never before heard anything like this; what I felt I cannot express, but my heart was most tenderly moved."

Menatschis then asked her, "What would you now wish to do? I would willingly know it."

Mamtscha answered, "I am glad that you ask me. I have waited for this. My wish is to love our Savior and believe in Him, but I should find it difficult without you. I cannot live here alone, nor can I part with you."

Menatschis replied, "I will not hinder you. For if I did and you should be lost, I should bring your guilt upon myself. Alas! I have enough sins of my own. God forbid I should do this! We will rather both beg leave to live here that we may hear daily of our Savior, learn to love Him, and become happy people."[102]

After they related their conversation to the missionaries and their assistants, the couple obtained permission to live at Huts of Peace. Seeing how it went with Mamtscha, her sister Mattamis then expressed her sensations during the reading of our Lord's sufferings by saying, "My heart tells me my sins have occasioned the torments, distress, wounds, and death of our Savior. When I, a child of hell, heard that Jesus had suffered all this to redeem me from Satan, sin, and eternal death, I felt that I ought to love Him and believe on Him. Otherwise

---

[102] He was baptized "Jacob" on 29 December 1765 and she "Rebecca" on 7 June 1767.

Under Attack at Wyalusing: 1765-1772

I should be lost, fail to obtain salvation, and miss His gift to me of everlasting life."

The assistants had no greater joy than when the conversation of the visitors afforded an opportunity to testify of the truth. One of the assistants, Joseph, one day spoke with the wife of the Delaware chief, Newallike. He told her about the love of the Savior for poor sinners and finished with, "I have experienced this love myself."

She answered, "All that may be true, but I cannot be forgiven, for I have sinned grievously against God."

Joseph replied, "Nevertheless, you may find forgiveness with our Savior. I formerly thought as you do, but found salvation despite my doubt. Our Savior has forgiven my sins though they were many and great. He is even now the same gracious Savior and has died, shedding His blood upon the cross for your sins also. As soon as you truly believe this, you will taste this love and be assured that He will forgive all your sins."

It was a custom at Huts of Peace to give any visiting captain a belt of wampum in recognition of the great honor of his position. One newly elected visiting captain, Chelloway,[103] returned the proffered belt to me saying, "I am concerned for my salvation. My sins, which are many, lie heavy upon me. Sometimes I despaired of all help, but when I heard that our Savior receives the worst of sinners, it encouraged me to hope that even I might be saved.

"I then prayed to our Savior, 'Have mercy upon me, and let me feel that there is grace, even for such a wretch as me.' He heard me, and I saw Him as crucified for me. I was convinced that I have wounded Him with my sins; this made me weep. I then prayed, 'Dear Savior! I desire to be healed and saved by thy wounds, and to be washed from all my sins in thy blood.'

---

[103] Baptized "Willhelm" 6 January 1771 at Huts of Peace.

UNDER ATTACK

"I often thought and felt that to be truly converted, I should bid farewell to the world. Therefore I returned the belt of wampum. I do not desire any such honor among the Indians. I only want to obtain mercy and forgiveness of my sins, become a child of God, and live happily among His people. Then I will have all my heart can wish for."

The heathen visitors were astonished at the great change in all those who believed in Jesus and were baptized. Many were obliged to confess, "The words of the Brethren must be true. Otherwise it would be impossible that the mere belief in the Brethren should make the believers willing and able to deny the world and every ungodly lust. Who could miss observing that they became serene and cheerful in their countenances and behavior?"

One evening a reputed sorcerer who lived near Huts of Peace came to visit. He would not even enter the chapel but stood outside and listened to the sermon. When it was over, he said to me, "Brother Johannes, I am indeed a very wicked man, and I know I have committed many sins. Yea, I am so loaded with them that they weigh me down. If I knew that Jesus would accept me and help me, I would pray to Him to save me."

One sinner after another came to Huts of Peace to hear the Gospel preached. One hearer said, "I am terrified when I consider that I have heard the Gospel so long and have not yet attained to saving faith."

However, not every visitor had good intentions, nor were all converted. Some suspicious characters who stayed in the village had evil designs, especially on the young people. Brother Schmick and Brother Rothe did not dare forbid these people to stay lest they be charged with trying to govern the Indians. They therefore chose some of the oldest and most respected assistants, like me, and commissioned us thus:

> You must meet and speak with all strange Indians who wish to become inhabitants of Huts of Peace. You

Under Attack at Wyalusing: 1765-1772

must examine their views and then declare to them, with kindness and firmness, that all people who are not truly desirous to turn unto their Creator and Redeemer should absolutely not dwell in this place.

This was done accordingly, and the faithful, prudent, and undaunted manner in which we executed our commission was very edifying. We had no respect of persons, nor did we spare our own kindred more than strangers. The good effects of our zeal were soon visible, and several dangerous people left the place.

While carrying out my charge to rid the town of these unwanted characters, I encountered one Nanticoke physician who did not turn out so well. Unnacoksi was named after a famous Nanticoke chief from the period when the tribe still lived in their homeland on the eastern shore of the Chesapeake Bay.[104]

When the Nanticokes came north, they brought along with them a repulsive custom. Whenever one of their tribe died, those at hand buried them. Then the relatives of the deceased would come at their convenience, dig up the dead person, scrape off the flesh, rebury it, and carry the bones off with them for idolatrous worship.

Because of this practice of worshipping the dead, one young Nanticoke who earnestly desired to live in Huts of Peace was denied entrance several times. The assistants were firm; he could not remain in the town unless he was baptized. He pled with them, "I have experienced something remarkable in my mind today. I have a great desire to be saved, but alas, I feel myself a slave of sin and Satan. It is as if he kept me fast bound, unwilling to release me. Though I strive to get away from him and become the property of our Savior, I cannot do

---

[104] *Nanticoke* means "people of the tidewater." The remnants of this tribe were driven north by relentless pressure from the settlers of Virginia, Maryland, and Delaware. The full name of the ancient chief was Unnacoksimmon.

UNDER ATTACK

it." Still the Brethren could not agree to baptize him because of how he clung to his pagan practices.

Upon another occasion, he burst into a flood of tears and said, "Brethren, have mercy upon me. I am the most wretched creature upon earth. Since yesterday morning, I have felt nothing but sorrow, anxiety, and perplexity. I can find no place where I can bear my existence. This whole afternoon I have lain like a dead man. I have no strength and am quite exhausted. Have mercy upon me. Oh, that I were baptized and washed from my sins in the blood of our Savior; that alone can help and give me rest." Hearing this earnest petition, it was at last impossible to refuse him. He became the firstfruits of the Nanticokes. On 10 August 1766, Brother David baptized him Samuel Nantikok. Samuel is faithfully serving the Lord among us to this day as a helper and lay preacher.

It did not go this way with Unnacoksi. He possessed the "poison," a deadly concoction of herbs and sorcery. By his own statements, he had already murdered several of his Nanticoke nation by his vile practices. Unnacoksi kept hanging around Huts of Peace. When I questioned him about his intentions in the future, Unnacoksi became angry. "I can stay here as long as I want," he shouted, "and if you make any trouble, I will breathe on you and kill you."

I was kind but firm. "Unnacoksi, you have no power over us other than the power of Satan. We have a much stronger power to guard us, our Savior and Redeemer. If you repent of your wickedness and turn to the Savior, you may remain here. Otherwise you must go away. All of us have agreed on this, and if you stay here, our God is able to punish you." Unnacoksi went away, still breathing out threats against me.

Then the assistants had to deal with another serious problem: the rum trade. Heathen Indians made frequent attempts to introduce rum into Huts of Peace, so the assistants introduced the following rules into the town:

Under Attack at Wyalusing: 1765-1772

If strangers come to the town, their goods will be examined immediately upon their arrival. If the visitors want to stay overnight, their rum shall immediately be secured until the next morning. When they proceed on their journey, they will be accompanied until they are a safe distance from the town. Whoever refuses to comply with this order is asked to leave the settlement without delay.

The assistants saw to it that these regulations were strictly attended to.

The white traders gave the most trouble to the settlement. They were not content to just trade in Huts of Peace either. A company of ten traders from Paxton wanted to make it a place of common resort. Their plan was simple and evident: to ruin the people with rum and then take their land. These disagreeable guests occasioned much dissipation among the young people.

I called a meeting with the assistants and the Paxton people. I spoke for the assistants. "The Iroquois have sent us several serious protests, warning us that we dare not allow Whites other than our teachers to live here or to build storehouses in our town. Furthermore, it is against our rules for you to remain in our town more than two or three days at a time. Therefore you must leave, or we will take all your goods and pass them out to the needy Indians who come through here."

The Paxton Boys flew into a rage at this ultimatum. "We can stay in this town as long as we like," they growled.

"We will have your land and your goods, whether you like it or not," Lazarus Stewart, the leader of the gang, threatened as he fingered his pistol.

But again, I was firm. "We are here with the consent of the Six Nations. We shall abide by their decrees. You must go at once. We are at peace with Pennsylvania and all the Indian nations. We do not war with anyone, but only mind the things of God. We trust in God

UNDER ATTACK

for our protection from those who would do us harm. If you, as a Christian people, would steal from us, you will have to give account to God for that."

"What will you do about the Connecticut people who come into the valley?" Lazarus Stewart asked.

"We have no quarrel with them," I responded. "They have not harmed us, nor we them. The Connecticut people are not the ones who killed the Conestogas, drove us from our homes, and wanted to kill us in Philadelphia. It is well known to us that those people came from Paxton and that there is a reward offered for the capture of their leaders. You would do well to leave us in peace."

Sullenly and silently the men left the meeting. Lazarus Stewart was the last to leave. "So you think the Connecticut people will take the valley from Pennsylvania, do you?" he asked. Then without further explanation he turned, kicked his boot in the dirt, and went off muttering curses. When the gang had saddled their horses, gathered up their goods, and boisterously made ready to depart, Lazarus Stewart threw a parting challenge to the watching villagers, "You will hear from us again." I sent two young men to quietly trail the Whites till they were sure the traders would not return to Huts of Peace.

In 1766, the Delawares in Goshchuenk on the Ohio, along with thirteen other nations, sent a solemn embassy to the Iroquois capital in Onondaga. They arrived in Huts of Peace and presented their message: "We wish to establish a general peace among the Indian nations and invite you to lay hold of the chain of friendship. If you refuse to do it, we declare you to be our enemies."

I gave the embassy a string of wampum and made a fitting response for the Brethren:

> Brothers, we at Huts of Peace have no part in war, neither in the past nor in the present. Our desire is to be at

Under Attack at Wyalusing: 1765–1772

peace with all men and to mind only the things of God.

We at Huts of Peace want to promote and share in a general peace among all the Indian nations. With this string of wampum, we lay hold of the chain of friendship you are taking to the Iroquois.

The embassy then proceeded on by way of Zeninge to Onondaga, and thence home again. The Brethren hoped the Iroquois also took hold of the friendship belt, for whatever it was worth. But you shall soon see they had good reason to suspect that neither the Iroquois nor the Whites really wanted a general peace among all the Indians.

The number of people in Huts of Peace increased quickly. The numbers who attended to hear the Gospel were so great that the believers had to build a more spacious chapel. The new building included glazed window glass in the openings and a bell atop the new chapel. Everyone loved to hear the bell announce the services throughout the town.

Many visiting Indians who constantly attended the services came from various tribes and nations: Mohawks, Cayugas, Senecas, Tutelos, Delawares, Mohicans, Wampanoags, Nanticokes, and Tuscaroras. Besides a hunger to hear the Gospel, a famine among the Indians also served to increase the number of people coming to Huts of Peace.

The generosity of the believers in sharing their food became well known among the Indians, and sometimes they received messages from distant nations telling of distress and famine among them. Thus it came about that seventy-five Tuscaroras from North Carolina and fifty-seven Nanticokes from Maryland came and stayed near the village for a number of weeks.

The famine proved an opportunity for the missionaries and the assistants to teach the Word of God. Some guests thanked God for the famine and said, "If we had not gone to Huts of Peace, we should

UNDER ATTACK

never have heard the Gospel of salvation."

The opportunity to teach the Gospel made the believers always ready to feed the hungry, even though some lazy and indolent people abused their generosity. They ate up scarce provisions while continuing to lead idle and profligate lives, never even paying attention to the Word of God.

In this way the selfless generosity of the Christian Indians was frequently followed by want, which the believers cheerfully bore as true children of God. They were not tormented by the cares of this life, but contented themselves with little. They relied upon the daily bread given them by their heavenly Father, who does not forget even the meanest of His creatures.

Upon one such occasion, a poor woman said, "I have been thinking how poor I am. I have nothing of my own. Where shall I get enough for myself and my child?

"This made me uneasy, and immediately I prayed thus to our Savior: 'Forgive my care and anxiety about outward matters. You yourself have been very poor in this world, and you did not even have as much of your own as I have.' This thought comforted me, and my heart was satisfied."

In this time of much need, one of our families with six children walked ten miles so they could feast on bilberries to sustain themselves.

Besides the want occasioned by the extraordinary number of visitors, the locusts did very great mischief to the fields and plantations. I can describe their swarms as covering the earth as in the plagues of Egypt. Yet in all the times of scarcity and difficulty, God provided enough so that no one starved.

The chief means by which the Indians provided a livelihood for themselves and their families was by hunting bear, deer, and elk, and by catching beaver, fox, and raccoon. The missionaries encouraged

Under Attack at Wyalusing: 1765-1772

the Indians to stay away from the heathen on such trips so they could help each other and meet sometimes in prayer.

One woman disregarded this advice and fixed her hut near the banks of a river which unexpectedly overflowed in the night. Water inundated the whole country to such a degree that she and her daughter were obliged to take refuge upon the roof. They almost starved before the waters subsided.

Evil Designs

The great success of Huts of Peace enraged many Indians against the missionaries. The Nanticokes of Zeninge were particularly exasperated because they believed Brother Schmick caused the Christian Indians to separate themselves and form a detached tribe of their own. Also, the believing Indians no longer practiced the customs peculiar to the Indians. Worse yet, Huts of Peace Indians successfully proselytized among the heathen Indians.

The Zeninge Nanticokes sent Brother Schmick a message saying, "Because you have so many Indians in your arms and hold them fast, and even endeavor to grasp more and thus rob us of our friends, we are going to kill you." The words of Hebrews 13:6, the reading for the day when Brother Schmick received the message, greatly comforted him: "The Lord is my helper, and I will not fear what man can do to me."

The message from Zeninge had no wampum with it to verify it as an official message. Later events made me believe it was just another Indian lie. Still, it reeked of trouble.

Not long after this foreboding message, Unnacoksi and a partner returned to Huts of Peace. Unnacoksi hung around the edges of the

UNDER ATTACK

town and spent his time visiting with those Indians whom he knew to be unsettled.

The two men repeated a tale several times throughout the village. "We have received full and satisfactory information from the chiefs at Zeninge stating that Johannes Papunhank is a dealer in poison. He has indeed caused the recent sudden deaths of several people, as well as the epidemic which raged in this country some time ago." Then the two hung around outside the town while the furor mounted.

By this wicked lie, the whole settlement was alarmed and in a great uproar for a whole week. Some looked upon me as innocent, but a greater number of them were doubtful. A few were so far misled by the slanderers that they even joined them and formed a party, having little less in view than to take my life.

Brother Schmick, convinced of my innocence, took all possible pains to inform and pacify the doubters and the evil party, but in vain. He then assembled the whole congregation, and I declared publicly:

> I never had any poison in my possession, nor do I understand the art of mixing it. While I did not love the Lord Jesus, my whole heart was full of wickedness, but now my soul has been washed by the blood of Christ and my sins pardoned. Ever since the time I received holy baptism, I have belonged to the Lord with all my soul and body. I love Him and intend to serve Him and cleave to Him all my life.

By my free and sincere declaration, the greater number were fully satisfied, but Unnacoksi and his party were rendered more bitter and even attacked me outside the settlement. When my assailants cornered me, they commanded, "Give up your poison or lose your life."

Under Attack at Wyalusing: 1765–1772

I appealed to them with great calmness and composure. "Look," I said, "I told everyone publicly that I know nothing about the poison. If you have honest charges to make, you should also bring them out publicly." Then I walked quietly away, and my enemies did not dare to execute their wicked design.

During this very dangerous period, I depended upon the sure protection of God, which filled my heart with confidence. I once said, "If the Lord permits that by these base lies I lose my life, I shall at once be delivered from all misery and go to my Savior. I should only pity my wife and child." My wife supported me, and we clung to the Savior, the best friend in every time of need.

To prove my innocence further, I sent two messengers with a belt of wampum to two chiefs in the Zeninge area. "I, Papunhank at Huts of Peace, desire to know if you have ever accused me of the abominable practice of having the poison."

The chiefs replied, "We are astonished at the message and solemnly declare we are ignorant of this whole affair."

My innocence was thus firmly established, and the diabolical malice of my accusers thoroughly exposed. The slanderers, Unnacoksi and his partner, now thought it most prudent not to be seen by the inhabitants of Huts of Peace, who sympathized with my unmerited sufferings.

All joined in praising the Lord for this discovery, which put a stop to a most detestable business. But the sorrow over those members who had been so grievously misguided by the seducers was also widespread. They acknowledged their transgression and publicly begged and received the pardon of the congregation, but it was a long time before they could recover rest and peace of mind. They served as a remarkable example of what a hideous and aggravated crime the sin of slander is in the eyes of a just and righteous God.

UNDER ATTACK

The Murders

After Unnacoksi and the Paxton Boys left Huts of Peace, things seemed quite peaceable and prosperous for several months. Then in the middle of January 1768, I received alarming news. A white man had killed ten Indians near Shamokin at the Forks of the Susquehanna. With Brother Schmick's consent, Anthony and I immediately got in a canoe and paddled south to check on the rumor.

At the Indian town of Shamokin, we located Little Cat, an Indian related to the murder victims. He was ready to talk. "It is indeed true," he growled angrily. "The white man called Stump and his helper, Ironcutter, murdered six Indians at his house." Slowly he named them: "White Mingo, Cornelius, John Campbell, Jones, and two squaws." Tears moistened Little Cat's eyes, and he faltered before he again gained control of his voice. He clutched his tomahawk. "Stump cut a hole in the ice and dropped the bodies into it. White Mingo floated down the creek into the Susquehanna and lodged on the shore at Harrisburg.

"The six murders were not enough for Stump and Ironcutter. The next day they went fourteen miles farther up the creek to White Mingo's cabin and killed his squaw, two girls, and a child. They threw them into the cabin and burned it down," Little Cat choked.

"When we had discovered all this, I found several other relatives. We went to Stump's cabin and chased him almost to Fort Augusta. But Stump did not go into the fort. We thought he went into the house of two women who lived close to the fort, but they declared they knew nothing of Stump. Since we could not find him in the house, we seized one of their cats, pulled out its hair, cut it to pieces,

Under Attack at Wyalusing: 1765-1772

and then we left."[105]

I offered my condolences to the aggrieved Indian and offered some wampum, as the custom was, to soothe the pain and appease Little Cat's need for revenge. "We do not want this act of a madman to start another general war," I said. "If this belt is not enough, when we return home we will take up a collection for you to share with the family."

"But why are you doing this?" Little Cat wanted to know.

"We serve the Creator God," I said. "We are a people of peace. Our God has told us in His Word, 'Vengeance is mine, I will repay.' We can rest easy, knowing that God's punishment in eternal fire will be far worse than anything we could do to Stump now. If we seek revenge through murder, we will reap bitterness and hatred the rest of our lives on earth and may also join Stump in the eternal fire."

Little Cat thanked us for the wampum belt and said, "The other relatives and I will think much about it. Perhaps we will come to Huts of Peace to hear more of the Gospel you teach."

Anthony and I then returned to Huts of Peace. We reported what we had found out. All rejoiced that perhaps our small journey had helped avoid a war. Then Billy Champion, a Delaware Indian, stopped at Huts of Peace with a message from Governor Penn. Brothers Schmick and Rothe called the assistants together in their house and listened quietly while Billy Champion laid the wampum on the table before him and faithfully "read" the governor's message to them.

> I am glad this Indian man, Bill, came down at this
> time, for it gives me an opportunity to inform you of a

---

[105] C. Hale Sipe, *Indian Wars of Pennsylvania*, p. 485. "[Stump] ran to a house occupied by two women whose protection he implored, alleging that he was pursued by Indians. The women did not believe his story, but he begged very piteously. They then hid him between two beds." Why the Indians did not hang around for some time when they knew their quarry was so close is something of a mystery. Or one wonders why the Indians did not pursue the murderer at a later date, unless something like Papunhank's offer made them lay their tomahawks aside.

UNDER ATTACK

melancholy affair which I have only heard of within these few days, and which fills the hearts of all your brethren with the deepest sorrow and grief. It is this: two or three families of Indians, namely, the White Mingo, Cornelius, Jonas, and John Campbell, three women, two girls, and a child, left Big Island in the spring and came and built themselves cabins on Middle Creek. There they lived and hunted and were often with our people and were always well received and kindly treated by them.

About ten days ago, they were at the home of Mr. William Blyth, who lives at the mouth of Middle Creek. He treated them kindly. From his house, they went to one Frederick Stump, a Dutchman, who lives in that neighborhood. There it is supposed some difference arose, but what it was we have not heard, but they were all found murdered, six of them in Stump's own house, and four at a cabin some distance from it. Stump says he killed them all with his own hands, and there was no other person there to offer him assistance in the brutal act.

Upon receiving this melancholy account, I immediately sent for the sheriff and his officers to hunt down this Stump and charge him with the murder. For their encouragement, I offered a reward of two hundred pounds, and I am in hopes he is by this time taken. May he suffer the same punishment he would receive had he killed that many white men.

I consider this matter as nothing less than the act of a wicked, rash man, and I hope you will also consider it in the same way. Do not imagine, since it was done by one man in the manner I have related it to you, that any other persons have been concerned in it, or that it has been in

Under Attack at Wyalusing: 1765–1772

any way encouraged by any of my people. I assure you it has not.

There are among you and us some hotheaded people who commit actions of the sort. Whenever it so happens, all that can be done is immediately to acquaint each other of them and to bring the offenders to justice. In this way, it may make no breach between us, but be considered as a rash, sudden act that could not be prevented. We now inform you further that we are going to send off a messenger immediately to the relations of the deceased people, who, we hear, live near Chenasse, to inform them and the Seneca nation, to whom they belong, of this murder. We will bury their bodies and wipe the tears from their eyes that it may not break the friendship subsisting between us and the Indians, but that we may live together and love one another as we did before this melancholy accident happened. This belt confirms my words.

I desire that this belt of wampum may be sent to any of our Indian brethren near you, that they may not be frightened or think the English are not their friends. Assure them to the contrary, and we will keep the chain of friendship entire and bright, notwithstanding this accident. To confirm this request of mine, I give you this string.

Given under my hand and the lesser seal of the Province of Pennsylvania; at Philadelphia, the 23rd of January 1768.
—JOHN PENN.[106]

When Bill Champion had finished delivering the message and left, I

---

[106] Pennsylvania Archives, Colonial Records. *Minutes of the Provincial Council*, Vol. IX, pp. 428–430.

UNDER ATTACK

spoke to the people. "The governor speaks with his lips, but not from the heart. His message is the same as the one he delivered when the Paxton Boys murdered the Conestoga Indians. He does not want an Indian war, but he also knows that Stump and Ironcutter will never be tried or put to death.[107]

"We must be watchful. If the Indian nations join to avenge this horrid act of cruelty, all Whites will be considered as outlaws. Our white teachers will risk being sacrificed to the fury of the enraged savages, for they never inquire whether anyone be innocent or guilty. If he has a white skin, it is deemed sufficient reason to take his life. Therefore we must not allow our teachers to be left alone, but must always keep a strict watch about their persons until the fury of this time be passed."

All the assistants voiced their approval of my suggestion.

Brother Schmick spoke next. "Brother Johannes, you are overly fearful. God has brought us to this place, and He will protect us. Governor Penn will shield us from the settlers, and the Iroquois will shield us from revengeful Indians."

"Brother Schmick," I answered, "the Iroquois will shield us from no one. They have not accepted the Gospel and are only interested in themselves. They will cheat, lie, and steal whenever they wish." I looked around the room at the other assistants as each one nodded his head in agreement.

This time Brother Rothe said, "Brother Johannes, we do not want to be blinded by race, hatred, and bitterness. God has made of one blood all the nations, and His grace can reach the Iroquois as well as the other Indian nations."

---

[107] The date of the governor's letter was 23 January 1768. The governor says in the letter that he hopes the sheriff has already captured the murderers. In what appears to have been a staged arrest, the murderers were delivered two months later to the Carlisle jail on 23 March. One week later, a company of settlers from his home area surrounded the jail, entered it with drawn pistols, and released the murderers. They were never again arrested for the crime, but soon went to Virginia, where Stump died at an advanced age. —C. Hale Sipe, *Indian Wars of Pennsylvania*, p. 486.

Under Attack at Wyalusing: 1765–1772

"Brothers," I continued, "I will explain further. Stump and the other settlers around him were settled on Indian lands not yet purchased from the Iroquois. Yet the settlers are there, and the general hatred for the presence of Indians living among them brings on these murders."

Brother Schmick again raised a question. "Did you and Brother Zeisberger not obtain a firm commitment from the Iroquois at Onondaga that they have permanently seated the believing Indians at Huts of Peace? They have given you the land as far north as Tioga. And God is with us."

"Brother Schmick," I said quietly, "the Iroquois cannot be trusted! I pray you are right, but I have not forgotten Canassatego, nor Teedyuscung, nor Lazarus Stewart, nor Governor Penn, nor Secretary Peters. Only God can spare us."

And all the assistants plainly agreed with me.

Soon after Governor Penn's message was delivered by Billy Champion, Sir William Johnson sent a special message to Huts of Peace.

> If you know any of the relations of those persons murdered near Shamokin, send them to me that I might dry up their tears, comfort their afflicted hearts, and satisfy all their grievances. I also request Huts of Peace to send delegates to an amicable convention of all the chiefs of the Iroquois and all the other Indian nations living on the Susquehanna and the Ohio.

I again spoke strongly to the missionaries, saying, "We have no inclination to go to such a political affair. Such journeys are always attended with more harm than good to the souls of those who go. Let us give a commission to the Cayuga chief to treat with the rest in our name."

Such an arrangement did not satisfy the enemies of the believing

UNDER ATTACK

Indians. They pretended that General Johnson and all the chiefs had resolved to count the believing Indians as enemies and planned to destroy them and their settlement.

When the truth was later discovered, they found that General Johnson had publicly praised our conduct and expressed a wish that many more towns like Huts of Peace might be found in the country. Thus, through General Johnson's benevolent exertions at the conference, peace between the Indians and the English was reestablished and the minds of the people were set at rest.

General Johnson also helped to settle the long-standing dispute between the Iroquois and the Cherokees. To bring this about, the King of the Cherokees was led in solemn pomp through the whole country of the Iroquois by the Oneida chief, and everywhere he was received as a friend.

They also came to Huts of Peace, and the Oneida chief used this occasion to declare the great joy which he and the whole Council at Onondaga felt when they considered that the Indians here learned to know God. The Oneida chief did not stop there, but exhorted the believing Indians to remain faithful and gave us a string of wampum.

I also gave them a string of wampum and said in reply, "Our chief desire is to grow daily in the knowledge and love of God our Creator and Redeemer. It is also our fervent wish that all the Indian nations might become acquainted with our God and Savior, for then peace and benevolence would infallibly reign among them."

Land Sale

The joy felt by the Indians at Huts of Peace because of the good overtures from General Johnson and the Iroquois was greatly lessened

Under Attack at Wyalusing: 1765–1772

by troubling news we received from the Delaware Chief Leekey from Great Island. I spoke with Leekey, and he was visibly angered. "In November, the Iroquois sold all the land as far west as the Ohio to the English. That includes all the lands in the Forks of the Susquehanna—Great Island, Shamokin, Wyalusing, and Wyoming."

"Are you sure this is true?" I asked Leekey.

"The Indians had a great council with the English. More than 2,200 Indians were at Fort Stanwix. We cannot be sure of anything about the boundaries because only the Iroquois talked to the English. But it is rumored the Iroquois received a payment of more than £10,000. Of course, the thieves kept all the money and shared none of it with the other Indians."

"But did the land sale include Wyalusing and Huts of Peace?" I asked.

"Papunhank, we cannot be sure since the Iroquois did not talk to any of the other nations, but the English are not fools and would not pay such a large sum for nothing."

"But," I protested, "Lydius of the Iroquois sold Wyoming and much land there to the people from Connecticut. The Iroquois have given us all the land as far north as Tioga. Do you think the Iroquois would really sell land they have already deeded to others?"

"Papunhank, you know the Iroquois claim all the Indian land by right of a fake conquest that never happened," Leekey continued. "The real conquest was when the French were driven out and the English conquered the Iroquois. Now the Iroquois have no choice but to do whatever the English want, for they have been conquered by the English. As surely as the sun rises in the morning sky, someday soon the English will take the land of the Iroquois for nothing."

"Leekey," I said sorrowfully, "if the Iroquois really have sold the land out from under us, it will give rise to many new troubles."

UNDER ATTACK

New Missions

Some of the many visitors to Huts of Peace went home and proclaimed with energy what they had seen and heard. In one such town, called Sheshequin,[108] located thirty miles higher up the Susquehanna, a great awakening took place. At the repeated request of all the inhabitants of Sheshequin, the Brethren appointed John Rothe to that post.

But before Brother Rothe moved to Sheshequin, the Brethren urged the Cayuga chief to ask permission from the Great Council at Onondaga for a white teacher to live at Sheshequin. The petition was successful, and the Cayuga chief added, "Now I shall go frequently to Sheshequin to hear the great word, for I am convinced that this is the right way to come to God and to learn to know Him."

Brother Rothe then moved to Sheshequin on 4 February 1769, and as the people requested, he regulated both the morning and evening services, which were numerously attended. Proofs of the grace and power of Jesus Christ prevailed at these meetings, and this encouraged him to boldly preach repentance and forgiveness of sins in His name.

Those who came to the services with their faces painted and their caps adorned with tinkling bells were asked in a friendly manner by their own countrymen to wash their faces and take off their bells before the service. In March, two Indian assistants also went to Sheshequin to assist Brother Rothe.

Sheshequin furnished a great contrast when compared with a neighboring town only half a mile away, where the savages kept their feasts of sacrifice. On these occasions, they roved about in their neighborhood like so many evil spirits, making such hideous noises and bellows that the air resounded with them both far and near. But even during

---

[108] The original name of the town was Tsehechsehequannink.

Under Attack at Wyalusing: 1765-1772

the feasts, the savages did not molest those at Sheshequin. In our town, the preaching of the Gospel continued uninterrupted.

The power of the Spirit of God was so manifest at Sheshequin that a white man who came to a meeting, and saw the Indians in tears, said to Brother Rothe, "I am baptized and call myself a Christian, but my heart is far from being touched by the Gospel."

The emotion which caused even the wildest savages to shed tears led one Indian to express himself thus: "Whenever I saw a man shed tears, I used to doubt whether he was really a man. I would not have wept even if my enemies had cut the flesh from my bones, so hard was my heart at that time. But now God has softened the hardness of my heart so that I can weep."

So many similar proofs of the power of the Word of God were manifested at Sheshequin that it appeared for a time as though all the people in the town and neighborhood would turn to the Lord. But then a division arose among the town chiefs and the neighboring country.

Chief James Davis became a follower of the Gospel, and on that account, was persecuted by the rest. The sorcerers threatened his cattle, then the Chief, and then Brother Rothe. Others were persecuted in the same manner by the heathen chiefs, the sorcerers, and their nearest relations.

These troubles, however, were not able to hinder the progress of the Gospel in Sheshequin. Brother Rothe had the joy of seeing Brother Schmick baptize Chief James Davis in Huts of Peace. Others were soon partakers of the same work of grace, and their cheerful countenances and godly walk fully proved the conversion of their hearts.

The glorious work of God also flourished in Huts of Peace throughout 1769. The believers grew in the grace and knowledge of our Lord Jesus Christ, and a great many of the heathen visitors were awakened

UNDER ATTACK

from the sleep of sin. Several of these had been robbers and murderers who now appeared hungry and thirsty for grace in the blood of Jesus, and their sincere declarations of peace and forgiveness gave everyone much satisfaction.

Brother Schmick asked one visitor, "Why do you weep so much, and what do you hope for?"

He replied, "Alas! I wish to obtain life eternal; my sinful heart longs for our Savior and His cleansing blood. You know I have often told you my desire, but today I have felt such an eager longing after our Savior in all the meetings, that I know not what to do for the uneasiness of my heart. I cry continually, 'Lord have mercy upon me! Remember even me, a wretched sinner. Forgive me all my sins, and wash me in thy blood. Take my heart, bad as it is, my soul and body, and save me.'"

Another visitor spent almost two whole nights in tears, and when Brother Schmick asked the cause of it, he answered, "Well may I weep when I do not feel our Savior and the power of His blood in my heart! Without this, I am lost and undone. I wish to be saved and to believe in and love Jesus.

"I considered what might hinder me. *Is it my wife,* I asked myself, *or anything else that is in the way?* My heart told me, *It is not my wife. If I had no wife, I should be contriving to get one. It must be something else.* Then I knew it was my own bad heart!"

When such poor and needy sinners, weeping for mercy, were afterward absolved in the name of Jesus and baptized, their joy and that of the congregation was inexpressibly great.

As to outward matters, the course of the congregation at Huts of Peace was very edifying. The missionaries and the assistants rejoiced to see industry, diligence, a desire to learn, and a benevolent behavior toward strangers become universal.

A chief residing on the Ohio had heard both good and evil reports

Under Attack at Wyalusing: 1765–1772

concerning Huts of Peace. He came to observe the Christian Indians and see for himself the changes taking place. He afterward said, "I had heard that when strange Indians come to you, you pay no regard to them, and that you are a disdainful set of people. But now I am convinced that this is a falsehood, and therefore I will not believe any evil report of this place."

Whenever any chiefs came to Huts of Peace, especially of the Iroquois, Brother Schmick invited them to dinner. They were unaccustomed to such hospitality from most Whites, and it left a good impression on them. This practice also gave the Brethren an opportunity to converse in a familiar way with the chiefs and to hear their scruples and remarks. For instance, the measuring of the fields geometrically made some suspicious this was a mysterious contrivance so the white missionaries could secure the land as their own property.

These questions gave Brother Schmick an opportunity to explain the practice and to open to them everything about the place. "We have nothing to hide," he told them, and he showed the chiefs everything in his house and the church. The paintings representing the life of Jesus, including the crucifixion, engaged their attention and gave Brother Schmick an opportunity to relate to them a brief history of our Lord. This awakened in some a salutary thoughtfulness. As a result, many chiefs became friends and defenders of the Brethren.

Thus a chief of the Nanticoke tribe, a prudent and sensible Indian, became convinced of the Gospel truth and behaved well toward the Brethren. He was then deprived of his office by his own people, but the Chief in Onondaga reinstated him with honor. Soon after this, he again visited Huts of Peace and said, "My people have indeed taken away my belts and strings of wampum, but they could not take away that understanding which God has given me. And I may still make use of it as I please, to do good."

UNDER ATTACK

Worthless Promises

I now found out from the visiting chiefs that the Iroquois had indeed sold to the English that spot of ground which they had given to the believing Indians in 1765. I asked of one chief, "What about the plot of ground the Iroquois earlier sold to the New England people?"

"The Chief declared the sale to Lydius was only a private affair and was not approved by the Great Council at Onondaga. Therefore they resold the same tract to Pennsylvania," the Chief explained.

I then decided to get Brother Schmick to draft a petition to Governor Penn. Brother Schmick agreed and together we drafted the following letter:

> FEBRUARY 7, 1769
> THE PETITION OF SEVERAL INDIANS TO HIS HONOR, THE GOVERNOR.[109]
>
> The petition of John Papunhank and Joshua the Mohican, in behalf of themselves and their friends, the Indians who live at Wyalusing, on the east side of Susquehanna, about sixty miles above Wyoming, humbly showeth:
>
> > 1. That the spot of ground whereon the said Indians are seated was originally the plantation of the said Papunhank, who with the consent and approbation of the Five Nations at Onondaga, received at his said place several families of Indians

---

[109] John Penn, a grandson of William Penn. He was commissioned their lieutenant-governor by the proprietaries of the province (Thomas Penn, his uncle, and Richard Penn, his father) in August of 1763, entered upon office in November of that year, and resigned in April of 1771. After his father's death, he became one of the proprietors and owner of a fourth of the province. He was governor a second time just before the Revolution. He died in Bucks County in 1795.

Under Attack at Wyalusing: 1765-1772

which came in the year 1765 from the Philadelphia barracks.

2. That the said Indians being about 180 men, women and children, are by their connection and intercourse with Christians become in some degree civilized, using agriculture and other domestic business, have built at the place aforesaid twenty-five good strong log houses and a handsome church or meetinghouse, and have cleared and fenced fields of several miles in circumference, in full expectation that they and their posterity should enjoy the fruits of their labor on a small glebe (plot) of their native country.

3. That about six miles above their aforesaid settlement, at a place called Massasiung, is a tract of about 300 acres where they make hay for their cattle, and on the west side of Susquehanna opposite their settlement is some good woodland, it may be 100 acres, proper for to get their fuel. These three tracts are so necessary for the support of their settlement that if either of them should be taken up by an old right, or people should come of their own accord and seat and improve them, the Indians would be obliged to remove farther up in their country.

4. That about six miles below their said settlement are two spots of ground, maybe 400 acres in the whole, which the Indians have no immediate occasion for, but are nonetheless apprehensive that some people looking out for good land might be tempted to seat themselves there and give the Indians opportunities to buy rum, which must tend to the utter ruin of our young people.

UNDER ATTACK

> 5. That your petitioners have no money to offer to the honorable proprietaries for these lands or to pay rents, but must confide in their Honor's wonted goodness who have always in their purchases reserved some lands for the Indians that had lived there before the purchase was made. Besides, that no grant of sale or lease can secure an Indian property when for the convenience of government, and to avoid disturbances, they should shortly be obliged to remove farther up in the country.
>
> And your petitioners humbly pray that the aforesaid lands may by a special warrant be surveyed, and afterward by grant be vested in trustees for the use of the said Indians, so that when the Indians for the good of the state must remove, the said trustees may sell the improvements for the benefit of the Indians, subject to the proprietaries' demands for the price of the land, and under such other reservations and restrictions as your Honor in your wisdom shall think fit."[110]

Brother Schmick wrote a similar petition for Samuel Davis and the Indians at Sheshequin. Then he wrote the following cover letter to go with the two petitions:

> A LETTER TO THE HONORABLE JOHN PENN.
> WYALUSING, FEBRUARY 13, 1769
> Honorable Sir,
> Since the last treaty by which the Indians have ceded the lands on the Susquehanna to the honorable

---

[110] This and the following three letters were taken from *Transactions of the Moravian Historical Society* by William C. Reichel, pp. 213–217.

Under Attack at Wyalusing: 1765–1772

proprietaries of this province, I have found a great deal of uneasiness among the Indians under my care, in regard of their present establishment here within the line of purchase, and on that account they have resolved to send down Joshua, John Papunhank, and Jacob as their deputies to lay their case before your Honor, in full confidence that your Honor will be pleased to secure to them their possessions, which have cost them great pains and labor.

I beg leave to recommend them to your kind favor, and am with the greatest respect,

Your Honor's most devoted humble servant,

John Jacob Schmick

Minister of the Gospel

In due time Joshua, Jacob, and I made the trip to Philadelphia and delivered our petition to Governor Penn. He received us in a kindly manner, heard our petition, and promised us he would respond to our request in writing. He kept his promise, and on 21 June, he wrote a letter to the Wyalusing Indians. When it came, Brother Schmick gathered the people together and read the letter to us several times.

> JOHN PENN TO PAPUNHANK AND THE REST OF THE WYALUSING INDIANS.
> PHILADELPHIA, JUNE 21, 1769.
> Brethren, the Indians of Wyalusing,
> I have heard that you are very uneasy for fear that your land at Wyalusing should be taken away from you. When some of you came to me a few months ago, I told you that as you were a peaceable and a quiet people and behaved very well, you should not be disturbed in your possessions

UNDER ATTACK

at Wyalusing. This is the word that I then gave, and you may depend that I may keep it; and I have accordingly given orders to the surveyors not to survey your lands nor any lands within five miles of your settlement. Therefore I would have you disregard all idle stories you may hear about your lands being taken away from you, and be satisfied that I will do all in my power to protect and secure you in the possession of them, so long as you behave yourselves well, and if any of the people of this province shall offer to disturb you, I will take care that justice shall be done to you.

One thing I must tell you, I expect you will not give encouragement to the New England people who have taken possession of the proprietaries' land at Wyoming. If you expect to be protected by this government you must not encourage the New England people who are endeavoring to take the land from the proprietaries.

I send this by Job Chilloway (with a string of wampum) who has promised me that he will do nothing to your prejudice; and I must do him the justice to say that he at first took up his land to secure it for himself and the rest of you. And as Job is well inclined to agree with you, I must advise you not to differ with him, but by all means endeavor to live together in a friendly manner.

JOHN PENN

The letter came to us in the midst of a severe Indian famine. In July, twenty families from Shamunk came to buy corn. Forty half-famished Indians from different points came for corn. Ten Cayugas came for the same purpose. There was also scarcity among the Christian Indians, so we ate only one meal a day, but we did not complain. The chapel bell

Under Attack at Wyalusing: 1765–1772

continued to call us to gather for worship services. Instruction, praise, prayer, and song continued unabated.

I pondered Governor Penn's letter and then talked it over with Joshua and Jacob who had gone with me to Philadelphia. I asked them, "Why did Governor Penn give a deed to Job Chilloway and fail to survey the land we asked for? I fear that his talk of keeping the surveyors away is only an empty promise that he cannot or will not keep. Like his lies in New Jersey when he sent me away, and his lies about the Paxton Boys, this message also is not to be trusted." I decided to wait and see what would happen next, but Brother Schmick wrote a kindly letter in our name to Governor Penn.

> THE INDIANS' REPLY TO JOHN PENN. AUGUST 1769.
>
> Honorable Sir,
>
> We received your kind letter of the 21st of June with a string of wampum on the 23rd of July by the hands of Job Chilloway, and thank your Honor for the good words that we shall not be disturbed in our possessions at Wyalusing, and that your Honor has given orders to the surveyors not to survey our land, nor any lands within five miles of our settlement, which has abated all our uneasiness; and we will not give ear to anything contrary to your Honor's good words.
>
> We love that which is good and hope we shall never be found unworthy of your protection. Those who will not behave well shall not live in our town.
>
> With the New England people, we have no connection at all. We have never encouraged them in their settlement and shall not do so now. But we pray your Honor not to believe every report of us. There are many bad Indians,

UNDER ATTACK

and all say they come from Wyalusing, as they pass through here. If we are charged with anything and we are asked about it, we will answer what is the truth.

We wish to live in a friendly manner with Job Chilloway and all men, and as far as we know everybody has been kind to him and his family. If he does nothing to harm us, we shall be obliged to him. But we never desired him to take up any land for us, and upon what account he could call Wyalusing his land, we do not know. We think that was to our hurt, for our worthy Brother John Papunhank was settled here two years before him. Job has but this year begun to clear some new land, and has the least judgment of us all; but we shall not differ from him so long as he behaves well and lays nothing in our way, and then we shall not make complaint against him.

Signed in behalf of all the inhabitants living at Wyalusing with our names and marks.

JOHN PAPUNHANK & JOSHUA

My doubts of the governor's promises were well founded. Before long, various Europeans came, pretending that the governor had either sold or given them the land reserved to Huts of Peace and Sheshequin Indians. Contrary to the written statement of the governor, surveyors came to measure the land. Only with much difficulty could I convince them of their error.

Not only did the surveyors come, but in general, the Europeans continued to settle closer and closer upon us, survey or no survey. And no one tried to stop them, neither the Indians nor Governor Penn. With the settlers also came the rum trade, which led to the debauchery of the young people.

In the 1769 fall hunt, we could not hunt to the south at Wyoming

Under Attack at Wyalusing: 1765-1772

because of a collision there between the New England and the Pennsylvania settlers. Neither could we go to the north because of the Iroquois.

Life at the mission continued with regular and special worship services. Amid bitter cold, we felled trees for a new schoolhouse. Around the middle of March, all were busily engaged in the maple sugar camps. On 6 June, we replanted the corn; the worms had destroyed all the first planting.

On 16 June, two Mohawks arrived carrying a message and a belt from the Six Nations to the New Englanders at Wyoming: "If you delay in evacuating the valley, we will come down and take you by the hair of your heads and shake you."

I shook my head at the message. "It's all empty talk. The Six Nations do not care who settles the valley. They have their money. They will not spill their blood for Pennsylvania."

Still, I was concerned. The Iroquois had sold my land to Pennsylvania. Governor Penn made hollow promises. Lazarus Stewart and the Paxton Boys had threatened us. Other troubled Indians from south of us brought reports of settlers forcing them from their lodges and told of the war in the Wyoming Valley between the Yankees and the Pennamites.[111] Both sides wanted the valley, and they thought they could not live together.

Colonel George Croghan and a Doctor Forbes came by Huts of Peace. They breakfasted with Brother Schmick and both attended a service at the chapel. Anthony and I accosted the pair afterward and started what appeared to be a friendly inquiry. "What do you think of the mission?" I asked.

Salamander George answered in smooth Delaware, "We are much gratified with the appearance of things at the mission. Everything is

---

[111] The Pennsylvania forces were called Pennamites, and the Connecticut forces were called Yankees.

UNDER ATTACK

orderly, clean, and peaceful."

"Where are you going when you leave here?" I asked next.

"We have some business in Wyoming first. When that is taken care of, we will move on to Pittsburgh."

At this point, the doctor excused himself, saying, "If you are going to talk in Delaware, I will begin my sketch of the town. I offered Brother Schmick to do one before I leave."

I pursued my subject. "Salamander George, tell us how things are going at Wyoming. You know we're neighbors, and what happens there affects what happens here."

Salamander George was expansive as usual. "Well, you know I'm allied with Pennsylvania, and I think Pennsylvania is going to win. Still, those Yankee dogs are putting up a good fight, so I want to have a look at it. Old Salamander George doesn't mind switching sides every now and then when it is to his advantage."

Salamander George laughed at himself and then went on. "That's the way Lazarus Stewart plays the game too. The Yankees offered him and his followers free land. The Penns want to sell land and charge quit rents. They themselves have huge estates they pay no taxes on. The idea hasn't caught on very well.

"Anyway, Lazarus Stewart and thirty men with him joined the Yankees. So far it hasn't worked out too well for them. Twice, the Pennamites captured them and marched them fifty miles to a jail in Easton. They immediately posted bail and returned to Wyoming, where the fighting continued.

"The Pennamites built a fort and brought in a cannon. The Yankees took the fort and hid the cannon. Then the Pennamites retook the fort, but the Yankees still had the cannon. So when Colonel Butler and the Yankees wanted to retake the fort, they got the cannon out and tried to shoot at the fort from the other side of the river. They couldn't hit it and never did any real damage."

Under Attack at Wyalusing: 1765–1772

Salamander George was thoroughly enjoying his story. He paused and smiled. "So what do you think those ingenious Yankees did next? You have to admire them. They built a bigger cannon out of a tree trunk and strapped steel bands around it. The first ball didn't make it across the river. On the next shot, they loaded her up good with powder. When the spark hit the powder, the explosion split the barrel, burst the bands, and made such a terrible thunderclap that the Indians at Wyalusing could have heard it."[112]

I laughed at the amazing story and then changed the subject. "I take it you were at Fort Stanwix when the '68 land sale was made to Pennsylvania. Did the Iroquois really sell the Wyoming Valley to Pennsylvania?"

"Papunhank, they did. When you want something badly enough, little niceties like prior agreements and sales don't mean a thing. The Iroquois just cancelled the former sale to the Connecticut people and took the English money. More than 10,000 English pounds! The English really wanted it badly, but that was the best deal I could get."

"So how did the Iroquois have the right to sell all the lands of the other Indians clear out to the Ohio?" I asked.

Salamander George didn't bat an eye. "By right of conquest! The Iroquois made women out of the Delawares. And if you don't like it, the Iroquois and the English will swat you down like you swat mosquitos."

I shook my head. "Salamander George, you do not understand. Our God is a God of peace, and we are His people. He will judge you and the Iroquois, but we will not fight you nor them. Yet I must warn you that it is a fearful thing to fall into the hands of the living God. To lie, steal, and kill is under God's condemnation. We, the Christian Indians, have nothing to do with wars and politics. We mind only the things of God."

---

[112] This incident is true, although I doubt the noise could be heard at a distance of fifty miles.

UNDER ATTACK

An Invitation to the West

In the spring of 1771, I was surprised when Wangomen, the disagreeable witch doctor from Goshchuenk, showed up at Huts of Peace. I remembered the man well from my earlier encounter with him, and I did not trust him.

Neither did Brother Zeisberger's reports from the new missions on the other side of the Allegheny say anything good about him. Wangomen has been the chief cause of moving the mission away from Goshchuenk, and then Lawhannek, to Peace Town near Kuskusky.[113]

Nevertheless, Wangomen and several other delegates brought this official message, with wampum, from the principal chiefs of the Delaware nation:

> To the Indian congregation at Huts of Peace and Sheshequin:
>
> Brothers, we invite you to the Allegheny country, that is, to the country on the Ohio. We, the Delaware chiefs, declare that we will receive the believing Indians into our arms as friends.
>
> We will allow you to choose a tract of land where you will be able to live together as Christians and dwell in peace and safety. You may also bring your white teachers with you, and they shall be considered as being of the same color as the Indians.
>
> Brothers, we are truly desirous that we and our young

---

[113] The complete story of these three Indian missions will be told in the fifth book in The Conquest Series, *War Chief Conquered*.

Under Attack at Wyalusing: 1765-1772

people might hear the Gospel. Therefore we wish that all of you might reside among us.

Because we wish you to understand that our invitation conceals no bad designs, and that it is honest and open, we have instructed Brother Zeisberger to write a letter to your deputies that confirms our honest intentions in this matter.

Brother Schmick read Zeisberger's letter to the assistants, but they still mistrusted the message. They therefore sent this short reply with the delegates: "We rejoice that Packanke and the other chiefs have thought on us with so much kindness, but we are as yet too heavy to rise. When we have lightened ourselves, we will send word to the chiefs."

A short time later, the head chief of the Delaware nation, Chief Newcomer, repeated the invitation in a strong and pressing manner. The Wyandots, who owned the land around Lake Erie, also invited the Christian Indians and their teachers to come and dwell among them, and added this tantalizing promise: "We will not sell the ground under your feet as the Iroquois have done to you." But the Brethren still came to no firm resolution as to what should be done.

Amid all the uncertainties surrounding the future of Huts of Peace and Sheshequin, Augustus, Daniel, Saul, and I took two canoes down the river to bring up some distinguished visitors. John Loretz and Christian Gregor had come from Europe to visit all the Brethren's settlements in North America. Bishop Nathaniel Seidel, a man known and respected by the Indians, accompanied these special guests.

Soon after their arrival, the delegation endured nearly constant rains. Then the river began to rise till it covered the entire farm, some of the houses, half of the garden, and the well. The people had to take to their canoes and look for higher ground. The water swept

UNDER ATTACK

away all the fences along the river and even some along the creek where we plant. A number of swine drowned. In twenty years, I had never seen such a flood.

After three days, the river began to recede, and the delegation continued with their investigation. They visited every family in the two congregations.

When they came to my house, Brother Seidel and I embraced and wept together. With wet, shining eyes, Brother Seidel told me, "It is a great joy to see you still serving the Savior. You have endured such great tribulations in Philadelphia, not to mention abuse in the white settlements and betrayal by the governor. As the overseer of the Unity in North America during that time, I suffered with you. And how does it go with you now, Brother?"

I could not help sobbing. "Brother Seidel, times are hard. I have been accused of having the poison and have been doubted by my own brothers. I have always been a man of peace and did everything I could to keep the peace. Yet it is all in vain. The Iroquois have sold the ground under our feet. Governor Penn fails to keep the surveyors and the settlers away. The Yankees and the Pennamites war over who shall have our huts and houses. Nobody cares. I find it difficult to love my enemies as our Savior has commanded."

The Brethren sat in silence for a half hour while the weeping continued. Then they laid their hands on my head and Brother Seidel prayed, "Lord, you see the heart of our dear brother. Comfort him. Give him strength. Help him to keep his heart and mind fastened on you and not on governors, councils, warriors, and chieftains. Help him to see the glory of the homes you have prepared for him in a heavenly city where lying and stealing and murder will not be found . . ."

The prayers continued for a long time as each of the three brothers prayed for me and the congregation at Huts of Peace and Sheshequin and Peace Town and Bethlehem and the Caribbean and Herrnhut.

Under Attack at Wyalusing: 1765-1772

Many, many names of Brethren were mentioned. The three asked repeatedly that the works of the evil one might be put down among the Brethren. I also prayed and felt the power of the Spirit and the joy of the Lord come upon me in that sacred hour.

When the prayers ended, Brother Seidel said, "Brother Johannes, you are not alone. The power of God and the Brethren around the world stand with you. When we have finished interviewing all the families, we will investigate your land difficulties. We support you. Be strong."

The joy at what the Brethren found as they went from house to house was great indeed. The European Brethren saw here, for the first time, a flock of Christian Indians. They could not sufficiently praise and thank God the Savior for the gracious work begun among these nations. For them, it was easy to see that even though the Indians suffered so many heavy trials, God had miraculously preserved them.

Then the time came for the conference. The missionaries and the assistants from both towns were present. I told them of my conversation with Salamander George and of his blatant defense of the sale of their land by the Iroquois. I mentioned the ongoing war between the Yankees and the Pennamites. I spoke of the governor's written promise that the land within five miles of Huts of Peace should not be disturbed and how the surveyors and settlers disregarded it. I told of the worrisome rum trade and how it promoted evil among the young people. Then I informed the delegation of the warm invitation from the chiefs in the West to come and live with them.

That was the big question, "What should we do about the invitation to move west?"

Brother Seidel asked, "What does Brother Zeisberger think of this proposal to move the missions from the Susquehanna? His reports to Bethlehem show that he has had much difficulty with his missions

UNDER ATTACK

at Goshchuenk and Lawhannek, sometimes to the point of extreme depression."

Brother Schmick answered, "Yes, a sorcerer named Wangomen has made life very difficult for Brother Zeisberger at both missions, but an amazing thing happened. Wangomen's blood brother, Glikkikan, has converted and has brought the new mission at Peace Town into the favor of Packanke, the head chief of the Wolf Clan. Things have gone better at Kuskusky, but because of land uncertainty there, Brother Zeisberger is still interested in moving that mission to the Ohioland."

"How far is it from Peace Town to Newcomerstown on the Muskingum?" Brother Seidel wanted to know.

"About three or four days on horseback," I answered.

"Brother Johannes, are you and your people willing to leave your homes and fields after seven years of toil here to move across the Alleghenies?" was Brother Schmick's next question.

"We would need to decide such a large question in the Council," I answered. "As I see it, this is the only way we may remain at peace."

The discussion continued for many hours until Brother Seidel proposed a plan of action. He said, "It is not good to think of moving directly to the Muskingum River where all is uncertain. First, we should think of moving to the Big Beaver where Brother Zeisberger has a town established. This fall, several families should move to Peace Town and lay out plantations for more families if they should come in the spring. This would show some regard for the message from the Delaware chiefs.

"In the meantime, Brother Zeisberger and the assistants with him on the Big Beaver should go to the Muskingum River and investigate the land and the real attitude of the chiefs about a mission. But the question of whether the whole congregation here should move across the Allegheny should be fully considered and decided by the

Under Attack at Wyalusing: 1765-1772

Brethren at Bethlehem."

Not long after the delegation returned to Bethlehem, they called Brother David Zeisberger to come from Peace Town on the Big Beaver to Bethlehem for a conference.

At the conference, the whole situation of the missions among the Indians was carefully weighed and considered. The Brethren were convinced that the Indian congregations at Wyalusing and Sheshequin could not long maintain themselves in those places. The reasons were easy to see:

- The Iroquois had sold the land and were making troublesome demands upon the believers.
- The contest between the New Englanders and the Indians of Wyoming affected the Christian Indians because of its proximity to them.
- The bad behavior of the Senecas (one of the Six Nations) gave the Christian Indians much trouble because the Whites were likely to suspect the Christian Indians as accomplices in evil deeds.
- The number of European settlers daily increased both above and below Huts of Peace.
- The rum trade tended to seduce the young people.

The conference then made a final resolution, stating, "We advise the Indian congregation to accept the proposal repeatedly made to them to move to the Ohio, and to consider it as proceeding from the gracious providence of God."

Brother Zeisberger then returned by way of the congregations on the Susquehanna and gave them the message. Both congregations, therefore, resolved to remove to Peace Town in the spring of 1772. Four families went thither in November to lay out plantations of Indian

UNDER ATTACK

corn for themselves and the congregations who were to follow them.

When the delegation visited Huts of Peace, they saw that Brother Schmick was worn down from his duties and not in good health. Accordingly, Bethlehem sent Brother John Ettwein to Huts of Peace. His mission was twofold: he was to relieve Brother Schmick and lead the migration to Peace Town in the spring.

The believers would suffer a great loss because of being forced to leave their many improvements at Huts of Peace. We now had proof of this, so I went with some of the assistants on a trip to Philadelphia to plead our case before the governor. Governor Richard Penn, in office while his older brother was gone to England, listened to us kindly and wrote us a letter the following day.

> Friends and Brethren, the Wyalusing Indians!
>
> I have taken into consideration what you said to me yesterday, informing me of your intention to remove to the Ohio and desiring some satisfaction for the improvements you are about to leave at Wyalusing. I am sorry for your departure at this particular time, because I am apprehensive it may be injurious to the government and the interest of the proprietaries. I wish it could have been convenient to you to remain where you are another year.
>
> As to making you any satisfaction for your improvements, I have no power from the proprietaries to do it. All I can do for you is to lay your case before them, which thing you may depend on me doing at my first opportunity. At the same time, I shall do you the justice to inform them of your orderly and quiet behavior since you have lived at Wyalusing. If they should sell the land for an advanced price, on account of the improvements you have made, I doubt not but they will, in justice,

Under Attack at Wyalusing: 1765–1772

order you to be paid the overplus.

Brethren! I now take leave of you, and I wish you a good journey, and that your removal to the Ohio may prove to your satisfaction.

I am your friend and brother RICHARD PENN.
Philadelphia, 15 May 1772.

On the following day, 16 May 1772, our delegation appeared before the Pennsylvania Assembly, and I made the following address:

To the Honorable Representatives of the Freeman of the Province of Pennsylvania.

The Christian Indians of Wyalusing and Sheshequin present their most sincere thanks for the notice and care hitherto taken of them, their wives, and their children in the time of their distress, especially when they were protected and maintained at Province Island and the Philadelphia barracks.

They shall ever preserve a grateful remembrance thereof, impress it upon the minds of their children, and relate your acts of humanity and benevolence to those distant nations among whom they are going to live.

They wish that the peace of God may be with the people of this province, and that ease and plenty may always be the lot of the industrious inhabitants thereof. They bid you the last farewell. They thank you for the present you have provided for them, and beg this only additional favor that you will always kindly remember the faithful and unshaken attachment of these Christian Indians to his Majesty's government in this province.

Signed in behalf of the said Indians by their deputies.

UNDER ATTACK

The present given to the deputies amounted to 100 Spanish dollars.[114] The deputies returned home and divided it among the heads of the families.

The Last Time

The decision had been made to abandon Huts of Peace and Sheshequin. Once the four families had left for the Big Beaver, every activity and every worship service took on special meaning. This was the last time they would celebrate Christmas here. This was the last time the children would go to school here. "The last time" became familiar and sorrowful words heard in the forests, the snug houses, and the chapel.

Despite the sense of impending loss, a semblance of life as usual continued. On 4 February 1772, a layer of snow three feet deep covered the town. This made it difficult to care for the seventy horned cattle and more than seventy horses. Without the haystacks, many would have perished. By 5 March, the snow was still unusually deep for that time of year. Nevertheless, on 10 March, the men began constructing canoes for the trip west. By 21 March, all the men, women, and children were busily engaged in the sugar camps.

At that time, the internal course of the congregations in both places was very pleasing and edifying. The children were not only remarkably diligent in their schoolwork, but also expressed great love to our Savior, frequently meeting of their own accord to sing His

---

[114] A Spanish dollar was a silver coin that served as legal tender in the United States until 1857. It is difficult to find any idea of value in terms of trade items in the year 1772. The present was probably given mostly by Quaker friends.

Under Attack at Wyalusing: 1765-1772

praises. Most of the believers were intent upon being as Jesus Christ was when on earth, and sought to walk in His steps.

A brother said one day to Brother Schmick, "I cannot express what I feel when I meditate upon our Savior, when as a boy He sat among the doctors in the temple; or as a teacher; or as laboring hard for our salvation and dying on the cross. All is important to me, and when I consider these things, I perceive a peculiar emotion within me."

As preparations for the departure continued, word spread to the surrounding nations. The chiefs of the Iroquois sent a message: "We have heard a little bird speak that you are removing to the Ohio. We are much displeased that you will leave us, and we wish to clear every former grievance in order to prevent this from taking place. In the future, the Indians on the Susquehanna shall be only one body and one vein."

I could not help smiling. "Do they really expect us to believe them?" I asked of the other assistants. "Can their treachery be so soon forgotten?"

So the Brethren sent a gentle message telling the Iroquois chiefs, "Your message has come too late. We are of a firm resolution to go to the Ohio."

The chiefs replied, "Our tears flow like a heavy rain because you will leave us. But you shall know that we will hold you in our bosom and remain your friends as long as the sun shines and the rivers run down to the sea."

The believing Indians returned the same promise. "We will remain friends after we leave the Susquehanna."

On 5 May, Brother and Sister Schmick took a tearful farewell of their beloved Indian congregations on the Susquehanna and returned to Bethlehem for some rest.

On 6 June, the congregation partook of the Holy Communion for

UNDER ATTACK

the last time and celebrated Pentecost with a baptism. Since I had been the first person baptized at Wyalusing in 1763, it now seemed fitting that my youngest daughter, dressed in white and seated in the front of the chapel, became the last person baptized there. Brother Ettwein baptized her as Anna Paulina. Hers was the 186th baptism performed there since the time those weary pilgrims had arrived at Wyalusing in 1765, only seven years before.

On 11 June, all being in readiness for the journey, the congregation met at Huts of Peace for the last time. The cattle and horses waited nearby. Thirty canoes floated at the river's edge, stowed with cooking kettles, a few utensils, some clothing, maple sugar, maize, and dried shad. The travelers packed only those items they would have taken when going on a hunt or to the sugar camps. Still, there was room for 120 passengers.

The crowd gathered in the chapel for the last time. All 204 souls, the women standing on the left side and the men standing on the right, started singing. Joshua led out, and song after favorite song rang out in that hallowed place of worship. Some songs were in Delaware, some in Mohican, some in German, and some in English. The tears came as the sweet memories of the Savior's work in that tiny chapel passed through their minds.

Brother Rothe reminded us of the great favors and blessings received from God in this place. He offered up praises and thanksgivings to God for His goodness and fervently entreated Him to grant His peace and protection on the journey. Brother Ettwein also prayed a long prayer. Fervent *"Kehelles"* and "Amens" rang out.

When Brother Ettwein closed the prayer, Brother Joshua started singing once more while the group slowly moved toward the canoes waiting at the river shore. As prearranged, those going by water stood with their captain. There were five captains, each one in

Under Attack at Wyalusing: 1765-1772

charge of six of the grand canoes. Brother Rothe stood with those going by water. Those traveling by land gathered behind their two captains. One group would walk with the horses and the other with the cattle. Brother Ettwein stood with that group.

I estimated there were 120 souls going by water and 80 souls by land. If all went as planned, those going overland by the shorter route to Muncy Creek would wait for those going by water. When the two groups met, they would sell the canoes and travel together across the mountains.

When all the groups had gathered behind their captains, those going by water entered their canoes. Anthony and I took the lead canoe, and Anthony began tolling the chapel bell that he held in his hands. We shoved off into the broad Susquehanna and drifted downstream, each captain with his group.

Anthony kept on tolling the bell. Those in the canoes and those on shore turned back and gazed at the thirty-nine log cabins, thirteen huts, the schoolhouse, and the beloved chapel. This was Huts of Peace they had built and lived in. Huts of Peace, the place where so many of them had met the Savior and been freed from their sins; the place where their bodies and souls had been nourished and sustained for seven years. And for me, it was simply home.

The bell kept on tolling as Huts of Peace faded in the distance. I placed my fingers to my lips and held them aloft toward the departing town. Those in the twenty-nine other canoes followed my example, raising their arms in a goodbye kiss and salute. Finally, those still standing on the river shore turned and did likewise.

As the lead canoe rounded the river bend, the bell stopped tolling. Only the surging waters of the Susquehanna disturbed the heated memories of the past. Resolutely and cheerfully, everyone turned and faced forward. A new life lay ahead.

UNDER ATTACK

Recorded by John Heckewelder
At Beautiful Spring, Ohio,
Sunday, 13 November 1774

No Gospel for the Iroquois

After being gone nearly two months on our journey to Bethlehem, Brother Johannes and I returned yesterday. We passed on our greetings from Bethlehem and other congregations to the brothers and sisters and assured them of their sincere love and participation in our joy and suffering. We also read a letter from Brother Ettwein which delighted everyone in the Indian congregation here and at Huts of Grace. The news and letters powerfully refreshed and strengthened the believers, and they felt the compassionate and motherly heart of the dear Unity toward us as her members.

I answered their questions the best I could, but I had many other things I wanted to know about the present situation in the Ohioland. First, I wanted answers from Brother Zeisberger to the questions Brother Johannes had raised on our trip. So after the morning service, we had a relaxed time together, and I worked the conversation around till my questions could follow unobtrusively.

"Brother David, when did you learn to speak Iroquois?"

Zeisberger laughed. "My first try at it landed me in a New York jail for fifty-one days. In 1745, at the age of twenty-four, I had just completed an Indian language school at Bethlehem under the tutelage of Christopher Pyrlaeus. So

Under Attack at Wyalusing: 1765–1772

Farewell

"This was the place where so many of us first met the Savior."
—Johannes Papunhank

UNDER ATTACK

the Mission sent Frederick Post and me to the village of Tyianoga, head chief of the Mohawks, to learn the language. Tyianoga treated us kindly and took us in, but Moravians were not an approved sect in New York, so Post and I did our language study in jail.

"After we were released, Schebosch and I accompanied Bishop Spangenberg and Conrad Weiser on a mission to Onondaga, where I was formally adopted into the Onondaga tribe as Ganousseracheri.

"I spent ten years in various mission posts studying and using the Iroquois tongue. I compiled two dictionaries: Iroquois-to-German and Iroquois-to-English."

"How did you use your knowledge of Iroquois to help establish missions among them?"

"That is the problem. We never established any mission among the Iroquois. In 1750, Martin Mack, Godfrey Rundt, and I went to Onondaga with a detailed plan for a mission among them. But Bishop Spangenberg told us not to say we wanted to evangelize them, only that we had come to study the language. During the 305 days we were there, we never held any religious meetings or proclaimed the Savior."

"Why did Bishop Spangenberg tell you not to evangelize when that was the whole reason you wanted to learn the language?"

"That was twenty-two years ago, and sometimes truth may be shrouded in the mist of time. But I will tell you some of the reasons I think could have been involved.

"The New York authorities were hostile to the Moravians and had actually succeeded in closing the mission at Shekomeko, forcing the Christian Mohicans to move to Pennsylvania. So for us to proselytize among the Iroquois would be an invitation to get thrown out of New York.

"The rum traders hated us. One actually beat me over the head and knocked me out in an unprovoked attack. He would probably

Under Attack at Wyalusing: 1765-1772

have killed me if other Iroquois had not restrained him. The rum trade flourished among the Iroquois, and I have seen terrible debauchery where whole villages were drunk for days at a time. In such cases, they had no hunger for the Gospel, but were entirely given over to the flames of hell.

"The French were making inroads in the West at this same time and trying to draw the Indians away from the English interest. The Iroquois wanted to maintain their independence and not become subject to either the French or the English. Everything we Germans did was regarded with suspicion by the English and the Iroquois.

"Maybe the main reason for the lack of interest in the Gospel among the Iroquois lay in the covenants of friendship Count Zinzendorf and Bishop Spangenberg made with the Iroquois. And Conrad Weiser, to the detriment of all the other Indians, pushed those agreements to favor the Iroquois."

"Brother David, do you believe the so-called Walking Purchase was a fraud that cheated the Delawares?" I watched him carefully on this key question that had often tormented me. He paused for quite a while before answering slowly.

"Brother John, we cannot undo the past. The past is in God's hands, and all men will stand before Him in judgment."

"That does not answer my question nor satisfy my conscience," I persisted. "If the Iroquois lie and cheat along with Pennsylvania and Virginia, is it right for us to go along with their sin? Did the Iroquois really have the right to sell Wyalusing to Pennsylvania?"

"Brother John, we always do right to submit to the order God has established. If God has established Pennsylvania as our government, we do well to submit to it. God uses the kingdoms of this world to keep order among the heathen."

"I thought Brother Zeisberger's answer evasive and unsatisfactory, but as his junior and helper, I felt it better not to push the matter further.

UNDER ATTACK

Recorded by John Heckewelder
At Beautiful Spring, Ohio,
Wednesday, 16 November 1774

The Gospel for the Delawares

Lord Dunmore had made his peace with the Shawnee and disbursed his armies, but the struggle between Captain White Eyes and Chief Watwees was ongoing. And the cause of it all was the mission and us white teachers.

On Monday evening, White Eyes and other Indians came from Newcomerstown for a visit and attended all our services on Tuesday. On Wednesday, we called a conference and invited White Eyes to attend so we could get his thoughts on the particular case at hand.

Brother David's Indian uncle came here several days ago. Yesterday, he and his wife visited us. Brother David had stayed in his home several times when his uncle lived on an arm of the Susquehanna above Zeninge. Their family consists of six adults, all of whom had been baptized on the Mohawk River. They begged us urgently for permission to live with us.

This is their story:

> We visited Brother Zeisberger and the mission at Goshchuenk five years ago and wanted to live at the mission then, but we did not think it feasible at that time because our children did not want to live as the Indians at the mission did. However, when we heard you moved the mission to Kaskaskunk, we followed you and intended to come to you. But when we got to Pittsburgh,

Under Attack at Wyalusing: 1765-1772

Hokolesqua persuaded us to go with him and live among the Shawnee. We lived with them for two years and always wanted to come live with you, but the Shawnee did not want us to leave.

Recently, the fear and terror among the Shawnee because of the war drove us away. One night we left all our food behind and fled. We were afraid someone might follow us, so we traveled through the bush instead of following the road. When we came to the Delaware towns, everyone offered to let us stay with them, but we refused all the kind offers and told no one where we really wanted to go. We are so happy to be here, and we hope you will not turn us away.

We told them about our policy. "No one can live here who is not concerned about the Savior and his salvation."

"Oh, we already know that," they responded. "That is precisely why we have come. We have spent the last five years since we were at Goshchuenk in great uneasiness about our hearts."

We asked White Eyes if he thought there would be any problem with the Mingo or the Six Nations if we allowed this family to live with us. He did not object, so several brothers thoroughly explained our rules to them and to White Eyes. The brothers also told them that anyone who does not want to submit to these rules must not be annoyed if we send them away. Hearing the rules did not deter the family in the least, but they continued asking even more insistently for us to take them in.

We explained the reason for each of the rules to White Eyes. He had heard much said against us because we often sent people away when they did not behave according to our rules. White Eyes understood everything and received it very well.

We especially testified to White Eyes that the Brethren's work

UNDER ATTACK

among the Indians was not the work of humans but of God. If it were the work of humans, it could not last. However, if it came from God, it would not only last, but would increase with time. It would also spread among other nations because what we now saw with our eyes was just the beginning. This pleased him, and he was quite happy about it because it is very important to him that the Gospel be extended among the Indians everywhere.

On the 16th, White Eyes met with Brother David alone and bared his heart. He did not want to do this yesterday in the presence of other Indians. He said, "My intention is to arrange things so the Delaware nation declares that it wants to accept God's Word, live in peace and friendship with the Indian believers and their teachers, and be given complete freedom."

Brother David told him, "If the Delawares want to accept God's Word, that is good. But you should not think all Indians have to become faithful and live as we do. This can hardly happen. Instead, let the Indian believers and their teachers enjoy the same rights and privileges as other Indians so they do not put obstacles in our way."

White Eyes said, "I already see that many Indians are against you and say the Indian believers have no right to be in the Ohioland. They say this because Chief Watwees has declared that the Delawares will not accept God's Word. Therefore I have separated myself from the Chief until he agrees to what I ask. I expect that the Chief will agree for the Delawares to accept God's Word, but if he will not, I will resign completely and leave him. In that event, I will help and support you.

"And," he continued, "after the primary issue is put right, I will try to see to it that the Indian believers receive their own district of land along with the other Indians. I have not yet revealed my project to any Indians and dare not tell them everything because they cannot grasp it all at once. Therefore I must work quietly and take one step at a time so that I can accomplish my goals without being noticed."

Under Attack at Wyalusing: 1765-1772

After giving Brother David more particulars about himself and his plans, White Eyes went on to Pittsburgh.

Recorded by John Heckewelder
At Beautiful Spring, Ohio,
Tuesday, 29 November 1774

Shining Stars

We granted the Onondaga family—Thomas, wife Maria, sons Nicolaus and Joseph, daughters Christine and Polly—permission to move here, but being short of space, we cleared out the schoolhouse for them until they can build their own house.

Thomas and his family speak Onondaga. Brother David is completely out of practice with the Mingo language, so they communicate in Delaware, which Thomas understands but cannot speak.

Brother David spoke to them about the crucified Savior who saves sinners. They and their children listened very attentively to what Brother David said, but they seem to have little life and feeling in their hearts. However, they do not miss any of the services and are always happy to be at Beautiful Spring. The children's conduct is as quiet and orderly as you will find among the Indians.[115]

One evening a trader who had been in the army and then stayed with the Shawnee after the army retreat, brought a good report of the Shawnee. He said, "They are now the best people, and it is safer to be

---

[115] All the family had been baptized on the Mohawk River, but apparently not by the Brethren from the Unity. But by the end of 1775, each of the family had been individually accepted into the congregation at different times without rebaptism.

UNDER ATTACK

among them than ever before. They showed me all love and kindness and promised to replace everything I had lost as soon as they returned from the fall hunt.

"Furthermore, the Shawnees said to me, 'We could not imagine Lord Dunmore would be such a kind and friendly gentleman. We gave him a horse to ride and a quantity of skins for shoes for his soldiers because we thought their shoes must be torn after walking such a long distance through the bush.' "

It seemed that ever since I returned from Bethlehem and Philadelphia, Brother Isaac was constantly travelling to and from Newcomerstown or the upper Shawnee towns. I wanted to catch up with him and see what really happened with Hokolesqua and Lord Dunmore and White Eyes and this business with Chief Watwees. In addition, I had a tiny bit of news I wanted to share with him. On my journey, I had made it a point to visit Friend Israel Pemberton, and I now knew the gold medallion had been sent westward.

In my heart, I desired the same kind of relaxed privacy we had enjoyed at our last meeting on the way to Kuskusky. Glikkikan agreed, and we settled on the old Post cabin as the site for our rendezvous two nights hence.

I knew it would be more than one day by canoe to travel up the Muskingum for twenty miles, but it didn't matter. I could expect some low water and some difficulties, but I was in the mood for it. I told Brother Zeisberger I was going upriver to Post's old cabin to reminisce for a few days. I picked out a small canoe and a good paddle, packed in a few extras, and set out, thirty-one years old, single, in good health, and free. The chilly air invigorated me.

When I arrived at the old cabin site, Glikkikan already had a fire going and a duck roasting on the spit. A bell tinkled occasionally as his horse foraged about. He said nothing, and I rummaged about in the remains of the cabin. I found a discarded book in the loft, a rat nest of

Under Attack at Wyalusing: 1765-1772

hickory nuts hidden behind a board in the corner, and an arrowhead. *That's probably from the arrow that sent me scurrying eastward twelve years ago,* I thought.

I looked around for the hard-earned garden patch Captain Pipe had marked off for Post and me. It was all grown over with young trees and brambles, but with some investigation, I found the swollen blazes on the large corner trees.

We spoke little while we ate our meal and let the memories come flooding back. Once we had washed our hands and were again relaxing by the fire, I said, "Many things change, and many things remain the same. Some wounds heal, and some fester and burst into open sores."

"Ah, Turtle," Glikkikan said affectionately, "you have said it well. Burying the tomahawk can stop murder and burning, but it never brings peace to the heart. For the tomahawk can spring out of the ground at any time. Lord Dunmore has stopped the war for the time being, but he has done nothing at all to take the wood out of the fire."

"Then you think there will be more war?"

"Turtle, I am certain of it. I have trailed along behind Hokolesqua, White Eyes, and Watwees throughout the talks of peace. Why did those large armies come from Virginia to the Ohioland? Why did those four hundred local settlers in McDonald's army come and destroy the Shawnee capital of Woaketameki? It was not because the Shawnee were invading Philadelphia or Williamsburg.

"Listen to me, Turtle. It was about the land. Both the Virginians and the Pennsylvanians want all the land west of the Alleghenies.

"When Hokolesqua and seven hundred Indians fought with seven hundred white savages at Point Pleasant and spilt some of their blood, it only made them more determined to destroy the Shawnee forever. And if Lord Dunmore had not drawn his sword on Andrew Lewis and ordered him to withdraw his army, they would have wiped out all the Shawnee towns and killed their inhabitants. There are still thousands

UNDER ATTACK

of ferocious, angry men intent on owning the Shawnee lands.

"Listen to me, Turtle. Those angry men will return. Now they are enraged not only against the Shawnee, but also against the British and Lord Dunmore."

"And what about Captain White Eyes and his struggle with Chief Watwees?" I inquired. "Has God placed him there to help and protect us from the ravages of the Virginians and the Delawares?"

"You see, Turtle, there is something that neither White Eyes nor Watwees yet understands. They think the Christian towns are the work of men. They do not see that it is the work of the Savior in the heart that makes it possible for us to live together in peace.

"Just the other day, when I was trying to mediate the dispute between Chief Watwees and Captain White Eyes, the Chief said, 'The believers have the *machtapassican* among them. They take in bad people and protect them, and then when these bad people live in their towns, they are considered believers and are respected.' What the Chief apparently didn't consider is that people like this could be transformed into good people if they renounced Satan with all of his black magic.

"Perhaps Captain White Eyes' understanding of conversion is a bit more advanced than that of the Chief's, yet he still sees our towns as the clever work of white men. Maybe God will use White Eyes to aid the cause of the Indians and help us secure land, but I am afraid he likes to be a leader of men. White Eyes can count noses, and he sees the Christian Indians as a strong, stable people to have on his side. He knows too that a secure homeland would please many Delawares, including me.

"So you see, Turtle, once again it's about the land, the Ohioland, rather than about changed hearts."

Glikkikan stopped and gazed wistfully out into the darkness. He said nothing, waiting patiently for me to speak.

Under Attack at Wyalusing: 1765–1772

"Brother Isaac, I guess you are wondering if it had to be," I began. "Did God want the Christian Indians to leave Huts of Peace on the Susquehanna so He could give them a permanent homeland on the Muskingum?"

"Well, Brother John, what do you think?" That was all the encouragement I needed.

"The actions of the Iroquois were evil. They sold the land to the people from Connecticut, and then they resold it to Pennsylvania. The Iroquois in turn seated the Christian Indians on all the land from Wyalusing to Tioga. Yet they secretly sold that same land to Pennsylvania.

"They sold the land as far west as the Ohio River and included Kentucky as land they claimed by right of conquest over the Susquehannocks long ago.

"There never has been a conquest of memory. Rather, it has been the other way around. The Wyandots and the French soundly defeated the Iroquois. The Iroquois cannot be trusted. They do evil. They do not want to hear the Gospel, but go on with their lying and warring."

I thought Glikkikan would agree with me, and he did. "Brother John, you say the Iroquois do evil, and where evil is done, we may be sure that the devil is present. Tell me, when Lazarus Stewart entered Huts of Peace to sell rum, was he innocent of evil and the Indians who bought it guilty?"

I answered him that both were guilty. Then he asked, "Which did the greater evil: the Iroquois who sold land that didn't belong to them, or the Penn government who bought it? After all, Pennsylvania knew the land did not belong to the Iroquois. Don't you think each side is equally guilty?"

"How do we know that all the accusations Papunhank made against the Paxton Boys and Governor Penn were true?" I countered. "Brother Zeisberger spoke and wrote English and corresponded regularly with

UNDER ATTACK

the Penn government throughout the Philadelphia captivity and the Paxton Boys' insurrection. Brother Zeisberger saw the big picture. He knew what was going on in Pennsylvania, in England, and in Germany, and he did what was best for the Christian Indians.

"Brother Johannes Papunhank saw only a small part of the big picture, so while he may have been perfectly honest and of good character, his perceptions on some of the bigger issues were flawed."

Glikkikan shook his head sadly. "Turtle, you can ask any of the Brethren who lived through the Philadelphia captivity if it was not exactly as Papunhank told you."

The fire sputtered onward while we waited in silence. Then the orator in Glikkikan gripped him. He rose to his feet, and the shadows on the forest behind him enlarged his powerful presence. He could have been preaching to a throng of a thousand people when he began. My heart fluttered expectantly.

> Brother Johannes Papunhank was a true prophet. He saw through the lies of his enemies and the injustice of being forced from his homeland, and he always clung to the Savior. Like Abraham, he saw beyond Wechquetank and Wyalusing to a place of rest in the Ohioland.
>
> Prophet Papunhank saw the big picture. We speak of the difference between good and evil. We speak of right and wrong. We speak of love and hate. We speak of war and peace. We speak of the land. All that is the big picture.
>
> Let us go back in time to when the Moravians first came to our homeland and brought the Gospel to us. We learned of the Savior and of His power to transform Indian lives and lift us out of misery and evil to a life of peace and prosperity. Those gentle, dedicated men said

Under Attack at Wyalusing: 1765-1772

they had no interest in land, yet at the same time the very foundations of their empire rested on the premise that it was not evil to *own* the land.

When Count Zinzendorf came across the Salt Sea in 1742, he wanted to buy 10,000 acres to establish a Holy Land in America with place names such as Nazareth and Bethlehem and Nain. And from whom did he "buy" his land? He bought it from the most crooked men of the time: evil men who by deceit, fraud, and force stole the land from those who rightfully occupied it, driving them away. I speak of the Penn government and their collusion with the Iroquois.

The Moravians may deny that they have been a part of this evil conspiracy to *own* the land, and for many, that would be true. They did it in ignorance. But in every case, there is the fixed premise that guns and bullets and knives can decide who *owns* the land. And it is the strongest, most violent government to whom we must bow if we are to live on the land in peace.

Some may say that the struggles of the Lenape to find a permanent homeland have nothing to do with land, but are about race or religion. That is wrong. It is the land that underlies all sorts of evils: greed, hate, murder, and war.

Remember Shekomeko. The surrounding settlers wanted the land whereon the settlement rested. They closed the mission and petitioned the government to allow them to kill all the Indians.

Remember Wyoming. Teedyuscung burned because he wanted to set aside a permanent homeland for his people. The Moravian elders, in conjunction with Conrad Weiser, twice bowed to the Iroquois for permission to

UNDER ATTACK

move the Shekomeko Christians to Wyoming. Twice they refused to go. It was about who owned the land.

Remember the Forks of the Delaware. Greedy men in the Penn government wanted to sell Indian land to the settlers, and they were willing to stoop to many kinds of evil to do it.

Remember the Philadelphia captivity. Settlers drove the Indians away, and the Penn government forbade any Indians to return to their homes in so-called purchased lands.

Remember Wyalusing. The Iroquois sold the land to Pennsylvania, and settlers drove us away because they wanted the land.

It was all about the land.

Now we, the Christian Indians, reside peaceably in the Ohioland. Perhaps God has given us this land as a new homeland for our people.

But make no mistake. Lord Dunmore's evil war and the war yet to come are both about the land—the Ohioland. And if all the scheming generals, land speculators, and settlers did not have their eyes set on land, there would be no war in the Ohioland.

Glikkikan closed his passionate speech and knelt close to me where I could see the firelight reflected in his eyes. He took my hand in his and said, "Brother John, you should learn from the past. Do not favor one side over the other in the war. Both sides are evil and doing the devil's work. If it is our lot to suffer and be driven from land to land for His name's sake, the Savior has promised us one hundred times as much in houses, lands, brothers, sisters, and mothers in this world, and in the world to come, eternal life.

"Let us not despair at the wars of the heathen. Let us not cower

Under Attack at Wyalusing: 1765–1772

Clear Vision

"I saw the gold medallion."

—Isaac Glikkikan

UNDER ATTACK

in fear and terror. Let us rejoice and praise God for the many great victories He has won among the poorest of men and women, and the proud chieftains He has humbled and brought into the battle for the Savior's kingdom. Men like Mewi, Wehund, Daskund, Glikkikan, Welooch, Mamawad, Leekey, Panhillen, Papunhank, Rex, Sakima, Wamapah, and more. Many of them were drunkards, liars, thieves, idolaters, and murderers. All were bound by sin and Satan and without hope. But now they have been redeemed, baptized, and changed: Abraham, Augustinus, Augustus, Petrus, Isaac, Jacob, Joshua, Salomo, Simon, Johannes, John . . . The night would not be long enough were I to recite the names of all these heroes of faith.

"Turtle, when I think of all these great victories, I want to rise up and shout, Hallelujah!

And so we did, "HALLELUJAH! HALLELUJAH! HALLELUJAH!"

The forest rang with our triumphant cries, and the echoes came bouncing back until they faded away. Our breath smoked in the cold night air as we gazed up into the star-spangled heavens. Stars, stars, and more stars. Stars of faith. Indians washed clean in the blood of the Lamb. Shining Indian stars. Brilliant Indian stars.

We sat down again and remained silent for a long time. We thought over the great glories God had wrought among the Indians and of the victories yet to come.

I laid my hand on Big Indian's knee. "Glikkikan," I whispered, "I saw the gold medallion."

He laid his big hand on top of mine and whispered, "Turtle, I saw it too."

Appendix A

Cast of Main Characters

Abraham—Sakima. Baptized 25 December 1765 at Wyalusing. Three years later, he and his wife Salome left Wyalusing to help found the mission at Goshchuenk.

Agnes—Glikkikan's wife of Mingo (wayward Iroquois) lineage. Mother of Phoebe from an earlier marriage, she had two children with Glikkikan, Jonathan and Benigna.

Anton—Baptized 8 February 1750 in Bethlehem. Nineteen years later, he and his wife Johanna accompanied Zeisberger to help found the mission at Goshchuenk. No children.

August Gottlieb Spangenberg—(1704-1792) Educated in Europe. Served the Unity many years in America beginning in 1735-1739. Ordained bishop in 1744 and returned to America at that time. Except for a two-year period, he was in charge of the Moravian Church in North America until 1762.

Christian Henry Rauch—German young man of twenty-two who founded the mission at Shekomeko, New York, in 1740.

Christian Renatus—First Indian baptized from Gomekah. He was falsely accused and imprisoned in Philadelphia. His wife, son, and father died while he languished in prison.

David Zeisberger—Sometimes called Good News in the story. Veteran missionary and leader of the Moravian missions among the Delaware Indians west of the Alleghenies.

George Rex—Mamanawad or Mamawad, a young chief from Meniolagomeka. Baptized as Augustus.

Appendix A

Glikkikan—Seventy-five-year-old Delaware war chief of the Munsee (Wolf) Clan. Head counselor to Delaware chiefs and a renowned orator. Possible father of two sons, Ludwig and Jonathan, both old enough to marry when baptized at Bethlehem in 1749. Also had two children, Jonathan (deceased in childhood) and Benigna, by Agnes. Glikkikan was baptized as Isaac in 1770 at Moravia, Pennsylvania.

Gudlop Buettner—Head missionary at Shekomeko. Won many souls and suffered much for Christ. Died and was buried at Shekomeko.

Hard Man—Gischenatsi or Natsi, a Shawnee chief known for his unbending opposition to white encroachment.

Hokolesqua—Cornstalk, head chief of the Shawnee and leader of the battle with Virginia forces at Point Pleasant.

Israel Pemberton—A wealthy Philadelphia Quaker merchant. He personally gave and also helped raise huge sums to adjust Indian grievances. Because of his leadership and influence in early Pennsylvania, he was known as King of the Quakers.

Johann Schmick—A former Lutheran pastor in Germany, he came to America in 1751, and at the age of thirty-seven, he married Johanna. Together they served in the Moravian Indian missions for twenty years, the last four at Huts of Grace II in Ohio.

John Gibson—(May 23, 1740 - April 10, 1822) Served in the French and Indian War, Lord Dunmore's War, the American Revolutionary War, Tecumseh's War, and the War of 1812. Gibson spoke the Indian tongues and traded with the Indians. He pretended to be friendly with the Indians and in many cases they trusted him. But in times of war, Gibson always fought against the natives, often serving as a commanding officer in the army.

Appendix A

John Heckewelder—(1743-1823) Came from England to America at age eleven. Started his mission training at the age of nineteen with Christian Frederick Post on the Muskingum River. He served as an adjunct of David Zeisberger until the end of the Revolutionary War. After the complete takeover of the Ohioland by the Whites, he returned to Gnadenhuetten as storekeeper and postmaster for a number of years. After his retirement and return to Bethlehem, he wrote much about the Indians and the former mission villages along the Muskingum River.

Knave Peters—A disenfranchised Anglican minister who served as secretary of the Pennsylvania governor's Council. He was instrumental in forcing the Indians from their lands and then profited from the sale of those lands to the settlers.

Nathanael Seidel—(1718-1782) Became bishop of the *Unitas Fratrum* in 1758; guided the Moravian Church in North America beginning in 1762.

Packanke—Custaloga, head chief of the Wolf Clan. He resided at the Kuskuskies on the Big Beaver River, near present-day New Castle, Pennsylvania.

Papunhank—Indian prophet and elder of the congregation at Wyalusing. Baptized as Johannes at Wyalusing on 26 June 1762. Served ably as a leader in the congregation at Huts of Peace in Pennsylvania and at Huts of Grace in Ohio. Accompanied Zeisberger on his investigative trip to Goshcheunk.

Salamander George—George Croghan, a risk-taking Irish trader who by bluster and guile created a trading empire on the Pennsylvania frontier. Known as King of the Traders.

Salomo—Allemewi or Mewi, blind chief at Goshcheunk known as Wise One. Baptized at Lawhannek 25 December 1769.

Wangomen—A blood brother to Glikkikan. Priest, sorcerer, and local leader at Goshcheunk. Invited Moravians to come west of the Alleghenies and open a mission.

Appendix A

Watwees—Original name, Netawatwees, means "skilled adviser." In English, he was known as Chief Newcomer. Head of the Turtle Clan and thus head chief of the Delaware nation. Died at Fort Pitt, 31 October 1776.

White Eyes—Koquethagechton, came to be known as Gray Eyes or White Eyes because of the mysterious gray matter in his one eye. A close friend of Glikkikan's who became head war chief of the Delaware nation.

William Johnson—Many Children Johnson. The King's agent in charge of Indian affairs. He managed to secure a large New York estate while favoring Iroquois dominance over all other Indian nations. It is claimed he fathered over one hundred children by his many Indian consorts.

Appendix B

Place Names

Beautiful Spring—Schoenbrunn. Moravian Indian mission founded in 1772, just outside New Philadelphia, OH. At certain times of the year, one can visit the partially restored village.

Beaver River—Flows south from New Castle, PA, to the town of Beaver, PA, where it empties into the Ohio River. A river route joining the Kuskuskies and the Ohio River.

Bethlehem—Moravian center, started in 1741 in Bethlehem, PA.

Cayahaga—A Wyandot town on the Cuyahoga River near the present city of Akron, OH. *Cuyahoga* means "winding river" in the Iroquois tongue. Flows north into Lake Erie.

Cowanesque River—Tributary of Tioga River, very close to northern Pennsylvania line at Knoxville, PA.

Fort Allen—On the Lehigh River. Weissport, PA.

Fort Pitt—English fort founded in 1758 on the Forks of the Ohio at present-day Pittsburgh, PA.

Friedensstadt—"Peace Town" marked on the map as Moravia. A Moravian mission on the Beaver River near New Castle, PA.

Goschgoschünk—Shortened to Goshchuenk in the story. Zeisberger's first mission west of the Allegheny Mountains. It was three miles south of Lawhannek and twenty miles northeast of Venango.

Huts of Grace—Gnadenhuetten on the Mahoning, Lehighton, PA.

Huts of Grace II—Gnadenhuetten II on the Muskingum, Gnadenhutten, OH. Twelve miles south of present-day New Philadelphia, OH. Mission founded there in 1773.

Kuskuskies—A region at the head of the Beaver River near present-day New Castle, PA.

Lawunnakhannek—Lawhannek in the story. The mission lay three miles upriver from Goshchuenk and over fifty miles east of present day Franklin, PA.

Appendix B

Meniolagomeka—Gomeka in the story. Delaware Indian village east of the Lehigh River in the Forks of the Delaware.

Muskingum River—Means "elk eyes." Currently, it flows from Coshocton to Marietta, OH. In the time of the story, the Muskingum included all of what is now known as the Tuscarawas River from its source to Coshocton, OH.

Nescopeck—Nutimus's town on the Susquehanna south of Wilkes-Barre, PA.

Newcomerstown—Gekelemukpechünk ("still water") on the Muskingum, eighteen miles east of Coshocton, OH. The largest town of the Delaware at that time with a possible population of seven hundred. Likely named after Chief Newcomer (Netawatwees or Watwees), the head chief of the Delawares.

Ohio River—At the time of this story, the river included all of what today is known as the Allegheny River from Pittsburgh to its source not far from Lake Erie. For a time, the Ohio marked the boundary between Indian land and white settlements.

Onondaga—Head council fire of the Iroquois confederation of six Indian nations. Located in New York State.

Pachgatgoch—A Moravian mission station near the Connecticut border.

Shekomeko—A Moravian mission among the Mohican Indians. It was located one hundred miles north of New York City and east of the Hudson River. Present-day Pine Plains, NY.

Sheshequin— Shortened from Tsehechsehequannink. A town thirty miles north of Wyalusing along the Susquehanna River.

Venango—A French Fort built where French Creek enters the Ohio (Allegheny River). Close to present-day Franklin, PA.

Wechquatnach—Moravian mission in this town close to the Connecticut border.

Westenhuck—Mohican capital near the Connecticut border.

Wyalusing—*Friedenshuetten* (Huts of Peace). A Moravian mission on the Susquehanna River, north of present-day Wilkes-Barre, PA. The town was abandoned in 1772, and the Indians relocated to the new mission towns in Ohio.

Appendix C

How Much of This Story Is True?

All the events and characters portrayed in this story are based on historical records and the Moravian Diaries. The events are true, but sometimes I have woven in imaginary details to make the story flow.

The canoe journey in chapter one is mainly taken from Heckewelder's actual diary. Many of the facts and observations that are presented in this story as having come from John Heckewelder's fictional diary are actually gleaned from the mission diaries written by David Zeisberger and others.

It is not certain that Glikkikan accompanied the group on the journey from the Kuskuskies to Beautiful Spring, although his experiences are in keeping with his past record. As in this example, I have sometimes placed Glikkikan where he may not have been, but it is exciting to see how often he was sent as an emissary to the Indian nations or served as spokesman for the Christians. At other times, the diaries may say he is off on "business" but give no indication as to the nature of that business.

Much of what is recorded as coming from Johannes Papunhank is taken from historical accounts and is backed by his *Life Work* as given by David Zeisberger at his funeral (See Appendix D.)

The events surrounding Lord Dunmore's War are clouded in confusion, with differing accounts of the same happenings. I have tried to faithfully present the characters and times as seen from the Indian viewpoint.

Many documents from varied sources leave little doubt that the main purpose of the Virginians and the rapacious settlers in the Ohioland was to either eradicate the Indians or drive them away so the Ohioland would be cleared for sale and settlement. Although

Appendix C

Pennsylvanians like Croghan, Mckee, and Gibson shared similar sentiments, they tried to generally appease the Indians so the atrocities committed by the Whites would not generate a united Indian war.

When war came to the Shawnee, the list of commanders and participants in the expeditions included all those from both sides, no matter how closely they were connected to former atrocities and land grabs: Greathouse, Cresap, Crawford, McDonald, McKee, Croghan, Gibson, George Rogers Clark, Daniel Boone... The list goes on and on. The immorality of the whole campaign in the name of making peace is revolting to me. The Whites had broken every promise made at former treaties with the Western Indians, and yet, these same people could participate in their dirty, immoral war. What most Whites wanted was the complete surrender of the Indians to all their demands.

Indians who did not want to fight were invariably squeezed into either retreat or annihilation, no matter how peaceful their actions or how good their promises.

Under Attack is not revisionist history where we rewrite facts to make former heroes look bad or attempt to make villains look good. Almost all people and events in the book are gleaned from historical records and interpreted as I believe the Christian Indians and their teachers saw them.

All references to the gold medallion are fictional.

I trust you will feel the injustices and the sufferings of true servants of the kingdom of God surrounded by evil men in an ungodly world. And I hope that you will rejoice with the triumphant saints who preached and exhibited the true way of peace to the ungodly around them.

Peace,
James G. Landis

Appendix D

The Life Work of Johannes Papunhank

When we laid our faithful brother Johannes[116] to rest on 16 May 1775,[117] a large procession, including many brothers and sisters from Gnadenhuetten, followed the body to the Lord's Acre. At the service, David Zeisberger gave a summary of Brother Johannes's *Lebenslauf* (Course of Life).

> I baptized Papunhank as Johannes on 26 June 1762, at Wyalusing[118] on the Susquehanna. Brother Johannes suffered the exile in Philadelphia, the fraudulent sale of his homeland at Wyalusing by the Iroquois, the move to Langundoutenünk,[119] and finally another move to Beautiful Spring. At Beautiful Spring, he continued to suffer hardship by his many enemies among the Indians who accused him of having the "poison." Although Brother Johannes suffered much, his heart was firmly attached to the Savior and the Unity. Brother Johannes faithfully took care of the external affairs of Beautiful Spring and did his work with great cheerfulness and faithfulness until the Savior took him to his eternal rest.
>
> About twelve days ago, Johannes got pains in his side

---

[116] Baptized with the name Johannes. Prior to his conversion, he was an influential Delaware preacher named Papunhank. Various spellings used for this man include Pepunhang, Papoonhoal, Wampoonham, Papoonhang, and Papoonham. I use only Papunhank.

[117] The burial took place at Schoenbrunn (Beautiful Spring) Ohio. Today, one can visit this partially restored Moravian mission village located close to New Philadelphia, Ohio.

[118] Papunhank called the place Machhachloosing. During the time of the Moravian mission, the missionaries called it Machwihilusing, M'chwilusing, and Wialusing. I use Wyalusing throughout the story. Heckewelder says the meaning of the name is, "the place of the hoary veteran."

[119] The names for this mission were Langundoutenünk (Indian name), Friedenstadt (German name), and Moravia (current English name).

Appendix D

and began coughing, which really bothered him. During his illness, he only talked about how he wanted to die, and he did not want to get well again. He said he loved everyone and did not hold anything against anyone. He then died with the blessing of the congregation, being about seventy years old.

Appendix E

The 1763 Murders in the Wyoming Valley

In doing research for *Tomahawks to Peace* and *Under Attack*, I have come to believe that the Paxton Boys, in collusion with officials of the Penn government, were responsible for the murder of Teedyuscung, the destruction of Wyoming, and the murder of the Connecticut settlers in the Wyoming Valley.

Historians offer various conjectures about who was responsible for these raids. At first reading, most writers attribute these events to Indian savages, even though the facts do not support their conclusions. But after multiple readings and an effort to combine the various accounts, I began to see that some writers did cautiously mention facts that pointed to White ravages and the collusion of the Penn government.

More recent writers such as Kevin Kenny in *Peaceable Kingdom Lost* have also brought to light more letters and files that strongly support my conclusions as presented in *Under Attack*. I would move what some writers suggest as a vague possibility to "near certainty."

Donald R. Repsher in his *Reasons for the Revolt of the Lenape and Shawanese 1722-1759* (2005) first suggested to me that perhaps Secretary Peters of the Pennsylvania Governor's Council was a party to Teedyuscung's murder. It was a thought not suggested in anything else I had read, but suddenly, many other clues began to point in that direction.

I must say right up front that I have not found any writing that claims to know for sure who killed Teedyuscung. This in itself is strange and a matter of suspicion. The date of the murder and some surrounding details are clearly known. Anthony F. C. Wallace writes in *King of the Delawares*, page 258:

Appendix E

On April 19, 1763, Teedyuscung was murdered. In the evening, as he lay asleep in his cabin (some say in a drunken stupor), the house was set afire from outside; he was burned to death within the flaming walls of the lodge which Brother Onas had built for him. Almost simultaneously, the twenty surrounding dwellings burst into flames. Within a few hours, the whole town of Wyoming lay in ashes. The surviving members of the community fled in terror, some of them to the Moravian mission at Wechquetank, not far from Fort Allen; some to Nain, near Bethlehem; and others across the mountains to Big Island in the West Branch of the Susquehanna.

An inquirer has reason to ask some questions. How can anyone know so many details about the murder of Teedyuscung and yet have no conclusive evidence about who the murderers were? Was Teedyuscung the only one murdered in the whole town, or were others also killed? In what language were the villagers warned to flee? Did no one see any of the raiders? There were certainly multiple attackers as all twenty cabins burst into flame at once. Did the survivors not talk? Did they have no suspicions about who the attackers were?

The same questions arise about the murder of the Connecticut settlers. The only testimony we have on record is the lies of commanders who said, "It looked like the raiders came from such and such a place, and they appeared to have gone in such and such a direction. We found a woman with a hinge burned into her hand . . ." Where is the testimony of the survivors? How do the dates and times of the raid match up?

Other disturbing facts are the repeated official denials of any involvement in the murders while letters and dates reveal impossible knowledge ahead of the actual event. The repeated statements by the

Appendix E

governors in which they always said, "The savages struck first without any cause," destroys the credibility of their statements. They knew better.

The important thing to those involved was that the public perception of unprovoked Indian cruelties would arouse the populace to support the war against all Indians, regardless of the truth. The Indians had no printing presses and no machinery to refute the lies and to present the truth. And the missionaries who knew the truth remained publicly silent while carefully recording events in their diaries.

The blatant murder of the Conestoga Indians could not be hidden from public view. But the feeble efforts to supposedly bring the perpetrators to justice lacked any teeth, and so the murderers went unpunished. The public was generally willing to accept even this heinous crime as a justified action in light of Indian savagery.

In later events, it was the land speculators (who were they?) who managed to pervert Pennsylvania justice and very cruelly attack and destroy Yankee settlers (Irby, State of Westmoreland). The Pennsylvania government and its officials were willing to continue the fraud of the Walking Purchase in the Wyoming Valley. They would steal the land by whatever means necessary.

So it is easy to say that the Penn government had motivations to burn the cabins and murder Teedyuscung: revenge, land ownership, contest with the Quakers over Indian affairs, and the whole issue of "using" (bribing) the Iroquois to sell land that did not belong to them. The Penn government also had previously shown that they had no scruples at casting aside Delaware claims to land, cheating, lying, or using outright treachery to gain control of land to sell to settlers. They had no intention of surrendering any Wyoming land to speculators or settlers from Connecticut. Pennsylvania would use force if necessary to obtain control of the Wyoming Valley.

In a commission to Colonel James Burd and Thomas [Alexander]

Appendix E

McKee on 2 July 1763, Governor James Hamilton uses strong language: "Use your best endeavors to persuade or drive away all the white people that you shall find settled . . . they shall all immediately depart and quit their settlements . . . and after their departure, see all their buildings and improvements destroyed . . . This government will never permit them to continue there."[120]

So already on 2 July 1763—the actual murders and the destruction of the Wyoming settlers did not take place till 15 October 1763—Pennsylvania had the motivation and the determination to drive the Connecticut settlers out of the Wyoming Valley. But what means would they use?

The Paxton Boys were ready and willing to destroy the Connecticut settlers. The Paxton Boys (Scotch-Irish) later demonstrated at the Lancaster murders (December 1763) and the Philadelphia confrontation that they had the will and the desire to inhumanely butcher all Indians. They believed the Indians were Canaanites whose destruction was ordered by God, so justice and humanity meant nothing to the Paxton Boys. They intended to kill all Indians or anyone else who got in their way. They wanted land.

Later events prove that the general populace shared the Paxton Boys' attitude. Maybe people felt the Paxton Boys carried things to excess, but they were generally glad to get rid of the Indian problem and never brought the murderers to judgment or punishment. Feeble rewards were offered, but people in authority claimed they didn't know who the murderers were, and no one ever turned them in or brought them to justice. All the noise amounted to nothing.

More curious facts related to the Paxton Boys and the murder of the Connecticut settlers are noted in Miner's *History of Wyoming*, page 56: "The dates on several letters from the commander of the Paxton

---

[120] See *Pennsylvania Colonial Records*, Vol. 9, p. 126.

Appendix E

Rangers, John Elder, to Governor Hamilton indicate they were written to Hamilton prior to the destruction of the Connecticut settlers on 15 October 1763. The letters from John Elder to Governor Hamilton on September 30 and October 10 talk about destroying the corn that was 'left' from the destroyed settlers so as to prevent the savages from benefitting from its use."

The problem and the giveaway is that the Connecticut settlers were not destroyed until the 15th of October. Presbyterian preacher and commander John Elder was lying. There was much more intended in the coming expeditions than just the destruction of the settlers' corn. They probably intended to destroy the Connecticut settlements and murder the inhabitants or at least drive them completely from the valley. The corn story was just a cover. But it is interesting that Governor Hamilton approved of destroying the corn that was "left."

Let us assume for a moment that Governor Hamilton and Commander Elder were using the term "corn that was left" as referring only to corn that was in storage from the harvest or corn that was still standing in the fields. If the Connecticut settlers had not yet been murdered and the Pennsylvania militia came to destroy their stores of corn to prevent the Indians from using it, would the settlers have stood passively by while this was going on?

Furthermore, the Wyalusing Indians were under the express protection of the government at that time. Yet it was a stated objective of the militia who marched to Wyoming that they would destroy the Wyalusing Christian Indian village. However, after these "brave" murderous soldiers "found" the Connecticut settlement destroyed on 17 October and "discovered" such barbaric cruelties as a dead woman with a hinge stuck through her hand, these same brave soldiers quietly returned home and forgot about the Wyalusing Indians. The official and public report was full of lies and laid the blame for the atrocities in the Wyoming Valley on Captain Bull and the Indians.

Appendix E

I believe the Connecticut settlers badly underestimated the hostility of Pennsylvania settlers, land speculators, and the Penn government. This hostility and complete lack of morals by many Pennsylvania soldiers was later revealed in three Pennamite and Yankee wars fought over the Wyoming Valley. Of one of the Pennamite Wars involving some of the same characters involved in the raid on the Connecticut settlers, the Wyoming historian writes that on "May 13, 1784, an operation commenced that would have made Sherman proud . . . The nightmare continued for fourteen days of Pennsylvania hell."[121]

Now let's return to events in the Wyoming Valley in the fall of 1763. On 17 October 1763, Commander Elder wrote to Governor Hamilton and said he could not recall the expedition commanded by Asher Clayton, Matthew Smith, and Lazarus Stewart—the latter two soon to be known as principals in the murder of the Conestoga Indians—against *Wyalusing!* (Kenny, *Peaceable Kingdom*, p. 144) as they were already at Wyoming. In the October 17 letter, Elder gives two reasons for the expedition: destroy the corn that is "left" by the Connecticut settlers so as to displease the Indians, and perhaps intercept the Indian raiding party from Northampton (8 October 1763). It is worth pointing out that according to Elder's letter of September 30, this expedition had already been planned "to destroy the corn that was left." At that time, no Indian raid in Northampton County had yet taken place.

In a letter dated October 10, 1763, Governor Hamilton expressly forbade Elder to destroy the Indian village on the Susquehanna at Wyalusing. It seems logical that the governor understood that the destruction of Wyoming and not Wyalusing was intended as well as other unwritten objectives. The stated objective of the leaders of the expedition was to destroy Wyalusing. It seems logical to me that Governor Hamilton's belated affirmation of his protection of the

---

[121] Richard E. Irby Jr., *The State of Westmoreland and the Pennamite-Yankee Wars*, pp. 1–14.

Appendix E

Wyalusing Indians was only an official ruse to cover the real purpose of the expedition (he had actually ordered it) which was to destroy the Connecticut settlement in the Wyoming Valley.

Were the Paxton Boys culpable in the destruction of the Connecticut settlements? Only two months later, about fifty Paxton Boys did their butchery at the Lancaster jail in public view. There was no need to guess who did it. What is less certain is whether officials could have prevented the murders.

A curious fact implicates the local officials in the murder of the Conestogas. According to a letter from Edward Shippen to his son, who served as secretary on the governor's Council, the Lancaster "prison keeper" had given him at least a day's notice of the impending murders. Magistrate Shippen failed to take any action to prevent these murders. Why?

There were Highlander (English) soldiers stationed in the town who could easily have prevented the break-in and murders. All the Lancaster magistrates sat idly by while the Paxton Boys, led by Matthew Smith and Lazarus Stewart, did their heinous, barbaric work (Kenny, *Peaceable Kingdom*, pp. 142-143).

This is some of the convincing evidence—there is much more—that led me to present the story as I did in chapters 3 and 4 of *Under Attack*. I believe the underlying facts and internal evidences strongly support the truth of the story as I have written it.

Appendix F

Christian Village Statutes and Rules

Agreed upon by the Christian Indians at Langundo Utenünk and Welhik Tuppek,

17 August 1772

Rule #1. We will know no other God but the one only true God, who made us and all creatures and came into this world in order to save sinners; to Him alone we will pray.

Rule #2. We will rest from work on the Lord's Day and attend public service.

Rule #3. We will honor father and mother, and when they grow old and needy, we will do for them what we can.

Rule #4. No person shall get leave to dwell with us until our teachers have given their consent and the helpers have examined him.

Rule #5. We will have nothing to do with thieves, murderers, whoremongers, adulterers, or drunkards until they repent of their bad ways.

Rule #6. We will not take part in dances, sacrifices, heathenish festivals, or sinful plays.

Rule #7. We will use no tshapiet, or witchcraft, when hunting.

Rule #8. We renounce and abhor all tricks, cheats, lies, and deceits of Satan.

Rule #9. We will be obedient to our teachers and to the helpers who are appointed to preserve order in our meetings and in the towns and fields.

Rule #10. We will not be idle and lazy, nor scold, nor beat one another, nor tell lies.

Appendix F

Rule #11. Whoever hurts anybody's goods shall make the damage good.

Rule #12. A man shall have but one wife. He shall love her and provide for her and his children. A woman shall have but one husband, be obedient to him, care for her children, and be cleanly in all things.

Rule #13. We will not admit rum or any other intoxicating liquor. The helpers shall take it from them and not restore it until the owners are ready to leave the place.

Rule #14. No one shall contract debts with traders or receive goods to sell for traders unless the helpers give their consent.

Rule #15. No one is to go on a journey or long hunt without informing the minister or stewards of it.

Rule #16. Young people are not to marry without the consent of their parents and taking their advice.

Rule #17. If the stewards or helpers apply to the inhabitants for assistance in doing work for the benefit of the place, such as building meeting houses and schoolhouses, clearing and fencing lands, and so on, they are to be obedient.

Rule #18. We will freely contribute when corn or sugar is gathered for love feasts or to entertain strangers.

Rule #19. No man inclining to go to war, which is the shedding of blood, can remain among us.

Rule #20. Whosoever purchases goods or articles of warriors, knowing at the time that such have been stolen or plundered, must leave us. We look upon this as giving encouragement to murder and theft.

The last two rules were added during the Revolutionary War and insisted upon by the native helpers.

–*Moravian Mission Diaries*, p. 563.
–De Schweinitz, p. 378

Bibliography

Primary Sources

Fliegel, Carl John. *Index to the Records of the Moravian Mission Among the Indians of North America.* New Haven, 1970.

Heckewelder, John. *History, Manners, and Customs of the Indian Nations.* Philadelphia, PA, The Historical Society of Pennsylvania, 1876.

Loskiel, George Henry. *History of the Mission of the United Brethren Among the Indians in North America.* Translated from German by La Trobe. London, England, 1794.

Schaaf, Gregory. *Wampum Belts & Peace Trees: George Morgan, Native Americans, and Revolutionary Diplomacy.* Golden, CO, Fulcrum Publishing, 1990.

Wellenreuther, Hermann & Wessel, Carola, eds. Julie Weber, translator. *The Moravian Mission Diaries of David Zeisberger 1772-1781.* University Park, PA, The Pennsylvania State University Press, 2005.

Zeisberger, David. *Journals & Diaries of David Zeisberger.* Gathered by Earl Olmstead, New Philadelphia, OH, Kent State University, Tuscarawas Campus, 1988.

General Sources

Alder, Henry Clay. *A History of Jonathan Alder, His Captivity and Life with the Indians.* Akron, OH, University of Akron Press, 2002.

Bailey, Kenneth P. *The Ohio Company of Virginia and the Westward Movement, 1748-1792.* Original: Glendale CA, 1939. Reprint: Lewisburg, PA, Wennawoods Publishing, 2000.

Barsotti, John J. *Scoouwa.* Columbus, OH, Ohio Historical Society, 1978. Original: Bradford, John. *An Account of the Remarkable Occurrences in the Life and Travels of Col. James Smith,* Lexington, MA, 1799.

Bibliography

Bronner, Edwin B. *William Penn's "Holy Experiment."* New York and London, Temple University Publications, 1962.

Carrell, Jennifer Lee. *The Speckled Monster.* New York, Dutton, 2003.

Chase, Thomas Christopher. *Christian Frederick Post, 1715-1785: Missionary and Diplomat to the Indians of America.* Pennsylvania State University, 1982. Doctoral Thesis from Internet, 199 pages.

Colonial Records of Pennsylvania, *Minutes of the Provincial Council of Pennsylvania,* Vol. IX. Published by the State. Available from Pennsylvania Archives Online.

Comfort, William Wistar. *The Quakers, A Brief Account of Their Influence on Pennsylvania.* University Park, PA, The Pennsylvania Historical Association, 1986.

Davis, Sheldon A. M. *Shekomeko, The Moravians in Dutchess County.* Poughkeepsie, NY, Osborne & Killey, 1858.

Demos, John. *The Unredeemed Captive.* New York, Alfred A. Knopf, 1994.

Deschweinitz, Edmund. *The Life and Times of David Zeisberger.* Philadelphia, PA, J. B. Lippincott & Co., 1870.

Dixon, David. *Fort Pitt Museum: Pennsylvania Trail of History Guide.* Mechanicsburg, PA, Stackpole Books, 2004.

Dixon, David. *Never Come to Peace Again: Pontiac's Uprising and the Fate of the British Empire in North America.* Norman, OK, University of Oklahoma Press, 2005.

Donehoo, Dr. George P. *A History of the Indian Villages and Place Names in Pennsylvania.* Harrisburg, PA, 1928. Reprinted: Lewisburg, PA, Wennawoods Publishing, 1998.

Dowd, Gregory Evans. *War Under Heaven.* Baltimore, MD, The John Hopkins University Press, 2002.

Duel, Newton, Elizabeth Klare, James Mara, Helen Netter, and Dyan Wapnick. *Out of the Wilderness: A History of the Hamlet of Bethel in the Town of Pine Plains, New York.* Vol. 5. The Little Nine Partners Historical Society, 1996 & 2008.

Bibliography

Eckert, Allan W. *That Dark and Bloody River.* New York, Bantam Books, 1995.

Ettwein, John. "Notes of Travel from the North Branch of the Susquehanna to the Beaver River, Pennsylvania 1772." *The Pennsylvania Magazine of History and Biography* (Vol. 25, January 1, 1901).

Fitzpatrick, Alan. *Wilderness War on the Ohio.* Benwood, WV, Fort Henry Publications, 2003.

Fitzpatrick, John C., ed. *The Writings of George Washington from the Original Manuscript Sources 1745-1799.* Charlottesville, VA, University of Virginia Library, Vol. 2.

Frank, Albert H. *Transactions of the Moravian Historical Society.* Vol. 26. "Spiritual Life in Schoenbrunn Village," Nazareth, PA, 1990.

Fur, Gunlög. *A Nation of Women.* University of Pennsylvania Press, Philadelphia, PA, 2009.

Gollin, Gillian Lindt. *Bethlehem Transformed: The Secularization of a Moravian Settlement.* <journals.psu.edu/phj/article/viewFile/23428/23197>

Grumet, Robert S. *The Lenapes.* New York & Philadelphia, Chelsea House Publishers, 1989.

Hamilton, John Taylor. *A History of the Moravian Church or the Unity of the Brethren During the Eighteenth and Nineteenth Centuries.* Transactions of the Moravian Historical Society, Vol. VI. Bethlehem, PA, 1900.

Harpster, John W. *Crossroads, Descriptions of Western Pennsylvania, 1720-1829,* Pittsburgh, PA, University of Pittsburgh, Digital Research Library 2009-12-22.

Heckewelder, John. *Narrative of the Mission of the United Brethren Among ... Indians, 1740-1808.* Philadelphia, PA, McCarty and Davis, 1820. Reprint: Arno Press, 1971.

Heckewelder, John. *The First American Frontier.* Arno Press and The New York Times, 1971.

Hindle, Brooke. *The Meaning of the Bethlehem Waterworks.* Bethlehem, PA: Historic Bethlehem Inc., 1977.

Bibliography

Irby Jr., Richard E. *The State of Westmoreland and the Pennamite-Yankee Wars.* Publisher unknown.

Jacobs, Wilbur R. *Diplomacy and Indian Gifts, Anglo-French Rivalry Along the Ohio and Northwest Frontiers, 1748-1763.* Original: Stanford, CA, 1950. Reprint: Lewisburg, PA, Wennawoods Publishing, 2001.

James, Alfred Proctor and Charles Morse Stotz. *Drums in the Forest.* Pittsburgh, PA, The Historical Society of Western Pennsylvania, 1958.

Jennings, Francis. *Benjamin Franklin, Politician.* New York, W. W. Norton & Company, 1996.

Jennings, Francis. *The Ambiguous Iroquois Empire.* New York, W. W. Norton & Company, 1984.

Jennings, Francis. *Empire of Fortune.* New York, W. W. Norton & Company, 1988.

Journals of the House of Burgesses of Virginia, 1773-1776. American Historical Association, licensed to JSTOR.

Landis, James G. *Tomahawks to Peace.* Berlin, OH, TGS International, 2017.

Landis, James G. *Homeland in My Heart.* Berlin, OH, TGS International, 2016.

Levering, Joseph Mortimer. *A History of Bethlehem, Pennsylvania 1741–1892.* Bethlehem, PA, Times Publishing Company, 1903.

Mancall, Peter C. *Deadly Medicine.* Ithaca, NY, Cornell University Press, 1995.

McNeal, Patricia. *Painters of the First Frontier,* Compiled from *Westsylvania Stories.* Gettysburg, PA, Lord Nelson's Art Gallery, 2002.

Merrell, James H. *Into the American Woods.* New York & London, W. W. Norton & Company, 1999.

Miner, Charles. *History of Wyoming.* Philadelphia, PA, J. Crissy, 1845.

Moravian Diaries, various pages 1749-1754, translated by Jeannette Louise Norfleet, Winston Salem, NC, 2013.

O'Callaghan, Edmund Bailey. *Documents Relative to the Colonial Records of New York:* Vol. 12. Albany NY, Weed, Parsons and Company, 1853-1887.

Bibliography

Olmstead, Earl P. *David Zeisberger–A Life Among the Indians.* Kent, Ohio, The Kent State University Press, 1997.

Paterek, Josephine. *Encyclopedia of American Indian Costume.* New York, W. W. Norton & Company, 1994.

Reichel, W. C. *Wyalusing and the Moravian Mission at Friedenshuetten.* Bethlehem, PA, W. C. Reichel, 1871.

Reichel, W. C. *Transactions of the Moravian Historical Society.* Nazareth, PA, Moravian Historical Society. Vol. I, 1876.

Repsher, Donald R. *Reasons for the Revolt of the Lenape and Shawanese 1722-1759,* 2005. A contemporary language version of: *An Enquiry into the Causes of the Alienation of the Delaware and Shawanese Indians from the British Interest* by Charles Thomson.

Repsher, Donald R. *"Meniolagomeka" – Annals of a Moravian Indian Village.* Dedication of Meniolagomeka Memorial, Monroe County, PA, 2011.

Richardson, C.B. *A Memorial of the Dedication of Monuments Erected by the Moravian Historical Society.* Office of the Historical Magazine, 348 Broadway, NY, 1860.

Sipe, C. Hale. *The Indian Chiefs of Pennsylvania.* Butler, PA, 1927. Reprinted: Lewisburg, PA, Wennawoods Publishing, 1994.

Sipe, C. Hale. *The Indian Wars of Pennsylvania.* Butler, PA, 1931. Reprinted: Lewisburg, PA, Wennawoods Publishing, 1995.

Sheafer, P. W. (1875) & Wenning, Ronald R. (2004). *Historical Map of Pennsylvania with a History of Indian Treaties and Land Titles.* Lewisburg, PA, Wennawoods Publishing, 2004.

Tantaquidgeon, Gladys. *Folk Medicine of the Delaware and Related Algonkian Indians.* Harrisburg, PA, Commonwealth of Pennsylvania, 1972.

Tehanetorens. *Wampum Belts,* Onchiota, NY, Six Nations Indian Museum, 1972.

Turdo, Mark A. *Common People, Uncommon Community; Lenape Life in Moravian Missions.* Nazareth, PA, Moravian Historical Society, 1998.

Bibliography

Volwiler, Albert T. *George Croghan and the Westward Movement, 1741-1782.* Cleveland, OH, 1926. Reprinted by Wennawoods Publishing, Lewisburg, PA, 2000.

Wallace, Paul A. W. *Indian Paths of Pennsylvania.* Harrisburg, PA, The Pennsylvania Historical Commission, 1965.

Wallace, Paul A. W., ed. *Thirty Thousand Miles with John Heckewelder.* Published 1958. Reprinted: Lewisburg, PA, Wennawoods Publishing, 1998.

Wenning, Scott Hayes. *Handbook of the Delaware Indian Language.* Lewisburg, PA, Wennawoods Publishing, 2000.

Weslager, C. A. *The Delaware Indians—A History.* New Brunswick, NJ, Rutgers University Press, 1972.

Wilson, Dorothy Clarke. *Bright Eyes.* New York, McGraw-Hill Book Company, 1974.

Zeisberger, David. Archer Butler Hulbert and William Nathaniel Schwarze, eds. *David Zeisberger's History of the Northern American Indians.* Marietta, OH, Ohio State Archaeological and Historical Society, 1910. Reprint: Lewisburg, PA, Wennawoods Publishing, 1999.

About the Author

by Fonda Joy Wadel

L ove for learning sparked early in my dad's life. Raised on Pennsylvania and Virginia farms by a professor father and a home-loving mother, his world formed in a place where work and study intermingled. Reading and history lessons captured his young mind in class while farm chores educated his hands at home.

After graduating from high school in 1960, Dad chose agricultural work for three years. But the yearning for book learning propelled him on to college. For another year he sharpened English composition skills and reveled in Bible and history lessons.

Dad enlarged his education with diverse experiences. For fourteen years he dairy farmed on Georgia plains. He taught high school students amid Pennsylvania hills. He wrote at a publishing house in the New Mexico desert.

From his West Virginia mountain home he edited educational newsletters and penned articles for farm magazines. Hobbies varied from chess games and singing to beekeeping, landscaping, and composting.

His agricultural, economic, and historical interests spurred travel to Central and South America, Europe, Africa, Australia, and New Zealand.

Dad prizes truth. He refuses to accept pat answers flipped to ethical questions. His beliefs demand Bible research, historical evaluation, and worldview consideration. He enjoys stirring minds through church periodicals, Sunday school classes, and Bible history lessons.

Dad's manifesto flies above the hearts of all seven of his children:

Drink knowledge. Hail adventure. Stand on truth.

About Christian Aid Ministries

Christian Aid Ministries was founded in 1981 as a nonprofit, tax-exempt 501(c)(3) organization. Its primary purpose is to provide a trustworthy and efficient channel for Amish, Mennonite, and other conservative Anabaptist groups and individuals to minister to physical and spiritual needs around the world. This is in response to the command to ". . . do good unto all men, especially unto them who are of the household of faith" (Galatians 6:10).

Each year, CAM supporters provide 15-20 million pounds of food, clothing, medicines, seeds, Bibles, Bible story books, and other Christian literature for needy people. Most of the aid goes to orphans and Christian families. Supporters' funds also help to clean up and rebuild for natural disaster victims, put up Gospel billboards in the U.S., support several church-planting efforts, operate two medical clinics, and provide resources for needy families to make their own living. CAM's main purposes for providing aid are to help and encourage God's people and bring the Gospel to a lost and dying world.

CAM has staff, warehouses, and distribution networks in Romania, Moldova, Ukraine, Haiti, Nicaragua, Liberia, Israel, and Kenya. Aside from management, supervisory personnel, and bookkeeping operations, volunteers do most of the work at CAM locations. Each year, volunteers at our warehouses, field bases, Disaster Response Services projects, and other locations donate over 200,000 hours of work.

CAM's ultimate purpose is to glorify God and help enlarge His kingdom. ". . . whatsoever ye do, do all to the glory of God" (1 Corinthians 10:31).

The Way to God and Peace

We live in a world contaminated by sin. Sin is anything that goes against God's holy standards. When we do not follow the guidelines that God our Creator gave us, we are guilty of sin. Sin separates us from God, the source of life.

Since the time when the first man and woman, Adam and Eve, sinned in the Garden of Eden, sin has been universal. The Bible says that we all have "sinned and come short of the glory of God" (Romans 3:23). It also says that the natural consequence for that sin is eternal death, or punishment in an eternal hell: "Then when lust hath conceived, it bringeth forth sin: and sin, when it is finished, bringeth forth death" (James 1:15).

But we do not have to suffer eternal death in hell. God provided a sacrifice for our sins through the gift of His only Son, Jesus Christ. "For God so loved the world that he gave his only begotten Son, that whosoever believeth in him should not perish, but have everlasting life" (John 3:16).

A sacrifice is something given to benefit someone else. It costs the giver greatly. Jesus was God's sacrifice. Jesus' death takes away the penalty of sin for all those who accept this sacrifice and truly repent of their sins. To repent of sins means to be truly sorry for and turn away from the things we have done that have violated God's standards (Acts 2:38; 3:19).

Jesus died, but He did not remain dead. After three days, God's Spirit miraculously raised Him to life again. God's Spirit does something similar in us. When we receive Jesus as our sacrifice and repent of our sins, our hearts are changed. We become spiritually alive! We develop new desires and attitudes (2 Corinthians 5:17). We begin to make choices that please God (1 John 3:9). If we do fail and commit sins, we can ask God for forgiveness. "If we confess our sins, he is faithful and just to forgive us our sins, and to cleanse us from all unrighteousness" (1 John 1:9).

Once our hearts have been changed, we want to continue growing spiritually. We will be happy to let Jesus be the Master of our lives and will want to become more like Him. To do this, we must meditate on God's Word and commune with God in prayer. We will testify to others of this change by being baptized and sharing the good news of God's victory over sin and death. Fellowship with a faithful group of believers will strengthen our walk with God (1 John 1:7).

Hardcover

$29.99
ISBN 978-1-947319-64-6

Softcover

$15.99
ISBN 978-1-947319-63-9